RETRIBUTION

WHO WOULD YOU KILL TO ESCAPE YOUR PAST?

DIANE DEMETRE

RETRIBUTION

Copyright © June 2018 Diane Demetre
ISBN: 978-0-6483324-4-2

ALL RIGHTS RESERVED

The author acknowledges Banjo Paterson as the creator of the poem, The Billy-Goat Overland.

Keep up-to-date by signing up for my no spam newsletter here
https://bit.ly/ddNews
For more information please connect with me at...
www.dianedemetre.com
https://www.facebook.com/DianeDemetreBooks/
https://www.instagram.com/dianedemetrebooks/
https://twitter.com/DianeDemetre

CHAPTER 1

*E*very Sunday, Jessie tried to walk down the stairs like a
civilian, but it was impossible. The trademark duck-walk
of a professional ballerina could not be disguised. Not that she
cared. Ballet was her life. In fact, ballet was the love of her life.
Unlike men with their petty jealousies and unreasonable
demands, ballet asked for little in return; just bloodied toes, hours
of bone-wrenching rehearsals and absolute commitment. A
worthy suitor, it allowed her to flourish onstage in a world of
make believe, where happy endings came at the finale of each
performance. Ballet was her perfect partner. Life was good.

Stepping out onto the leaf-littered street, she shivered and
dragged her coat collar up against the sudden, bitter wind
Melbourne turned on for the evening. Four seasons in one day
was the capital city's unofficial slogan and one which it invariably
lived up to. When she'd headed into her weekly yoga class this
evening, the early December sun had warmed her skin. Now, no
more than two hours later, a plunge into an autumn-like chill
reminded her of the city's fickleness.

Against a pewter grey sky, drab buildings lined the grimy
bitumen, their dark shadows slanting as night fell. Virtually

deserted, Rathdowne Street stretched like a city runway before her, its street lights guiding wayward pedestrians. Jessie clutched the mat roll on her shoulder while the wind ripped water-starved leaves from the oak trees lining the median strip. Despite the flurry around her, the post-yoga peace lingered which meant she'd sleep well tonight and not wake up swamped by terror. Relieved by the thought, she headed briskly towards her car.

She spied him standing in the same place, under the awning of the fruit shop on the corner. Like her, he'd tugged the collar of his black leather jacket high around his jaw and dug his hands deep into the pockets. Reminiscent of a brooding 1940s movie hero, all he needed was a fedora and a cigarette. He leaned against the rust-red brick wall of the dilapidated storefront, and with one leg cocked behind him he looked ready to launch into action at any moment.

Each Sunday, he occupied a mat in the back of the room for yoga class. He left class before Jessie, never stayed or talked to anyone. Yet each week he hung back, propped under the awning until she came down. He didn't appear to be waiting for anyone. Just standing and staring into space.

As usual, she nodded on her approach. "Good night."

"Good night," he said, with a reciprocal nod and continued his vigil.

For months, she'd wondered who he was and why he stood there, but she never ventured to ask. It was none of her business. But tonight, the mystery tugged harder at her curiosity, and she stopped. "Hi. I'm Jessie Hilton. We do Aimee's yoga class together."

"Brad Jordan, but everyone calls me BJ. Pleased to meet you." He didn't offer his hand, just a short, sharp nod.

"Good to meet you…BJ." She lifted a brow and gave him a wry grin.

"I know…the initials could mean something else, but BJ's a nickname my mates gave me, and it stuck."

"That's okay." She paused, becoming serious. "I don't mean to be rude, but why do you stand here every week after class?"

"Just checking…" He scanned the darkness, the seriousness of his expression unchanging.

"Checking for what?" She swivelled her head and joined in his apparent reconnaissance.

"Not sure. Just checking." Although hidden in the shadows, she could see his rugged face sported scruffy, straw-coloured stubble and it accentuated his solemn countenance. Though his lips softened into what could almost be called a smile, his brows knitted, and he offered no further explanation.

Jessie shuffled, pulling her collar higher with a nonchalant shrug. "Okay. Well. I guess I'll see you next week then."

"Yes, you will. Good night." A brighter, easier half-smile creased his face, and she relaxed.

"Good night." Waving a cheery farewell, she walked away, her low-heeled boots clicking a staccato beat. He was definitely different—handsome, in an unkempt sort of way. She wondered what he'd look like if his scraggy, golden hair was released from its rough ponytail and stylishly cut, and his strong abrasive jaw was clean shaven. What fascinated her most though was his brooding presence. He somehow didn't belong on the suburban streets of Melbourne. Not at all like the male dancers she hung out with. A phrase her mother used whenever she'd swoon over the movie star, Robert Redford came to mind. *A man's man. That's who he was.* Jessie hadn't met many of them in the ballet world.

She scurried to where she'd parked her car down a side street. Even in the darkening, ambient light, her cobalt blue Volkswagen beetle gleamed. She'd had her faithful little bug for years and had named it "Penny" in homage to the motely moggie cat who'd been her childhood pet. Together they'd travelled far and wide, clocking up thousands of kilometres on Jessie's annual trip back home. Poor Penny now sat squashed between two bigger, brasher cars that had her jammed in tight.

"Damn. It's going to take me forever to swing out of there," she said out loud.

She dumped her bag on the bonnet and rummaged inside for her keys. She could hear their cheeky rattle in the bottom of the bag along with her make-up, phone, brushes, ballet slippers, sewing kit, and other assorted necessities.

Losing patience, she shoved her hand after them, just as another determined hand grabbed her shoulder. As a ballerina she'd been pulled and shoved by lots of male partners throughout the years when they threw her in breath-taking lifts, but this was no *pas-de-deux*. Fear darted up her spine like a startled spider. Her dancer's strength engaged, and she kicked back, hoping to connect her boot heel with his knee cap. She missed. While his other hand tried to secure her, Jessie's heart hammered against her ribs, and she fought frantically to be free. *Scream, for God's sake, scream.* Stripped of moisture, her mouth and throat squeezed shut. But the primal fight-or-flight response torpedoed her adrenals, releasing her panicked shriek. But he held firm. Gathering up her bag in both hands, she whirled around like a hammer thrower, intent on hitting attacker's head.

"Piss off, or you're a dead man." The menacing growl reverberated off the side of Jessie's face. She half-turned to see BJ lift the attacker off his feet as if he weighed no more than her and fling him across the road. The mugger sailed through the air and landed with a thud on the bitumen, his limbs spilling wide and his head lolling forward. BJ stalked towards the moaning, crumpled mass on the road. Jessie shuddered. In that instant she felt a little sorry for the poor fellow. Having BJ's menacing form advance towards you would be anyone's worst nightmare and the damage it promised to inflict obviously jolted the mugger from his daze. By the way he recovered and scrambled to his feet, she thought he must have been no more than a teenager. Before BJ reached him, the kid was up and running down the road, all arms and gangly legs, with his hoody hiding his face.

Not bothering to chase him, BJ returned to the VW. "Are you all right?"

"Yes. Thank you. A little shaken, but okay." She breathed in a long, slow breath and tried to stop trembling.

"Good to hear. I'll wait while you get in your car, if you like."

"Yes, please. Thank you. That'd be good." Taking a moment to collect herself, she fought off the fear that scratched at her consciousness. The same sense of panic that woke her from frequent nightmares. She swallowed hard, blew out a breath and plonked her bag back on the bonnet to find her keys. Once more, her hand swirled unsuccessfully around inside.

"You know, you really ought to get another bag or have a keyring strap sewn in, so you can find your keys easily. Then you wouldn't be a sitting target for those sorts of clowns."

She turned to BJ, who peered over her shoulder, and stiffened under the force of his stare. His electrifying cobalt-blue eyes matched the colour of her VW. Uncanny. For the second time since meeting him, Jessie shuddered.

At last she found the wretched keys and retrieved them. "You're right. I'll have to get a new bag or something." A sheepish smile edged her lips while she tittered at her own stupidity. God, she sounded incapable of any intelligent thought.

"Come on." He escorted her to the driver's side in silence. After she unlocked the door, he held it open and she slid in.

"Make sure you lock yourself in, okay?"

"I always do. Thank you." After fumbling with her seatbelt, she jammed it in the buckle. "BJ?"

"Yes?" He leaned down closer, their faces level. A mountain of a man, he dwarfed the car. His icy blue gaze fused with hers.

My God, those eyes. She swallowed and bit her lower lip a little too hard so as not to be distracted. "Were you following me?"

"No. Not really."

"So how come you were right there when that guy tried to mug me?"

"Trouble and I seem to go hand in hand. Wherever it is, I'm usually just a step or two behind. You take care now. See you next Sunday." Straightening to his full height, he closed her door and stepped back. With a grateful smile, she triggered the lock, and he nodded in approval. She eased Penny out of the tight parking spot while he looked on. Except for a gust of delinquent wind whipping the stray strands of his hair, he could have been carved from stone. She drove away, leaving him on the desolate footpath with the wind as his companion.

CHAPTER 2

*T*he black Jeep Grand Cherokee confirmed lock-down with a high-pitched chirrup. Like most Melbournians, BJ had little choice but to park his pride and joy on the street—too many people, not enough space. Although he'd been back for a few years, he still struggled with big city living. He missed the sense of vastness, of land stretching endlessly to the horizon, devoid of a city skyscape. He missed gazing up at the brilliance of billions of stars in the night sky. He missed a lot of things.

After confirming the street's absence of loitering would-be felons, he walked over to his property's pedestrian gate, punched in the security code and pushed it open. When it closed with a clunk behind him, he checked his two-metre-high fence. A compound to keep out the rest of the world is what he'd wanted and that's what he got. With a nod, he strode up the four front steps to his unassuming house with its fortified front door. He plucked the key from his pocket, frowning at how easy it was for him to find his keys—unlike Jessie. *Some women just don't get how dangerous it is.* But at least she didn't freeze under attack. She fought back and recovered well. *She's got spunk.*

Shaking the incident from his mind, he turned the key, opened the door and prepared for the onslaught. Bolting up the hallway towards him like she did every time he returned home came his dog. All amber eyes and happy face, she danced and pranced, speaking an exuberant welcome through her doggy larynx.

"How're you doing, Whiskey? You miss me?" Reaching down, he rubbed his black and white Border collie's lopsided ears. "You're the most beautiful girl I know. Come on, let's chow down." He strode down the narrow hall of his weatherboard cottage, weaving from side to side, careful not to step on her paws. "What did you get up to this evening? Been protecting the castle?" He opened the fridge door, grabbed a bag of beef brisket bones and tossed it on the kitchen bench. He'd left the lights on out of habit, rather than for Whiskey. If there was light around him, the darkness within was somehow easier to bear.

Scanning the back yard, he checked the perimeters that he'd planted with impenetrable, skyward-reaching bamboo. He never knew what he expected to find. Maybe he hoped it was all a bad dream and that everything would return to the way it was. But nothing would be the same again. Regret tore at his heart as he tore open the plastic bag of bones. "Here you go, girl. Take it outside. I'll grab a beer and join you."

Whiskey clasped the bone and darted to the back door. As soon as BJ cracked it open, she sprinted to the grass and began devouring her dinner. Shortly after, he slumped into a well-used, canvas director's chair on his back deck, beer in hand. He hoisted his feet onto the timber railing, slurped a long tug of Crown lager and delighted in watching his dog.

Reflecting on the two hours he and Whiskey had spent together at training that morning, he uplifted his bottle in salute. "You did good today. Cheers."

The dog's head snapped up at the sound of his voice. Her eyes locked on him, waiting for further instructions. "Eat, Whiskey. Eat." He motioned his hand up and down, and she returned to her bone.

When they'd started training together some months ago, he'd wondered if she would ever overcome her instinct to herd everything in sight—low-flying swallows, smaller dogs, ducks on the lake, curious hares, and even the trainer on one occasion. But with diligence and determination, she and BJ had finally graduated from the obedience, personal protection and attack training classes. Now in specialist training, they underwent more focused practice, advancing their skills set with the end goal of becoming a search and rescue team.

During his combat years, he'd watched and admired the fearlessness, loyalty and vigilance of the bomb squad dogs. If not for them, many a soldier would never have returned home. Figuring search and rescue might give him a renewed purpose and aid in his assimilation back into civilian life, he'd bought Whiskey. Although many scoffed at his choosing a Border collie, he'd felt sorry for the runt of the litter and gave her a chance to prove herself. Much like the second chance life had given him.

Lifting her head, Whiskey tilted her ears as if picking up a clearer signal and growled.

"Hey, buddy, you home?" A familiar voice called through the house.

"Yeah, Ricky, out the back. Grab yourself a beer on the way through."

"Righto." Ricky made a pit stop in the kitchen then folded into the only other chair on the deck, beer aloft. "Cheers."

"Cheers, mate." BJ raised his bottle in the customary salute.

Both men savoured the hoppy brew for a moment in silence. Buffered by the backyard bamboo and the imposing concrete front wall, minimal sound penetrated BJ's small suburban sanctuary. Only the rustling wind and the barely audible thrum of distant traffic interrupted the evening's quiet.

"You know, buddy, you really ought to keep your front door locked…" Ricky regarded his mate with a look of bemused concern.

"Just because you and I could scale the front wall, doesn't mean any other bastard could. Besides, you're the only other person with a set of keys and the gate code. I lock up when I go out or go to bed."

"Maybe…but here in the city we lock the door, so the lunatics can't get in in the first place. Even if you are a big, strong bloke, you don't need the grief."

"Old habits die hard. Survival, evasion, resistance and a quick escape plan. Eh, mate?" BJ winked at him. "Besides, I've got Whiskey. She'll look after me."

"Yeah, right. Like she's going to do much good? All she does is run at people and lick them to death."

"That's where you're wrong." Rising to his feet, BJ set his bottle on the hand rail. "Whiskey, heel." Without hesitation, she discarded her bone and charged up the back steps to his side. "Sit." She set her butt to the floor. Eyes narrowing, he taunted his mate. "So, you think she's going to lick people to death, do you? Let me show you what we've been working on recently in her training. Just don't make a move."

With the hard edge of authority, BJ spoke the next command, directing his dog's attention to the possible perpetrator. "Defend." Putting a visual lock on Ricky, Whiskey curled her lips, bared her teeth and snarled. "Hold." Gripped in the command, the dog waited, body quivering in anticipation.

BJ returned his attention to Ricky. "I can either have her stand down or proceed. Which would you prefer?"

Visibly impressed, Ricky remained silent, still and steady.

"Release." BJ's hand sliced the air.

Whiskey reverted to her loving, doggy personality, tongue lolling from her mouth, making goo-goo eyes at her master. "Good girl. Good girl." He gave her an affectionate ear ruffle then hurled a tennis ball into the back yard with a final command. "Go play, Whiskey. Go play."

Ricky whistled and rubbed his chin. "Well, I'll be damned. I can see why you're not too concerned about the front door. I wouldn't like to be on the receiving end of her if you sent her on the attack."

"I told you. She's really improved. I'm hoping we'll make the search and rescue unit by next year." He collected the ball Whiskey dropped at his feet and threw it again.

"By the teamwork you two have going on I reckon you'll be a shoo-in. She's certainly come up well." Ricky shoved up to stand beside him, both enjoying the game of ball with the dog. After a couple more throws, BJ sent Whiskey back to her bone, and they settled down to finish their beers.

"How's yoga going? I can't believe you're still doing it. I guess it must be helping?"

"Yeah, it keeps my head together. I'm a little more relaxed most of the time. Though tonight I could've killed the dumb bastard who tried to mug one of the women from the class at her car."

"And you just happened to be there I suppose?" Ricky shot him a shrewd glance.

"Yeah, well. What am I supposed to do? I'm bored out of my brain a lot of the time. Doing a little recon helps." A wide grin split his face. He and Ricky Alvarez had done a lot during their time in the Australian Special Forces. "Tricky Ricky" was what they used to call him on tour. Not just because he was a damn fine soldier and spotter, but his Spanish heritage and swarthy good looks made him a real ladies' man. A tricky character both in and out of combat.

"And this woman you helped out—I guess she's the prettiest in the class?" Ricky asked. "Oops, sorry, buddy. I didn't mean…"

"Hey, it's fine." BJ raised his hand, his voice tinged with resignation. "I guess she is the prettiest, but I'm not ready, and I'm not looking. The only girl for me is Whiskey." At the mention of her name, the dog lifted her head, ready for another game. On command, she returned to her bone once more.

"What happened? With this woman and the dumb bastard?"

BJ gave a quick recap of the event. "All I can say is I'm glad the bloke decided to run…"

"Yeah. Lucky for him. I wouldn't like to clean up the mess after you finished with him. Want another beer?"

BJ nodded, and Ricky returned with two more beers. "You've done a good job with this place, buddy. You should be proud. It's come up really well."

"I'm happy with it. It's small, but it suits Whiskey and me. I don't need anything bigger." BJ had sold everything shortly after the accident. He'd drifted for a few months, until he'd stumbled across this renovator's dream and snapped it up for a good price. Donning his handyman belt, he'd gutted it, opened the interior, keeping only one bedroom and a study. He'd installed a swank new kitchen, even though he didn't cook much, and treated himself to a big bathroom with a spa bath. An investment project that well pleased him, the renovation had kept his mind and hands busy over the past months.

After rubbing her face on the grass, Whiskey joined them on the deck and nudged into his leg to receive an instant head massage. "What's your week shaping up like? Got lots of cougars to train at the local gym?" BJ gave another salute of his bottle.

Close to the same height as him, Ricky was less bulk and more speed. Athletic, ropey-muscled and fast on his feet, he was a terrific trainer and modern-day warrior. A hard one to land a punch on and if anyone happened to get one in, Ricky's abs could damage a man's fist. But his best civilian asset was his looks. Sometimes mistaken for Ricky Martin, he played on the resemblance and with his natural rhythm, the swooning ladies lined up for a dance. Like moths to a flame, Tricky Ricky burned so bright, BJ joked he had to wear sunglasses whenever he accompanied him on one of his tomcat prowls.

"Very funny…" Ricky pulled a face at BJ's dig about his female clients. "I have to use the local gym, because unlike you, not everyone can afford a set-up like this." He gestured towards the rack of ultra-heavy free weights and Smith machine that stood on the other side of BJ's back deck. Especially built as his home gym, the space also boasted a stationary bike and an assortment of balls, ropes, bars and a punching bag; all squeezed strategically together. An impressive statement, but for BJ it wasn't about vanity. Training hard saved him from the insidious depression that had laid claim to him not so long ago. His gym acted as his torturer and saviour, a place to gain a psychological advantage over his enemy—the darker version of himself. "It's a terrific set-up, buddy. I enjoy training here better than at the local gym."

"You didn't answer my question. How many cougars this week are you training and how many will end up in your bed?"

"From last count, I think I've got six hot bods and, fingers crossed, a couple will make all the hard work worthwhile." They joked about Ricky's lucky week ahead while Whiskey stared at her master with doe eyes.

"See, who needs a woman, when you have love like that?" BJ ruffled her ears.

Ricky set his empty bottle on the outdoor table between them. "I do. And so do you. How long's it been now?"

BJ's lungs deflated. He gritted his teeth and inhaled slow and steady, then drained his bottle, placed it beside Ricky's on the table and dragged a hand across his bristled chin. He spent most of his time trying not to think about it, but that also meant he wasn't dealing with it. He knew Ricky only wanted to help, but this was something he had to do in his own time. It just wasn't getting much easier. In the outside world, he got on with life. But inside, the rat of guilt gnawed at his brain.

"Two years, ten months and three days." With his gaze once more locked on the bamboo perimeter, his gut twisted.

"Buddy, it's time. It's not your fault. You weren't here. There's nothing anyone could have done."

"If that prick hadn't been drunk, Rachael and Tiffany would still be alive." He hissed the words as his hands clenched the railing, whitening his knuckles. "If I hadn't been in that hell hole of Afghanistan, none of this would've happened."

Rachael and he had been married three years. Three terrific years. They'd met in Perth after he'd been accepted into the Special Air Services Regiment, and they'd married a couple of years after that. God, she was beautiful…tall, leggy, brunette. And smart. She'd been a successful accountant before she got pregnant and then decided to start her own business from home after Tiffany was born. Tiffany. Daddy's princess. How she'd captured his heart, wrapped it in her tiny, chubby hands and pulled at its strings with sheer joy. At one year old, with her blonde curls and piercing blue eyes, she'd resembled a pretty baby doll.

He remembered when he left for his last tour of duty, a sinking feeling had roiled in his gut. He thought it was because his ticket was about to be punched. But he was wrong. Back home, some drunken loser swerved onto the wrong side of the road and killed his wife and daughter. Killed his family. Killed him, as sure as he'd killed them. His heart rate accelerated. *Control the fear, bury the anger, and avoid exposure.* A sniper must be mentally strong.

"BJ." Ricky's tone sounded more command than request.

His face twisted, and his lips clamped shut, like he'd sucked the life out of a dozen lemons. He forced himself back from the bitter memory. Releasing his grip on the railing, he tilted his neck until the familiar sound of snapping tendons signalled his tension had dispersed. "I'm fine, mate, really, I am. I'm getting better. And training with Whiskey helps a lot. So does the yoga."

"Are you still seeing the army shrink? What's his name?"

"Dr Thomson. I go and see him every now and then. But he just wants to feed me a stack of anti-depressants, and I'm not taking that crap. I need to keep my wits about me." Instinctively, he checked the perimeters once more.

"You're the boss. I'm just the guy who looks out for you." Ricky clapped a firm, friendly hand on his mate's shoulder.

"Thanks."

Ricky glanced at his watch. "I better get going. I've got an early in the morning. Six am she's turning up." Laughter and locker-room humour ushered them to the front door while an innocent Whiskey trotted at their heels.

"Make sure you do what I used to…" BJ grabbed his friend in a powerful forearm handshake.

"I will. And you remember what we said in the forces, it's better to burn out than fade away. You need to start burning again, buddy. I'll pop in during the week, and we'll do some training together."

"Thanks. I'd like that. See you."

"Later." Ricky gave a thumbs-up, turned, and in sharp, fast strides paced to the gate disappearing into the night, just like he used to do in the desert.

On a deep exhale, BJ closed and locked the front door. If it wasn't for Ricky, he didn't think he would have made it this far. In his darkest hours, he could have easily turned a gun on himself. End it all. But Ricky had been there, keeping an eye out for him. Like a good spotter in combat on surveillance for the enemy, he'd identified BJ's emotional enemy time and again. He'd saved him from blowing the mission, from blowing his brains out. As much as BJ hated how he still ached, he was no coward. His current search and rescue mission was himself. *Live in the moment and take one step at a time.*

Feeling an insistent paw at his leg, he looked down at Whiskey's ever-happy face beaming up at him. "Come on, girl. You can watch me shower."

Beyond excited, Whiskey ran circles around him on the way to the bathroom, her enthusiasm lifting his spirits. He'd got used to her being the only female in his life, his house, and his bathroom; and he wasn't ready to change that just yet.

CHAPTER 3

here did that big bastard come from? Whoever he was, that guy really ticked me off. She was mine. I had her. Her perfect, delicious body was in my hands. I was going to snap her open like a spring harvest pea pod and nibble out all her sweet goodness. It's not like I hadn't done my planning. I've been watching her for ages. She parks in that street like clockwork every Sunday and returns alone at the same time. All I wanted to do was get to know her better. But no! Some hero comes along and pokes his nose into my business. I hate those types of guys. Jocks, is what they used to call them at school. Girls swoon over them. Open their legs for them. Groan when they bed them. He had no right sticking his nose in where it didn't belong.

I hate him. And I hate this rat-hole my landlord calls an apartment. *Recently- refurbished, my arse.* This place hasn't seen a paint brush since before Christ was born. That Communist prick will be next on the list. The Chinese are taking over this country, buying up properties. I'm calling that poor excuse for a landlord tomorrow and demanding a new stove. And if he doesn't give me one, then I'll make him sorry.

Every time I think of her, my body tingles all over, especially down there. But I don't dare touch myself. I'm keeping myself only for her. I bet the big, interfering hero wanks off over her. I bet he tried to persuade her to go home with him tonight. I watched him leaning into her car, making eyes at her. *Bastard!* But she didn't. I saw. She drove away by herself. Left him on the footpath by himself. Serves him right. Anyway, it doesn't matter. *Where's there's a will, there's a way,* that's what my mother used to say. *Where's there's a will, there's a way.* The dancer will be mine soon enough.

CHAPTER 4

*W*ith but a hitch of breath, Jessie launched into a *grand jeté*, her powerful legs exploding into a mid-air split, her sinewy arms floating upward like silk ribbons. Glimpsing herself in the mirrors, she tilted her chin up a little more and breathed in. *Hold, hold, hold.* She willed her body to resist gravity, to hover airborne, until inevitably she conceded, and her feet touched down on the timber floorboards with the merest tap, tap, tap. She pattered across the stage space into imaginary wings and caught her reflection in the mirror. Her face wore an expression of bliss, the sheer bliss of being a ballerina. Despite the physical stress ballet placed on her body, it was only when she danced that she truly felt at one with her essence, her purpose for being.

Clapping of hands stopped the music. "Thank you, Jessie. Thank you, everyone. Good rehearsal. See you all tomorrow." The diminutive head ballet mistress collected her papers from the top of the piano, then nodded a farewell to the pianist, and left the studio in deep conversation with the artistic director. He'd watched these final rehearsals of "The Nutcracker" and would give his notes tomorrow.

Bare except for a ballet barre that lined three walls, the rehearsal studio's key feature was the mirrored wall in front of which the dancers performed. Like the famed mirror in Snow White, it reflected who was the fairest of them all and who was flawed. What the head ballet mistress or artistic director missed, the mirror reported. Mirrors were both friend and foe of dancers. As such, Jessie pushed on pointe, catching her breath. Overarching her insteps, she prepared and snapped off a couple of *pirouettes*, scrutinising her technique one last time. Not entirely convinced she'd performed her best today, her mouth screwed into a tight crimp.

With her hands on her hips above her frothy rehearsal tutu, she waddled across the studio, heading for her dance bag. She, like the rest of the dancers, shone with the lustre of perspiration, but few allowed themselves the privilege of looking exhausted. She nodded goodbye to those of the company who chatted together in small groups while they stretched and tugged at their tired limbs. Others jammed their gear into their dance bags and scurried from the studio, while a few simply preferred their own company as they reflected upon their rehearsal performance, or lack thereof. Sliding down into a second split, Jessie savoured the coolness of the timber floorboards through her stockinged legs.

"God, that was a tough day." Jasmine dropped to the floor beside her like a broken marionette doll. Spinning around on her bottom to face Jessie, her eyes sparkled. "But you were fabulous...You dance the Sugar Plum Fairy much better than Tabitha. I'm sure they're going to offer you the principal role for next year. Really I am."

In a wide leg split, Jessie rolled her body forward and back, releasing her hips. "Who knows? Don't underestimate the politics of this place though. Tabitha is as strong a dancer as me, maybe better, particularly as the Sugar Plum Fairy, and she's very chummy with the powers that be." She darted a furtive glance at her competitor nearby, whose foot was hoisted above her head in a standing split. It was no secret Tabitha Simpson had been campaigning for the top job and her dancing was impeccable. She and Jessie were alternates as the Sugar Plum Fairy in the company's forthcoming Christmas season of "The Nutcracker". Like Tabitha, Jessie knew her performance in this role, more than any other to date, influenced the likelihood of being promoted to principal ballerina next year. Make or break time for both her and Tabitha's careers.

"Forget about Tabitha's dancing." Jasmine waved a dismissive hand. "Just focus on you. Don't pay any attention to her. We're breaking for Christmas holidays soon, so they'll have to announce before then." She shoved her belongings in her oversize bag and sprang to her feet. "Let's go to Salvatore's. Grab something to eat. What do you say?"

"I'm in. I've got nothing in the fridge anyway." Jessie rose from the floor in one fluid movement. Like the rest of the female dancers, her limbs appeared disproportionately long and thin, barely held together by sinewy muscles and encased in a polished alabaster skin that seldom saw sunlight. Despite the gruelling rehearsals, she floated across the studio, a picture of composed elegance. Try as she might to be a little less reserved and more boisterous like Jasmine, ballet's grace was loaded into her DNA. She hoped the decision makers at the Australian Ballet Company would see that and it would tip the scales in her favour. Although she never voiced her burning desire, she prayed it would be her name on next year's programs as principal dancer.

"You danced really well today, Jessie." Tabitha sidled up beside her, the tight pinch in her voice matching her bright bottle-red hair pinned in a tight bun. Unlike most dancers, Tabitha wore lots of make-up to rehearsals. *Probably to show off the perfect symmetry of her exotic face*, thought Jessie, disappointed with her own ordinary round eyes, her too-wide mouth and too-square jaw.

"And you did too, Tabitha. Your pointe work was perfect,"

Jessie said, as Jasmine tapped her foot, obviously impatient to leave.

"Well, it won't be long now. One of us will be principal dancer and the other will remain a senior artist next year."

"And what will you do when Jessie becomes principal?" Jasmine tossed her head.

"I wouldn't count your chickens before they're hatched. I have it on good authority that the role may not go to Jessie." A smirk turned Tabitha's exquisite face into a mask of spite.

"Well, if I were you, I wouldn't believe everything you hear." Jasmine stepped in, thrusting her chest forward.

"Seriously, Jasmine, you can be so…" Tabitha jutted her chin higher.

Like a referee, Jessie sliced her hands between them. "Listen, you two. Let's not argue about it. We just have to wait for the final decision. Okay?" She glanced at each of them in turn.

"Okay," they murmured, eyeing each other suspiciously.

"Good. See you tomorrow, Tabitha, and all the best with the selection." Jessie tried for a genuine smile, but knew she failed. Liking Tabitha proved challenging. She seemed to go out of her way to be confrontational, except to her superiors who almost fawned over her when she was at her compliant best. "Come on, Jasmine. Let's go." She grabbed her friend and together they hurried from the studio.

"Tabitha gets me so mad. She thinks she's queen bee." Jasmine threw her pointe shoes into her locker, slammed the door and locked it.

"Don't let it bother you. It's no big deal." Taking her time, Jessie wrapped her pointe shoe ribbons neatly around each shoe before locking them safely in her locker.

"I don't like her. And I don't trust her."

"That's obvious. But why?" Worried they might be overheard in the change room, Jessie pulled her friend aside.

"Pure and simple, she's a bitch." She stripped off her tights and leotards. "Tabitha is someone not to be trusted. I've seen those types before. She'll do anything to get the top job. I'm telling you, Jessie. Watch your back." She shoved her damp gear into her dance bag with a punch and dragged on her street clothes. Still incensed, she continued her tirade. "She's Snow White on the outside, but the Wicked Queen on the inside. She's evil, through and through."

Jessie giggled. "Oh, Jasmine, you should have been an actress, not a dancer. Your gift for the dramatic is amazing." She loved how her friend always stuck up for her, but she could certainly blow things out of proportion.

"Regardless of whether you think I'm exaggerating or not, I don't like Tabitha Simpson. She's bad news."

Shaking her head, Jessie sighed. "But I do envy her self-confidence. There is no doubt in her mind, the job's hers." She peeled off her sweaty dance gear and rubbed her throbbing, inflamed toes. At least, they weren't bleeding today.

"Rubbish. Stop putting yourself down. You're every bit as a good a dancer as she is. Better." She leaned over and grabbed Jessie's shoulders, giving them a slight shake. "You need to give yourself some credit. Stand up for yourself a bit more. This is as much a mental game as it is physical, you know. You need to storm her defences like she does yours."

Pulling free of her grip, Jessie rose and began dressing. "Sorry. That's just not me. I'd rather keep a lower profile and let my work speak for itself."

"Well thank God you have me. I'll storm that bitch's defences until she crumbles in a heap." Striking a pose with hands on hips and legs wide, she reminded Jessie of Peter Pan, full of confidence before taking on the evil Captain Hook.

She giggled again. "Jasmine, you are wicked, but I love you."

She stretched her arm around her best friend's shoulder in a tight squeeze.

"Ditto." Jasmine returned the hug.

Now changed into their street clothes, they finished grooming in front of the mirrors. Freeing her buttery blonde hair from its tight rehearsal bun, Jasmine rubbed her scalp hard. "God, that's better." She tugged at her hair as if trying to uproot it like a nuisance weed. After a quick finger brush, she tossed her straight mane behind her shoulders and applied a bright red lipstick. Meanwhile, Jessie brushed her shoulder-length brunette locks, allowing the natural curl to bounce back. After applying a neutral-coloured lip gloss, she brushed her cheeks with a stroke of blush. Both dressed in blue jeans, loose-fitting blouses and sneakers, Jessie thought they resembled book ends.

"Ready?" Jasmine picked up her bright red parker.

"Ready." Jessie reached for her navy pea coat.

"Let's go eat some pasta." With jaunty resolve, Jasmine led the march to the best café and pasta ristorante in town.

At peak hour, the short walk up Kavanagh Street bustled with professional types conversing on their phones while they rushed to get home.

"You're not going to believe what happened to me last night after yoga," Jessie said, over the hubbub.

"What?"

"I was at my car and…"

"Hey, watch where you're going." Jasmine snapped at the business-suited man who bumped into her without apology. "Stop texting and watch where you're walking," she called after him, hands to mouth. But his head remained bent forward, oblivious to their contact.

"Come on, over this way." Tugging her friend's arm, Jessie

manoeuvred them away from a widening procession of IT-crazed workers. "Don't make a scene. We're nearly there."

"But people can be so rude…"

"I know, but it's not worth having an argument in the street."

"All right," Jasmine said, as they ducked and weaved through the burgeoning crowd.

Barely five metres from the restaurant, a sudden downpour of rain spewed from a lone cloud and the pedestrians bolted, their phones no longer the centre of attention. Bucketed in water, the girls dashed through the restaurant's glass doors.

"Miss Jessie, Miss Jasmine. Welcome. Welcome." The cheerful voice of Salvatore Bacci, owner and pasta-maker extraordinaire, greeted the dancers as they burst into his café.

"Bloody weather." Jasmine shoved wet strips of hair from her face. While she and Jessie shrugged off their coats, Salvatore offered them a hand towel each. "Thanks, Salvatore. How's it going?"

He pouted and shook his head in disappointment. "Oh, not so good. Not so good. Only one hundred and twenty-three covers today." He blinked his big, brown puppy-dog eyes, obviously wanting sympathy while they wiped the last of the water away.

Jasmine slapped him on the shoulder. "Get out of here. That's a great day, Salvatore. And you know it. Thanks for the towels."

"You are most welcome." He folded the crumpled wet towels over his arm like a five- star maître d.

"Have you got a table for us?" Jessie asked.

"*Si, si.*" He flourished his arm, directing the way. True to the Italian stereotype, he wore his love of pasta on his belly and rolled like a barrel between the two dozen undressed tables and bright red chairs. A favourite with the locals, Salvatore's café with its trendy atmosphere, rustic tables and red theming, buzzed with bright conversation and animated diners. Similarly, Salvatore thrived on playing pseudo-father to the dancers from the ballet company. For many of them, eating at Salvatore's was the closest thing to home, and for Jessie and Jasmine, their preferred haunt.

"Here you go." He pulled out a chair for Jessie, while Jasmine sat opposite.

"Thank you, Salvatore." She mirrored his smile.

"You are welcome, Miss Jessie." Cocking an eyebrow, he leaned closer. "Any news yet?"

"No, not yet, Salvatore. You'll be the first to know."

"I am sure they will pick you, Miss Jessie."

"Thank you, Salvatore." She squeezed the strong dough-making hand with which he patted her shoulder. *If only all fathers cared this much for their daughters.*

"Skippy will be here shortly to take your order." In a flurry of customer service, he hurried away to attend another couple entering the restaurant.

On his retreat, they decided on their usual—entrée-sized vegetarian lasagne for Jessie, main fettucine carbonara for Jasmine, and a litre of sparkling Santa Vittoria between them.

"Now what were you saying about last night, after yoga?" Jasmine picked up a bread stick from the basket on the table and bit into it.

"Well, this guy tried to mug me."

"What?" Half-masticated breadcrumbs spilled from her mouth. "What happened?"

"Long story short, this guy tried to snatch my bag when I was at my car. But one of the other yoga students, Brad Jordan, happened to be there and threw the mugger across the street."

"And?" Brushing the crumbs off the table, Jasmine gnawed at the breadstick like a voracious rabbit.

"The mugger was so scared, he got up and ran away."

"God, Jessie. Are you okay?"

"Yes. But I'm not sure what would've happened if BJ hadn't been there."

Jasmine lips curled upwards into a cheeky smile as she

swallowed the last mouthful. "BJ is it? And is this BJ tall, dark and handsome?"

"No…" A coy smile forced its way onto Jessie's face, try as she might to stop it. "He's tall, *blonde* and handsome."

"Ah, ha. So, when are you seeing him again?"

"I'll see him at yoga next Sunday, like I always do. Nothing more."

"Pity. You could do with a bit of tall, blonde and handsome."

"What do you mean?" Jessie pouted.

"You're too wound up for your own good. I love you to bits, but you need to relax more. Let yourself enjoy life. And a hunky man could be just the tonic."

"Despite what you think, I don't need a hunky man or any man for that matter."

"Really? Here have a breadstick." Jasmine shoved the basket across the table.

"No, thanks." She waved the offer away.

"Why not?"

"Because I have to be careful what I eat."

"For God's sake, Jessie. There's nothing of you now but lean muscle and bone. One breadstick isn't going to hurt." She scowled at her friend. "This is what I'm talking about. You're too uptight. Thinking a breadstick is going to impact your weight is crazy. Loosen up a little. Jump into bed with this BJ guy…"

"Absolutely not. Seriously, you can be so…"

"Coarse?"

"No, I don't mean that…"

"Jessie, I worry about you." She reached over and squeezed her hands. "You're too tightly wound, like a watch ready to bust a spring."

"I'm fine, really I am." Jessie squeezed back. "I just have to get the principal role next year and then I'll relax. I promise."

"Yeah, well you say that now, but when next year comes, you'll probably be even more stressed out." She withdrew her hands and flopped back in her chair.

"No, I won't. I promise. Come on. Let's order."

Skippy shambled up to their table as if on cue. "Hi, J-J-Jessie. Hi, J-J-Jasmine. How's th-th-things?"

Poor Skip Norton suffered from a speech impediment which, along with his red hair, made him the brunt of snide comments from some of the other dancers. No one except Jessie called him by his christened name—Skip. Somehow the misnomer of Skippy had stuck, which only added to his obvious embarrassment. In direct contrast to the bright, hoppy nickname, Skip moved with an awkward gait. Dressed in oversized jeans and shirt, he wore his sorry state for the world to see.

"We're good, Skip. How have you been?" Jessie had witnessed the effect of school bullying on her friends, twin sisters Mia and Kate Jones. Like Skip, they'd inherited bright red hair and freckles. Mia and Kate's problems had been further compounded by their need for glasses and bulky braces. By early high school, life became a living hell for them. Although Jessie didn't know much about Skip's history, she could guess enough from his slumped posture and downcast eyes.

"Oh th-th-things are pretty good. We've b-b-een b-b-busy here and..." he began.

Just as his tone brightened and his hooded lids lifted to reveal opaque blue eyes, Salvatore scurried over. "Now Skippy, don't go disturbing Jessie and Jasmine. Just take their order. We have more people arriving. Come along now." With fatherly affection, the owner patted Skippy on the shoulder, but his message was clear. Move on.

"Yes, Mr B-B-Bacci. Right away." Shut down like a toy box lid slammed by a bratty child, Skippy winced and wrote their order on his pad. Then with a lame smile, he retreated towards the kitchen.

"God, I feel sorry for him." Jessie watched him shuffle off. "It must be awfully difficult to stutter and not be able have a simple conversation."

"Yeah, he seems nice enough. How old do you think he is?"

"Maybe our age… in his twenties, I guess. You know, if he stood up straight, got a different haircut and found some confidence, he's quite a good-looking young man."

Jasmine spun around in her chair to eyeball Skippy, while his attention was elsewhere. "You think? Maybe? Not my type though." She swivelled back to face Jessie and snickered. "I like men with muscles and strong, powerful arms to throw me around the bedroom."

"For goodness sake, Jasmine. Who has time for men or sex?"

"I do. I know you don't, as all you think about is ballet. But I'm not going to make the corps de ballet for much longer and in a way I'm glad. I'm twenty-six years old, which is ancient in ballet years. I need to have some fun."

"But won't you miss it?" Jessie couldn't think of life without ballet.

"Of course I will, but I need to think about what I'm going to do with the rest of my life. And I want a man, a real man to settle down with."

The sound of falling plates and the scream of a customer disturbed their conversation.

"Skippy…" Salvatore dashed over to the customer who now wore Skippy's fully laden tray. Tomato-based pasta, coffee and salad rested in the woman's lap, like an ugly nest of bird guano. With a look of horror on her face, she blinked, hurling expletives at Skippy, who was on his hands and knees, collecting the broken crockery and ducking from the abuse. "S-s-sorry, s-s-sorry." His stutter worsened as his stress elevated.

Jessie's heart sank. She wanted to get up and help him but thought better of interfering. With effusive apologies, Salvatore escorted the woman to the ladies' restroom. Shooting a death stare back over his shoulder at Skippy, the owner sealed the young waiter's humiliation. With the evidence of his clumsiness returned to his tray, Skippy struggled to his feet and scuttled to the kitchen for his reprimand.

"Oh, God. Poor Skip. How terrible for him," Jessie said.

"I feel sorry for him too. But I hope he gets it together before he brings out our pasta." Jasmine's mouth curled in an irreverent grin, which drew a giggle from Jessie.

"Mum, you know I can't get there now. We're about to do the final season. I'll be there as planned for Christmas." The weekly phone conversations with her mother were taxing, but tonight's was tortuous. Jessie always notched up multiple circuits pacing around her unit whenever she spoke to her mother. Mostly it worked to quell her anxiety. Tonight, not so much.

"Well, I just hope your father pulls through, Jessica. Otherwise he won't be here when you come home for Christmas."

"For goodness sake, Mum. You said Dr Bruen told Dad today to take it easy, rest and wait for the results to come back. He didn't say it was urgent, did he?"

"Well, not yet. But it could be…" Joanna Hilton continued to criticise her daughter over her indifference to her father's health. It had always been this way. Dad came first as far as her mother was concerned, then her younger brother, Richard, then Coodravale Homestead, and finally her.

"Listen, Mum, this is my last chance to impress as a senior artist. I can't come home now. But as soon as the season is over, I'll be there as planned. I promise." Jessie waited for the obligatory pause and heard a sniffle on the other end of the phone.

"Very well, Jessica." *Oh God, she's doing mother martyr again.* "I understand. It's not that I don't want you to succeed and be a star in the Australian Ballet Company. It's just that I thought you

might like to know about your father's health. After all it is
Coodravale Homestead that financed your dream, you know."

Jessie bit her tongue. Joanna Hilton, the dominatrix of guilt. "I
know. And I'm eternally grateful to you and Dad for getting me
here. But I've got to finish it. I need to know if all your sacrifice
has been worthwhile. I need to give it my best shot at becoming
principal in the company. Surely you understand?"

Joanna's tone softened a little. "Of course I understand, Jessica.
You're right. I guess I'm just overwrought. I don't know what I'd
do if your father died." Then in a meek voice, she added, "I do
miss you, you know."

"I know, Mum. But I've been gone a long time now. Anyway,
Richard's there. He's helping out, surely?"

"Yes, your brother helps, but he doesn't love Coodravale like
your father and me. I guess your father's health scare has made me
realise I'm not prepared to handle this place on my own. Richard
won't stay, you know. He wants to move to the city. Start his own
life. He's got his sights set on being an accountant like your
cousin, Tom, and he's almost finished his study. He'll be leaving
soon I expect, once he finds a job in Sydney."

Despite their frequent spats, Jessie felt sorry for her mother.
The time would come when the life she'd lived at Coodravale
would crash down around her. "Mum, you have to stop worrying
about what's going to happen in the future. Take each day as it
comes. I'll be there in a couple of weeks. And we can talk about
everything then. Okay?"

"Okay. I'm sorry we can't be there to see you perform this
time." The hint of longing whined in her mother's voice like it did
whenever they discussed Jessie's career. Her mother had once
been a ballerina with a promising career but had not pursued it. "I
know you'll light up the stage as the Sugar Plum Fairy. You always
do in whatever role you dance. Good luck, darling. I'm sure they'll
offer you the principal role for next year. I just know it."

"Thanks, Mum. I hope so. Give Dad my love, and I'll see you

soon. Bye now." She ended the call on the tenth circuit of her unit. *Shorter than some, longer than others.* She set her phone on the kitchen bench and checked her Fitbit for the number of steps she taken today. At least the conversations with her mother added to her overall step count.

With a sigh, she wandered over to the window and peered out into the murky evening. Thick tears of rain smacked the window pane of her humble, third-floor unit. She had no balcony, so her unit and her life were enclosed in a bubble of her own making. Devoid of city noise, the only connection to the outside world was through the glass. Like Alice, she viewed life from inside her unit, wondering what it was like on the other side. Although ballet was her love, she wondered what it would feel like to be free of its responsibilities and experience earth-shattering romantic love. To not be so driven to achieve her dream. But that wasn't the life she chose. She would see this through. She had no other option. Her eyes watched the rivulets of water weaving this way and that down the window pane. She wished she could cry like the rain.

On Friday afternoon of opening night, a knock at her door had Jessie running to answer. "Who is it?" She never opened the door unless she knew who stood on the other side. Living alone in the big city made her cautious.

"The landlord sent me. I've come to fix your kitchen cupboard hinges." The deep, throaty resonance of a man's voice filtered through the timber. Since he knew specific details about the cupboard hinges, she decided he was legitimate and opened the door.

"I'm from Baker Builders and... Jessie?"

"BJ?" She cocked her head and blinked.

"Twice in one week I get to help you out. First a mugger and now cupboards." Sporting a cocky grin, Brad Jordan stood in her doorway.

"Are you a builder?"

"No, I work for Trent as a handyman. Baker Builders is his company. Can I come in and fix your hinges?"

She stepped back. "Sure. Sure. Come in. Kitchen's just here on the left."

"Thanks."

He strode past her, and she admired his easy saunter and imposing body. His muscled torso bulged beneath his cotton work shirt, while his jeans cinched tight at his trim waist. Dragging her attention away from his impressive body, she pointed to the culprits. "The three up the top. Be careful when you open them though. They'll just fall off."

"Okay." He pulled a cloth from his tool box and laid it on the bench. On it, he unpacked the necessary tools for the job. "Nice little place you have here."

"Thanks." As the yolky summer sunlight diffused through the window and chased away the lingering shades of grey from the rain, she followed his gaze into the living area. The butterscotch-coloured couch, her personal favourite, and the four-person dining setting came from a discount store, as did the bent glass coffee table and table nest. Accented with a few aqua throw cushions and rug, it was designer chic on a budget. Looking at her unit as if for the first time, she noticed she had no personal memorabilia on display. No pictures, no books, no programs from the ballets in which she'd performed, no hint of who she was or what she liked. The whole place screamed no-fuss, functional and impersonal. *Much like me.* Maybe Jasmine was right. She needed to loosen up a little.

"So, Jessie, what is it you do?" he asked over the whirring of his cordless drill.

"I'm a senior artist with the Australian Ballet Company."

The sound stopped as his hand froze mid-air. "A ballet dancer?"

"Yes, that's right."

"Wow. I bet it takes a lot of discipline and talent to be a ballerina. Tough work, I reckon. And with the Australian Ballet Company…" A low, appreciative whistle escaped his lips before he returned to his task.

"Yes, it does. I have no other life really. Just ballet. But that's okay because I love it." She strolled over to the other side of the bench to watch him work.

"What about you? Is this what you do?" She had a feeling it wasn't.

"For the moment, yes. I'm sort of in between things in my life, so I'm filling in time doing odd jobs." He tested the first cupboard door and then moved to the second.

"By the look of you, you obviously do more than yoga…" She didn't mean to pry—or did she? But she figured since he was in her unit, fixing her cupboards, it was a perfect opportunity to find out more about him.

"Yeah, I do a lot of training. I recently renovated my house, a little place in Carlton North. I installed a home gym. Helps me burn off steam."

"I know what you mean. Aside from ballet, I do a gym workout twice a week. Takes my mind off things and gives me more strength for my ballet." Leaning on the bench top, her feet pointed and stretched, as if all the talk of working out triggered them to limber up.

Having tested the second cupboard, he began repairing the third. "I hear you. Working out clears my head, too." The drill whirred, and she admired the grace with which he went about the mundane task. Nothing seemed to require any effort for him. "There you go. All done. Three cupboards with new hinges." He packed up his tools and leaned across the top of his tool box. "I guess I'll see you at yoga on Sunday, unless you need help tomorrow?" A soft, easy chortle rang from his generous mouth.

She huffed and rolled her eyes. "Very funny. I'm sure I'll be fine. Thank you very much."

"Jessie?" He paused. "Would you like to come to my place after yoga on Sunday? See my home gym?"

She hesitated, but Jasmine's voice echoed in her head to accept.

He hurried on. "Not on a date or anything. Just come over. Maybe grab something to eat?"

While she considered his offer, she busied herself with the unnecessary arrangement of three tins of tea at the edge of the counter. Jasmine's lecture on loosening up still resounded in her mind. Maybe she could take a night off, do something different. BJ seemed trustworthy, what with his recent heroics and respectful handyman behaviour. And...there was something else about him, something intangible that reminded her of herself. Perhaps it was his discipline to train hard, or that he balanced it with yoga. Whatever it was, she decided to take a chance. "Sure, why not? I could do with a change of scenery and some other company aside from dancers."

"Terrific. I'll see you at yoga, and you can follow me back to my place. I'll organise the rest. Okay?" With a grin, he bundled up his tool box and cloth.

"Okay. Can I have your number in case something comes up, and I can't make it?"

"Sure." They swapped phones and punched in their numbers.

"Thanks. See you Sunday." She ushered him to the door.

"See you then." He headed out along the landing and jogged down the stairs of the three-storey walk-up.

She watched him disappear, thinking he seemed brighter today than he had last Sunday night. Maybe like her, he longed for someone outside of his world to connect with. She glanced at her watch. *Damn...* Twenty minutes to get to the theatre before warm-up. She grabbed her dance bag and pea coat, and after slamming the door behind her, fled down the stairs.

"Hello, Jessie." The gravelly voice of Ron Jacobs, the building's middle-aged, bespectacled gardener greeted her as she dashed out onto the footpath. A fit-looking, gregarious sort of fellow who loved to chat.

"Hi, Ron." A quick grin tilted her lips.

"Have a look at these pansies. Don't you think they give the old building a bit of a facelift?" He guided Jessie towards the street planter box which burst with a rainbow of colour.

"Yes. They're lovely. You did a good job." She fidgeted, keen to be on her way. Ron always seemed to be around just at the time she headed to the theatre. She was sure the building's garden maintenance couldn't take more than one day a week, but still he was there nearly every afternoon, wanting to chat.

"I planted them in winter, so they'd be flowering now." He reached down, picked a deep purple pansy and handed it to her.

"Thank you." She held the flower to her chest. "The whole garden is lovely."

"Not as lovely as you," he said. "I've booked my ticket for "The Nutcracker". I can't wait to see you perform." Behind his fine-rimmed glasses, his dark eyes crinkled at their edges.

"That's nice. Nutcracker is such a festive ballet." She shifted her weight from foot to foot, hoping he'd get the message.

"I'm coming to the first matinee. Will you sign my program afterwards if I come to the stage door?"

"Of course, I will. Now, I have to be going." She glanced at her watch. "I don't want to be late for warm-up. Thanks for the flower." With a farewell smile, she stepped aside and powered along the footpath. *Poor Ron, he seems so lonely.* But she didn't have time to think about other people's problems. She needed to get to the theatre, and fast.

CHAPTER 5

*W*ith the glow of the street light behind him, his body cast a shadow over Jessie, leaving her classically sculpted face bathed in the early evening light. Her enchanting crisp scent crowded around him. She smelled like fresh, green apples and the fragrance triggered happy memories on his uncle's farm. He smiled. It had been a long time since he'd noticed any woman, let alone notice they were pretty. He'd been right last Sunday when he told Ricky she was the prettiest in the yoga class. With her gilt-flecked, hazel eyes, creamy skin and glossy brunette hair, she was damn pretty. "I have to warn you, I have a killer dog inside." BJ punched the code into his security gate.

"Dogs love me," she said. "Besides, you invited me over so it's your job to protect me."

"What, again?" Laughing, he escorted her to the front door. "Get ready."

She stepped behind him, peering around his upper arm.

When he opened the front door, Whiskey came bounding up the hallway, ready to herd whatever stood in her path. Screeching to a halt at his feet, she cried her welcome and then darted around, assessing his visitor with an intensive sniff fest.

"Whiskey, this is Jessie. Jessie, Whiskey."

"Good to meet you, Whiskey." She offered the back of her hand to Whiskey's investigative nose. After a couple of sniffs and tentative licks, the dog turned her attention to her master.

"Looks like you're in. Come through. Just be careful she doesn't trip you up. Come on, girl, out the way." He nudged the dog in front of them.

"Wow. This is stunning. You renovated this?"

"Yeah. It took me about six months or so. Do you want a drink? I've got beer, white wine, sparkling water…"

"I'll have a white wine spritzer. Thanks. Goodness. Look at this kitchen…" Jessie's fingers feathered along the black marble bench top. "I'm so embarrassed you had to come to my little hobbit hole of a kitchen to fix three cupboard hinges."

"Don't be. Look around if you like while I feed Whiskey and fix the drinks."

Circling the space, she stroked the luxury brand appliances and sighed. "If I could have the kitchen of my dreams, I'd have Miele appliances too." When she leaned over the hot plate, he sneaked a sideways glance. Thick hair cascaded over her shoulders like a silken shawl. Soft and shining. The blush pink of her lips and cheeks gave her face an innocence and fragility that belied the tenacity she obviously needed as a dancer. "Oooh, what a sink…" Jessie appeared to float around his kitchen, unaffected by gravity. He'd never seen anyone move like her. He liked it.

"I don't use the kitchen much," he said. *It was Rachael who wanted a designer kitchen. I made it for her.* Biting his tongue, he returned to the drinks, forcing the looming melancholy back into its box.

"That's a shame. It's stunning." While she continued admiring his handiwork, he gave Whiskey her bone and released her to the back yard. He picked up and drinks and nodded to the door. "Come out the back. I'll show you the gym I told you about."

Once on the deck, he stepped aside allowing her to join him.

"This is an amazing set-up. You've certainly done a terrific job with your renovation."

"Thanks." A sense of pride lifted his spirits. Up until now, he hadn't realised how much he'd missed having a woman appreciate his efforts. Living a solitary life with no one to talk to or share things with made for a lonely existence. Handing her the wine spritzer, he motioned towards the director's chairs on the opposite side of the deck.

Drink in hand, she moved to the farthest chair and melted into it. "How often do you work out?"

"Maybe five times a week." Sitting down, he hoisted his feet on the railing, nodding for her to do the same if she wished.

She drew her chair closer and mirrored his posture. "You work nearly as hard as me," she teased, reaching over to chime her glass on his bottle.

"No argument from me on that one." He tugged his beer, and a companionable silence enveloped them, broken only by Whiskey's enthusiastic bone cracking.

"How old is Whiskey?"

"Just over two."

"She's a beautiful dog."

"Yeah. She's got the best nature, and she's smart as hell."

He flicked another furtive glance at his guest while she watched Whiskey demolish the bone. With her long legs, lithesome body and delicate face framed by waves of maple sugar brown hair, Jessie was the most unusual house guest he'd had—unusual in a feminine, gentle way. One not only pleasing on the eye, but also on the spirit. "So, tell me a little about yourself. Aside from being a senior artist with the Australian Ballet Company, what makes you tick?"

The insistent pealing of the gate buzzer interrupted them.

Whiskey raced from the grass and hurtled down the hallway on high alert.

"Easy, Whiskey," he called after her. "Sorry. I wasn't expecting anyone. I'll go see who it is." At the front door, the dog sat on command and waited. BJ peered into the wall-mounted intercom screen and unlocked the security gate. "Angel, come in, mate."

When he opened the front door, he beamed at the tall, quietly-spoken man who grasped his hand in both of his. "BJ, how are you?"

"Terrific. I haven't seen you for a while. Come in. I've got company, but that's okay."

"Are you sure? I don't want to interrupt." Dressed in jeans and a blue chambray shirt, around which draped a white designer scarf, Angel oozed sophistication and style. The only child of Iranian parents who'd fled to Australia years before his birth, his swarthy looks and intense manner often unsettled people, but Aaban Naser possessed the most kind, even-tempered nature BJ had encountered in anyone.

"Not that sort of company. A friend. She's a ballerina from the Australian Ballet Company. We do yoga together." He closed the door behind them. With Whiskey bringing up the rear, he led Angel out to the back deck. "Jessie, this is a good friend of mine. Aaban Naser, the best crown prosecutor in the country."

"I'm not sure I'm the best." A self-deprecating smile played on his lips. "Hello, Jessie. Call me Angel. Everyone does." He offered his smooth, well-manicured hand.

"Hi, Angel." She accepted his welcome hand shake. "That's an unusual nickname."

BJ motioned for Angel to sit next to Jessie while he got a beer for his new guest.

"My mother called me her angel when I was a baby and it somehow stuck. Caused me no end of grief at school whenever she'd come to collect me. But as I grew up, I found the nickname

Angel was less culturally divisive than Aaban in social situations. You know how it is?"

"I can never understand why people are so afraid of differences."

"It just takes some people longer to change, and to realise the similarities we have as a human race, rather than our differences."

"I guess so, but that sort of discrimination or prejudice doesn't help..."

"That's why I got into law, to be a positive influence in the justice system. Now, enough about me, BJ tells me you're a ballerina with the Australian Ballet Company?" He accepted a beer from BJ, who angled in front of them to side-straddle the railing.

"I was just about to find out a little more about Jessie... By the way, what is your last name?"

"Hilton. Jessie Hilton." She smiled. "I grew up on Coodravale Homestead, about an hour's drive from a small country town called Yass, in South-West New South Wales. Coodravale was the home Banjo Paterson jointly owned with the winemaking Lindeman family between 1908 and 1911. Because of its history and cultural importance, my father and mother renovated it into a bed-and-breakfast and have been operating the business for years now. I won a scholarship to the Australian Ballet School when I was fifteen and moved to Melbourne. I was accepted into the Aussie Ballet Company when I was nineteen and am now a senior artist, hoping to become principal dancer next year. That's it in a nutshell." The men clapped her presentation, and she offered a coy smile over the rim of her wine glass.

"Wow. That about covers it I think," BJ said.

"Your turn," she said, holding eye contact.

Angel tilted his head at BJ, who responded with the merest of head shakes.

"Mine is a little more complicated I'm afraid..." BJ scratched the back of his neck. He didn't really want to tell her. Not yet.

He'd worked hard to keep his past shrouded in secrecy with only a select few in his inner sanctum of trust. Angel was one of them. He'd been instrumental in getting the drunk driver who killed Rachael and Tiffany sent to jail for a long time. Not long enough in BJ's mind, but as long as the law permitted. While he contemplated what to say, Jessie's phone trilled.

"Sorry." She glanced down at the screen. "It's Mum. I better get it. Dad's been sick." Standing up, she squeezed past them and trotted down the stairs into the back yard, out of earshot.

BJ took advantage of the reprieve and exchanged a look with Angel.

"She doesn't know?" Angel arched a brow.

"No. All she knows is I do handyman jobs for Baker Builders and the same yoga class as she does."

A thoughtful smile creased the crown prosecutor's face. He leaned back and steepled his fingers together under his chin. "Are you going to tell her?"

"What do you think I should do?"

"Your call. But what do you want from her? Friendship or something more?" With the accuracy of a skilled surgeon, Angel cut to the heart of the matter.

BJ rubbed his knuckles against his jaw, his thoughts racing. "Friendship. I've got too much of my own shit to sort out. I'm not ready." He gave a conclusive nod and seconded his decision with a slug of beer.

Angel fixed him in a cool stare. "Don't wait too long. Sometimes it helps to have someone on your side to see it through."

"I do. I have Ricky and you and…"

"That's not what I mean. A woman's love can work more magic than mateship."

"But that's what Rachael did for me." The bitter taste of loss and longing filled his mouth. Even another mouthful of beer couldn't wash it away.

Jessie hurried up the stairs, breaking the tension. "I'm sorry. Mum says Dad's had a stroke. I've got to go. I'll have to drive home to Yass tomorrow."

"Is there anything I can do?" BJ snapped to attention while Angel rose elegantly to his feet.

"No. I'll have to organise special leave from the company tomorrow. Then I'll drive straight to Yass Hospital. Sorry about this." She blinked up at him, her face a grimace of impending doom. He'd seen the same expression on the rookies' faces during their first desert night patrol. A gut instinct of serious shit about to go down, with no way out.

"If you need anything, call me. Okay?"

"Thanks." She managed a half-smile at Angel. "Nice to meet you."

"You, too. Be safe, and I hope everything works out for your dad." Reaching out, he clasped her hand in both of his.

"Bye, Whiskey." She ruffled the top of the dog's head as she sat beside her master.

"I'll see you out," BJ said, and they double-timed it to the door in silence. "Anything you need. I'm happy to help."

"Thanks." As tears misted her eyes, she pivoted and departed in a whirlwind of emotion.

BJ let out a breath. He was disappointed she had to go. Her presence had reminded him of how simple and enjoyable life could be. On his return, Angel met him in the hall. "I'm going to head off too. You look like you could do with some R & R."

Although he hadn't acknowledged it, BJ was dead tired. Harbouring rage, resentment and revenge for all these years bankrupted him emotionally and physically. "Okay. Thanks for dropping by." He locked eyes with him. "That drunk bastard is staying in jail, isn't he? You didn't come here to tell me he's appealing or anything?" Unrequited revenge churned in his gut.

"No appeal. He'll be there for a long time yet. I just dropped by to see how you were."

"Good. I hope he dies in there with some bastard up his arse..."

"From what I know about our penal system, your wish might just come true. Try not to dwell on him, eh? It's time to think about you and your future. Good night."

The soft snoring of Whiskey as her head lay beside him on a pillow prompted an affectionate smile on BJ's face. He knew he shouldn't allow her on the bed, but it was a Sunday night treat— for them both. Since moving into the house, they'd become staunch companions, and he figured she deserved to share his bed as much as any live-in partner.

Without a woman's touch, he'd decorated his bedroom in an unembellished theme of grey, black and white. Due to his forces training, he kept a kit packed and ready to go in his wardrobe. Just in case of what, he didn't know. Aside from two black bedside tables and a couple of monochromatic abstracts on the walls, his bedroom appeared almost unlived in—except for the pictures. Framed photos of him and Rachael on their wedding day, of Tiffany cradled in their arms at the hospital, of them playing with Tiffany at the beach, of Rachael bathing Tiffany, feeding Tiffany, changing Tiffany. So many pictures, so little room on the bedside tables.

He lay next to Whiskey, gazing at the frame in his hands. A photo of Rachael and Tiffany taken just before Tiffany's first birthday. Perched in her highchair, with creamy sponge cake all over her tiny hands and cherubic lips, she looked the essence of mischievous delight with Rachael leaning in and laughing. Rubbing his thumb over their framed faces, he relived the joy...a bittersweet memory.

Hot tears pooled in his eyes and he pressed the frame to his chest. God, he missed them. No matter how punishing the training had been to graduate as a SAS soldier, it didn't compare to the endless torment he'd experienced since losing his girls. In the forces, they used to say the easy day was yesterday. And for him, now, it was true. Each yesterday was easier than the present day in which he lived. Try as he might to swallow down the burning emotion, to store its rage in his gut, tonight it defied his command. Short, sharp hiccupping sobs loosened his self-control. Like a fleet of long-range patrol vehicles, the pain, loss and injustice rolled forth, gaining momentum. Low, desperate moans shuddered from deep within. Unable to withstand the emotional battle any longer, he surrendered and wailed into the night.

CHAPTER 6

*D*isjointed thoughts tumbled in Jessie's mind like too many clothes in a dryer as she vaulted the stairs two at a time to her unit. Her father having a stroke couldn't have happened at a worse time. Hopefully, the company would understand her predicament and grant her special leave tomorrow. In a couple more weeks, she would've been able to get away easily. But now, Tabitha Simpson would dance the part of the Sugar Plum Fairy for the entire season, giving her the edge to secure the role of principal dancer for next year. *God, why me? Why now?* Striding along the landing to her unit, she scrounged in her bag for her keys. Her lips suppressed a smile. She still hadn't followed BJ's advice and got a key strap or changed bags. Just as her hand found her keys, a sense of foreboding crawled over her. The door to her unit was ajar. When she'd left this afternoon, she knew she'd locked it.

She clutched the keys, so they wouldn't jingle. Should she go in? No, that's what all those stupid heroines in the movies do. That's just asking for trouble. Should she call out? No, another stupid thought. Whoever broke into her unit could still be in there. *Back up. Back up. Get away now.* With the stealth and confidence of a cat, she stepped one foot behind the other, then slowly turned and sprinted down the stairs to where Penny was parked on the street. Slipping inside and slamming the door behind her, she gulped down big breaths of air and rummaged in her bag. *Bloody bag...* Finally ripping the phone from its hiding place, she scrolled through her contacts and jabbed one. Ringing, ringing, ringing. *Pick up, pick up.*

"BJ?" The pause at the end of the line signalled she'd disturbed him, but still she rushed on. "I'm sorry. But someone's broken into my unit, and you're the first person I thought of. Can you help me please?" The fright in her voice whined on the last word. She hated how desperate she sounded.

"Where are you?"

"I'm sitting in Penny on the street."

"Who's Penny?"

"Sorry. My VW. I call her Penny. When I got home after leaving your place, my unit door was open, so I just ran back down the stairs. And now I've locked myself in the car."

"Good. Stay there. Have you called the police?"

"Not yet."

"I'm on my way. Call the police and wait for them to arrive. Do not get out of the car."

"No. I won't. Thanks." But the connection had ended. He was already on his way. After a deep inhale, she dialled triple zero and gave them her details. Nothing to do now but wait. Jessie tipped her head back on the headrest and sighed. *What the hell is going on in my life?*

A gentle tap-tap-tap at the driver's window startled her. Beside the car, BJ stood in all his towering glory. In that moment, she understood the whole thing about white knights on horses rescuing princesses. His quick response made the break-in episode less frightening, although no less real.

"Thanks for coming. I didn't know who else to call." She climbed out of the car and locked it behind her. "My friends are all dancers, and I doubt they'd be much help."

"I'm pleased you did. I'll go up and have a look around. Did you call the police?

"Yes. They should be here soon."

"Good. I've brought my tools, so I can change your lock once they've finished." He lifted his tool box as confirmation. "How about you stay here and wait for me?"

"No. I'm coming up with you." Her mouth twisted in defiance.

"Okay then. But promise you'll do everything I tell you? Agreed?"

"Agreed."

He hefted his tool box, turned and led the way. She scurried behind trying to keep up. For a big guy, he sure moved fast and silent. Creeping up the stairs, she realised she still knew nothing about Brad Jordan. Yet, he'd been the first one she'd thought of to call. Probably because he was damn good at damage control. He certainly acted like he knew what he was doing. Setting his tool box down in the landing alcove, he placed a finger to his lips. "You wait here in the alcove. If anyone is in there, I don't want them seeing you if they run out. Got it?"

"Got it." She backed into the shadows.

He stepped up to her unit's semi-closed door, eased it open and disappeared into the darkness of her unit. Jessie watched and waited. *One, one thousand; two, one thousand; three, one thousand.* Her ears strained, trying to catch any noise. Nothing. After ten seconds, she took a timid step out of the shadows and froze.

"What are you doing? I told you to wait in the alcove." Disapproval growled in BJ's voice as he paced over to collect his tool box. "It's clear. You can come in."

She gave him an apologetic grin and followed him into her unit, switching on the lights. Their bright blaze turned the dark, nightmarish event into something less sinister. On initial inspection, her neat little unit looked undisturbed. Miffed at overreacting to the entire incident, she shook her head in self-reproach. *God, I've spent the best part of my life looking after myself without a man and the first thing I do at the scent of trouble is ring one I don't even know that well. Seriously?*

He interrupted her inner scolding, his voice serious. "It doesn't look like anything's been touched. But only you'll know that once you've had a closer look. But I did find this." He held up a sealed pink envelope that he'd skewered on the tip of one of Jessie's kitchen forks. The wary expression on his face kindled a spark of fear in her.

She eyed it with suspicion. "What is it?"

"I'm not sure, but it was propped up on the pillows on your bed. It's addressed to you. I haven't touched it."

An icy shiver skidded down her spine and slammed into her stomach. "You open it." She rubbed her arms a little too fiercely.

"Do you have any gloves? If this has got fingerprints on it, I don't want to contaminate evidence."

"Yes. Under the sink in my bathroom. There're disposable gloves in a box." She cocked her head in the direction, indicating he should go and find them. Her legs trembled, and she feared that if she tried to go, she'd fall flat on her face.

Within a minute or two, he returned with a pair of gloves. "You'll have to put them on. They're too small for me."

Jessie rubbed her hands, stalling for time. She reached for the gloves and braced herself as if expecting them to send an electric shock up her arms. Doing her best to remain calm, she pushed her hands into the gloves, finishing each with a snap.

"You have to open it, Jessie. If you don't want to read it, leave it on the table and walk away. I'll read it if you like."

Her hands shook as she plucked the envelope from the fork. The back of it peeled up effortlessly, and she imagined the person who had left it, licking it with their vile tongue and sealing it with just enough of their wetness, but not so much as to stick it tight. She swallowed down her revulsion before gagging on it. Reluctantly, she opened the envelope and eased out an innocent piece of squarely folded pink paper. Flattening it out, she wrenched her gaze away, before she accidentally read its contents.

BJ leaned over and read the note. The silence stretched on until his gaze lifted, his expression intense.

"Well? What does it say?" she asked, unwilling not to know.

"Once I read it, you can't un-hear it. You understand?"

"Yes." Jessie locked her arms across her chest, as if this small action would defend her against the letter's message.

In a gentle, almost comforting voice he read aloud…

> *They say it takes a minute to find a special person*
> *An hour to appreciate them*
> *A day to love them*
> *And an entire life to forget them.*
> *Soon, we will be together for our entire lives*
> *I'm coming for you soon*

A love letter. In fact, a beautiful, romantic love letter which any woman would be thrilled to receive if it had come from her lover. Not from someone who broke into her unit and left it on her pillow. A stalker. *God, someone is stalking me.*

She staggered and collapsed backwards onto her couch. Panic slammed into her, forcing her face downward as she clutched her stomach, rocking and moaning. Her mind blurred. *Oh God, I'm going to faint, I'm going to faint.* The sensation of dread drenching her body reminded her of the terror in her nightmares.

Beside her, the couch sank as BJ eased his weight down. "Jessie. Listen to me. Jessie." He waited, but she continued spiralling. "Jessie. Look at me." The force with which he spoke stopped her free fall. She blinked at him and bit her lip. "Good.

Now pull yourself together. You're going to go into your bedroom and bathroom to check if anything is missing. Keep the gloves on. Okay? I'll wait here in case the police arrive."

Without a word, she nodded and rose to her feet. *I can do this. I can do this.*

On approaching her bedroom, she hesitated at the threshold. To think someone had been in there, touched her things, maybe smelled her clothes and fondled her underwear made her skin crawl. Another shudder gripped her body, but she forced herself onwards. Inching into her inner sanctum, she noted the items on her dressing table were where she left them. Hair brush, a plastic basket with some lipsticks and eye shadows—though she couldn't remember how many of each was there before she left tonight. Half a bottle of mineral water, assorted pens and writing pads, a postcard picture of Coodravale Homestead and a couple of James Patterson's books. *At least in his stories, the bad guy is caught.*

She reefed up the bed ruffle and peered into the sinister blackness under the bed. Resting peacefully lay her winter slippers and a lost sock she'd been searching for. Ignoring its lonely plight, she straightened and approached the wardrobe. Although certain BJ would have checked everywhere, she still slid open the doors with childish caution.

She inspected her clothes. Everything seemed to be in order. As her fear dissipated, anger bubbled up to take its place. *How dare someone break into my unit?* With each drawer she opened in the wardrobe, her rising anger slammed it shut. *Wait 'til I get my hands on this freak.* Short- and long-sleeve T-shirts and tops were all accounted for. *He'll be sorry he messed with Jessie Hilton, that's all I can say.* Underwear. Check. No. Wait. Where were her apricot G-string and matching bra? Rifling through her knickers, bras and socks, she couldn't find them. But she'd just washed them, so they should be there. She battled to dislodge the laminate drawer, swearing at its defiance. With a vicious tug and a grunt, she yanked it free, nearly toppling backwards.

Spinning around, she upended the contents on the bed and scratched through them like a dog after a bone. "Where are they? Where are they?"

"Jessie, what's wrong?" BJ stood at the doorway.

With hands madly paddling on the bed, she wailed. "I can't find them." Burning tears streamed down her cheeks. "I can't find them."

Strong, sympathetic arms engulfed her. "I promise you're safe. What's wrong? What can't you find?"

"He took my favourite underwear. They're not here. Oh God. What's happening? Why would anyone do this to me?"

"I don't know. But we'll find out. Listen...Do you want me to stay the night? I'll sleep on the couch."

She nodded meekly. "But what about Whiskey?"

"She'll be fine. I'll get up at dawn, go home, let her out and be back before you know it. No one will be lurking around at sunrise. These bastards are back in their coffins before day break." His attempt at humour lightened her mood a little, as did the assurance of his smile.

"I'd feel safer if you were here. I don't really want to stay alone tonight." The thought of this lunatic returning triggered a new wave of fear in her. The whole episode reminded her too much of her nightmares. The terror of being trapped and unable to escape was shocking enough when asleep, let alone if she was awake.

"Come on. Let's have a tea or something stronger if you have anything."

Dazed, she crawled off the bed. He tucked her under his arm, and they walked to the kitchen. "I only have herbal tea, I'm sorry."

"Tea is fine. You put the kettle on."

Rap, rap, rap. "Hello. Officers Charles and Wentworth responding to a break and entry."

BJ hurried to the door. "Hello, officers. This is Jessie Hilton." He waved Jessie over. "It's her unit."

Officer Charles was a tall, dark haired woman, while Officer

Wentworth was her male counterpart. Both looked like they could stop a truck.

"And who are you?" Officer Charles cocked a brow at BJ.

"Brad Jordan."

"He's a friend," Jessie said. "I called him for help. Please come in and sit down." The presence of the police steadied her nerves.

"Actually, we prefer to stand. Can you give us your account of what happened here, Miss Hilton?" Officer Charles asked, her voice official yet kind. Officer Wentworth extracted a notebook and pen, readying to take notes.

Jessie explained, trying to recount every detail as clearly as possible. Then they questioned BJ who retold his part of the story. Over the next hour, the officers inspected Jessie's flat, and tagged and bagged anything that might give them a clue as to the identity of the perpetrator. A forensics team arrived shortly after and set about unpacking their gear to dust for prints throughout the unit.

At the dining table, BJ pointed to the note. "This is the letter I found on Jessie's pillows."

The officers peered down at it and then at Jessie. "Can you think of anyone who would do this? Maybe an ex-boyfriend or someone who has a grudge against you? Perhaps someone you've jilted?" Officer Wentworth asked.

"No. I can't think of anyone. I don't have time for relationships..." She tried to think, but her mind was a fog.

"Very well. In the meantime, here's my card." Officer Charles handed her a white business card. "If you think of anything else, be sure to let us know. You may find over the next couple of days you remember things that will help us in our investigation. In the meantime, be careful."

"Thanks. I will." Jessie's voice was as stiff as her smile. Officer's Charles warning reinforced the possibility that she could still be in danger. Real danger.

"Very good then. Once forensics has finished, you can touch anything you like. Thank you. Jessie. Brad." Officer Charles nodded curtly and with Officer Wentworth behind her, strode from the unit.

After they left, Jessie returned to the kitchen and fumbled around with the routine task of getting mugs, boiling water and making tea. The sense of safety she'd valued as a single woman living alone in a big city had been ripped away from her. In its place, the stark reality of a demented stalker landed with a thud. One thought looped in her mind. *This can't be happening.* But it was. They say life imitates art, but now in her case, life imitated her worst nightmares. She moaned. Her body sagged. Broken and paralysed, she ground to a halt, staring out into space.

"Jessie. Jessie. Forget the tea..." BJ's soothing voice drifted to her from afar. A moment, or was it an hour later, he nudged beside her. "Jessie, honey. Time for bed." Cradled into his side, she shadowed his lead and trundled from the kitchen. But she was numb. Disembodied. Somewhere else.

"Excuse me, guys..." BJ called to the team dusting the door lock. "Have you finished in Jessie's bedroom? She needs rest."

"Sure. Go ahead. We're nearly done out here as well. But you'll need to replace this lock. It's been tampered with."

"Thanks. I'll get onto it when you leave."

Once in the bedroom, Jessie waited while BJ found some sheets and remade her bed. He helped her up and removed her shoes. "Lie down." Obediently, she lay back, and he folded the top sheet under her chin. "I'll be in the living room, on the couch. You're safe. I'm here. You're safe."

The last thing she remembered before sleep rescued her were the well-cut lines of his face and the golden bristle of his jaw. His wild blue eyes gazed down at her while he traced his thumb across her cheek. "Sleep," he said. But when he turned out the lights and left the room, her senses sharpened, and the slimy serpents of dread entangled themselves in her stomach.

~

Out of the shadows a familiar evil slithered, all groping hands and probing fingers. A man, always a man. Licking wetness—a vile tongue lapped at her cheek. Pledges of love and threats of death whispered in her ear. *No, no, no.* Fear cleaved her in two. A scream clutched in her throat, tight and scorching. In her mind, she could hear it shrieking for freedom, but it never escaped her body. Jessie jolted upwards. She heaved awake, head spinning, mouth dry. Behind her ribs, her heart hammered as if she'd just danced the dawn variation from the ballet "Coppelia". Her head hung in her hands, and she swiped away the futile tears cried in her sleep. Before tonight, wakefulness had been her ally. Her only escape from the haunting nightmares. But now, with a stalker lurking around not just in her mind, but in her waking life, when would she ever find relief? When the panic lifted, resignation took its place, leaving Jessie to wonder how her once ordered life had spiralled so far out of control.

CHAPTER 7

How easy was that? Breaking into her unit was a piece of cake. I was in before I knew it. Lucky that old lock didn't put up much of a fight. That's why I have three heavy-duty deadlocks on my door. No one will ever get in here without a fight. Bloody landlord tries, but he can go screw himself. This is my unit, and possession is nine-tenths of the law.

She has such a neat little home, nothing out of place, just like her. I made myself comfortable. On the couch, I buried my face into the cushions and smelled where she sat. It reminded me of the talcum powder my nan wore. I lay there for a while, just breathing her in. Next stop was the bathroom. I tried her lotions and creams, rubbing them hard into my skin. It felt good. I even sprayed her perfume down there. But I got so hard, I thought I would burst. It hurt like hell, but I don't dare touch myself.

When I went in her bedroom with its pretty girly things, my heart skipped a beat. Make-up, books, clothes…her precious things. Things she touches and treasures. Then, I found her lace bra and knickers, so pretty, so delicate. Just like her. And they smell good too. Soapy and fresh. I imagine how they must look on her lean, supple body. The way the thong cuts into her round, tight arse and between her long, silky legs. How excited it must make her as it rubs and rubs and rubs. When I wrap my tongue around that tiny piece of fabric and suck really hard, I can taste her. *Mmm...salty and sweet. My favourite flavour in the whole world.* I can taste the journey my tongue will take into her when we are finally together. And her pert breasts that fit snugly into the frilly bra. I will lick and nip them until they are red and raw. Oh God, it makes me tingle, but I don't dare touch myself.

Patience is a virtue my mother used to say when she made me wait for a slice of the cake that she baked. It was stale by the time she finally gave me some. But I got real good at patience. Soon, my dancer, you will come to me, soon. We will have such fun together. Soon.

CHAPTER 8

$\mathcal{B}$y the time she showered, changed and ambled into the living room, early morning streaks of marigold yellow dissipated some of the previous night's terror. Gone were the insipid charcoal hues from the previous days of rain, instead replaced by the vibrant shades of summer glittering on the city's skyscape. While a sweltering, hot day prepared to broil the city, Jessie's spirits lifted. The smell of toast and tea wafted to greet her, as did the pleasing sight of BJ's back flinching under his skin-tight, white T-shirt.

As if detecting her presence, he turned, a grin spreading across his face. "Good morning. Feeling better?"

"Yes, thanks. How's Whiskey?" She wrapped her fingers around the steaming mug he pushed across the kitchen bench towards her.

"Overexcited, overactive and now overfed. I bought some groceries. How do you like your eggs?"

"Just one egg for me thanks. No toast."

"You've got to be kidding. After all the calories you burned up with last night's stress, you need food. Real food. Two eggs, one piece of toast and nothing less."

She opened her hands in submission. "Okay. Okay. Sunny side up. Thanks."

Amused, she watched him fry eggs, butter toast and pour more tea in a well-rehearsed routine. All the time, he talked about ordinary, everyday things. The more he talked about nothing, the more her muscles relaxed and the terror from the previous night slipped away. Within minutes, they were seated at the dining table, with the first hot breakfast she'd eaten in twelve months. The last had been one she'd allowed her mother to make when she returned home to Coodravale last Christmas. On BJ's side plate teetered four pieces of toast to match the four eggs sunning themselves on his dinner plate, all of which he hungrily set to.

"Do you always eat this much?" She shook her head in awe of his appetite.

"Absolutely. How do you think I stay this big? Not by eating bird seed." He chuckled at his own joke before returning to the task at hand.

"Thanks for staying last night." She hoped he knew how much she appreciated it.

"No worries. The forensics guys left shortly after you went to bed. I've installed a new lock on your front door." He shoved another forkful of eggy toast into his mouth and chewed contentedly. He reminded Jessie of Whiskey, and she giggled. *They say owners pick dogs that mirror themselves.* "You've still got no idea who might have broken into your unit?"

"No. I thought about it this morning in the shower, but I can't think of anyone." She wasn't interested in eating, so she fiddled with her cutlery.

"Does someone have a grudge against you? Or is jealous of you?"

"I don't know. I've always gone out of my way to be friendly and not upset anyone. I've no idea who'd want to do this to me." Fresh tears bit her eyes.

He reached over and patted her hand. "It's okay. I'm sure the police will find this sicko. Now, what do you have to organise with the Aussie Ballet, so you can get home to your dad?"

"I'll get in there early and see David. He's the artistic director. Hopefully he'll grant me special leave. I'll catch up with my best friend, Jasmine and then head off to Yass around lunchtime. It's a six-hour drive, and I want to be there before dark."

BJ scooped up the traces of egg from his plate with the final quarter piece of toast. "Okay. Here's the deal." He gulped it down and sculled the last draft of tea. "If you like, I'll drive you to Yass, and I can stay if it suits. I don't like this stalking shit any more than you do. Until the cops get a handle on this, I think having me around is at least a deterrent. But there's one condition..."

"What's that?" she asked, wide-eyed at his offer.

"I have to bring Whiskey. I've got no one to look after her. So, where I go, she goes." He reached over to clear the plates and scowled at Jessie's. She hadn't touched the toast and had eaten only one egg, just as she ordered.

She trailed him into the kitchen and began rinsing the plates. Although she liked the idea of having him around, she wasn't sure how Joanna would cope. Her mother was difficult enough without trying to explain BJ's reason for being there. But she had six hours to work out a reason that might satisfy her. "What about your work? Won't your boss mind?"

"Trent's a bit of a grouch at the best of times, so he'll be pissed. But since he hasn't lined up any real work for me, I figure he won't miss me too much. I need a bit of time off anyway. What do you say?"

"Okay. You're got yourself a deal." Jessie's shoulders sagged as if she'd just dumped her heavy dance bag on the floor. It felt good not to carry everything alone.

"Terrific. Now if you don't mind finishing off, I'll go organise a few things. I'll meet you back here in two hours. I've got a key for your new lock, and I've left yours on the bench here." He slid the new door key towards her. "If anything changes, call me. Okay?"

"Sure." She stopped washing dishes and fixed him with a sincere gaze. "You know. All I seem to do is say thank you to you. I'm an awful nuisance…" She hesitated, her expression saddening. In the week they'd known each other, she'd been nothing but an inconvenience. Not the way to start a new friendship.

"Don't be silly. It's been a long time since I had someone to look after, aside from Whiskey. Actually, I'm kind of enjoying it." Planting a kiss to her forehead, he shot her a sunny smile to match the light streaming through the window. "See you soon." He collected his tool box and departed.

Now the hard part. With another steaming cup of tea in hand, she gazed out of her living room window and planned the best approach with the artistic director.

"Come in, Jessie. How may I help you?" David Fitzgibbons, the artistic director of the Australian Ballet Company for the past five years, waved her into his office. A tall, horsey-looking man, he'd performed male lead roles in famous ballets around the world before taking up this post in his home country. Aside from establishing himself as a legendary performer, he possessed both creative genius and a savvy business sense. A rare breed. Like a god, he was worshipped and feared by the company and media alike.

Pushing a few strands of hair behind her ear, she walked over to sit in front of his formidable desk. As a child, she'd loathed being in the school principal's office. Now, sitting in the visitor's chair in the artistic director's office proved even more daunting. Sweaty palms and silent prayers accompanied her fidgeting feet.

"Thank you for seeing me, David. The reason I asked for this meeting is that my father has had a stroke. Unfortunately, I need to get home straight away. I hate not being able to stay and perform in Nutcracker, but I must go. He may not pull through."

With his autocratic gazed fixed on her, the artistic director drummed his fingers on his wood-grain desk. "I'm sorry to hear your father is so ill, Jessie. That's very sad news. When do you wish to leave?"

"Straight away, please. I won't be able to perform tonight. I'm sorry."

The finger drumming grew faintly louder. "And do you think you'll be back before the season ends?"

"I'm not sure at this stage."

The drumming stopped. "You understand this means Tabitha Simpson will perform the role of the Sugar Plum Fairy for the entire season then?"

"Yes, I understand." Jessie lowered her head.

"And you know this may affect the principal ballerina selections for next year?"

"Yes." She picked at the cuticle on her thumb.

"Very well. Off you go, and I hope your father improves so you can return to at least dance some of the season for us."

She lifted her eyes to see the artistic director push back his chair and offer his hand, brusque and final. She accepted his reluctant permission with a shake, almost curtsied, and scurried from the office before heartbreak shattered her poise.

Jasmine rushed toward her. "How'd it go?"

"They're giving me the leave. Legally, they can't refuse, I suppose. But I could tell by the look on his face, my chances to be a principal next year just got shredded. I was so close." Jessie grabbed her friend in a tight neck hug. She wanted to cry. Everything she'd worked for came crashing down around her because of her father. *Why couldn't he be less sick?* Running the memory newsreel backwards, she reviewed the last ten years she'd been away from home. In all that time, her father hadn't shown any real interest in her or her ballet career. Sure, he'd come to see her perform at times, but she was convinced that was because her mother made him. Not once had he ever said he was proud of her. Yet now, she was expected to go rushing to his bedside because he might die any minute. It wasn't fair.

Jasmine rubbed sympathetic circles on her back. "It's not over yet. Come on. I've got thirty minutes until the next clean-up rehearsal. Let's grab a quick coffee before you go."

Downcast, Jessie broke the embrace. She stared at the polished concrete floor, half-expecting to see her future scattered in pieces at her feet. *My life is falling apart and there's nothing I can do to stop it...*

"Hi Jessie, How's it going?"

She groaned. Michael James. With matted hair and eyes rimmed in dark circles, he looked like he'd just got out of bed. The sickly scent of cheap aftershave wafted around him, unsuccessfully concealing his body odour.

"Not now, Michael. Jessie's had some bad news." Jasmine wrapped Jessie's shoulders in a protective hug.

"I'm just saying hello. What's got your knickers in a knot?" He glared at Jasmine.

"Sorry, I can't stay and chat. My father's sick, and I have to go back home." Jessie forced a thin smile while trying to keep the peace between her best friend and one of the junior lighting technicians from the company. He'd asked her out whenever they crossed paths, and although she'd repeatedly refused, he didn't understand she had no interest in him.

"Oh, I'm sorry to hear that. How long will you be gone?" He stepped in closer.

Jessie shrugged. "I'm not sure."

"Maybe when you get back, we could go out and..."

"Listen. In case you don't get it. Jessie doesn't want to go out with you." Jasmine was curt.

"You can be such a bossy bitch Jasmine Longford."

"Stop it," Jessie said. "Michael, I have to go." She grabbed Jasmine's hand, pivoted and walked away.

"Okay then," he called after them. "We'll catch up when you get back."

"What doesn't he understand about no?" Jessie asked.

"Got me. The guy's an idiot." Jasmine sneered over her shoulder. "Anyway, forget about him. Let's grab a coffee. You look like you could use one."

"You've no idea."

With little time to spare, they jogged to Salvatore's, arriving damp and reddened not just from the effort, but from the day's mounting temperature. Dropping into a chair, Jessie scanned the restaurant for service and on spying Skippy cleaning glasses behind the counter, waved him over.

Beaming an eager smile, he shambled towards them. Although his oversized clothes still hung from his body, he appeared better groomed than usual. His hair less dank, his skin less freckled, his eyes less ghostly.

Jessie leaned closer to Jasmine. "At least life seems a little better for Skip at the moment. Check out the grin he's wearing."

"That's because he runs at a slower speed to the rest of the world. When you move and think that slow, there's no time to be stressed."

"Stop it." Jessie tapped a good-humoured slap on her friend's hand. As Skippy sidled beside her, she managed a brighter smile than her mood. "How are you, Skip?"

"I'm g-g-good, Jessie. An-n-d you?" The concentrated furrowing of his brow demonstrated the care he took in speaking with her.

"I'm good thanks, Skip. You look particularly happy this morning?"

"I g-g-ot some g-g-good news yest-t-terday." Even more than usual, Skippy stumbled over his words as excitement rang in his voice.

"What was it?"

"A f-f-f-friend of mine from s-s-chool is c-c-coming to visit me. A f-f-female f-f-friend." He puffed out his chest like a mating pigeon on display.

"Hey, Skippy. That's great. Way to go," Jasmine said from across the table.

"Yes. Her n-n-name is Chr-Chr-Chrissy. I like her a l-l-lot."

"Well, I hope you have a lovely time with Chrissy when she gets here. Now, can we have two cappuccinos, please?"

"Two c-c-cappuccinos, c-c-coming right up." With a decisive tap of pencil to pad, he confirmed their order. His repetitive nod of understanding reminded Jessie of the bobble-head toys that people glued to the rear parcel shelves of their cars. Skip's almost child-like delight at being of service prompted both girls to smile.

Reaching up, she touched his forearm. "Thanks, Skip. Now hurry. We don't have a lot of time."

Obviously thrilled by her encouragement and probably the thought of Chrissy's visit, Skippy gathered speed on his way to the counter.

"He is rather sweet, isn't he?" Jasmine watched him retreat.

"Poor Skip, he has a lot of challenges, yet somehow finds something to be glad about in his ordinary day. His attitude could teach us all a thing or two about appreciating what we have in life."

"Yeah, maybe you're right. I hadn't thought of Skippy like that before."

He soon returned victorious with their coffee. Without spilling a drop, he placed their cups and saucers on the table. "There you go, J-J-Jessie. J-J-Jasmine."

"Excellent. Thanks. I may not see you for a couple of weeks because I've got to go home. My father's sick." His face fell. "You have a nice holiday and enjoy Chrissy's visit. Okay?"

"O-o-kay." Reverting to his downtrodden demeanour, Skippy shuffled back to the kitchen.

"Now you've done it." Jasmine brandished a breadstick at her. "You've upset him. You and your strays."

"Actually, there's something I need to tell you…" Jessie turned her coffee cup around and around on its saucer.

"What now?"

"Well…" While they sipped their coffees and Jasmine ate another two breadsticks, Jessie briefed her on last night's unit break-in, the hideous calling card of her stalker, and BJ's offer to drive her to Coodravale today.

Jasmine blinked wide-eyed like the proverbial possum. "Are you kidding me? Why didn't you tell me all this sooner? Thank goodness your father is deathly ill, and you've been called home. I don't know how you could go on performing the Sugar Plum Fairy under these conditions."

"Don't be silly. Of course I could. I'd have to. I only wish I could stay and keep performing. This is the biggest opportunity of my life. I hate that I've got to leave and give up my chance to be principal next year. It's such a mess." She rubbed her forehead and then glanced at her watch. "Shit. I have to go." She launched to her feet, leaned over and kissed Jasmine's cheek. "I'll call you."

"And I'll call you when they announce…"

When she spun to leave, Jasmine grabbed her wrist. "Jessie, be careful."

"I'll be safe as houses," she said, not feeling as confident as she sounded.

"Houses can be broken into, burned down or blown up, as you've already seen with your unit. Just be careful. Okay?" Jasmine exchanged a look of grave concern with her.

"I'll be careful. I promise." She leaned over once more to brush a kiss across Jasmine's cheek. "See you soon."

Snapping an about-face, she set off in the direction of home. First her unit, her once loved little sanctuary in which now, she no longer felt safe. And then Coodravale Homestead, her childhood home. *But I never felt safe there either…*

CHAPTER 9

"So that's where we're up to. What do you think?" While BJ finished explaining last night's events over hands-free, he glanced into his rear-view mirror and changed lanes.

"I'm sure the police will be thorough. If you like, I can follow them up and see how their investigations are proceeding?" Angel's smooth voice filtered through the cabin of the Grand Cherokee.

"That'd be great. Thanks."

"Leave it with me. I'll keep you posted."

"I owe you."

"Jessie has no idea who might be stalking her?"

"I asked her again this morning, but she reckons she can't think of anyone. Maybe it's a sick fan or a disgruntled dancer who never made the grade? All I know is that I can't let her do that six-hour drive to Yass alone."

"You're a good man. Always the hero, hey?"

BJ imagined the droll grin creasing the prosecutor's face. "Cut it out. I'm just doing what any decent bloke would do." He steered the Jeep into a tight street park outside his house.

"No mate. You're wrong. Many a decent bloke would like to do it, but few would. That's what makes you different. You actually go out on a limb to help someone."

"Thanks. Talk to you later." BJ switched off the engine and got out of the car. He punched in the code at his security gate, then strode up his front steps two at a time. When he inserted his key into the front door lock, the door drifted. He knew he'd locked it before leaving this morning after he'd fed Whiskey. Had someone broken into his house? Was the same stalker now following him? Flattening his bulk against the door frame, he stiffened; his hands frustratingly empty. *Where the hell is your weapon when you need it? And where is Whiskey?* Jagged thoughts bounced off the walls in his mind. *Maybe they killed her?* This one thought alone tore open a Pandora's Box of hate and revenge. Heart slamming in his chest, he crouched, eased the door further open and slinked inside.

The back door was closed, so maybe they were still in the house. Compressing himself against the wall like a gecko, he edged along the hallway. Steady, muffled thuds came from his back yard. *Someone digging?* He checked the bedroom, bathroom and study, and then approached the kitchen, still undetected by whoever was outside. Peering around the corner of the kitchen, he spied Whiskey prone on the grass. From this distance, he couldn't tell if she was breathing or not. He refocused and edged further around the corner to gain full view through the kitchen window. That's when he saw him, bench-pressing on the deck. BJ flung open the back door. "What the hell are you doing here, Ricky? I could've killed you, man."

Ricky halted the bar mid-air and swivelled his head towards him. "If you recall, we organised to train this morning. It's Monday, you know."

BJ slumped and consciously switched off his tactical training. "Shit. I completely forgot. Sorry, mate." By now the familiar, hairy head of Whiskey nuzzled his thigh wanting affection. He crouched and cupped her wolfish face. "I thought someone'd killed you. Good to see you, girl." A long, wet tongue greeted him across his lips, and he wiped away her love. "You're lucky she didn't bail you up."

Ricky rose, flicked his towel from the bench and wiped the perspiration dripping down his arms and torso. "Initially, she thought it was you when I opened the door. I guess because she knows my smell and since I'm here a lot, she allowed me in. I have that effect on the ladies. She couldn't resist me." A cheeky glint flashed in his eyes. "Where were you?"

"You're not going to believe this, but it was that woman again."

"What? The one from yoga? What trouble did she get herself into this time?"

"Come inside while I make a coffee and tell you all about it."

"I need to grab my kit, throw Whiskey and her gear in the car, and get back there. Sorry, mate. I've got no time to train. But use the gym while I'm away." BJ rinsed out the coffee mugs and wiped the benches, so the ants wouldn't have a festive season of their own in his absence.

"I'm not letting you go off to Yass without at least meeting this bothersome wench of yours."

"What? Now?"

"I'll follow you into the city. Then you can introduce me before you two set off into the wild blue yonder." He clapped BJ's shoulder.

"Unbelievable." BJ shook his head in amusement.

"Just doing my job, buddy. I'm the spotter, you're the sniper. I scope them out, and you hit the target. Sounds to me like this woman may become your target, so I need to scope her out first." His throaty laugh echoed in the kitchen, harmonised by BJ's deeper chuckle.

By the time they arrived, Jessie was waiting on the footpath in front of her building. While Whiskey remained propped in the back seat of the Jeep, BJ and Ricky crossed the busy street to where she stood.

"Hi, BJ." She looked relieved to see him.

"Is everything okay?"

"Yes. As good as can be expected, I guess." She glanced at Ricky.

"Jessie Hilton, this is Ricky Alvarez, a good mate of mine. We go way back."

"Hi, Ricky, good to meet you." She managed a half-hearted smile and offered her hand.

Picky pumped it a couple of times. "You look pretty good considering you've had a break-in and got yourself a stalker."

BJ scowled at him. Ricky smirked back.

"I don't feel that good. But the show must go on. I suspect it's much the same for you and BJ, although I have no idea who you are…" She cocked her head and glanced from one to the other.

"I'm sure he'll fill you in on the details. I hear you've got quite a drive ahead of you," Ricky said.

"Yes, we do." Her voice sounded thin and tired.

"You got everything you need?" BJ glanced at the duffel bag at her feet.

"Yes. I've locked my unit, but I didn't have time to clean up that black fingerprint dust. It's awful stuff. You touch it and it goes everywhere."

"If you want, I'll clean it up for you while you're away?" Ricky said.

Jessie frowned. "That's very nice of you, but…"

"I can vouch for him. He's a neat freak. Loves to clean. Don't ask me why." BJ shrugged.

Jessie reached up to whisper in BJ's ear. "Are you sure?"

He nodded. "Absolutely."

"Okay. Offer accepted. But it's not necessary. I can do it when I get back."

"Of course you can, but you won't want to. Leave it to me." He rubbed his hands together as if eager to begin.

"You can have my key, mate. Let Angel know you've got it in case the police want to get back in. Is that okay with you, Jessie?"

"Sure." She waved a dismissive hand. "This whole business makes my head spin."

BJ fished out his key and handed it to Ricky, who locked an unwavering gaze on him. "Target scoped. Your turn to lock and load. Have a good trip, buddy."

"What on earth…?" Jessie said, but her attention wasn't on the banter between the two men.

"Jessie, Jessie," another voice called out. It belonged to a blonde-haired young woman who ran up the footpath with the lightness of a gazelle.

Skidding in beside them, she regained her composure and fluttered her eyelashes. "Hi, I'm Jessie's friend, Jasmine. Which one of you is BJ?"

"I am. Pleased to meet you." He eyed Jessie who shrugged as if to say she had no idea what Jasmine was doing here.

"And I'm Ricky, Ricky Alvarez." Like a kitten angling for a cuddle, he edged closer to Jasmine. Wearing a cutaway training T-shirt and jeans, and under a fine layer of perspiration, his body rippled and shimmered in the late-morning heat. BJ shook his head, entertained by his friend's talent not to miss any opportunity with a new, attractive young woman. The gods-of-lucky-meetings certainly bestowed good fortune on Ricky Alvarez.

"Jasmine, what's wrong?" Jessie reached for her friend's hands.

"Tabitha Simpson has fallen and sprained her ankle. Just now, in class." Jasmine's voice trilled. "The Company doctor is on his way. You may still get the role of principal. Don't give up hope,

Jessie." Holding onto her hands, Jasmine jumped up and down on the spot.

"That's terrible news. Poor Tabitha." Despite Tabitha's bitchiness, Jessie couldn't think of anything worse than being injured when such an important decision was at hand. She'd hate to be in her shoes...literally.

"No, it's not. It means you may still be in with a chance. Stop feeling sorry for her and think about yourself for a change. Anyway, Kelly, your understudy will dance the role in the meantime. I'll keep you posted."

"You know you won't be able to get me on mobile at Coodravale. Just land line." Jessie wagged her finger.

"Yes, I know. I've got the number." Jasmine rolled her eyes in return.

BJ interrupted. "Listen. We need to head off if we want to be there before dark. See you soon, mate. You better get that landline number off Jasmine before she heads back. Keep in touch, okay." He grabbed his mate in a tight bear hug, and they slapped each other's back a couple of times.

"Thanks, Jasmine. See you soon." Jessie embraced her friend, both holding tight.

"Right. Let's hit the road." BJ stooped to collect Jessie's bag. Turning to the other two, he flipped a wave. "See you when we see you."

He ushered Jessie across the road and threw her bag in the back while she climbed into the front passenger's seat.

"Hi, Whiskey." Reaching back, she stroked the dog's chest as BJ slid into the driver's seat. With Whiskey's head pushed between them, he put the Jeep into gear and drove off with a toot of the horn.

Looking in his side mirror, he clucked his tongue. "Check those two out, Ricky and Jasmine. Flirts, the two of them."

She swivelled around and stared out the back window. "Yes. You're right. At least they're having fun. I don't expect there'll be much fun on this trip back home." Unenthused, she slumped back in her seat.

"Who knows? Maybe it'll turn out better than you expect?"

"We'll see. But based on everything so far, I'm not getting my hopes up."

BJ glanced at her, but she averted her gaze out the passenger window. Without further conversation, he manoeuvred the Jeep through the traffic and hoped tomorrow would be the easy day for Jessie.

CHAPTER 10

Doesn't this guy have anything else to do with his life? I can't believe he's shown up again. After all the trouble I went to finding just the right love poem, printing it out, breaking into her unit and leaving it on her pillows, he shows up again to spoil everything. *He's really ticking me off.* He's hanging around her like a bee to a honey pot. Has the man no honour? He needs to find a girlfriend of his own and leave mine alone.

But it doesn't matter. I have what I wanted. It was all I was looking for when I let myself in…her delicious underwear. I have her G-string with me always. Here in my jockey shorts, curled around me, reminding me of what delights are in store. Oh, it makes me tingle, but I don't dare touch myself.

But that big hero is ruining everything I planned. Now they're off on some road trip by the look of it. I saw them drive away. They didn't see me in my car, watching them. But I'm here, keeping my distance. I've done this before. I know how not to be seen, in and out of the traffic. He doesn't even know I'm here. Him and his big, black car. He thinks he's hot shit, but I'm way smarter than he is. As my mother used to say, *you can't keep a good man down.* Well, I'm a good man, and he won't keep me down.

Soon, my love, we will be together. I'm coming for you soon...

CHAPTER 11

*S*canning the Jeep's rich leather interior, Jessie suspected BJ wasn't just the action-man type, but he also appreciated luxury. The way the soft, leather seats hugged a person's body, the touch of sophisticated wood trims and the cluster of state-of-the-art instrumentation, screamed top-end luxury. The Grand Cherokee was the perfect fit for BJ. A bit of GI Joe meets James Bond.

"How did things go with your artistic director?"

"He wasn't happy I had to leave, which is understandable. I just hope I can get back and dance at least a few performances, particularly now Tabitha is out."

"I'm sure it'll all work out. Had any more thoughts about who might have broken into your unit?"

Jessie frowned as she remembered what Officer Wentworth had said last night. "Well, there is this guy Michael. He's a lighting tech' at the Company. He keeps pestering me to go out. I've told him I don't want to, but he doesn't take no for an answer."

"Anyone else like that around? Pestering you?"

She reflected on the last few days. "There's my building's

gardener, Ron. But he's just a lonely, middle-aged man who likes to chat."

"Listen. You need to call the police with these two guys' names. At least, give them something to go on. What about this dancer, Tabitha? Do you think she might do something like this to unnerve you to get the principal role?"

"Tabitha can be a bitch, but I don't think she'd do anything like this?"

"You never know. People do odd things when someone stands in the way of their dreams."

Jessie's thoughts went into a tailspin. Surely, she couldn't be so hated or Tabitha so jealous that she'd do something as horrible as this? "But I don't want to get Michael or Ron or Tabitha into trouble. Can you imagine the back lash after the police question them?" She tugged at her hair. The thought of causing all this fuss made her head hurt. It could destroy her chance at becoming the principal dancer in the Company, forever. David would be appalled. She just wished it would all to go away.

"Call the police. Give them the names."

She scowled at him, but knew he was right. If someone was planning on doing her real harm, she needed to tell the police, despite the repercussions. "Okay. Okay." She fumbled in her handbag, retrieved Officer Charles' business card and made the call. After a ten-minute conversation, she threw her phone back into her bag and let out a ragged breath.

"Now, sit back and relax. Try not to worry about it anymore."

BJ's reassurance soothed the tension in her shoulders, and she settled back for the ride. Within no time, they escaped the city limits and powered along the M31. The heat of the midday sun blasted through the windscreen only to be thwarted by the air conditioning, which maintained a comfortable temperature in the cabin. Clear skies promised a hassle-free trip, while easy-listening music set a stress-free driving mood. Like a kid on her first holiday, Whiskey sat bolt upright, ready for the forthcoming adventure.

Jessie glanced across at BJ. "I don't know how to thank you for everything you've done for me over this past week. You really are the proverbial knight in shining armour, aren't you?" She stared at the attractive planes of his face as his eyes focused on the highway. Even his scraggy hair tied in its trademark ponytail and scruffy stubble that needed a tidy-up did nothing to hide his good looks. Dressed in rough, almost tattered blue Levis, scuffed tan suede boots and a grey chambray shirt, rolled at the cuffs, he looked like he'd just ridden in on a horse and swung from the saddle. Yet it was the concentrated effort which knitted his brows that intrigued her most. She sensed a troubled mind was caught behind his rugged handsomeness. A mind mulling over a problem that refused to be solved.

"God, no. I'm no knight. Just a bloke who doesn't like to see someone, particularly a lady, take unnecessary risks."

"Really? I think there's a lot more to you than you're willing to say. But we have about six hours until we get to Yass District Hospital. Plenty of time for you to finally tell me the Brad Jordan story..." She extended her legs deep into the foot well and clasped her hands behind her head. Flashing him a radiant "gotcha" smile, she waited. Judging by the twist of his mouth, she wondered if she'd pushed too hard. But since he was trapped behind the wheel, he had to tell her something. She hoped it would be the truth.

"I guess what with the mugging, your unit break-in, meeting Ricky and Angel who both like you, and most importantly based on Whiskey's approval..." The dog turned to him on cue. "It would seem you can be trusted."

"Of course, you can trust me. But why so secretive?"

"It's a long story, but as you say we have plenty of time." His swift sideways glance of cobalt blue sealed the deal. Chasing the sun up the highway, he repositioned his sun glasses and began. "I don't talk much about my childhood. But here goes...I grew up in

Melbourne and like most kids, both my parents worked. Nothing fancy. Just ordinary, everyday people doing ordinary, everyday jobs. I was the eldest of two boys. I was twelve when my younger brother drowned. He was ten..."

She drew a sharp breath and darted a glance at him, but his focus never wavered from the road. In a steady, flat voice, he explained. "We were swimming at the local public pool on the Christmas holidays. Mum had gone to get ice creams and left me in charge of Tony. We were both strong swimmers. We competed in the school swimming carnivals, usually placing in the top three. I figured he didn't need looking after too much. Instead of watching him, I clowned around with some other boys. When I couldn't see him, I started yelling for him. Tony was floating face-down in the pool. They tried to revive him, but it was too late. I remember how blue his lips were. His skin, cold and damp. No one could work out why he drowned. But I knew. It was my fault. It was my fault for not looking out for him. It was my fault he died. Everything turned to shit from that day." As BJ retold his boyhood story, his voice held no emotion, no inflection.

Lifeless, she thought. Exactly how poor Tony must have looked to his older brother who shouldered all the blame for his younger brother's death. "But you were only a boy. You can't really blame yourself..."

"That's what everyone said, except my father. He blamed us both. He left Mum and me not long after that. We never saw him again. It fell on me to look after Mum and do her proud. To somehow make up for Tony's death and Dad's leaving."

God, how awful. What do you say to someone who's lived such a traumatic childhood? She glanced at the air con display, expecting the temperature to have dropped, but it remained steady. The chill filling the cabin was the haunting legacy from BJ's past. Unsure as what to say, she decided on silence.

"As I got older, I spent weekends at my Uncle Bob's place on the Mornington Peninsula. My mother's brother, not my father's.

Uncle Bob taught me about being a man, about responsibility, about perseverance. When I was old enough, I joined the army. It's where I belonged. But because most of the other guys didn't really want to be professional soldiers, I felt out of place a lot of the time. I wanted to be the best soldier I could be. After a while, I needed more. So, I applied and was accepted into the SASR—Special Air Services Regiment, which is a special missions unit within the Australian Defence Force."

"Oh, I see…" Her mind teased apart the small details it had unconsciously stored.

"See what?" He glanced across at her.

"Your size, the way you can creep up on someone without making a sound, the constant scanning of your surroundings, your gym at home and the ease with which you threw that mugger in the air…it all makes sense now. It's your training in the SAS."

"Like your ballet training affords you extraordinary skills, my SAS training has done the same for me." He nodded then returned his attention to the road.

Jessie recalled their first meeting. He'd said that he and trouble seemed to go hand in hand. Based on what he'd just told her, it certainly appeared to be the case. No wonder he was only too eager to help. He probably felt duty-bound to do so.

"After three years, I ended up deployed to a number of combat zones including Afghanistan, as a sniper."

Her skin prickled. *A sniper.* Being in the SAS was one thing, but a sniper? She gazed out the window and tuned into the drone of the rubber on the highway, while the East Wangaratta countryside whizzed past. Parched from recent drought, plains of brittle, dust-covered grasses blurred into a grim landscape of death. *A trained, highly skilled killer.* Someone specialised to kill others to protect their own. She had no idea how to process that information.

She was a vegetarian for God's sake. Not for health reasons, but for ethical ones. She refused to eat any flesh because it upset her to think a life had been taken just to feed her. And here she was sitting beside a trained killer, an SAS sniper. *God knows how many people he's killed. How many lives he's taken?* Was he some crazed serial killer exploiting war to kill other people, or just a noble guy doing an extraordinarily difficult job? A job he chose— no doubt as some sort of penance for not saving his brother all those years ago.

She let out a heavy sigh and sneaked a peek across at him. Obviously sensing that she needed time to process, he focused on the road, on the job of getting them there safely. *That's what a sniper does. Makes sure the team gets there safely.*

Jessie forced her mind to stop dramatizing, to take a more positive approach. She backtracked on everything since meeting him. Her previous thought about him being a GI Joe type was closer to the truth than she'd expected. And she'd just got through telling him he was like a knight in shining armour. On some level, she'd been correct. For the men and women who counted on him to protect them when they risked their lives on war-torn streets, he was. His accuracy, skill and unwavering sense of duty protected them.

She cast him a nervous glance which he caught with a nod and an upward curve of his lips. That was enough. She didn't need to know more. She didn't need to know how many people he'd killed or what war was like. He did what he had to do. It was none of her business. Her business waited for her at Coodravale Homestead.

She reclined the seat, closed her eyes and trusted him to get her there safely.

CHAPTER 12

*A*ll in all, he thought Jessie took the news of his being an ex-SAS sniper well. She'd not commented or passed judgement, which he took as a plus. Like his mates from the unit, he'd got used to not telling anyone about his past. People's reactions were mixed and difficult to judge. The ghoulish voyeurs pumped him as to what it felt like being in a war zone, "plugging off the enemy". They made his skin crawl. And the holier-than-thou types reviled him as nothing more than a paid assassin. They never understood that without him and the other troops, the freedom they took for granted could soon be usurped. *But it takes all types.* He had no one to answer to but himself.

He raked his fingers through his hair, dislodging another section from its ponytail. Through all those years of complying with army regulations, he'd taken to not cutting his hair or shaving as an act of rebellion. Rachael hated when he came home on leave, and got "shabby", as she called it. But since he had no one left in his life to impress, he wore shabby like a badge of honour.

With the tender memory of Rachael came the familiar tug at his heart. Automatically, he reached his hand between the seats, and Whiskey nuzzled into his palm. "You're a good girl." He appreciated how her affection lessened some of his longing.

The orb of the sun slid towards the western horizon. A cracking summer spectrum of burnished oranges, reds and yellows flared across the windscreen, and he flipped down his sun visor. Glancing into the rear-view mirror, he noticed a car trailing behind them. Not unusual for other cars to be on the highway, but his sixth sense piqued. He strained to identify the make and colour, but in the afternoon's heat haze, the vehicle remained distorted. Despite returning his attention to the road, he checked the rear-view mirror more often on the last leg of the journey than the first.

"Jessie, wake up. We're almost there." He reached over, nudging her from sleep.

Blinking, she rotated her neck, stretched and returned to consciousness. She tilted her seat upright, still groggy. "I must have been asleep for hours."

"A while." An indulgent smile tugged at his lips.

"Sorry. That's so rude of me. Here you are driving me all this way, and I just fall asleep." She dragged both hands through her hair. "Didn't you have to stop to give Whiskey a toilet break?"

"Yes, but you were dead asleep. I just left the engine running. You didn't stir."

"I'm so sorry. I usually don't sleep well at all. I can't believe I've slept all this way."

"You've been through a bit, so you needed to sleep. No big deal." He shrugged and steered the Jeep through the round-about and up Yass's main street.

Like many country towns, the traffic flowed patiently while cars slipped in and out of unmetered angle parking on either side of the two-lane road. Rows of turn-of-the-century buildings dressed in pastel shades of egg shell, muted apricot, parchment grey and porcelain white snuggled between more modern buildings of nondescript red and cream brick. They performed their roles of bank, café, Returned Services League Club, supermarket, library, court house and second-hand shops without fanfare, giving Yass a quiet, circumspect atmosphere.

"Not much changes here by the look of it," he said, charmed by the town's timelessness.

"It's your typical country town. There're the locals, whose families have lived here for generations, and just enough tourists to boost the economy."

BJ hung a right into Rossi Street and drove up the hill, passing the Yass District Police station on his right and the white picket-fenced Methodist Church built in 1871 on his left.

"There it is. Yass District Hospital." He nodded to the one-storey brick building at the top of the hill. "Are any of your family going to be here?"

She glanced at her watch. "Maybe Richard, my brother, will be here. Mum's probably gone home by now. She doesn't like driving once it gets dark."

He noticed her face blanch. "Are you all right?"

"I'm not sure. I haven't seen Dad for nearly a year and the last time I did, he was his usual brusque self. In charge, telling people what to do. Now that he's had a stroke, I'm not sure how he'll be. Or for that matter, how I'll be."

He parked the car, switched off the engine, and swivelled to face her. "Listen, I've seen some awful shit in my time and nothing prepares you for it." He paused. She swallowed. "It doesn't matter how much you psyche yourself up, until you get there, face to face with it, you never know how you'll react. But what I can tell you is, you'll cope."

"How do you know?"

"Because you're tough, Jessie Hilton. Whether you know it or not, you're tough." He meant it.

"I'm not so sure." She screwed up her mouth. "They say seeing someone after they've had a stroke is a real shock. They can't talk properly, they don't know who you are, and they got no muscular control…" Her fingers fidgeted in her lap until one of them sacrificed itself to her mouth, taking the brunt of her anxiety.

He gently reached out to rescue Jessie's finger and pressed on. "Sure, it'll be tough, but you're tougher. Do you want me to come in with you?"

"No. It's fine. You take Whiskey for a walk. I'll go in to see Dad. Maybe Richard's there. I'll call you when I'm ready. Thanks for the offer though." She squeezed his hand and managed a thin smile.

"That a girl. Remember, your worst enemy is your own self-doubt. As Nike says, just do it. Don't think about it too much. Just go in and front up. Okay?" He added extra emphasis to his message. Many times in combat, he'd led his unit into situations they'd instinctively avoid at all costs. With bullets that would rip a man in two cracking around their heads, he'd control the fear and take charge. He applied the same leadership strategy here, hoping it would spark Jessie's natural determination and dancer's discipline.

"Thanks. You're right. All I can do is front up and do my best." Brightening with resolve, she opened her door as he slid out of his and wrangled Whiskey from the back seat. With his dog leashed beside him, he escorted Jessie to the entrance of the hospital. "If you need anything, just call me. I won't be far away. Whiskey and I'll just wander around here 'til you're ready to leave. Okay?"

"Thanks…Again." She stressed the final word.

"Forget it. Go see your father. Even if he hasn't been the dad you wanted, he helped you get this far, and he's still here for a while longer." He hoped his comment didn't patronise her, but she still had a father. Something he'd lost years ago.

Stretching up on tip-toe, she cupped his face in her hands and inclined it forward. With a tender touch, she pressed her lips to his forehead. "See you soon." She pivoted and walked towards the glass doors of emergency.

He swiped at where her lips touched and smiled. "Come on, Whiskey, let's walk." Heeling beside her master, Whiskey kept pace while he strolled across the hospital's green front lawn and headed down the hill. "So, what do you think, Whiskey girl?"

Like any good mate, Whiskey kept her own counsel, allowing BJ to make his own decisions. Along the way they stopped for a toilet break and a quick inspection of the Methodist Church now painted in shades of garish blue, which BJ thought sacrilegious on such a magnificent piece of architecture. At the bottom of the street he chucked a U-turn, and they began the incline back up to the hospital, past the white-washed courthouse with its trading hours blazoned boldly on its side wall, and the police station, which looked pristine and unused. "I'm not sure if anyone gets into trouble here in Yass, Whiskey. It's a pretty lazy town."

By the time they arrived back at the hospital lawn, dusk was stealing the heat of the day and preparing to replace it with a balmy summer's evening. The energy of Yass shifted down a gear as townsfolk knocked off work and made for home. Settling onto the park bench where he figured patients and visitors contemplated their lives, or coming lack thereof, he stretched his legs in front of him, while Whiskey lay down beside his heels, head on paws. "We'll wait here a while, girl. Jessie will be out shortly."

Releasing the leash, he clasped his hands behind his head and leaned back to watch the last of the cottony clouds skitter across the late afternoon sky. A deep breath filled his lungs, and, on its release, he registered something he'd not experienced for a long time. A sense of peace curled in his stomach, like a cat curling up in front of a blazing fireplace on a winter's night. For the first time since losing Rachael and Tiffany, calmness took up the tiniest residence in his body.

Maybe it was because of the nearby hospital. In war, he and

some of his mates had sensed a strange energy around an army hospital. No one really spoke about it too much. They didn't want to broach the subject of departing souls and stuff like that. Besides, if he'd stopped long enough to consider an afterlife, or heaven, or hell, there'd have been no way he could've done the job he did. It all came down to who had the strongest will to live. Back then, danger was his constant companion. But now, there was no danger. He didn't have a visible target or ops mission to execute. All he had to do was kick back and wait for Jessie. If doing that reintroduced him to a forgotten sense of peace, he'd happily sit here all night long.

CHAPTER 13

"Can I help you?" A kindly voice drifted from behind a sickly green reception desk at the hospital entrance. Squeezed into a uniform she'd obviously outgrown, a middle-aged nurse blinked up at Jessie.

"Oh, yes. I'm here to see Ken Hilton. I'm his daughter, Jessie."

"Your father is down this corridor in Room 11." The nurse raised her mutton arm in the direction of the opposite corridor. "He's probably just finishing his dinner, so you can go in."

"Thanks. Do you know if any of my family is here at all?"

"I couldn't say, dear. I've just come on shift myself." She tugged her cardigan around her bulging waistline in a futile effort to cover herself.

"Okay. Thank you." She offered the nurse a meek smile, set her shoulders and headed for the hospital room.

Nothing much had changed since the last time she'd visited this hospital years ago when her grandmother died. Buffed green and white linoleum floors butted into scuffed skirting boards. Overhead fluorescent lights flickered as if struggling to remain energised, mimicking the plight of the patients lingering in the beds. *What a terrible place to die.* She shivered and expelled the thought from her mind. The asphyxiating smell of eucalyptus disinfectant permeated everything. Its unpleasant tang stung Jessie's mouth and nostrils. She wondered how such an invigorating, natural scent could smell so sickening. Similarly, although painted in a cheery peppermint green, the corridor walls held no pleasure. Pain and suffering lurked behind them, barely hidden by the hum of silence.

She hesitated at Room 11. The courage with which she'd endured the past week's events vanished, leaving her hostage to her fears. She didn't want her father to die, but she was powerless to stop it. Rooted to the spot, she glanced down at her hand, willing it to the doorknob. Bit by bit the handle rotated, and she edged her head into the room. Backlit by the fading afternoon light, a human shape reclined against a tower of pillows in the far bed as a nurse prattled on about what a good job he did eating his dinner. "Come in. Come in. Are you here to see Mr Hilton?" The nurse waved Jessie into the room.

"Yes. I'm his daughter." She rubbed her clammy hands on her thighs and she moved towards the bed.

"Well, he's just finished his dinner. I'll leave you alone for a visit." Collecting the dinner tray, the nurse bundled out of the room while Jessie lowered herself onto a cold aluminium chair. Whoever lay in the bed did not resemble her father. Frail and withered, the patient barely supported the layers of bed linen weighting his body. Gone were the rugged, square features of a robust man in his sixties, replaced instead by gaunt hollows and a hawkish nose. A grotesque caricature of the man she called father. Piping-hot emotion lodged in her throat.

"Dad, it's me. Jessie. Can you hear me?"

His head juddered as he turned towards her. With wiry, grey strands of hair sticking out from his balding pate and tattered eyebrows, he was a man forlorn. A man cast adrift from life.

"Oh, Dad. What's happened to you?" The lump in her throat burned.

"Jessie. Is that you?" Through twisted lips, a timid, raspy voice drifted towards her.

"Yes, Dad. It's me. How are you feeling?" Her warm hands reached under the bed covers and found his cold skeletal fingers. Dragging his hand on top, she clutched at it, stroking the decaying skin.

"I'm not so bad."

Distressed to see spittle seeping from the corner of his mouth, Jessie grabbed a tissue from a nearby box and dabbed at it. "I came home to see you." She blinked back the tears, noticing her father's eyes peer at her as if through a haze of confusion.

"I'm sorry, Jessie. I'm so sorry."

"You don't have anything to be sorry for, Dad. Everything's going to be fine."

"I'm sorry. I'm sorry." Tiny convulsions rattled her father's chest.

"It's okay, Dad." She reached over and dabbed more spittle. *Oh God, my father is dying. He's dying.* The realisation of what was happening rose from the soles of her feet, leeching into her body. A dam of memories burst. As a little girl, she and her father had huddled together after returning from a freezing winter's day in the paddocks. With steaming mugs of hot chocolate in hand and their chilled feet propped up in front of the open fireplace at the homestead, they'd warmed themselves from their soles all the way through. But now the heat surging up her body wasn't comforting or pleasurable. It was the burning fire of truth, of the inevitability of death. Desperate, unprepared and unwilling to let him go, she sat speechless, clinging to his hand, watching him nod to sleep.

"Hi, Jess." A voice whispered close to her ear, while stale cigarette smoke wafted under her nose. She turned and saw another familial face she'd not seen for almost a year.

"Richard." Delighted, she sprang to her feet and hugged her younger brother. Not that they'd been close as siblings, but somehow with her father so ill, she took comfort in his presence at the hospital. "Look at you." She thrust him back at arm's length, assessing him. "You've grown up even more."

"Cut it out, Jess. I'm nearly twenty-three, you know." He wriggled from her grip with a pout.

"I know you are. But that doesn't mean your older sister can't give you a hug." Ignoring his reluctance, she captured him once more and squeezed.

"Stop it." Shrugging her off, he moved to the foot of the bed. "I see you came." The bitterness in his voice sliced the air. Richard had inherited their mother's ability to parry a happy reunion with one verbal thrust.

Pressing a finger to her lips, Jessie slipped in beside him. "Keep your voice down. Of course, I came. When Mum called saying Dad had a stroke I came as quickly as I could."

"And what about your precious ballet company? What are they going to do without the great Jessie Hilton?"

Again, she shushed him. "Dad's sick. Is this all you can do? Bitch, whinge and complain. I take it back. You haven't grown up at all." Fixing her brother with a withering glare, she returned to sit on the bedside chair. She grasped her father's hand, willing him to stir. Richard remained at the end of the bed, pursed his lips and folded his arms in a sulk.

"Has Mum gone home?" she asked.

"Yes, she left about an hour ago. I was just outside having a cigarette."

"I noticed. Still can't give them up, I see?" She cocked a disapproving eyebrow.

"Maybe I don't want to give them up." He cocked one right back at her.

"Oh, well. It's your choice. You usually do what you want, anyway." Having made her point, Jessie's attention returned to her father who opened his bleary eyes. She glanced back at Richard. "If you want to go, I'll sit with Dad for a while longer and then come home."

"Okay. I'll let Mum know you'll be on your way."

"And tell her I have a friend with me, so if she could put us in the Garden Wing that would be best."

"A friend? Who?" For the first time, he sounded interested.

"Just a friend. I'll introduce everyone when we get back to Coodravale later. Okay?"

"Okay," he said, obviously peeved at her refusal to divulge anything further. Strolling to the other side of the bed, he bent down and kissed Ken Hilton's cheek. "See you tomorrow, Dad." When he straightened to leave, Jessie noticed her brother's misty eyes. Despite his resentment at being trapped at home, Richard adored his father. "See you at home later, Jess." In a lame effort of farewell, he lifted a hand and left.

Although his eyes remained closed, Ken Hilton's mouth twitched. Unsure whether he was awake or asleep, Jessie decided to take advantage of this private moment with her father. "I'm doing well at the Company, Dad. I might even make principal dancer next year, you know. And it's all because you and Mum supported me for all those years while I chased my dream. I can't thank you enough for that. I'll always be grateful…" Gentle sobs fell from her lips. "I know you loved Richard more than me. That's all right. Fathers and sons are like that. I tried to make you love me. Horse riding, target practice, orienteering—but in the end, I wasn't a boy. I was a girl who wanted to dance. Like Mum. But I loved you, Dad. I loved you…" She couldn't stop the flow of hot, childhood tears any longer. This might be the last chance she had to tell her father how much she loved him. "Oh, Dad, why didn't you love me?" Great heaving sobs erupted as she buried her face into the bed.

"I did." Ken Hilton's anguished voice floated above her head. "I just didn't know what to do. I'm so proud of you, Jessie. So proud." Tears trickled down his cheeks, while his body remained inert.

"I love you." She wrapped her arms around his limp shoulders and squeezed tenderly. "I love you."

"I love you too. I'm so proud of you. I'm sorry, Jessie."

She straightened, peering down into her father's distorted face. Employing fresh tissues, she swiped the tears away and finished with another dab at her father's dribbling mouth. His lips twisted a crooked smile. "Go home and help your mother. She needs you."

"Okay. I'll see you in the morning."

"Sure. I'll be here."

"See you then." Clutching his hand, she managed a weak smile. Not one of hope, but of sympathy.

Behind her, the door opened. "Hello, Ken. It's Father Conlon. May I come in?"

On hearing their old priest's voice, Jessie drew a surprised breath and turned to see him hovering in the doorway. "Of course, Father. Come in. It's me, Ken's daughter, Jessie."

"My, my Jessie. How you've grown up." He walked towards her and clasped her hands in his. "It's been a long time…"

"Yes, Father. It has." She lowered her eyes. The last time she or her family had attended church was when she was a little girl. Although she recalled many happy memories of her church days, she couldn't remember why they stopped going. Something to do with her father. She lifted her gaze and noticed the last two decades had layered the priest's face with a network of fine lines but had not lessened the intensity of his green eyes. Even as a girl, she'd believed he could see right into her heart.

The priest moved to the other side of the bed and leaned closer to Ken. "How are you feeling, today?"

"Not too bad, Father."

"That's good to hear." A serene expression graced Father Conlon's face as he patted Ken's shoulder. Both men stared at each other for a moment, as if conversing in a silent language. Jessie frowned, wishing she knew what they were saying.

"Jessie, will you give me a minute with Father Conlon?"

"Sure. I'll wait outside."

She leaned back on a chair in the corridor and closed her eyes. Father Conlon's presence worried her. Normally, priests are called when the chance of survival is low. She prayed this wasn't the case with her father. She wanted him to get better. If he died, how would she, her mother and Richard cope? Another whirlpool of worry swirled in her mind, and she began to understand her mother's distress during last week's phone conversation. She stared at her restless hands, deciding which cuticle to attack. Three of them were already inflamed from her constant picking and gnawing. A terrible habit. But whenever her anxiety escalated, she picked at her fingers. Father Conlon's reappearance beside her saved the intended digit.

"Do you mind if I sit with you a moment, Jessie?"

"Of course not. Please."

The priest folded into the other aluminium chair. "Your father loves you very much. And he wants me to tell you that despite everything, he's only ever tried to protect you."

Her brow creased. "Is Dad going to die, Father?"

"That I couldn't say, but he wanted me to make sure you knew how much he loved you."

"Thank you." She reached for the comfort of his hands.

"Although your father stopped being a practicing Catholic many years ago, he's been a good man. May I say, one of the best. I know for a fact, he's always had your best interest at heart." The look on the priest's face gave her the impression he wanted to say more. Instead, a long pause separated them. "Now, you go in and say good-bye. I'll sit with your father a while longer when you leave."

"Thanks." She crept back into the room and touched her father's arm. "I'm going now, Dad. I'll see you tomorrow." She leaned over and pressed a soft kiss to his forehead. Though her father's lips moved, she couldn't hear him, but a voice in her head said, *Goodbye, Jessie.*

CHAPTER 14

a gentle touch on his shoulder stirred BJ from his contemplation as Jessie slid in beside him on the park bench.

"How did it go?" He straightened, turning to face her.

"It went better than I thought. Dad looks terrible, but he at least knew me. All the same, it's sad to see how much he's deteriorated, but he seemed in brighter spirits when I left."

"That's good then. Maybe he'll improve enough to go home. They do some really good stuff with medicine now."

"We'll have to wait and see how he goes." She shrugged, but still seemed pessimistic. "My brother Richard was there, but he's gone on ahead. And the family priest Father Conlon who I haven't seen in years arrived. Anyway, we better get started. It takes another hour to get to Coodravale."

"Okay." With Whiskey at his heel, he walked with Jessie to the car. He noticed her nose and eyes reddened from crying. But he'd been right. She was tough. By the look of her, she hadn't collapsed under the pressure, but used it to strengthen her resolve.

"We turn right on the main street and head the other way out of town. I'll direct you from there," she said. "Just be careful of the kangaroos. They come out around dusk. You don't want to hit one of them, trust me."

"I hear you. Slow and steady it is." He flashed a shrewd smile at her as she snuggled back into the seat. Something stirred in his stomach. Hunger, he must be hungry. Or maybe it was pleasure? He'd spent so long in pain he'd forgotten what pleasure felt like. Thumbing back through his memories, he couldn't quite capture the full extent of it, but he sensed happiness lingering on the edge of his consciousness. A glimpse of a happier past he seldom unwrapped. A promise of a future he might one day deserve.

As they drove out of Yass, familiarity swirled in his gut, reminding him of when he was a young teenager, visiting his uncle's farm. Kerb and channel gave way to a simple sealed road, lined with wisps of spinifex grasses whispering to each other as the Jeep sped past. A watercolour wash of deep violet blue bathed the sky foretelling the night to come. He exhaled a breath of escape, pleased to shrug off city life.

The mountainous terrain to their left and right looked like a giant hand had clutched the earth's crust, leaving it crumpled in soaring ridges and folds. Further down, uninterrupted green pastures carpeted every hillside, broken only by the intricate tracing of meandering sheep tracks and family homesteads. Noisy ducks fought for dominance in the brackish water on the dams below, only to be usurped by other visiting birdlife. Amid this endless display of nature's beauty, massive electricity and telecommunication towers dotted the landscape—incongruent giants buzzing the verdant landscape of Wee Jasper Valley.

"Everything's so green here," he said, quietly awed.

"Normally it's dry this time of year, but Mum said they had unusually heavy rain over the past month, so everything's come alive again. I love the valley when it's like this."

The Jeep crested the next hill sending a flock of low-flying yellow-crested white cockatoos upward in a cloud of wings, squawking their irritation at being disturbed.

Jessie pointed out to the right. "That's the Murrumbidgee River."

He gazed down at one of Australia's best-known rivers, cutting its course through the valley like it had done for millions of years.

"And above the river are the Brindabella Ranges."

The ranges slid down from their great heights to the river's banks, where clusters of trees sipped the icy waters from the Snowy Mountains. Nourishing each other, every aspect of the landscape worked in harmony. That's what he felt—the harmony of the land. He loved this country. That's why he fought for it. That's why he killed for it. Great southern land.

"What's with all the rocks?" He pointed to thousands of craggy outcrops forcing their way through the lush green pastures like nasty acne on a teenager's face.

"This valley was once a vast inland sea. Those rocks are limestone formed over four hundred million years ago. The whole place is full of marine fossils and limestone caves. It's quite a famous geological site, you know. When Richard and I were little, Dad taught us all about caving. It's like an alien world under there, filled with spectacular flowstone, rock shawls, stalagmites, stalactites and lots of other spectacular rock formations."

He whistled a high-pitched note. "Wow. You certainly know your stuff. You sound like a geologist."

"Not really," she said. "But Dad taught us well. Hopefully, if we get time, I'll take you to Carey's Cave. It's open to the public."

"That'd be great." He steered the Jeep across the Teamas Bridge under which the mighty Murrumbidgee flowed.

"Watch out." She pointed to the furry grey face of a kangaroo, poking up from behind a roadside rock. BJ slowed, waiting for the 'roo to decide whether to move or not. "You can never tell what they'll do. That's why we don't drive through here at night. The head lights attract them, and they dart out in front of the car."

"Yeah, I noticed a few of them as road-kill along the way."

Deciding to remain behind the boulder, the kangaroo bobbed

down to hide, and they drove on. With the light fading fast, Jessie indicated to drive onto the dirt road ahead, ignoring the quaint white-washed Wee Jasper Bridge to his right. "We're nearly there. Coodravale is just down here."

Though he tried to navigate around them, dirty pools of evaporating water splashed up mud on the Jeep. Every time a thud of red clay hit his wheel arch, he winced. He'd be spending serious time blasting this stuff off.

"This is the driveway. Turn here." She pointed to an almost concealed white gate about thirty metres off the road to their right. A crooked sign proclaimed they'd reached their destination…Coodravale Homestead.

The Jeep's wheels rumbled over the cattle grate. With no driveway lighting, BJ steered down the double dirt tracks, careful to stay on the well-worn grooves. Oversteering into the brimming gardens on either side would seriously scratch the paintwork. Rounding the driveway bend, he slowed the Jeep and gave a low sigh.

Set back on an expansive green lawn and rebuilt in early nineteenth century architectural style, the single-storey homestead sprawled in historic splendour. Flanked by an assortment of other smaller buildings and sheds, the red brick farmhouse wrapped itself in a wide veranda of white-painted timber railings and bullnose tin roof. In front of the sweeping side veranda, an enormous oak tree towered upward from the front lawn. Its vast canopy of countless leaves counterbalanced the property's proportions as if drawn by a master artist's brush. The whole scene reminded him of those immortalised on any number of famous Australian paintings.

"This is it," she said. "This is Coodravale."

CHAPTER 15

*W*hat a bastard of a day. My butt's sore and my back's stiff. *I hate driving.* Tailing them along that highway all afternoon and trying not to be seen wasn't easy work. It got even harder when they stopped at that bloody hospital. I had to park far enough away not to be seen, but close enough to know when they left. *And that bloody dog. What's that all about?* I hate dogs. There was that little black poodle that used to yap at me every time I passed its house on my way to school. It belonged to Mrs Springfield. Muffin she called it. Stupid, bloody thing. But I fixed it. When no one was watching, I took Muffin and put her where she belonged. In. The. Oven. That fixed it. Mrs Springfield never knew where Muffin went. Now I'm going to have to work out a way to get rid of the hero's damn dog as well as him. *Why couldn't he just mind his own business?*

Then they hightailed it out of Yass as if on some sort of bloody car rally. *I hate driving.* That's what I wanted to yell at them as they headed off. But I had to turn back otherwise he would have spotted me. I drove back to town, grabbed a coffee and came up with a new plan. As my mother used to say, *be thankful for each new challenge, because it will build your strength and character.* Well, I built lots more strength and character today.

These country people think they're so smart, with their trendy little cafés and friendly welcomes. But they're stupid. It took me all of two minutes to find out where my dancer lives and how to get there. All I had to do was say I was a friend of the family. People are stupid. Why didn't the waitress ask that if I was a friend of the family, why I just didn't call them for directions? Stupid bitch.

Doesn't matter. I know where my dancer lives now. Some place called Coodravale Homestead. I'll drive out there later tonight. Have a look around. Work out what I'm going to do. There's no rush. *The hero and his dog aren't going to get away from me with my precious dancer.*

Planning is something I'm good at. I'll work it out. There's plenty of time.

CHAPTER 16

Once more, mixed emotions flooded Jessie's body. The excitement of coming home to the sights, smells and sounds she enjoyed as a child growing up in the country were swamped by anxiety and disappointment. Previously, her mother's seeming displeasure and her father's brusque, indifferent attitude tainted her happy home-coming. But this time, with her father ill in hospital and his admission of love and pride for her, she hoped the relationship with her mother would equally soften. Despite the tension between them, she longed to be closer to her, to have a mother she could confide in and share her deepest feelings. She prayed this trip would turn out better than expected, just like BJ foretold.

Standing at the front door, with Richard propped behind her, Joanna motioned to park the car under the *port cochère*. With the Hilton family cars parked in front of the garages on the far side of the homestead, the vacant undercover space waited for the Jeep.

"That's Mum, and behind her is Richard," Jessie said, her apprehension rising.

"And who am I?"

"Oh, God, you're right, we didn't discuss that, did we?" Jessie braced herself as she caught the puzzled expression on her mother's face. She hoped her animated smile would assuage some of her mother's obvious confusion. With her rich brown hair twirled in a top knot and dressed in pale blue Capri pants, matching short sleeve knit sweater and navy-blue ballet flats, Joanna Hilton wore her fifty years well. Elegant, tall and slim, she'd bestowed good genes on her only daughter for which Jessie was grateful.

When BJ switched off the engine, Jessie sprang out of the car, dashing to her mother. "Mum. How are you holding up?" She hugged her tight, receiving a limp squeeze in return.

"Pretty good." But her mother's puffy face and red eyes conveyed a different story. "Richard told me you had a friend with you, but he didn't mention it was a man." Even though bloodshot, her cool grey eyes scrutinised BJ as he lowered from the cabin. It never failed to amaze Jessie how her mother could ignore what was in front of her to pursue what interested her more. In this case, finding out who the strange man was she had brought home without her prior knowledge.

"Hello, Mrs Hilton. I'm Brad Jordan, but everyone calls me BJ." In two long strides, he greeted her with an outstretched hand and charming smile.

Jessie watched her mother tilt her head to meet his piercing blue eyes with a steely gaze. "BJ's a friend of mine from yoga. He offered to drive me here…"

"…And help out with the homestead until Mr Hilton gets out of hospital. My uncle has a farm on the Mornington Peninsula, and I know how much work goes into a property. With your husband so sick, I thought a couple of extra hands might come in handy." With Joanna's small hand now firmly in his grasp and a hesitant smile replacing her suspicious scrutiny, Jessie began to relax.

"That's very kind of you. But if your mother wanted you to be called BJ, she would have written it on your birth certificate. Nice to meet you, Brad." Joanna's sculptured eyebrow arched in obvious disdain for nicknames. "This is Jessica's brother, Richard." She stepped aside to present her son who lounged against the door frame. Jeans scrubbed with dirt on both thighs from persistent hand rubbing, mud-caked boots and a threadbare T-shirt missing the sleeves, torn not cut from their seams; all embellished his look of overworked and underpaid. A look Jessie knew to be unwarranted. Joanna would never have allowed her to look so grimy with company about to arrive. Jessie stewed in silence. Richard had obviously just stubbed out another cigarette because she could smell it from where she stood. Her nostrils flared, trying to expel the odour.

"Hi." Richard tipped his hand in a half-hearted salute.

BJ reached over and received a limp hand shake in return. With the same cool gaze as their mother's, Richard scanned him from head to foot accompanied by a slight twitch of his lips.

"Well, I think we'll settle in and then we can catch up? Is that okay, Mum?" Jessie desperately wanted to get moving.

"Mrs Hilton, I had to bring my dog, Whiskey. Jessie said it would be okay. Whiskey's trained and very obedient." He motioned to the back-passenger window of the Jeep where Whiskey's effusive face blinked behind the glass.

"Well, as long as she doesn't tear around causing trouble, I suppose it's all right." Joanna cast a not-so-subtle reproachful glance at Jessie. "You can leave your car here. Jessica will show you to the Garden Wing. I've made up both beds." She swivelled her head from Jessie to BJ searching for any tell-tale signs of a sexual liaison.

"That's great, Mum. Thanks. We'll unpack then." Blowing out a breath, she rushed to the back of the Jeep where BJ helped her grab the bags.

When the passenger door opened, Whiskey sprang to the ground, clearly thrilled to be released. "Heel, Whiskey." She halted at BJ's feet. "Thanks very much, Mrs Hilton. I promise

Whiskey will behave, and if I can be of any help you just let me know."

"Thank you. Come on, Richard. You can help me with dinner."

Jessie waited while her straight-backed mother turned and herded Richard into the house, closing the door behind them. With a feeble smile, she upturned her face to BJ. "Welcome to Coodravale, one of the unhappiest places on earth."

Heaving up both bags, he gave a humourless chuckle. "She's certainly a tough woman. Now I know where you get it from."

Struggling to reclaim her duffel bag, Jessie bristled. "I'm nothing like her."

"You're a lot like your mother." He relinquished Jessie's bag and stepped in time beside her. "Come on, Whiskey. With me." Frantic to explore the property, Whiskey's feet danced on the spot, but she obeyed her master and remained close. "You're both similar in looks, posture, strength of will, and you're both tough."

"Well, maybe you're right with a couple of things, but I'm not aloof or self-absorbed like Mum is." She stopped and frowned at him in demand of agreement.

"Mmm, maybe it's just a matter of semantics. Some might say you're reserved and overly-focused on your ballet career? Could be misconstrued as being aloof or self-absorbed?" A taunting smile tugged at his lips.

"Now you're just being smart. I can't be bothered debating this right now. But you're wrong. Joanna Hilton is a difficult woman to please, or to love for that matter. She alienates people with obsessive expectations..." She clamped her lips shut. *Oh God, am I that much like Mum?* This wasn't the time for a deep and meaningful, either with BJ or herself about the similarities between her and her mother. She was tired. She needed a hot shower, something to eat and, if she was lucky, a good night's sleep. Tomorrow, when she had more time, she might reflect on what BJ had just said. Not now. "Doesn't Whiskey need a toilet break?"

"Yes, but is the homestead fenced all the way around?"

"Yes. She won't be able to get out. The gates are closed before dusk."

"Whiskey, go pee." He lifted his arm, pointing into the near distance. Delighted at finally being able to investigate, the dog raced to the fence line, sniffing and burrowing her nose into the earth. After finding a spot, she relieved herself and galloped back to them.

"Follow me." Jessie picked up the pace. The red gravel pathway leading to the Garden Wing crunched underfoot, shattering the velvety space between day's finale and night's prelude. With everything tinged in soft greys and purples, early evening bridged the seen and unseen, before the curtain of nocturnal peace descended on the homestead. The same sort of peace yoga gave her.

"Wow. This place goes on forever." The awe in BJ's voice drew her attention, and she shot him a proud smile.

"Yes. Coodravale is pretty special, isn't it?" *I just wish it didn't come with all the other stuff family brings with it.*

She turned the corner of the homestead and strode up four, uneven, concrete block steps. "This is the Garden Wing." The timber veranda echoed with their footsteps as they traipsed towards the double French doors at the far end. "It's where paying guests usually stay, but since Christmas is so close, the bookings are low. It's got a small kitchen, living room, bathroom and separate bedroom. I'll take the bedroom and you can have the bed nook. I thought we'd be better here than in the main house. Less tension, if you know what I mean." She opened the door, folded back the floor length damask curtains and ushered him inside.

CHAPTER 17

"Whiskey. Sit. Stay." BJ motioned for her to remain on the veranda before he went inside.

"This is your bed." Jessie pointed to the queen bed tucked into the bed nook just inside the French doors. Trimmed with white *broderie anglasie* lace, the bed reminded him of his grandmother's. He recalled the happy times he'd spent on her bed, listening to her read bedtime stories. *Life was simpler back then.* On top of the shabby chic bedside tables either side of the bed rested Tiffany-style lamps. Against the far wall, a matching shabby chic bureau caught his attention because of the ornate white vintage basin and jug perched on top.

"You did say there was a bathroom, didn't you?"

"Yes. And don't worry, it has hot running water. Come on. I'll give you the tour."

Dumping his kit on the bed, he followed her.

"My bedroom's down there." She pointed to the opposite end of the living room which separated the space. "Kitchen and bathroom are through here." On their right, a kitchen and separate bathroom fitted into what he suspected was originally a sun room but was now enclosed for functionality and privacy.

"This is a terrific layout." He poked his head into Jessie's bedroom for a quick reconnaissance. It had one window and a timber-and-glass panelled exterior door, locked with an old-fashioned key. One medium-sized sliding window hung in the kitchen and bathroom, while two large windows stretched above his bed. In total, two door exits and five windows. He'd check their locks later when she wasn't around.

He didn't want to alarm her, but he felt sure that the car he saw this afternoon tailing them on the highway stayed with them into Yass. The last thing he did when they left town was check his rear vision mirror, but it was gone. Logic said he was being too suspicious, but his gut told him otherwise. Some may say he was overly cautious, but he knew better. Being alive, proved that. Many times in combat, his instinct had stopped him from taking a step to the right or left, saving him from being blown up by an unexploded incendiary device. And this afternoon it told him something was off with the car behind them.

"Check this out. Mum left a bottle of wine in the fridge," Jessie called from the kitchen, obviously surprised and delighted at her mother's preparedness. "Let's unpack, and we'll have a glass to steel our nerves before dinner." Taking her own advice, she headed into her bedroom.

BJ crossed the cosy living room admiring the stone and mortar fireplace. On the mantle rested the complete works of Banjo Paterson bound in two large leather volumes. *Maybe I'll get time to read one of Banjo's poems.* Except poetry didn't interest him much. Chuckling to himself, he unpacked his bag and pulled out a change of clothes. "Do you want to use the bathroom first?" he shouted across the living room towards Jessie's bedroom.

"No, you go ahead. I'll jump in after you."

After a scorching hot shower, he felt brand new dressed in clean jeans, shirt and tan boots. "It's all yours."

"Thanks…" She barrelled from her bedroom with an armful of clothes before disappearing into the bathroom.

Inhaling deeply, he strolled out onto the veranda. "Come on, Whiskey. Let's get your gear and give you some dinner." He strode down the steps, his dog dancing by his side.

An inky black night had descended on Coodravale, reminding him of his tours in the Afghanistan. His senses sharpened. A dry wind gusted up the Wee Jasper Valley and swirled around the homestead, interrupting the silence. BJ hesitated at the bottom of the stairs, ears pricked by the eerie whoosh of the wind. He called Whiskey to heel, and she lifted her nose into the wind's direction. His heart rate quickened while he waited for any of his dog's tell-tale signs of concern—a low growl, a strain for release or a rigid body of alert. Instead, she rested at his side, attentive to his next command. Reassured, he stepped off. With the outline of the homestead barely visible, only the white veranda railings gave depth to his surroundings. Like the nights in the desert, the country night plunged Coodravale into chilling darkness. The crunch of the gravel underfoot guided them along the path to the car, so he picked up pace with Whiskey beside him.

He grabbed her gear and tucked it under his arm. "Here you go, girl. I've got your bed and food, so let's get you sorted." With an about-face, he marched his dog back to the Garden Wing.

∾

"Ah, that's better."

BJ turned towards the French doors where Jessie stood, white wine bottle in one hand and two glasses in the other. Barefoot, dressed in blue jeans and a floating cotton shirt, she appeared refreshed and relaxed and smelled of soap.

He eyed the bottle in approval. "Now that's a good idea. Here, let me open it." Taking it, he poured the wine and handed a glass to her with a "cheers".

"So, what do you think of Coodravale?" She slipped into one of the regency-striped wingback chairs on the veranda, curling her legs beneath her like a swami.

"It's a pretty place from the little I saw today. Whiskey and I are keen to get a better look at it tomorrow in full daylight." Before pulling the other chair closer to the railing, he glanced at her. "Do you mind if I put my feet up?"

"Sure. Go ahead."

Once positioned, he folded into the chair and hoisted his feet on the railing. With his legs stretched before him and Whiskey by his side, he settled in for a few minutes of pre-dinner R & R.

He caught a movement from the corner of his eye and glanced over to see Jessie upending the bottle. Although he had plenty left, she refilled hers to the top, swallowed a long gulp and replaced the bottle. *Slugging back the booze. Tonight's family dinner will be fun.* His lips tightened.

"How are you feeling after everything that's happened?" He kept his voice easy, his tone light.

"I'm fine. That sleep I grabbed in the car helped."

"Good to hear." Grappling with his next course of action, he resigned himself to living dangerously. "Jessie…"

She turned to face him, her eyes wide in child-like wonder. "Yes?"

"Are you sure you're okay? A lot has happened. Last night you got a call about your father having a stroke. You race home to find your unit's been broken into; someone's left you a sick love letter on your bed and stolen some of your underwear. Today we drive to Yass to visit your father in hospital. Then we arrive here to a frosty greeting by your mother. Now you're throwing back the wine before you go in for a family dinner. Maybe you want to slow down a little, talk about it?"

She glared at him. "You know what? I never asked you to drive me here. I could've done it myself. But it was very kind of you to offer. And thank you for all the other help you've given this past week. But it doesn't give you the right to judge me, or to pry into my feelings. I don't need to talk about anything, and I don't need you judging my drinking habits."

Terminated. He'd been shot down with little warning and minimal fuss. *She'd make a bloody fine sniper.* Careful to restrain the amused tilt of his lips, he narrowed his focus.

"I'm sorry. You're right. But you've had a few unusual shocks over the past twenty-four hours. I just thought you might like to talk about it. My apologies." He scratched the back of his neck and waited.

She responded with a tense *harrumph.*

Although the gold flecks in her hazel eyes flashed in annoyance, she pursed her lips, turned her head and sipped her wine. *At least, she's sipping. That'll do.* Better to win the battle than lose the war, so he said no more.

nother dump of a place. Crappy carpet, grimy microwave and a bathroom that doesn't look like it's seen a lick of disinfectant since Adam was a boy. If my mother was here, she'd whip the motel housekeepers into shape. *Best Eastern Motel, my arse.* If this is the best Yass has to offer, then more fool them. Anyway, it'll have to do. It's not costing me much. I'll lay low here for a while and work out the rest of my plan. Let's see if this Guide to the Yass Valley or the tourist maps that I collected at reception help. There it is. I go along the tourist drive on Wee Jasper Road and keep going a bit further to Coodravale. How easy is that?

God, I get hard just thinking about it. Soon I'll have my dancer all to myself. Right. Time for a little recon' work. Just like I did with her unit. Get in and get out. Maybe leave a calling card. I'll give it a few hours. Wait 'til they're asleep. I've even got time to write another poem. I bet my dancer loves my poems.

Wonder if the TV in this dump works? Maybe "The Bachelor" is on? God, there's some good-looking women on there. Not as good as my dancer, though. She's got real style and class. *Why don't these motel remote controls ever work?* Probably needs new batteries. Nope. There we go. How lucky is that. Now what station is it on? There it is. I'll stretch out on the bed for a bit. *Mmm...not too hard and not too soft. Just right. Like Goldilocks.* Geez, I'm a crack up. Oh-oh, look at her. Blonde hair, fake tits and goldfish lips. She thinks she's hot shit, but she's an ice maiden that one. Bet she'd just lay there like a starfish, cold and limp.

I bet my dancer's no starfish. I bet she bucks and sucks and hollers like a rodeo princess. Every time I think of her, I get hard, but I don't dare touch myself. I'm keeping myself only for her. It won't be long now...

CHAPTER 19

As Jessie examined the room, every feature held a memory. Crafted from tongue-and-grooved timber, the mint-green painted walls angled into an ornately-decorated cream ceiling. Her mother's tireless research had assured the authentic colour palette, despite her father's aversion to green. Many a debate had ended in a showdown between her parents over it. From the picture rail skirting hung sepia-coloured prints of men on horseback at muster, sheep droving along the Murrumbidgee and turn-of-the-century homesteads built in the Wee Jasper Valley. All collected by her father on his many excursions to garage sales. When Jessie was a little girl, he'd spent hours framing and hanging them, while she handed him nails. Happy times.

Although her mother cleaned like a tyrant, the familiar smell of old timber and stale dust still lingered in the air. Probably due to the tired tapestry rug that lay claim to the wheezing dark timber floors. She wondered why her mother kept the rug at all. Furnished with an impressive Tasmanian oak dining table, eight chairs and two side boards, Coodravale's main dining room existed in a time warp.

Little had changed over the years. Unlike Richard, who'd transformed since their arrival. Now wearing tight black jeans, polished snakeskin boots and a clinging black T-shirt, he no longer resembled an overworked farmhand. She couldn't understand why her brother chose to dress so outlandishly for a small family dinner. But then again, she didn't understand a lot about Richard.

She gave her brother a slight smile while flicking the pressed cream damask napkin onto her lap. "Mum tells me you're nearly finished your accountancy course. What do you plan on doing then?" She hoped tonight's dinner would be civil.

"I don't know. Maybe I'll get a job with Tom. I'm not sure."

"He's our cousin who lives in Perth," Jessie said to BJ, who sat across the table.

"This isn't the time to be making plans. We'll have to wait and see how your father recovers before you go leaving Coodravale." Joanna's curt tone closed the topic. She then nodded to Jessie, who lifted the platter of sliced roast lamb and vegetables and offered it around the table. "What is it you do for a living, Brad?"

"At the moment, I work for a builder friend." He forked three slices of lamb and two spoons of vegetables onto his dinner plate. Remembering how much he'd eaten for breakfast that morning, Jessie frowned at his meagre portion. She caught his reciprocal scowl and smirked. He was obviously trying to make a good impression on her mother by not taking too much food. Despite his earlier comment about how she sculled her first glass of wine, she warmed to his old-fashioned ways. His thoughtfulness at the table strengthened her resolve to disregard her mother's overbearing comments tonight.

"I see…" Joanna stretched across to retrieve the serving platter from her. "Aren't you having more than that, Jessica?" She eyed her daughter's plate with disapproval.

Jessie glanced down at the two Brussel sprouts, two pieces of cauliflower, two baby carrots and two boiled potatoes. The only item breaking the symmetry was a spoonful of peas.

"You can't possibly survive, let alone dance on that. Jessica, eat some meat, please."

"No thank you, Mum. I haven't eaten meat in years, and I've survived and danced just fine." She hated the dining table lectures over her eating preferences and diet. With an audible huff, she reached for her glass, slurping a hefty gulp of merlot. Now, she didn't feel like eating anything. With her resolve shattered and only the awkward sound of cutlery scraping the plates, silent tension rippled through the room.

"Coodravale Homestead is beautiful, Mrs Hilton," BJ said. "Is there anything that I can help with tomorrow?"

"I've got everything handled. You're not needed." Richard swatted his offer like a nuisance fly.

"There's no need to be rude." Jessie shot her brother a critical scowl. "BJ was only trying to help."

"We don't need his help. I don't understand what he's doing here. Dad's lying in hospital, and you bring some stranger into our house. Who is this guy?" He banged his cutlery on the table.

"Now, Richard. Calm down. Coodravale is Jessica's home too." Instead of reproaching her son for his rudeness, her mother simply tried to pacify him. He sat at the other end of the table, full of himself, like the head of the household in her father's absence. Jessie bit her tongue, but inside she seethed.

"Jess, I demand to know who he is?" With his arms folded and face reddening, Richard glared at his sister.

In normal circumstances, she would have fought back, told her brother to mind his own business, but her life no longer resembled normal circumstances. Telling her mother about some crazed lunatic stalking her wasn't what she'd intended to do on this trip. Exhaling a shuddering breath, she half-frowned at BJ. He nodded, but she disagreed with a shake of her head.

"Jessica, what's going on?" Concern seeped into Joanna's voice as she swivelled in her chair to face her daughter.

Again, Jessie shook her head. Again, BJ nodded.

"Mrs Hilton, I am a friend of Jessie's, but there's a bigger reason why I've driven her here…"

"No. Don't say anything," Jessie said.

"What bigger reason?" Joanna asked, her full attention now on BJ.

"I'm sorry, Jessie, but under the circumstances, your mother has a right to know."

Jessie hung her head and twisted the dinner napkin in her lap. "All right. You can tell her." She raised her gaze and stared hard at her mother. "But I don't want you to worry. You have enough going on with Dad."

"Will someone please tell me what's going on?" Joanna's head turned right to left in demand of an answer.

"Jessie had a little trouble last night. Someone broke into her unit. The police are currently on the case, but they suspect she has caught the unwanted attention of a stalker."

Joanna gasped. "Oh, that's awful. My poor darling." She pushed back her chair and rushed to her daughter's side, wrapping her arms around her shoulders.

"Shit, Jess. I'm sorry. That's terrible," Richard said.

"It's okay. Really. Don't fuss." Jessie waved her mother away.

"I offered to drive Jessie here to see her dad. I figure if someone's stalking her, having me around would at least be some protection until the police find out what's going on."

Joanna returned to her chair and poured more wine. "Thank you for playing my daughter's body guard. But friends don't normally place themselves in harm's way for each other." She tossed back a mouthful of red.

"Maybe in our world, friends don't do that, but in BJ's world of friends, they do." A grateful smile tipped Jessie's mouth. "Like I said, no need to worry. Our concern is Dad. No more talk about me. I'm sure the police will take care of everything. Now, what did the doctor say about Dad and his recovery?"

Joanna fluffed around with her napkin and shifted the cutlery on her plate. "But I am worried about you. It's very chivalrous of Brad to stand by you like this, but still…"

She caught the sheen in her mother's eyes. She was holding back tears. An event she'd rarely witnessed in her life. Jessie went to her mother and wrapped her arms around her. "Mum, I'll be fine. BJ's keeping an eye out for me. It's you and Dad I'm worried about. Now tell me. What did the doctor say?"

Dabbing the napkin to her eyes, Joanna straightened in the chair resuming the posture of matriarch once more. "Dr Bruen isn't sure. He said we'll know over the next few days. Richard and I are going back to the hospital early in the morning."

"Then I'll come with you." She held her mother's hand.

"Thank you, Jessica. I'm sure if we all go together it will lift your father's spirits. We can talk to the doctor then and see what we need to consider next. I'm so pleased you came home, darling. Forgive Richard for being so nasty. And me. The stress is getting to us. Having you here really helps." She squeezed her hand and smiled a humble apology.

"Yeah, sorry, Jess.' Richard wore a hang-dog expression.

"That's okay."

"Now let's eat before everything is cold." Joanna waved her fork in the air to signal the resumption of dinner.

"You were right. Even with Dad so sick, things are turning out better than I expected." An easy smile graced Jessie's face as they wandered back to the Garden Wing, with Whiskey prancing beside them. "Tonight ended up quite normal. Once Mum settled down, and Richard stopped being so rude, dinner ended up being quite pleasant, considering the circumstances."

"I'm sorry about taking the lead on the stalker thing, but I thought it would be better to tell them, than not."

"That's okay. Good call on your part. My family can be strange, as you've no doubt noticed. I wasn't sure how they'd react. I think because you told them and not me, they handled it better."

"Family can be tricky. It's a lot harder than friendship. There's nearly too much closeness, too much past good and bad with family that just doesn't come into play with friends. With friends there's an unspoken line in the sand… respect, loyalty and integrity. With family, there's usually someone who crosses that line despite the damage it may cause. Being a friend is easier than being in family. Way easier…"

"But it's a shame it takes something like an illness or some big drama to bring families together." She glanced up at the night sky remembering the happy, childhood times she'd spent with her father counting the stars. *If only Dad and I could go back there, now.* She scratched her head, trying to work out why that loving father-daughter relationship had changed. A distance had grown between them over the years, yet her father had told her today how much he'd always loved her. And Father Conlon had impressed the same assurances upon her. So confusing.

"They say you never know how good you've got it until it's gone. I know for a fact that's true, not just for families, but for everyone."

"Yes, you're right. You just never know what the future will bring…" When they reached the stairs up to the veranda of the Garden Wing, she stopped and faced him. "I'm sorry I snapped at you before we went to dinner. You were only trying to help, but I get so on edge when I come back home. Forgive me?"

"Of course. No problems."

"Thanks." She stepped up one stair and stopped again. Flashing a mischievous grin, she blocked his way. "You must be starving..."

"On that point you're one hundred percent correct." He rubbed his belly.

"I got you a doggy bag from dinner." She held up a plastic bag triumphantly.

He peered inside and saw two large takeaway containers filled with lamb and vegetables. "God, I hope you didn't tell your mother I was still hungry?"

"No, silly. I'm cleverer than that. I told her it was for Whiskey." She giggled like a school girl. The heady glow from the half bottle of white wine and the couple of glasses of merlot warmed her skin.

"That's great. Thanks."

Was it the alcohol, the blast of his icy blue eyes or the closeness of his body, that shifted her equilibrium? She couldn't tell, but she listed like a boat running aground. Just before she lost her balance, BJ grabbed her arms and saved her from tumbling off the step. She righted herself, but he didn't release his grip. Standing face to face, she didn't move and neither did he. He was so damn good-looking, so kind and so powerful. *But I don't have the time or space in my life for a man, even if I wanted to.* He'd become like part of the family. No. She wouldn't jeopardise their friendship by opening herself up. *But, God, he's so...*She swayed sideways again.

"Are you all right?" Shaking her lightly, BJ snapped her from her swooning trance.

"I'm fine. Just a little giddy." That stupid giggle again. *God, I hate when I sound like that.* "Must be the alcohol on an empty stomach. I need a good night's sleep. Let's get some of that food into you before we go to bed. Come on." She did what she considered was a damn fine impression of a sober about-face and marched up the stairs.

"Whiskey. Bed." BJ pointed to the dog's bedding on the veranda near the French doors. The dog circled and dropped, her happy face turned upward. "Good girl. Now you keep guard, and we'll see you in the morning." He ruffled her ears in a final good night.

"Good night, Whiskey." Jessie stroked the dog's head. "Don't go chasing wombats."

"Wombats?"

"I'll explain while you eat the rest of your dinner."

CHAPTER 20

*S*oft amber light slanted across BJ's chest while he lay in bed staring at the ceiling, with his hands clasped behind his head. The glow from the Tiffany lamp beside him offered just enough comfort to interrupt the murky depths of midnight. He disliked darkness—the darkness of a starless, new moon night, the darkness of not being able to see the encroaching enemy, and the darkness dormant in his soul. The presence of light not only minimised risk in times of rapid response, it enhanced his chances of emotional healing, of one day living a brighter future. For him, light meant hope, and hope kept him going.

Tilting his head, he listened to the noises of the night. The incessant scratch of wombats burrowing at the nearby fence, the scamper of possums racing up and down the fruit trees and the hoot of a lone owl calling for a mate harmonised together in a strange, nocturnal lullaby. Familiarising himself with the sounds, he sensed the homestead hunkering down for sleep.

His mind wandered to what had nearly happened on the steps with Jessie. He'd been taken as much by surprise as she seemed to be. For in that instant, he thought they might kiss. But how could he possibly do that? How could he cheat on Rachael like that? *But*

Rachael's not here anymore. The thought hurt, brutal in its honesty. Rachael wasn't here anymore. At the end of January, it'd be three years since Rachael and Tiffany died. Three long years of grieving —of denial, anger, self-recrimination and depression. *Was it enough? Was it ever enough?* Dr Thomson said that over time the suffering would lessen. Eventually, BJ would come to accept the loss and move on. *Is that what's happening with Jessie? I'm moving on?* But Dr Thomson never spoke about the guilt, the confusion or the anxiety of moving on. *What a clusterfuck...* He made a mental note to book another appointment with the doctor on his return to Melbourne. In the meantime, he decided not to complicate his life, or for that matter Jessie's, with spontaneous acts of uncontrolled emotion. Despite his growing affection for her, he'd keep his promise to be her friend. To protect her. Nothing more. With the owl hooting his loneliness, BJ closed his eyes and joined his feathered friend in his sleep.

Whiskey's barking snapped him awake. Jumping up, he went into overdrive, dragging on jeans and T-shirt.

"Jessie. Brad." A distressed female voice called out their names between Whiskey's aggressive barks and snarls.

BJ flung open the French doors to find a dishevelled Joanna standing at the bottom of the stairs with Whiskey refusing her any further entry. "Whiskey. Release. Heel." The Border collie immediately broke from her defence and rallied beside her master. "Mrs Hilton. Are you all right?" He rushed to her, and she collapsed into his arms.

"Dr Bruen just rang. It's Ken. He's dead."

"Oh no..." He virtually carried her up into the living room, where he propped her in an armchair. "I'll wake Jessie."

But she stood at her bedroom doorway, her face that of a frightened child's. "It's Dad, isn't it?" She appeared paler and thinner than when she went to bed, almost ghostly. With her long brunette hair cascading wildly over her shoulders, she wore the same dazed expression he'd witnessed on her face only last night. His heart went out to her. Twice in the same number of nights, the world Jessie knew and depended on had disintegrated around her.

"Your father's had a massive stroke. Dr Bruen just rang. There was nothing anyone could do." Joanna pulled the flimsy cotton shawl tighter around her shoulders and swallowed hard. Mother and daughter faced off across the room. Both too shocked, and he suspected, too shaky to move. As he stood silent sentinel between them, Joanna's shoulders began to shudder, and Jessie's lips to quiver. Breaking the stalemate, Jessie rushed to her mother, fell to her knees and buried her head into Joanna's lap. "Oh, Mum. Oh, Mum..."

"It'll be all right. Really it will." With her head lowered, Joanna stroked her daughter's hair, reassuring her through tremulous sobs.

Giving them their privacy, BJ retreated to the kitchen. Minutes later, he returned with mugs of hot tea. "Drink this. My grandmother always made black tea with lots of sugar. She used to say it was the best remedy for all of life's woes." Managing a regretful half-smile, he handed a mug to each of the women who sipped in compliance.

"That's most kind of you." Joanna nodded in strained appreciation.

"Thanks." Curling up at her mother's feet, Jessie clutched her mug as if it was a life preserver. A dreaded silence descended which BJ knew only too well. With death came the countless items of business to be organised, so the deceased can be properly farewelled. The Hilton family would have little time for grief until arrangements were made.

He leaned against the fireplace mantle, sipping his own tea. "How's Richard doing?"

"He's getting dressed. We'll drive in to the hospital now and see Ken before they..." Joanna choked on the remainder of the sentence. Fortuitously, the mug of tea drew her focus, and she returned to its steamy distraction.

"Richard's probably pretty shaken up as well. Why don't I drive you all in? It's a long hour's drive into town in the dark. We can all go in the Jeep, and I'll bring you home once you've arranged everything."

"Thank you. I'll speak with Richard." Before rising from the chair, she kissed the top of Jessie's head. "You get dressed, and we'll leave as soon as we're ready."

He escorted Joanna to the door and by the time he returned, Jessie had retreated to her bedroom to change. Sitting down on the side of his bed, he laced on his black stealth force boots and combed and tied back his hair. Catching a glimpse of his reflection in the mirror above the bureau, he wondered who he'd become and what he was doing here. Somehow, in the turmoil of these last few years, he'd unexpectedly found a place where he could be of service. Here, with the Hilton family at Coodravale. Like any other mission, he'd see this through, and only then consider himself and his future. He shrugged on his leather jacket and strolled outside to wait for Jessie. Commanding Whiskey back to her bed, he explained she had to stay by herself for a few hours. After he dropped a handful of dog kibble in her bowl, he sensed Jessie edge in beside him. "Ready?"

She nodded.

"Okay then. Let's go." He raised his arm and wedged her under his wing. Locked together they treaded down the stairs. The wind had died, but dawn had not yet broken. An early morning chill refreshed the air as if telegraphing the clear, summer's day to come. A day he knew from personal experience that would be hard, long and unfortunately, unforgettable.

CHAPTER 21

What the hell are they doing? I drive all this way out here in the middle of the night to find this bloody place and just when I'm getting out of my car, Coodravale lights up like a Christmas tree and that bloody dog starts barking. *I hate dogs as much as I hate driving, particularly at night.* Now, I'm just going to have to wait until they leave.

Right, here they come, up the driveway. And there he is…the interfering hero behind the wheel with my dancer beside him. Who's that bundled up in the back? Must be her family. *Maybe the father died in hospital? Could I be that lucky?* Nothing like a death and a funeral to keep everyone occupied. It's amazing how little people notice what's going on around them when there's a death in the family. You can get away with murder when everyone is boo-hooing over a lost loved one. I'll wait just a few more minutes to make sure they don't turn around. Then I'll go in. Take a look around. *I wonder if they took that dog with them?*

…Okay, that's long enough. I should have brought my jacket. It's bloody cold out here. Who says summer in the country is hot. It's freezing. Hey, pretty place. White roses lining the driveway. Wonder if the dancer's mother is the gardener? My mother was a terrific gardener. I remember the rose bushes she planted in the front garden. Those roses were her pride and joy. Beautiful, big blossoms. And when the roses died, she used to cut the stems and ... *I hate roses too.* They hurt, especially if she left the thorns on them.

I'm going to have to stay off this gravel path though. Makes too much bloody noise. I'll just tip-toe around here and ... *Fuck, that bloody dog scared the shit out of me. Better get out of here in case it chases me.* Run, run, run. My mother used to run after me yelling about monsters living inside me, whipping me with her thorny rose bush switches. *I've got to get out of here. I've got to run from the dog, from the rose bush switch. No, Mummy, no. Run!*

CHAPTER 22

"So that's about it, Jasmine. I'll be staying here until after the funeral and things get sorted." Jessie stood outside under the awning of Rosie's Café, talking on her phone. The mid-morning sun bore down, punishing the tin roofing and guaranteeing a scorcher of a day. Having grown up in this heat, Jessie was accustomed to the dry rasping air coursing in and out of her lungs on every breath. Every part of her crackled like withered leaves.

"When's the funeral? Do you want me to come out?" Jasmine asked.

"That's sweet of you, but it's too far. Besides, you need to stay for the end of the season. I can't be responsible for you taking leave. Anyway, we're not too sure when the funeral will be yet. Mum's got to find out when the rest of the family can get here. It's all up in the air at the moment."

"Are you okay?"

"Better than I thought I'd be. It's hard to believe really. I guess I'm still in shock. Maybe at Dad's funeral it'll hit me. BJ's been a great support. I'm pleased he's here. He's been a rock..."

"And his mate, Ricky, is pretty cute too."

"Really?" The image of Jasmine's cheeky smile beamed in. No matter how dull or down Jessie felt, her friend always knew a way to cheer her up. Even with six hundred kilometres between them, Jasmine remained an optimistic and dependable touchstone in her life. "Go on. Tell me."

"Ricky and I ended up grabbing a coffee after you two left. We're going to clean your unit together and after that we're going out on a date." She was quite smitten with BJ's mate. But Jasmine was easily smitten by any handsome, athletic and charming young man.

"I knew it. The way you drooled over him, I just knew you'd hit on him. Well if he's anything like BJ, you could do a lot worse." She paused to wipe perspiration from her top lip. "Is there any news on the principal role for next year yet?" She held her breath. *No news is good news.*

"Not yet. We'll know more about Tabitha's ankle in a day or two once the swelling goes down, and they do an MRI. But she's still off and spitting chips from what I hear."

"I would be too. At least, I'm not injured. But I wish I could get back there and dance the season. Oh, well. It is what it is. I'll have to stay here until everything gets sorted out. I don't know how long that will take, though. Anyway, keep me posted on Tabitha's ankle and if they announce. Talk to you soon. Have fun with Ricky. Love you."

"Love you too. I'm here if you need me. Bye."

"Bye." Jessie ended the call. She dragged her hand across her damp forehead and prayed she'd be able to get back and perform before Tabitha. She turned and pushed through Rosie's glass-panelled door into the cool air-conditioned café. The smell of freshly brewed coffee lifted her spirits. Unlike her family, the morning diners chatted happily above the sound of Adele singing yet another one of her hits. The place reminded her of Salvatore's... happy people, happy times. She returned to where BJ, her mother and Richard sat, finishing brunch.

"Any news yet? BJ rose as she approached the table.

"News on what?" Joanna turned her reddened face towards Jessie. Ken's death had trowelled years on her mother's appearance in a matter of hours. The once stylish woman Jessie knew had crumbled into an exhausted, anxious middle-aged widow. She brushed her hand affectionately on her mother's shoulder before sliding into the chair beside her.

"The news about the principal role for next year. I'm up for it against Tabitha Simpson. Remember? But they haven't announced yet. So, I'm still in with a chance." Managing a thin smile, she changed the subject. "Unless there's anything else you need to do, maybe we should go home and call the rest of the family from there. What do you think?"

"Yes. I'm very tired. I need to rest." Joanna clutched her hand.

"I'll pay the bill, and we'll head off." Ignoring their objections, BJ strode to the counter.

Once outside, Jessie stepped in beside him while her mother and brother lingered behind. "I can't thank you enough for everything you're doing for us. Having you here makes things easier. I'm certain Richard and I would've been squabbling by now."

"You know your brother's gay, don't you?"

"What?" She staggered from the bombshell he'd dropped on her. "Why would you say that?"

"Because he told me. When you were on the phone, and Joanna was in the rest room, Richard came out with it."

"You've got to be kidding. How didn't I know this?" She cast him an incredulous stare and slapped a hand to her heart.

"Because he was terrified that if he came out while your father was still alive, your dad would disown him. He thought you might have suspected and wanted me to broach the subject with you…"

"Oh my God." She quick-stepped up next to him, and they paced a little faster. "No wonder he's shitty about everything. The pouting and the bitching, it all makes sense now. Why didn't he tell me?"

"That's a question you need to ask him." Holding his remote towards the Jeep, BJ triggered the door locks. As Joanna and Richard approached, Jessie eyed her brother. In his jeans, polo shirt and riding boots, he appeared the same lean, attractive young man he'd always been. But when they locked eyes, she registered the hell her brother had been living. Not until today had she'd even suspected anything more was amiss than Richard being a petulant, whiny, self-centred young man. *Dad's death is certainly bringing the skeletons out of the closet.*

On their arrival home, Joanna escaped indoors to call relatives while BJ checked on Whiskey, leaving Jessie to some private time with Richard. Sister and brother took shade under the sprawling oak tree, sitting side by side on the white wrought-iron garden seat on the front lawn.

"Do you remember Dad telling us how old this tree was?" Jessie peered upward at the tree's massive branches and its tens of thousands upon thousands of leaves.

"Yes. He said it's nearly ninety years old." Richard tilted his head up, mirroring his sister.

"That's a long time to live, not only for a tree, but for a person. Imagine having to live that long and not be who you are?" She narrowed her eyes. "Why didn't you tell me you were gay? Out of everyone, I would've understood." She watched him flinch and hoped he wouldn't shut down.

"I guess because you were the star of the family. You were so talented and beautiful and perfect. I couldn't possibly compete with that. Telling Mum and Dad I was gay would've made everything even worse." He rubbed the heels of his hands into his eyes. After a cursory glance at her, he reached into his jeans pocket for his cigarettes. Thrusting one between his lips, he lit up. "Sorry, but smoking's about the only thing that keeps me sane."

She nodded absent-mindedly at the cigarette while digesting Richard's point-of-view. "You've got it all wrong, Richard. I'm not the star of the family. You've always been the favourite."

"Not from where I sit." He dragged a long, deep inhale. Closing his eyes, he allowed the smoke its freedom. "I'm sure I disappointed Dad. No matter how hard I tried to be a man-of-the-land like him, I couldn't do it. I pretend to do the dirty, torn, rough-house act, but it's not me. I'm not a man's man. For as long as I can remember all I wanted was to get out of here, like you did when you were fifteen. Ballet set you free. But here I am. Still stuck here. I'm nearly twenty-three years old." He inhaled another long, hard pull of smoke into his lungs, obviously trying to quell his frustration.

"I'm sorry you felt trapped here all this time. Maybe if you'd told me I could have helped?"

"How? How could you've helped?" An edge of bitterness returned to his voice. "I was barely thirteen when you left. You only came home once a year. Your ballet was more important to you than your family, than your little brother." He launched from the garden seat and ground his cigarette underfoot.

Jessie sprang up beside him. "I'm sorry. I never meant for you to feel like I'd just left you here, alone."

He tossed her a glare. "I know you didn't, but that's how I felt." His voice suddenly softened, and his eyes blurred with tears. "It's just that you were my big sister and then you were gone. I missed you like crazy. When you left I had no one. It's not your fault you got the chance of a lifetime with your ballet, but that didn't stop me from feeling lonely."

Jessie reached for her brother's hand and for the first time, he returned her gesture with a reciprocal squeeze. "I'm sorry."

"It wasn't long after you left, I realised I was gay. That really sealed the deal. Trapped in a town where I didn't fit in and with no one to talk to." He dropped to the seat, pulling her down beside him. "And to make things worse, Mum and Dad have been just the best parents. How could I tell them about their gay son who felt stuck in the home they worked so hard for? I just couldn't do it."

Jessie nodded. "I understand. But why tell BJ today?"

"I knew he'd say something to you. And I guess there's only Mum to disappoint now that Dad has died." He hung his head.

"I think you've been too hard on yourself all these years. Mum and Dad loved you. I'm sure if you'd told them, they would've understood."

"Maybe, but up to now, I wasn't willing to risk it, especially with Dad."

She nestled her head onto her brother's shoulder. "To think that all this time I thought you were the golden child, and you thought I was."

"Yeah. Not as smart as we like to think we are..." He rubbed his cheek on her head.

Jessie sat up and hardened her gaze. "I don't want us to bicker or fight anymore. I hate it when we constantly snap at each other. Can we start again?"

"I'd like that."

She wrapped her arms around his neck and held tight. "I love you little brother."

"And I love you. It's good to have you home."

She broke the embrace and brightened. "I promise I'll try to get home more often. If not, you can stay with me in Melbourne during the year. Okay?"

"Deal." Brother and sister shook hands, and in that moment, Jessie released days' worth of tension, maybe years' worth. Losing her father was awful, but at least Ken's death had brought her closer to Richard.

"What are you going to tell Mum?"

"That I'm gay and that once I've finished my accountancy

course and find a job, I'm going to leave Coodravale and live my own life." A look of anguish passed across his face.

Jessie's heart ached for him and her mother. A lose/lose situation for them both. "Do you want me to be there when you tell her?"

"Thanks, but no. I have to do this myself. I may be gay, but I'm still a man with integrity. I'll sort it out when the time's right."

"But we're going to have to find a way for Mum to manage Coodravale when you leave." Jessie stared out across the neighbouring paddock, praying for a solution.

"Trust me, I've been trying to find one."

"Maybe there's enough money in the estate so she can hire someone to do the outdoor and maintenance jobs when you go?"

"Maybe?" He leaned down to collect his crushed cigarette and wrapped it in some packet foil. "Mum hates it if I leave my butts lying around."

"You're a good son, despite what you think." Jessie patted his leg. "Anyway, I'm here if you need me." She leaned over and pecked a kiss to his cheek.

"Thanks." His expression relaxed, and she mirrored his expanding smile. Side by side, they sat in silence for a while, revelling in their new sibling connection.

After a few minutes, she turned to him, a playful grin edging her lips. "So? Do you have anyone? A boyfriend?"

"Hell, no. I'm stuck out here in no man's land—literally. No good country boy is gay around these parts." His imitation of a thick country accent made her laugh.

"So…?" She cocked an eyebrow and glanced at his crotch.

"What do I do about sex? Mrs Palmer and I are good friends." He waved his right hand in the air. She laughed again. "Whenever I can, I escape to Sydney or Canberra. Nobody knows me there, so I usually hook up with someone for a few days. It's better than nothing." He sighed. "By the way, sorry about my behaviour with BJ. I guess I was jealous you brought home such a good-looking man…" Mischief flashed in Richard's eyes.

"Stop it. What? You have the hots for BJ?" She gave his shoulder a short, sharp slap.

"I would if he was gay. But he's not. Still, he's a real hottie." The inflection of his voice rose and fell effeminately, giving Jessie a rare insight into the humorous side of her brother.

"Well, you just keep away from him. He's not in the market."

"Or not *on* the market? Maybe you two are an item, and we don't it know yet?"

"We're not an item. We're friends. Good friends."

"Well, is he on the market or not?"

"I don't know."

"Well, you can't be that good friends, if you don't know that." His lips pursed as his brow cocked pointedly.

"Listen, there's been a lot more going on than talking about his availability."

"Still…?" His voice trailed, leaving Jessie to ponder his remarks —and more importantly, her sudden, vehement response to them.

With the sun past noon, she kissed her brother and set off to find BJ. Skirting the Garden Wing, she found Whiskey and him playing some sort of hide-and-seek near the privet bushes. He held a finger to his lips which stopped Jessie in her tracks.

"Whiskey. Find the ball. Find the ball." Lifting his arm, he released his dog, watching her as she set off on. Around she went, sniffing low on the ground and high in the air. Under bushes, up on an old weathered table, around the base of nearby trees and in empty plant pots, her nose twitched following the scent trail of the ball. Passing the Daphne shrub at the foot of the stairs, she propped, snorted and back pedalled. With nose diving into the greenery, she scrounged a little longer. Satisfied, she withdrew her head and sat back on her haunches. Giving a happy bark, she spun her eager face to BJ. "Good girl, Whiskey. Good girl." Repeated praise followed by a treat sent the dog's tail into frenzied delight.

Jessie strolled towards them. "Wow. She's good."

"Yes. She's improving all the time. One day, she'll make a terrific search and rescue dog. I'm sure of it. This may look like a game, but it's all about positive reinforcement, practice and play."

"If you've finished, would you like a swim? I bet Whiskey would." Staring down at the dog, Jessie could have sworn Whiskey nodded in agreement. She laughed, and faraway kookaburras laughed back.

"That's got to be the best sound I've heard in days."

"What? The kookaburras? They're noisy, aren't they?" With a glance over her shoulder, her eyes skimmed the distant hill where kookaburras laughed intermittently at their own private jokes.

"No. Not the birds. It's good to hear you laughing."

"I haven't had many things to laugh at over this past week or so but having you and Whiskey here certainly lightens the mood. How about that swim? Meet you out here in five minutes."

Snapping a turn, she raced up the stairs with the sound of him light-footing it behind her.

Due to the unseasonal rains the month before, the grass outside the main homestead flourished thick, unmown and luxuriant. Cool and inviting, it brushed the sides of Jessie's sandaled feet, reminding her of childhood days. Back then, she used to run barefoot through the grasses until her mother had threatened that Jessie's budding ballet career would be over if she damaged her feet. Many a battle between them had been waged over Jessie's barefoot antics.

Overhead, across a Delphinium blue sky, fairy floss clouds

raced each other to some unknown destination beyond the Brindabella Ranges. With BJ and Whiskey strolling beside her, she almost forgot the tragic reason why she was here at Coodravale. A brief respite from the day-to-day drama, their presence gave her pause...and peace. She led the way down through the homestead gate and between the white blossoming crab apple trees. The thrumming of industrious bees caught Whiskey's attention, but her animal instinct stopped her from investigating further. Jessie glanced up at BJ, and they shared an intimate moment. *Unspoken words are often the best.* Unlatching another gate, she ushered them onwards. When they crested a nearby knoll, she stopped. "There it is. The Goodradigbee River. Its waters come all the way down from the Snowy Mountains then flow into the Murrumbidgee. The cleanest, purest waters you'll find anywhere in the world. And if you're lucky, Murray cod will tickle your feet while you swim."

"Wow. It's like an oil painting from the 1900's—like stepping back in time. No wonder Banjo Patterson bought this place. Righto, Whiskey. You're on your own. Go swim." Understanding playtime was here, Whiskey leaped from his side and bolted to the banks of the river. Launching into the air, she splayed forward and aft legs, bombing the water with a loud smack.

"Come on. We better get in too. The current's pretty strong. You don't want Whiskey half way to the Murrumbidgee." Jessie peeled off her light sun frock and sprinted to the river. By the time she splashed in and spun around, BJ had swum past her, calling Whiskey to come. The dog turned course and swam back until the three of them paddled in a cove on the outer limits of the current.

"How do you ever leave here and go back to the rat race in Melbourne?" he asked, while keeping one eye on Whiskey.

"It's a beautiful place to come home to, but it's not where I belong. The city is where the stage and ballet are. That's where I belong."

"I get that. But this place sure is peaceful."

With the sun glancing off each ripple of the bark-brown tinted water, the charm of the Goodradigbee River and its surroundings couldn't be denied. An untouched magic she'd forgotten. "Yes. There's a special kind of peace in the country. I guess because there's usually some kind of family tension whenever I come home, I miss the real beauty of the place."

Gazing at the opposite bank, she watched the unhurried sheep heading towards the river to quench their thirst. Hushed and patient, the straggly herd picked their way down the serpentine tracks. Bridal veils of weeping willow branches dipped to the water's edge in quiet repose as if beckoning the sheep to join them. Nature was the grandest stage of all, and Jessie had grown up on it without even realising. "With Dad gone, I'll have to get back here more often to see Mum. She's going to need the support."

"Did you talk to Richard?"

"Yes. It was the most honest conversation we've ever had. He told me how abandoned he felt when I left to go to Melbourne. I had no idea."

"He's been hurting a long time."

"Yes, he has. But, at last, I've got my brother back." She tried to reel in the words, but it was too late. "I'm sorry. That was insensitive of me."

"It's okay. I'm happy for you. Younger brothers are gold. I wish I could get my mine back. But it is what it is."

She waited a few moments before continuing. "Aside from telling Mum he's gay, Richard's going to tell her he can't stay here. He wants to leave as soon as he's got a job." She swept her hands to-and-fro through the chilly water and sighed.

"How do you think that will go down?"

"Who knows? What I do know is that death changes everything."

"You'll get no argument from me on that one. Nevertheless,

Coodravale is a special place for you and Richard to come home to. I'm sure your mother is more than capable of managing whatever has to be done. It'll work out." He gave her a wink. "Now, how about you show me these man-sized burrows you told me the wombats dig along the river banks? I promise to keep Whiskey from tunnelling after them."

"Okay. Follow me." She stroked to the easiest edge of the river, and balancing on slippery river rocks, she stepped ashore and walked up to where they'd dumped their towels. When she glanced back, her breath hitched. BJ rose to his feet like a mythological god of the sea. Wet, golden hair streaked down his neck, and his burnished body, perfect in its symmetry, rippled as if honed by a master stone mason. The occasional glint of sun danced off the water trapped in his beard and trickled down the plane of his chest. But when he flicked his head back and dragged his fingers through his hair, her stomach virtually somersaulted. Sporting a luminescent smile, he turned around and hollered for Whiskey. Emblazoned across his formidable back, a mighty dragon tattoo breathed fire, its flames encircling both shoulders and upper arms. *A mighty warrior.* She had no doubt BJ had been as destined to be on the stage of war, as she on the stage of ballet. A comforting thought, but she couldn't understand why. As man and dog ambled up to join her, she threw on her sun frock and towelled her hair.

"Okay. I'll give you the tour of the wombat burrows. Then I'll check on Mum. If she's okay, we'll grab a bottle of wine and come back here for sundowners and watch the sunset."

"Sounds like a plan to me." While he stepped into his shorts, Jessie sneaked in a couple more furtive glances. Beside them, Whiskey executed a full body shake, sending streams of water in every direction. Spontaneous laughter rang out from the banks of the Goodradigbee River, and the kookaburras in the distance joined in the joke.

In that otherworldly space, clammy hands slithered down Jessie's arms. She withdrew as far as she could into the abyss behind her, but still the disembodied hands followed, elongating bizarrely towards her. A familiar dusty smell penetrated her senses. What did it remind her of? Then it was gone. While the claustrophobic darkness continued to consume her, menacing hands touched and probed and prodded. *Get away. Get away.* Finally, her strangled cry for consciousness escaped in an ear-piercing scream. At last, she was awake. She bolted upright in bed and heaved in great gulps of air. Thwack! Her bedroom door flew open and smacked into the wall behind.

"Are you all right?" BJ stood silhouetted in her doorway, alarm in his voice. Flicking on the light switch, he scanned her room, looking for the cause of her panic.

"I'm fine. Just a nightmare." She steadied her breathing, but the dark emptiness of her nightmare lingered.

"Must have been one helluva nightmare…" He walked over and sat on the edge of the bed, and she noticed he wore only a pair of jockey shorts. "Do you want a glass of water?"

"No. I'll be okay." She punched her pillows, nestled back and dredged up a weak smile. "I've had nightmares since I was little. Everyone said I would grow out of them, but they're still there."

"How often do you have them?"

"Maybe twice or more a week."

"Have you seen anyone about them?"

"Yes, I tried hypnotherapy and counselling, but it never does any good. They just come back. That's why I slept so long in the car on the way here. I think I'm chronically tired, but since I don't know what it's like to be untired, I don't know." She shrugged, and her heart rate settled back to normal.

"That's how we lived our tours of duty, catching sleep whenever we could. We spent months physically exhausted with only adrenaline keeping us going. Sleep deprivation is terrible torture."

Her eyes roamed his face. "Do you think the police will find the person who broke into my unit?"

He clasped her hand. "Yes. I do."

"But why haven't we heard anything yet?"

"It takes time. Trust me, Angel's on the case. If the police find out anything, he'll be the first to know. Then he'll contact us. There's nothing else we can do but wait. Let them do their job."

"I don't know how much more of all this I can take. My entire life is falling apart and there's nothing I can do to stop it. I can't even escape into sleep without some stalker finding me there as well." The more she spoke the tighter she squeezed his hand. Like a ticking time bomb on rapid countdown, she teetered on the brink of exploding into a million pieces.

"I know everything feels like it's too much to handle, but it'll pass. Your life will get back to normal. It'll just take some time. I promise."

"Really?" Her sense of panic lifted a little, and she loosened her grip.

"I promise." He brushed a stray strand of hair from her face.

She heaved a breath until the tension passed. "Thanks. You go back to bed."

"Are you sure you don't want anything?"

"Just a good night's sleep." She joked, but internally prayed her wish would come true.

"Maybe you'd sleep better if you thought about me being just out there." He cocked his head in the direction of his bed. "No one can get you with me around. I promise."

"Thanks. I'll give it a go. Good night." She slinked down and scrunched her pillows into a comfortable position.

"Good night." He rose and moved to the door. Just before he switched off her light, he caught her gaze. "Sleep tight. I'll see you in the morning."

Behind a forced smile, she gritted her teeth. Another opportunity to return to the monsters in her sleep wasn't something she eagerly anticipated. As he closed the door with a soft click, darkness reclaimed her bedroom. She craned her neck and noticed light still crept in under the door. *He's left his light on.* She wondered if that was for her or if he also didn't like the dark.

Rolling onto her side, a soft smile loosened her lips. The thought of him being out there, ready to spring into action pleased her. *Nothing like having your own warrior on call.* A giggle tickled her throat. Despite how heroic it all seemed, knowing he was there eased the fear of falling asleep. Willing herself to relax and with the memory of his near-naked silhouette filling her mind, she drifted into a long, deep and undisturbed sleep.

CHAPTER 23

*S*hadowed from the morning sun by the nearby eastern hills, Coodravale awoke with an air of cool, dry crispness. Birdsong rang throughout the valley, each voice competing over the other. Waking up in country Australia had a bright, cheery atmosphere to it—one that reminded BJ of his teenage years at Uncle Bob's farm in Victoria. Listening to the cacophony of sound, he wondered how he could attract birds into his yard back home and decided to investigate which plants he'd need once he returned to Melbourne. Padding into the kitchen, he passed Jessie's open bedroom door, but there was no sign of her. *Where was she?* He gathered pace into the kitchen, the bathroom, back through the living room and jogged towards the French doors. Flinging the curtains to one side, he spied her outside on the veranda and breathed a sigh of relief. In front of her, Whiskey sat entranced, head tilted.

Dressed in figure-hugging ballet gear, Jessie moved her body in the most astonishing ways he'd ever seen. With one hand grasping the veranda railing and the other floating mid-air to her side, she unfolded her leg beside her ear, her foot pointing above her head. The movement reminded him of a butterfly delicately unfurling its wings when breaking free of its chrysalis. He knew it must take an extraordinary amount of strength, yet when she released her grip on the railing, her leg remained suspended, without the slightest trace of unsteadiness. After the longest time and minus the railing's support, she lowered her leg, wedging it in a tight lock with the other. The only hint to the effort this exercise required was the broad expansion of her ribs when she breathed. Springing onto the balls of her feet, she snapped a half-turn and caught sight of him staring through the glass doors. She scowled at him, wagging her finger. "What are you doing?" Her lips mouthed the words.

Sporting a sheepish grin, he opened the French doors and wandered out onto the veranda, where Whiskey wasted no time in slipping beside him for a morning welcome.

"Sorry. I didn't mean to disturb you, but I couldn't help but watch. I've never seen anybody do that before. You're amazing." He did nothing to conceal the admiration in his voice.

"That's because you haven't seen anyone do ballet, I guess." In her gear, she seemed transformed. Confident, powerful and accomplished, she'd discarded last night's panic. In front of him stood a highly skilled and talented young woman.

"You're right on that count. Never seen ballet at all. Let alone someone as good as you, right here within arm's reach. How on earth do you do that?"

"Years of practice, persistence, sweat, bloodied toes, tired and aching muscles… Need I say more?" Her face glowed.

"No need. I get the picture. How about I do us some breakfast while you keep practicing?"

"That'd be wonderful. Thanks. You know my order." She mocked him with a small snigger.

"Yes. One egg, no toast." He paused, reciprocating a smug smile. "But I'll still cook two eggs, sunny side up and a piece of toast, just in case you change your mind."

"Whatever. But I'll just eat the egg."

"I live in hope." He chucked a wave and retreated to the kitchen.

~

"Where are we going? What are we doing?" Jessie double-timed to keep up with him, while underfoot the gravel path crunched as if they wore jack-boots.

"I'm going to show you what I do." He flashed a big, easy smile at her.

He'd calculated the risk of doing this, both environmental and psychological. He'd not worn the sandy beret of the SAS for over three years. Only those closest to him knew of his past identity and since he'd already told Jessie, he reasoned showing her a little more wouldn't threaten his or her safety. The only other person he'd ever done this with was Rachael, and she'd understood. He figured Jessie might too. "You said Richard's gone into Yass to buy groceries, and your mother is at a friend's place, correct?"

"Yes. There's no one here except us." She raised an inquiring eyebrow.

"Good." He opened the back of the Jeep, leaned in and unlocked the concealed, rear floor tray, then lifted out the one and a half metre long aluminium case. He spun it around in front of them and unfastened the clips.

"You practice ballet. This is what I practice." Reverently, he opened the lid. There snuggled in black foam padding lay his .308 rifle. He heard her muffled gasp and out of the corner of his eye, caught her take a small step backwards. He waited. When he sensed her initial shock subside, he faced her. "Ballet is your skill. Shooting is mine."

"But what are you going to shoot?"

"Targets. I shoot targets. To keep my eye in." He flashed another easy-going smile, hoping she'd respond with less alarm.

"Oh…" Her eyes jerked from the rifle to him. "You don't kill anything?"

"No. I don't kill anything. Those days are over."

She blew out a breath. "So how does this work then?"

"Do you have a shovel?"

"What for?"

"I need to shovel a mound of earth up behind the target, so the bullet doesn't travel anywhere except into the dirt."

"There'll be one in the shed, I think. I'll go get it." She hurried off in search of the tool.

Staring down at Whiskey, he stroked her lopsided ears. "What do you think, girl? Will Jessie be able to cope or not?"

Tongue lolling from her mouth, Whiskey beamed up at her master.

"I hope so, too." He leaned into the case and set about the well-rehearsed ritual of cleaning the rifle and checking the bullets and magazine.

"Here you go." Jessie returned, shovel in hand.

"Terrific. Now does anyone or anything go into that paddock over there?" He pointed to the paddock on the other side of the fence, directly in front of the oak tree.

"No. It's empty. Only goats visit in the afternoon."

"Okay. I'll go set up. You keep watch in case some goats start their day early."

Grabbing the shovel and a small leather pouch from the rifle case, he set off. Through the old paddock gate, he paced out five hundred metres across uneven ground. Dotted with clumps of spinifex grass and fallen tree branches, the paddock stretched away out of sight to the river on one side and the road on the other. As he'd suspected, five hundred metres brought him to the base of a soaring poplar tree growing on the near side of the paddock.

He placed his kit on the ground and began digging the compacted earth into a rough mound about a half a metre high and wide. When that was done, he retrieved a long, thin rope from his pouch and threw it over a suitable tree branch. Fiddling with the rope, he spied a stone and tied it to the end of the rope, so it hung directly in front of the dirt mound. With the set-up sorted, he collected the shovel and marched back. At the Jeep he lifted his rifle, two pairs of ear muffs and stowed the magazine and bullets in his pockets.

"Whiskey. Sit. Stay." The dog obeyed, although obviously disappointed not to be joining the fun. "It'll be too noisy for her next to us. She's got to stay here. Take these." He handed a set of ear muffs to Jessie. "Okay. Let's go."

In long strides, he paced back to the paddock gate. Laying his rifle on top of one of the old, drystone gate pillars, he arranged the bullets and magazine in the exact formation which afforded him the most proficiency and speed. Despite the deadly result this ritual had delivered in combat, each time he executed this preparation, his body involuntarily produced a powerful high. *Better to be judged by twelve, than carried by six.* The familiar mantra played in his mind as the adrenaline kicked in. *Better to be judged by twelve, than carried by six.*

"But where's the target?" Jessie stared out towards the paddock. "I can't see anything except the mound of dirt."

"Look closer. See the rope coming down from the branch?" He snuck behind her, aligning with her line of sight and pointed.

"Barely." Straining, she leaned forward.

"Look at the bottom of the rope. In front of the pile of earth. There's a stone tied to it. See it?"

She spun her head around, blinking up at him. "You're kidding me, aren't you?"

"No. I'm not. The stone is my target."

"But how can you possibly hit that? I can barely see it."

"That's because you're a ballet dancer, and I'm a sniper." He sensed her body flinch. "You remember me telling you I used to go to my Uncle Bob's farm after my Dad left? Uncle Bob taught me how to shoot. This is how I used to practice. Every weekend, I'd pick off stones from the rope. And every weekend, the stone got smaller and smaller. I became so good at it, it's the reason I eventually became a sniper."

"But you killed people?"

"I admit it wasn't easy, but I was trained not to see it that way. As part of the coalition forces, we were deployed on covert missions to high value targets. My job was to support operations by delivering precision fire from concealed positions and to observe and gather information. You've got to understand that when they call in the SAS, it's not to negotiate. It's to resolve the situation with violence." He locked her in an intense gaze. "There's no good that comes from any war, Jessie. It's happened. I've got to accept it and move on. That's the job."

"But it all seems so senseless. How do you deal with it?"

"I tuck that crap away in a compartment in my head or I'd go insane. If you're not prepared to take the risk or get the job done, then you shouldn't wear the sandy beret."

She shuddered. "It seems so black and white, so cold and heartless."

"Not that much different from the Aussie Ballet Company I suspect, except no one gets killed going for the high value target, for the top job?" Flashing a half-smile, he cocked his eyebrow.

She screwed up her nose. "I get your point about the Company and it being just as ruthless, but I'm not sure it's really a good comparison..."

"Aside from all the ugliness of war, there was a lot of good that came from my days in the military. Apart from the skills and leadership training, I finally found the family I needed. Those I shed blood with and the pain we shared, bonded us as brothers. Like me and Ricky. He helped me get over the loss of Tony. In some ways, he's like my replacement brother. I found a lost part of myself in the SAS. For that, I'll be forever grateful." He'd not revealed this level of vulnerability for a long time. Nor had he planned to delve this intimately into his past or his feelings. Because of Jessie, his tongue loosened, and his heart cleaved open just enough to let some of the pain go. In that moment, he surrendered and fell captive to the spell of a country summer's day. "Do you want to see me do what I'm good at?"

"Okay." Her casual shrug indicated the time had come.

With Jessie by his side, he explained the complex requirements of weapon maintenance, sighting the rifle, shooting posture, loading the magazine and a range of other processes in which she seemed genuinely interested. "Now put on your ear muffs. This is pretty loud."

"I've heard a rifle before. Dad had a .202."

"But this is a lot louder. Ear muffs."

With a pout of reluctance, she obeyed.

Hunkering down on the gate post pillar, he tucked the rifle butt into his shoulder. *Better to be judged by twelve, than carried by six.* While his skin prickled with excitement, his focus sharpened. His limbs and muscles settled into place, ready. *Better to be judged by twelve, than carried by six.* Sighting the scope, he eyed the stone, drew and held his breath. Forfeiting all other awareness except for the target, he squeezed the trigger. The crack of a single bullet ricocheted around them, loud and forceful. He remained motionless, locked in his firing position, watching the rope swing. A proud smile tipped his mouth as he rose to face Jessie.

She blinked. "Shit. You're good."

He shrugged. "That's what they paid me for." Lowering back to his position, he aimed and fired again and again. While the sound fractured the serenity of the valley, it activated his steely focus. He became lost to everything except the target. The smell of gunpowder, the warmth of the weapon, the snap of the spent casings as he slid the pump action and the imperceptible jolt in his shoulder, all conspired to transport him back to the battlefield. *Better to be judged by twelve, than carried by six.* Not until the magazine emptied its bullets, did he recover. Free of its stone weight, long shattered by his expertise, the defeated rope swung limp and frazzled.

Removing his ear muffs, he turned to her. "Would you like a try?"

"It's so freakin' loud. Even with the ear muffs. Look." She lifted her shaking, clammy hands. "Being this close to something so dangerous makes me really uncomfortable."

"It's just anxiety. You get used to it."

"I'm not so sure. I've got danger signals going off in my head everywhere." She rubbed her hands on her thighs and shuffled from foot to foot.

"Fear is a good thing if you can control it. Here let me show you." He signalled for her to replace her ear muffs and stand in front of him. He loaded the weapon with a single bullet and manoeuvred her into position. "Make sure you keep the butt jammed hard in your shoulder." He held her tight, demonstrating how much counter force she needed. "Look through the scope with both eyes open. Line up the red dot at the bottom of the mound of dirt. Then squeeze the trigger. But hold the butt tight into your shoulder."

When he released his guiding hands, she inhaled a lungful of air. With concentrated effort, she took her time, aimed and fired. Holding firm, her shoulder rebounded only slightly. A conscientious student, exactly as he thought she'd be.

"Good. You shot the ground, which is better than sending a bullet into the air."

"Here. Thanks. You can have the gun back." Trembling, she handed him the rifle, and he promptly dropped the barrel downward. "I have no idea how you guys do this. Day after day. It's a wonder you're not all deaf."

"Well, deaf is better than dead." He checked his weapon and collected the spent casings. Coodravale eased back into relative silence, its natural state restored. Birds conversed once more, staking claim to their rightful position in the trees. With a whistle and release hollered from her master, Whiskey bounded from the Jeep to join them. Whining a greeting, she ran headlong into BJ's legs. After a quick pat, she turned on Jessie, knocking her to the grass.

"Whiskey. Sit." Holding the dog to one side, he dropped down on the grass beside her. "Are you okay?"

"Yes. I'm fine." Propped on her bottom, Jessie rubbed grass clippings from her jeans. She paused, sweeping him with her eyes. "God, BJ...it wasn't until I saw you pick off that target, time and again that...To think, of all those people, all those wasted lives. I never appreciated what you all must have gone through, serving your country."

"Maybe the easiest way for me to explain it is...you have nightmares when you sleep. We lived the nightmare, day and night. Every tour of duty was a nightmare. But we all chose to do it. No one forced us to enlist or become SAS. Anyway, it's all in the past now." He tilted his head, regarding her. With sunlight glancing off her sleek, dark curls and highlighting the copper flecks in her eyes, she was a natural beauty. A woman almost fragile in appearance but with a blinding magnetism. In the brief time BJ had known her, he suspected Jessie had no idea of her loveliness or the effect she had on people, particularly men. Because of that, he wanted to protect her even more.

"You're an amazing man, Brad Jordan. I'm not sure who or what brought you into my life, but I'm glad you're here." She leaned over and pressed her lips to his cheek.

"Me, too." Slinging his arm over her shoulder, he gazed at the poplar tree where the rope dangled. In no hurry to collect it, he gave her a hug. Today, for the first time in a long time, he'd bared a part of his soul. And the best of it was that the person he'd shared it with, hadn't gone away. It was a good day.

CHAPTER 24

What a wealth of information Richard was. I couldn't believe my luck when he sauntered into Rosie's and gave me the look. "Where are you from?" he asked all coy and sexy, while we waited at the counter to give our orders.

"I'm from Melbourne." I figured he's a local and could be useful to my plan. "What's your name?"

When he said Richard Hilton, you could have knocked me over with a feather. The dancer's brother. I bought us coffee each, and we sat chatting for ages in the café. He told me all about his family buying Banjo Patterson's old property called Coodravale Homestead.

Another idiot! Prattling on about his father who just died and how he can't wait to move to the city. Hinting at me he's gay, making innuendos about us catching up while I'm in town. Ugh. He made my skin crawl. *What a freak!* But I played along, pretending to be interested in his country-bumpkin arse. I needed as much information on my dancer and the big hero who's with her. Richard couldn't help me with that. He didn't know much about him. Keeps a pretty low profile he reckons. But he did say that bloody dog was well trained. Nearly took his mother's arm off when she got too close. *I hate dogs...*

Horny Richard was stupid enough to tell me what I needed to know and more than I expected. Now all I've got to do is bide my time. Watch and wait. Get everything ready. When the opportunity appears, I'll strike. It's a bit like planning a military mission, I guess. I tried out for the cadets when I was at school, but I didn't make it. *More idiots!* They said something about me not fitting the profile. Well, I showed them I fit their bloody profile. I planned and executed my own mission. It was me who drowned that pretty dancer back then, but they couldn't prove it. I'm good at this shit ...

CHAPTER 25

"Uncle Frank, Aunt Hilda and your cousin Tom will arrive tomorrow, and we'll have the funeral on Tuesday." Composed and in control, Joanna Hilton once more claimed her matriarchal status at the head of the dining table. A sheaf of paperwork with margin notes scribbled in red fanned before her. Jessie and Richard sat either side of their mother, listening to the specific arrangements of their father's funeral. "Frank, Hilda and Tom will be staying in the other guest quarters for a few days before and after the funeral. Any questions?" Her head swivelled from daughter to son, a little like the laughing clown heads at the Royal Easter Show. Jessie scolded herself for such an irreverent thought at such a terrible time.

"Is there anything we can help with?" Jessie asked, concerned that her mother had shouldered the entire arrangements on her own. Not that Joanna wanted or asked for any help. After the initial shock, she'd simply forged ahead, as was her way. Tonight was the first time Jessie or Richard had known their mother had finalised so many funeral details.

"Well, I'm putting together a tribute to your father, so if you'd like to go through some old photos and choose a couple of your favourites that would be a great help." She reached for the pair of cardboard storage boxes on the table and opened the lids to reveal decades of unrelated 4 x 6inch memories piled high. Jessie wondered how there could be so many hard copy photos with the world so digitalised. But she didn't dare mention it. Her mad, keen photographer father had adored taking "real" photos, and as such, he'd amassed a collection of chaotic imagery. She heaved a sigh of resignation. *Nobody's bothered to catalogue or sort these since the beginning of time.*

"There's so many, though." Richard moaned.

"Well if it's too much to ask …" Joanna's indignant tone silenced him.

"No, Mum, it's okay. I'll take this box, and you start on that one, Jess." He shoved the other equally full and heavy box towards Jessie who clasped her hands around it, reconciled to the task.

"How many photos can we choose?"

"No more than four each, please." Joanna's expression softened.

"We can do that. Can't we, Richard?" Jessie fixed him in a stern gaze.

"Yes. Yes. We can do that."

"By tomorrow morning, please…" Joanna's pause caught Jessie's attention.

"What is it?"

"I wasn't going to tell you, but I think you should know. I found this in your father's papers today." Joanna handed a folded document to Jessie, while Richard circled around to read it over her shoulder.

"What is it?" he asked.

"It a loan agreement between your father and Uncle Frank. When the bank loaned us the money to buy Coodravale, it included an extra one hundred thousand dollars. Your father then loaned this extra money to your Uncle Frank under the proviso it be paid off within a few years. I know we've paid off the bank loan in full."

Jessie stared hard at her mother. "But you bought Coodravale before I was born."

"Yes." Joanna's voice faltered. "And from what I can make out by that agreement, your uncle still owes us the money." Joanna nodded to the document in her daughter's hands.

The hairs on Jessie's neck bristled. "Why hasn't he paid it back?"

"I have no idea." Joanna scraped her chair back from the table and began to pace the room. Gnawing at her thumb, Jessie perused the document, but she couldn't make much sense of all the legal jargon.

"But Uncle Frank will pay it, won't he?" Richard asked.

"He should've paid it back years ago, but he hasn't. It means I'll have to discuss this with him while he's here. It's not a conversation I'm looking forward to though. Money is never a good topic to discuss at a funeral."

"When you do, Richard and I will be there if you want." Heat warmed Jessie's cheeks. *How dare Uncle Frank...* "I wonder if Aunt Hilda knows anything about it?"

"Knowing Frank, I doubt it. If your father kept it secret from me, I'm sure Frank did the same with Hilda." Circling back, Joanna dropped into her chair.

"But why would Dad lend money to Uncle Frank?" Jessie asked.

"No idea. But he needs to pay it back. This debt is over two decades old."

"Don't worry. I'm sure it will get sorted out." Richard walked around to stand beside his mother, hand on her shoulder.

"I hope so." She spread her hands on the table, head bowed.

"Don't worry. Richard and I will do whatever it takes to help." Jessie pushed from her chair to reassure her mother, bookending Richard on the other side.

Clutching their hands, Joanna glanced up at her children. "Thank you. I'm going to finish up here. I'll see you both in the morning. Good night, darlings." Proffering one cheek to either child, she managed a thin smile. Jessie and Richard lugged their boxes from the dining room and retired to their rooms to choose appropriate memories with which to honour their father.

Friday dawned bright and clear under the blinding glow of the summer sun. While BJ and Whiskey explored the back paddock, Jessie sat alone on the veranda. With a gloomy anticipation of her father's forthcoming funeral replacing the shock of his death, her emotions descended to melancholy. Tears pooled in her eyes as she half-expected to see her dad walk across the far paddock.

She'd not quite reached a quarter of a century before losing her father. Twenty-four years had sped past like an express train and all she had to show for it were some bittersweet memories and the four photos in her lap. The first photo of Dad and her rolling on the wet grass after the rains when she was little, reminded her of how she used to love the rain. Now it annoyed her. Studying the image, she wondered whatever happened to the gold chain with its swan medallion hanging around her neck in the photo. She'd loved that little chain but had somehow lost it. She heaved a disappointed sigh and flipped to the next photo. A snapshot of her father and Jessie squatting around a blazing fire, toasting marshmallows when she was about ten years old, told of a time when she didn't think about what she ate. Back then, the threat of sugar held no power over her. *Ah, how times have changed.* A flicker of irony tugged her lips.

The last two photos showed her father standing beside her in Melbourne outside the Australian Ballet School when she first arrived and then on the following Christmas at the dinner table. For Jessie, both images rekindled mixed emotions, but little overt joy. Rather, they acted as a timeclock punch to her life. Embittered tears burned behind her eyelids as she realised there were no recent pictures of her and her father—just distant images of a girl long ago with a man who never told her how much he loved her until the day before he died.

But she was as much to blame as he was. As soon as she could, she'd escaped into her ballet world, leaving anyone and anything to do with Coodravale behind in a blur. Inspired to carve out her own life, she never looked back for too long. Being here, being home, hurt. And although she could never work out why, it didn't lessen the pain. Coming home stung time and again, like picking a scab off a wound until it felt better to just leave it alone. With her father's funeral only a few days away, her old scab had been scraped off once more. But for the life of her, she didn't know why. *Selfish, that's what I am*, she thought, grinding her teeth. *Instead of thinking about Dad, I'm thinking about myself.* A wretched girl. But as the last thought skidded through her mind, she wondered where she'd heard that before.

In early afternoon, the beeping of a car horn triggered a series of barks from Whiskey. "That'll be my relatives," Jessie said, unimpressed at being disturbed. Nestled into the wingback chairs on the veranda, she and BJ had spent the last hour or so reading, relaxing and chatting. "I better go and greet them with Mum and Richard. Do you want to meet them now, rather than later?"

"Sure." He rose and heeled Whiskey beside him.

Jessie approached each relative with a quick kiss and brief hug. After an exchange of sympathy over Ken's death, she waved BJ forward. "This is a good friend of mine, BJ, and his dog, Whiskey. This is my Uncle Frank, my Aunt Hilda and my cousin Tom." She stepped aside allowing him to perform the required pleasantries.

"Pleased to meet you, sir." BJ pumped Frank's hand.

"BJ? Is that correct?"

Jessie rolled her eyes as she watched her uncle try to assert his authority by puffing up like a bullfrog. He'd always been like that, even with her father. Because Frank was the older brother of the two, he flaunted his seniority at every chance he got. Even though BJ stood a full head taller, Frank inflated himself in an unsuccessful display of dominance.

"I call him Brad," Joanna said, and Jessie wished the ground would just swallow her up.

"Then Brad it is." Uncle Frank pumped BJ's hand hard.

"Fine by me, sir." Turning towards Aunt Hilda, he leaned forward. "Pleasure to meet you, Mrs Hilton."

Jessie loved her aunt. Kind, demure and blithe of spirit, Aunt Hilda wore an endless expression of sweetness and compliance. Just as well, because her husband performed the counter role of tyrant only too well.

"A pleasure to meet you too, BJ." She offered him her hand, the best scone-making hands in the country as far as Jessie was concerned.

"And Tom. Good to meet you." BJ flashed a wide smile at the well-dressed, city slicker in his polished tan boots and crisp white shirt tucked into neatly pressed jeans. Confident and successful, Tom beamed back, accepting BJ's hand in a firm grip.

"Nice to meet you. Where are you from?"

"Melbourne."

Knowing BJ was a man of few words and liked keeping his personal story to himself Jessie interrupted. "So why don't you settle in, and we'll meet for sundowners by the river before dinner?"

"Good idea," Joanna said. "Richard, help them with their bags, please."

"Yes, Mum." Richard fell in line, and the Hilton clan tramped to the guest quarters.

Jessie lingered, shaking her head. "And I was having such a nice time."

A soft chuckle tickled her ear. "Not to worry. It's only for a few days." BJ edged closer beside her.

"I don't understand how you find any of this amusing."

"It's life. There's always some bloke who thinks he's boss, another who's on the up and up and wants to be the boss. Then there are the followers, the peace-keepers, those not willing to rock the boat. Peace at any price is their motto. Whether it's the army, business, family or community, the hierarchy is about the same."

"And where do you fit in this pecking order?" she asked.

"Me? I'm the rookie. The new kid. I just do what I'm told, unless…"

"Unless what?"

"Unless someone steps over the line…"

"But how does anyone know where the line is?"

"They'll know. Trust me. They'll know."

Her ears pricked at the lightly veiled ominous tone. She recalled the first night she'd met him. How he'd surfaced from nowhere to save her from being mugged. Back then, she'd shuddered at the thought of what he might do, but now she knew who he was and what he was capable of. She also knew that if he ever lost control, his reprisal would be swift and absolute.

CHAPTER 26

"What is it you do for a living?" One of those pushy guys, Tom Hilton wanted to know everyone's business. BJ felt a little sorry for him really. Tom's father was a boorish man, a man BJ instantly disliked. In his mid-sixties, with grey, receding hair, an ageing goatee beard and beady, blue eyes, Frank Hilton tried to dominate everyone around him. BJ suspected Frank had made his wife's life hell for their entire marriage. Figuring his son had had little choice but to mirror his father's officious behaviour to escape ridicule or a beating, Tom Hilton played a brash mini-me to Frank. They were like characters from Dickens' *A Christmas Carol*—the ghosts of Hilton past and Hilton future. Aunt Hilda seemed to be the only one present with any real goodness.

"At the moment, I work for a builder friend of mine. What is it you do, Tom?" Leaning back in his chair, BJ crossed his leg over his knee and steered the conversation.

"I work as a senior accountant for Campbell's in Sydney. I've been there for a few years." Obviously thrilled to have an audience, Tom chatted about his work while the Goodradigbee River burbled in the background. A Hilton family tradition, sundowners by the river gave BJ the opportunity to observe both sides of the family interact. So far, the tension rose to no more than a simmer, but BJ's gut warned that it'd only take the smallest irritation to reach boiling point. From the corner of his eye, he caught Frank's disapproving glances at Jessie. She upended the second bottle of wine into her glass and drank its contents twice as fast as anyone else. Knowing wine and Jessie's empty stomach were not the best combination, BJ decided to place himself in the firing line. He reached over and gently rested the bottle from her hand. "Would anyone like some more wine?"

'I would." She held her glass aloft.

He drizzled a little in her glass and then proceeded to top up the other glasses. When he set the bottle on the table, she nailed him with a scathing stare. He winced. She sculled her glass, reached for the bottle and poured the last of its contents into it, which she likewise sculled.

"Tell me, Brad. What did you do before you joined this builder friend of yours? You strike me as someone who can look after himself."

Frank's question and smug expression rankled BJ, but he kept his tone polite. "Well, Mr Hilton. I've done a few things in my time…"

"Uncle Frank, I think it's time to move inside. The mosquitos are swarming." Jessie's voice sounded brittle and sharp.

"Yes. I think you're right, Jessica. Let's retire inside. I've got to check the chicken anyway." Joanna rose, the others joined her, and they strolled up the property to the homestead. Frank glanced back over his shoulder with a distinct look of disdain for his niece's behaviour. BJ ignored him, leaned over and offered Jessie his hand.

She snarled and slapped it away. "How dare you embarrass me in front of my family."

"I was trying to *stop* you from embarrassing yourself. You've got to go easy on the wine."

"Why? Why do I? I have every right to have a few drinks. For God's sake, my father just died, I've got some crazed stalker after me, and I might not make principal dancer. My life is going down the toilet. I think I'm entitled to drink as much as I want!" The crescendo of her voice splintered the evening's serenity.

"But drowning your troubles with alcohol isn't going to help." He kept his tone even, trying to diffuse the situation.

"What would you know?"

Stony-faced BJ stared at her. "Come on. I'm taking you inside." He reached over to help her from the chair.

"Don't touch me. I can walk back by myself." She tossed her head and stormed off.

"Come on, Whiskey." He leaned down and ruffled her ears. "We better get going." In reluctant strides, he walked up to the Garden Wing with Whiskey by his side.

When he closed the doors behind him, Jessie paced to the other end of the living room. She snapped an about-face and glared at him. "Do you mind telling me what that was all about?" She flung her arm in the air and pointed in the direction of the river.

He inhaled a long, steady breath and met her frosty gaze. "You're drinking too much. I know you're going through a rough patch, but you can't keep drowning it with booze."

Obviously spoiling for a scene, her intoxicated bad mood pulsed in the vein in her neck. "You're not my keeper. I can do what I want. You make it sound like drinking too much is the worst thing in the world."

He locked eyes with her. The nerve she'd unknowingly struck sizzled like badly wired electrics. *Yes, drinking too much is the worst thing in the world.* Remaining cool and in command, he readied himself. "I need to tell you something."

"What?"

"This wasn't the way I wanted to tell you, but I'm hoping once you hear what I have to say you'll understand why I don't like watching you drink too much."

She folded her arms and huffed. "Go on."

"I was married. My wife's name was Rachael and we had a baby daughter, Tiffany."

"You were married? With a daughter?"

"Three years ago, when I was on a tour of duty, they were killed in a car accident by a drunk driver. That's why I hate watching you drink too much. It reminds me of the condition that bastard must have been in when he killed Rachael and Tiffany."

Jessie's arms dropped by her side and she sucked in air. "And you didn't think that the death of your wife and child was important enough to tell me until now?"

"I'm sorry. I wasn't deliberately withholding this from you. You've had enough going on. Besides, it's not something I go around telling people."

"But you told me about your brother, Tony. You told me you were an SAS sniper. Why not tell me about Rachael and Tiffany?"

An electrical storm erupted in BJ's mind, sending shock waves in all directions. He dragged a hand across his mouth and tried to swallow the words, but they won their freedom, fleeing desperately from his mouth. "Because you keep thanking me, and telling me I'm some kind of hero, but it's not true. What hero lets his younger brother drown? What hero can't protect his wife and baby daughter?"

"But, none of it was your fault…"

He cringed. There it was, the expression he never wanted to see on Jessie's face. The same expression he'd seen on the faces of other people when they discovered his tragic past. Pity. He hated that people felt sorry for him. Most of all, he hated to see it on Jessie's face now. He turned away, but he could still feel it burning into his back. "When the accident happened, I resigned my command and moved to Melbourne."

"Resigned your command?" Her voice sounded reedy and thin.

He swivelled around but stopped himself from snapping to attention. "Lance Corporal Jordan. Leader of a special black ops unit responsible for some of the biggest snatch and grabs…"

"Stop!" She rubbed the heels of her hands across her forehead. "I don't care about your military past or that you were in the SAS. I care about you, as a man."

"Don't you see? The only thing I did right was the military. There I had control. Everything else I fucked up. Watching you get wasted on booze reminds me of what I couldn't control all those years ago and look what happened to Rachael and Tiffany. I'm sorry, but I made you a promise, and I don't want anything bad happening to you. I'm trying to protect you."

She slumped into an armchair. "God." Holding her head in her hands, she leaned forward and moaned. "I really don't think I can go in for dinner tonight." She glanced up. "Will you tell Mum we're not coming?"

"Are you all right?" He moved towards her, concerned by the glassy look in her eyes.

"I'll be fine. You go tell Mum. I'll grab a shower and then we can talk some more when you come back."

Tension coiled in BJ's gut. "You sure you're okay?"

She lolled back and closed her eyes. "Yes. Yes. I'm fine."

"Okay. I'll see you in a couple of minutes." BJ paced out of the Garden Wing and commanded Whiskey to his side. "I don't think that went very well, girl." Man and dog set off at a brisk pace. "The timing sucked."

Unintentionally, he knocked too hard on the main house's front door. A startled Joanna answered. "Whatever is the matter, Brad? Where's Jessica?" She peered from side to side.

"I'm sorry, Mrs Hilton. Jessie's not feeling well, she's very tired. She's asked me to send her apologies. She won't be coming to dinner."

"Oh, that's a shame. But you will join us won't you?" She opened the door further to welcome him inside.

"No thanks, Mrs Hilton. I think I'll take a rain check too. Just stay in and watch some TV. Grab a sandwich or something. Keep Jessie company." He tried for a nonchalant demeanour but didn't quite succeed. A familiar sinking feeling churned in his gut, telling him to get out, fast.

"I understand. It's very kind of you to look out for Jessica this way. I cannot thank you enough…"

"No need to thank me. I'll see you in the morning then. Good night." With a curt nod, he turned and paced away while Joanna called her good night after him. He didn't care if she thought he was rude. His sixth sense screamed danger. His initial concern of leaving Jessie alone, even for a few minutes escalated to high alert.

No longer in sight of Joanna, and with Whiskey by his side, he sprinted back to the Garden Wing. He slammed through the French doors. "Jessie. Jessie." He raced from room to room. Gone. *Shit. Shit. Shit.* He bolted to the wardrobe and tore open his kit, grabbed and checked his torch, shoved his hunting knife into the back of his jeans and threw on his military vest. Racing into Jessie's room, he scrounged around her bed, locating what he needed—her pyjama pants. Using two fingers as a pincer, he picked them up and strode into the kitchen. He opened and slammed drawers until he found a zip lock plastic bag into which he dropped her pants, then went back outside to where Whiskey waited. His lungs locked solid as if someone had poured concrete into them. A familiar feeling. One he'd learned to ignore.

"Whiskey, we trained hard, so we could fight easy. This is it, girl." He opened the plastic bag and the scent of Jessie's pyjamas wafted under Whiskey's nose. He fused his focus with his dog. "Find Jessie, Whiskey. Find Jessie."

CHAPTER 27

"I can't believe he didn't tell me." Still fuzzy from too much wine, Jessie wandered down the property to the river, talking aloud. She needed fresh air to clear her head. Although she had no torch, she moved with confidence. Night was falling, but a sliver of daylight still skirted the landscape with a faint periphery glow. "How could he not tell me something as important as that?" Stopping in her tracks, she rubbed her temples. She needed water and lots of it. *BJ's right. I've got to stop drinking like this. I only ever do it when I come home.*

Gazing up towards the ranges, her scalp prickled. The witching hour where day and night honoured a short truce just before the day relinquished dominion to the night. She dug her fingers into her trapezius muscles and rotated her neck. Stretching her arms wide, she sighed. As the enormity of BJ's loss dawned on her, she crumbled to her haunches. She settled back on the ground and tucked her knees under her chin, encircling her legs with her arms. *Poor BJ. He's off at war, doing his duty and his wife and daughter are killed in a car accident. He's putting his life on the line and everything back home is taken away from him. No wonder he didn't want to talk about it. Some secrets are just too painful.* The longer she pondered his tragedy, the more disappointed she became with the way she'd behaved. As much as she didn't want to admit it, maybe she was just as self-absorbed as she judged her mother to be.

"Shit, it's getting really dark now. I better get back." Springing to her feet, she brushed off her skirt and turned back to the homestead. She could just make out the veranda lights peeping through the trees. "I certainly have some apologising to do." Striding off with a swing of her arms, she began to formulate an acceptable apology.

"Jessie." Off to her left a familiar voice whispered her name.

Her head snapped in its direction, thoughts racing. "Who is it?"

"It's me." Barely a few feet away, a gangly figure grew up from the ground like a ghost from a grave.

"I can't see you very clearly." She squinted trying to sharpen her focus, but her mind couldn't place who it was.

"It's me. I've come for you, Jessie." Out of the dark he appeared, looming over her, a white cloth in his hand. Clamping the wet, smelly fabric over her mouth and nose, he pressed hard, while his other arm gripped her tight. She opened her mouth to call out, but it was too late. She squirmed, gulping for air. Her limbs slackened, the panic subsided, and everything went black.

CHAPTER 28

've got her. I've got her. What a stroke of luck. I thought I'd have to stake out that bloody place for days to get an opportunity like that. Obviously, the big hero left her alone for just a few minutes, and bingo! She walked right into my arms. Serves him right. He's lost her now. She's mine…forever.

Look at her, my dancer, sound asleep on the back seat. How pretty she is. Light as a feather she was to carry. Nothing to her. Renting this four-wheel drive from one of those country idiots was a brain storm—as was cutting the fence wire on the neighbouring paddock to the homestead so I could drive along the lower river bank. Stroke of genius. *That's what I am…a bloody genius.* My mother used to say *there's no great genius without a touch of madness.* When she was mad and laid into me with the rose bush switch, she used to make me recite it over and over again. It was a tough lesson. But I learned my mother was a genius. And now, so am I.

Look at her breathing like a little lamb, asleep on the back seat. I've prepared a special place just up there, over the ridge, where no one will find us. It'll take us a little while to get there, but I know the way. You don't have to worry. It's a special place I made for us. It's so romantic. I hope you like it. There's not a person around for miles. We'll be all alone to get to know each other better without any interruptions. Now, you just stay asleep on the back seat for a while longer, my pretty dancer. I promised I would come to get you. We'll be there soon. I've waited a long time to make you mine. I'm so excited, but I don't dare touch myself. I'll leave that to you. *Soon I'll carry you across the threshold.*

CHAPTER 29

*T*he light from BJ's torch shone in a wide arc in front of Whiskey as she set off. He hoped she knew this game well enough to play it in the dark. Finding a ball in the daytime was easy, but now at night, and with Jessie's life at stake, Whiskey was in new territory. She'd not trained before with finding a human being. Still he had no other option, but to put his trust in his dog. Working as a team, he patrolled behind her while she smelled the air. The saturation of Jessie's scent added to the difficulty. She'd left a trail everywhere on the property—easy for Whiskey to follow, but difficult to discern which was most recent.

Man and dog zig-zagged down the property in the direction in which Whiskey was most interested. Now and again, the dog alerted with a sharp prop and plonk of her bottom. While she waited, he investigated the spot for signs of struggle or a fall. Once satisfied the spot held no significance, they moved on. When they crested the knoll, Whiskey became more excited, running ahead, sniffing the air with loud snorts.

"Jessie, are you there?" BJ shone the torch into the darkness. Whiskey's short, sharp bark told him to hurry up. The dog alerted, remaining fixed in her trained position. Illuminating the ground, he kneeled, and his heart clutched. Signs of struggle raked the grassy earth. Two sets of fresh footprints, one small and one larger. *Fuck. She's been taken.* With no drag marks cutting through the grass, either Jessie had got away or someone had overpowered her.

BJ rewarded Whiskey with a quick ear rub and a treat. Wasting no time, he removed a tracking card from his vest pocket and marked the spot. Once more he opened the plastic bag to refresh Whiskey's nose. "Come on, girl. Find Jessie. Find Jessie."

Head lifted, the dog galloped down towards the river bank. After a few metres, she wavered, trying to pick up the scent. Then she took off to her right. Within moments, she alerted with a bark. BJ palmed the treat as he dropped to his knees. His gut twisted. *Tyre tracks.* Powering to his feet, he switched off his torch and stared off into the night. Straining his eyes, he scanned in all directions. *Nothing.* But before he returned to marking the spot, he glimpsed red lights in the distance on the road leading up to the ridge. A vehicle's brake lights. But where were the head lights or tail lights? *They're not on because he doesn't want to be seen.*

"Whiskey. Heel." With his dog running beside him, BJ sprinted back to the homestead, loaded her into the Jeep and leaped in. He gunned the car down the driveway, sending a spray of gravel into the air and prayed no kangaroos played tag with him tonight. Driving on instinct, he headed in the direction of the brake lights disappearing over the ridge. With the Jeep's headlights on high beam, he hoped it would give him the advantage of speed, but he knew as soon as the other vehicle topped the ridge, the driver would flick his lights on for a swift escape. Left and right he swerved, taking the country road curves as fast as he dared. Whiskey dropped to her belly on the back seat for balance. "Hang in there, girl."

Despite the breakneck speed, the Jeep didn't seem to make up any distance. The fiery red from the other vehicle's brake lights snuffed out. Pushing further, BJ prayed their guiding glow would return. Surely there was another curve the bastard had to take. Surely. But they were gone. Into the night, BJ powered on, in the direction his instinct led. Fury gripped him, so too did the sinister fingers of guilt. *Predict rather than prevent. That's what I've been trained to do. I'm a fool. I shouldn't have left her alone. I shouldn't have left Tony or Rachael and Tiffany alone. My fault. It's all my fault...*

CHAPTER 30

*C*old, damp and hard—wherever she was, it wasn't her bed. Scattered thoughts whirled in her head while she searched for recent memories. A pungent smell lingered in her nose wakening her further. It reminded her of science class. What was it? Chloroform? Crunched on her side, her body cried for movement, and she strained to focus on her surroundings. But she couldn't. She was groggy and dazed and there was no light by which to see. Exhausted, she heaved her hand in front of her face, but she couldn't see that either. As if it wasn't there. Absolute, petrifying blackness. A nightmare. Another nightmare. But she knew it wasn't. Now fully conscious, Jessie pieced together the memories—the argument with BJ over her drinking, his telling her about Rachael and Tiffany, her walking down to the river to clear her head, and then…*Oh, God.*

Now she lay somewhere dank and cold, in pitch blackness. Her inability to see prevented any chance of escape. Even if she began to crawl, feeling her way, she might tumble down a precipice or a staircase. She didn't even know whether she was lying on the ground or on something man-made. Hard, cold and a little uneven. *He's left me here, alone, to die.* The thought scared her even more than her captor returning.

She rolled carefully onto her back. Stretching her body, she used her hands and feet to check that she wasn't about to roll off wherever she lay. Once assured she was safe, she relaxed a little. Deep, controlled breaths cleared her mind and nose of whatever drug he'd used. With no idea how long she'd been unconscious, she existed in an abyss of unknown time. She struggled not to panic. As she stared into nothingness, her sense of what was up and what was down destabilized. The subtle illusion of losing her balance teased her inner ear, increasing the fear. She managed to roll over onto her hands and knees and correct her equilibrium. Head lolling forward, she froze— humiliated, helpless and hopeless, overcome with despair. Minutes slipped by or was it, hours?

A faint glow leaked into the space from the right—a torch. Its beam brightened on approach, until it shone in Jessie's face, blinding her. She dropped her head to protect her eyes and relief washed over her. At least now there was some light by which to see, to plan an escape. She watched his feet walk past and stop to her left. Hearing the flick of a lighter, she waited, looking beneath her. She knelt on a narrow ledge of compacted, red earth, not quite a metre from the floor below. Soft, filtered light filled the void, encouraging her to lift her head. With eyes now adjusted to the light level, she examined her prison. Her heart sank. He'd interned her in a limestone cave. Invisible fingers of doom clutched her heart. *How am I ever going to get out of here?*

Off to her right, she assumed the tunnel through which he'd entered led to the outside world. That was where hope lay. Around her, stalagmites, stalactites, columns and flow stone decorated the small cavern, which under normal circumstances would have been breathtakingly beautiful. Nevertheless, the nature of this cave spelled disaster for Jessie. Razor-sharp edges promised serious consequences for any misjudged movement. For the first time, she realised she was shoeless. He must have removed them as an extra precaution to impede her escape. A high cavernous ceiling stretched upward, curving back to the ground encasing her in a giant egg-shaped vault. Dread backwashed her throat as she registered her plight.

Beneath Wee Jasper Valley tunnelled mazes of caves. Only a few operated as tourist caves, while others were wild, unexplored and unvisited, perhaps even undiscovered. And she was in one of them. Alone with a madman. With his back to her, he finished lighting the dozen or so candles on the grand floor-standing candelabra. In their luminescent glow, the red, orange and yellow tones of the cave intensified, filling the grotto with a romantic atmosphere. Like a scene from "Phantom of the Opera" when the villain took Christine to his underground lair, proclaiming his love. She shuddered at the thought. *This will be my underground tomb.*

"I'm sorry, Jessie. I didn't want it to come to this, but you left me no other option."

She knew the voice. But it lacked its usual deference—instead replaced by a condescending, smug tone of superiority.

Composing herself, she assumed a Japanese sit pose; her back ruler-straight, hands in lap and chin high. Her captor turned to face her. Fusing him in an unwavering gaze, she admonished him in a school teacher tone. "Well, Skip. I don't know what all this is about, but I suggest you return me to Coodravale, and we'll just call it a silly little game."

Skip Norton's diabolical laugh sent shivers over her skin. This wasn't the young, timid man she'd come to know. Locking her with obvious evil intent, he hissed. "This is not a silly little game."

She swallowed hard. "Skip, why aren't you stuttering? What's happened to you?"

He gave a sarcastic snort. "The stutter was an act. As was the poor Skip Norton, downtrodden young waiter working for bombastic restaurant owner, Salvatore Bacci. All an act." He spat vehemently at his feet.

"But you were so kind, so sweet. I really cared for you. Why would you do this to me, of all people?"

"It's exactly why I did. Because you were the only one who did care. You noticed me, you talked to me, and you were interested in me. Jessie, you're the one for me." While he rattled off his reasons, Skip's voice softened to a grating whine. Climbing up next to her, he huddled in close, like a puppy trying to please.

Oh, God. Oh, God. Swamped by disgust, she suppressed a scream while he rubbed against her rigid body. Although panic-stricken, she knew her only chance was to keep him agreeable in the hope she could talk her way out. "But Skip, kidnapping me is no way to treat someone who cares for you or who you care for, is it?"

"Maybe not, but I knew if I asked you out, you would've said no." He pouted at her, portraying the affable, sympathetic persona she previously knew.

"But Skip it's not that I wouldn't have gone out with you. I don't go out with any boys. I don't have time, with my ballet and everything." She managed a conciliatory smile and sympathetic expression.

Yowling like a wild beast, he thrust his face up to hers, breath stale and stinking. "So, who's the big hero with you, then? If it wasn't for him, we would've been together on Sunday night a couple of weeks ago. But no, he had to stick his nose in, didn't he?"

She blinked, her head reeling. It had been Skip who grabbed her on the street that night after yoga class. She evicted the thought from her mind. "But Skip, I'm not going out with him. He's just a friend."

"You're lying. You lying bitch!"

Jessie's face stung with the venom he spat on each word. Her heart hammered, desperate to be free as he leered at her throat and décolletage. *Keep him talking.* She forced her voice to sound calm. "But Skip, what happened with your old school friend who was coming to visit for the holidays? What was her name again? Chrissy?"

He barked a cynical laugh. "Chrissy. That was just to get you interested. I thought if I talked about a female friend of mine, you might like to meet her? Then, when you agreed, you and I could be alone."

"There's no Chrissy?"

"Oh, there was a Chrissy." Another sinister laugh burst from his mouth. "A long time ago. She was a right bitch, that one. A stuck-up ballet dancer she was." Jessie bit her lip, wishing she'd never mentioned it. "We were in the same class at school and when I asked her out, she laughed at me, in front of everyone. Bitch! But I showed her. She didn't go out with me, but she didn't go home either." His watery blue eyes danced maliciously. Then he leaned over and licked Jessie's cheek. The same repulsive saliva which sealed his love letter in its pretty pink envelope now sealed her fate. "But you're not like her, are you?"

"No. No. Of course not, Skip. Not like Chrissy at all. I'd be happy to go out with you."

Skip slid his index finger down to the top button of her blouse, then along the inner lining of her bra and whispered in a sing-song voice, "That makes me happy, Jessie. Very happy." Choking dryness corked her mouth. All she could do was grit her teeth. Ignore his touch. "Now, I have something for you, which I hope will make *you* happy." A secretive smirk curled his lips. He leaped down from the ledge, in willowy, agile movements. Not like the clumsy, awkward movements she remembered from the restaurant. A brilliant actor. He could have been a star on the stage rather than a psychotic kidnapper. Skip pulled his "gift" out from behind a nearby rock and presented it on a clothes hanger. Jessie moaned.

"These are for you. Put them on." Swinging on the hanger were her apricot G-string and bra.

"Skip…"

He picked up her G-string, wrapped his disgusting tongue around them and sucked. "I've had your knickers inside mine, getting myself ready for you. You taste so delicious." Wanton lust flamed in his eyes. Then he roared. "Put them on."

"Skip, can't we just talk about…" *Oh God. I can't breathe. Oh God. I…*

"Now!" As the bellow of Skip's voice thundered in the cave, the world spun, and she collapsed.

CHAPTER 31

Actually, I'm kind of pleased she fainted. It's been go, go, go since I got to this God-forsaken place, and I need a good night's sleep. I'll pour a little more sleepy-bye drug on this cloth to help her along. She can do the underwear modelling and everything else I've got planned when we're both fresh tomorrow. There, she's stopped squirming…and a bit more for good measure. "Breathe deep, Jessie. That's a good girl."

Look how pretty she is. I think all women are prettier when they're asleep. No talking, no complaining, no nagging. And their eyes are closed as well, so they can't see what you're doing. *She's so fast asleep she doesn't even know what's happening.* I'll just explore a little bit, not too much. I don't want to spoil things for tomorrow. Oh, her breasts are so warm and soft. When I cup them in my hands they're just right. Like Goldilocks, Jessie is just right. Look how her nipples bud when I squeeze them. They want me, I know it. And my cock wants her too. It's so hungry and hard, but I don't dare touch myself. I'll leave that for Jessie to do, tomorrow. But a peek under her skirt couldn't hurt. See how her legs meet at the top under those pretty white knickers. If I take a big breath, I can smell her sex, calling out to me. She's ripe for the picking. How I would love to touch her, to suck all the sweetness out of her. Slurp until she goes dry. But it's no fun if she doesn't know what's going on. Much more fun when she's awake and able to enjoy it. Much more fun.

I wonder what happened to the big hero. I got the best of him, I did. The dancer's mine now, and he's missed out. He'll be going crazy trying to work out what went wrong. Well, I can tell him what went wrong in his bloody life... Skip Norton, the genius.

"Good night, Jessie. I'm going back to my motel to get some sleep."

She'll be safe here. I'll put this blanket over her and a pillow under her head. I don't think the rats will nibble her. She's too warm. There, I've tucked her toes in. She looks like a fairy tale princess waiting for her prince to return.

"I'm blowing out the candles now, Jessie. You sleep tight. No one will find you here. I'll be back with breakfast in the morning. Then you and I can get down to some serious business. Good night, my lovely dancer."

CHAPTER 32

BJ hurtled on until he crested the ridge where he saw the vehicle disappear. Jamming on the brakes, his eyes scanned the landscape. Nothing but distant lights glimmered from the homesteads dotting the hillside. He'd lost them. He'd lost Jessie. *Fuck!* He flung open his car door and jumped onto the road. He grabbed the small pair of night binoculars from his vest and strained to see through them. With no idea where they went or whether they were near or far, he jammed them back in his vest. Raking his hands through his hair, he lifted his face to the sky and roared like a mighty lion wounded in battle. He yielded to his anguish and guilt, but only for a moment before returning to the fray. Back into the Jeep, he spun it around and sped back to Coodravale.

Careering down the driveway, he spotted Joanna and Richard standing at the front door. BJ slammed to a stop and released Whiskey from the back.

"What's going on?" Joanna asked.

"Jessie's been taken. I need to use the phone." Striding past them, he entered the main residence, heading for the landline telephone.

"Taken? What do you mean taken?" She followed behind him, her voice shrill and panicked.

"Probably, the stalker who broke into her unit. I don't know. She wasn't in the Garden Wing when I returned from speaking with you. I searched for her, but she was gone." As his hand reached for the phone, he winced at the pained disbelief creasing Joanna's and Richard's faces. He'd seen that look on his mother's face when they'd hauled Tony from the swimming pool. The same look on his father's face the day he'd left him and his mother standing at the front door. *He'd let them down. He promised to look after Jessie, but he'd let them down.* "I have to make some calls. I'll put it on hands-free, so you can listen in." His fingers jabbed the keys and the line connected. "Ricky, is that you?"

"Buddy. I was just about to call you..."

"I've got you on hands-free, mate. We've got a problem."

"What is it?"

"Jessie's been taken."

"Shit. When?"

"About an hour ago."

"This might help. I've just got off the phone with Angel. It seems the cops found a decent set of prints on an empty Coke bottle thrown into the street garden outside of Jessie's building."

"Go on."

"Ron Jacobs, the gardener, found it after the cops questioned him. When they put the finger prints through the system, they flagged as prints from a closed file."

"Closed file? What do you mean?"

"A juvenile file from years ago. Because the guy was underage, the authorities closed the file."

"So how does that help me?"

"Angel got the file opened."

Good for you, Angel. "And?"

"Seems this kid had a history of animal cruelty and possibly murder. He wasn't convicted of anything, but a lot of evidence pointed to him with the drowning of a young girl from his school who was a ballet dancer, a Chrissy Potomac. It was deemed an accidental death, but suspicion sat heavily with the kid. They couldn't prove anything though."

"What's his name?"

"Skip Norton. But get this…he works as a waiter at the restaurant Jessie and Jasmine go to. Jasmine's with me now, and she's told me all about him."

"What's he look like?"

"In his early to mid-twenties, red hair, freckles, strange-looking blue eyes, stutters. He's not all there in Jasmine's opinion."

Throughout the conversation, BJ watched Joanna and Richard while his mind pieced together possible scenarios. When Richard's face paled, he knew something was wrong.

"What is it, Richard? What?"

"That sounds like a guy who picked me up at Rosie's Café the other day…"

"Picked you up?" Joanna said, aghast.

"Not now, Mum. He said his name was Peter. Didn't give a last name. Said he lived in Melbourne and was here on a holiday."

"And?"

"He wanted to know where I lived, and…" A pasty expression settled on Richard's face as he recalled the meeting. "Oh, God. Aside from me telling him where we live and how to get here, he wanted to know about nearby limestone caves. Which ones were open to the public, which ones weren't and how to get to them? Oh, God. I led him right to Jess."

"Don't worry about that now," BJ said. "What else did he say? Think."

"He said he was staying in a motel in town. He didn't say which one though…"

"Okay. He introduced himself only as Peter and he's staying in town. Have you got that, Ricky?"

"Yeah, I've got it. I'll get onto Angel now to alert the Yass police. What are you going to do?"

"I'll go through what Richard said about the caves around here and see if we can narrow it down. If not, I'm going into town to find this motherfucker." He glanced an apology to Joanna.

"Just don't kill him, buddy. Okay?"

"Got it. Later..." He ended the call and turned to Joanna. "Mrs Hilton, have you got a map of the area?"

"I think so. Ken used to keep maps in the hall dresser. And for God's sake, call me Joanna." She rifled through the drawer, grabbed the map and handed it to him.

"All right. Dining room." He led the way with Joanna and Richard in tow. She snatched the centrepiece away while he laid out the map. BJ hunched over the table, hands spread wide. His gaze fused with Richard. "Speak to me. Tell me word for word whatever you can remember about this sicko."

"I told him about the limestone caves here." He pointed to a crescent on the map, not far from Coodravale.

"Right. Where else?"

"There're also a couple of caves up over the ridge. Here." When his index finger marked the spot, BJ knew this was the direction in which he saw the brake lights disappear.

"That's it. Tell me more."

"Well, there's an old cave system there that stretches back into the rock. The entrance is difficult to find unless you know what you're looking for. Jess and I went up there with Dad when we were kids. Only the locals know about it."

"Not any more. My gut tells me that's where he's taken her." He gripped Richard's shoulder. "It's not your fault. It's mine. I shouldn't have left her alone."

"There's no one to blame here except the man who took her," Joanna said. "But what are we going to do?"

"We're going to find her. Richard, you're going to get some gear together for me. I'll tell you what I need. And Joanna, you're going to go into the Garden Wing and find me some more of Jessie's clothes. They need to have been worn. Preferably smelling of her so Whiskey can get a strong scent. Take a pair of tongs with you to pick them up and a zip lock bag to put them in. I don't want your scent on them. Okay? Let's go."

Before Joanna turned to leave, she locked him in a steely stare. "By the way, who are you really?"

"I used to be Lance Corporal Brad Jordan, sniper in the SAS, ma'am."

"Doesn't surprise me one bit." A relieved smile lit her face and she hurried off.

"Right, Richard. Let's get to it."

CHAPTER 33

*W*hen Jessie regained consciousness for the second time in her inky tomb, she knew exactly what her future held. No longer concerned with the principal role in the Australian Ballet Company, she gritted her teeth for a far greater role—to stay alive. With no idea how long she'd been comatose this time, she shook off the drug's impact, determined to escape. Though free and unsecured, she remained motionless and listened, her hearing acute. Aside from the rhythmic beat of dripping water smacking the cave floor, she could hear nothing else. On top of her rested a blanket, under her head, a pillow. Not the sort of thing he'd do…unless he'd left and planned to return later. *Bastard! Does he think I'm just going to wait here and play victim until he comes back? Well, he's got the wrong girl!*

Outraged at Skip's arrogance and fuelled by defiant self-preservation, Jessie leaped into action. Sitting up, she yanked off the blanket and removed her blouse. Tugging it with all her strength, she managed to rip it into two pieces which she wrapped around each hand as protection against the sharp edges of limestone. A little dizzy, she paused to rebalance her inner ear. She braced herself and visualised in her mind's eye what she

185

remembered of the cave. Once ready, she secured the pillow in her teeth and threw the blanket to the ground below. Wiggling to the edge of the ledge, she dangled her legs, spun on her bottom and let go. Thud! She hit harder than expected. She realised that because she couldn't see in the pitch blackness, she lacked depth of vision. The jolt twinged her ankles, but nothing a good rub wouldn't fix.

Deciding on a more cautious approach, she remained on her hands and knees. Shuffling to her right, she faced in the direction where Skip had entered. Leaning back on her bottom, she removed her knickers and used them to secure the pillow to her head like a miner's helmet. She held onto a corner of the blanket, tossed it in front of her and waited for it to settle to the ground. With pain-staking care, she crawled over the blanket, keeping her head lowered so the pillow would take the first impact if she crept into anything. Repeating this laborious process, she inched her way along the cave's floor. On each occasion when the limestone scratched or bit her, she cursed. But the pain was little price to pay for freedom. Her father had taught her that if she ever got lost in a limestone cave it was pointless calling for help. Sound doesn't echo or carry in the caves. So, all she could do was continue in her slow procession with the blanket, praying she hadn't taken a wrong turn and was heading deeper into the cave system.

Thirst roared in her throat giving way to a sinking feeling of fear. In the suffocating darkness and unable to see or run away, she was transported back to her recurring nightmares. The unending darkness, the whispered threats in her ear, the hands touching her. *Calm down, calm down.* But fantasy and reality blurred. Overcome with confusion and terror, she cried out. Her arms flailed into the air, scraping against nearby limestone columns which tore off skin as effortlessly as coral branches. The smarting pain brought Jessie back from her twilight zone with a sudden shock. Thick, warm blood smeared her arms and confirmed the damage. She dabbed her wounds as best she could so as not to leave a blood trail, for either Skip or the rats. Despite everything, she had to get out. She would not die in this hell hole.

Rubbing a bandaged hand across her leaking eyes, she blinked to clear them of grit. Self-pity sobbed from her mouth, but she crawled on. Suddenly, ahead, light filtered from above. *A daylight hole.* They open to the ground above. Sometimes, big enough for a person to climb through. Daylight meant hope. It also meant she could make out her surroundings a little easier as precious shards of shadowy light spilled downward. *It's not daytime yet. Maybe just coming dawn.*

Encouraged by this new turn of events and now able to discern shapes more easily, she stood up. Still using the blanket to protect her feet, she shuffled closer towards the light cast by the hole and peered upward. Her only option. To continue through the tunnel meant she would lose all light and possibly run straight into Skip on his return. Climbing up and through the daylight hole was her only feasible, timely means of escape.

She clenched her fists, readying herself for the dangerous, painful climb. With only a thin skirt and bra protecting her body, and her hands bandaged in her ripped blouse, she reassessed the pillow's usefulness. Deciding to discard it, she stepped back into her knickers. She sacrificed the cotton blanket on an especially sharp edge of limestone and hacked it into enough pieces to fashion primitive footwear. She knew none of what covered her body would be much protection. It would be her dancer's training —her agility, strength and balance, which would be her greatest assets.

Reaching for a nearby outcrop, she found the least painful handhold, grasped it and sprang from the floor. Her foot sought a suitable cavity and deftly locked into position as her other arm stretched upward to the next ledge. Hand over hand, she grasped, scraped and cursed. She mustn't stop. Stopping meant defeat, meant she wasn't good enough. She could do this. She had to do this.

Her breath came in sharp bursts as she hung outstretched like the bats inhabiting the Wee Jasper caves. *Only a little more. Only a little more.* But then a terrible thought struck. Because the cave ceiling curved over like the inside of an egg shell, she'd have to edge upside down along the ceiling just to get to the hole. *Dear God. What am I going to do?* Hope dripped from her with every bead of perspiration.

Suddenly, a light splashed the walls in the cave below. Terror gripped her. Though the limestone bit with hundreds of needle-sharp pricks, she flattened herself hard against the wall. *Please don't let him find me. Please...*

CHAPTER 34

*B*loody kangaroos. *It's taken me nearly two hours to get back to Yass.* Stupid animals. Jumping out in front of the car. Bloody near killed myself swerving to miss one of the bastards. If hitting them wouldn't cause so much damage to the car, I'd have run the mongrels over. But it's a rental. Can't draw any attention to myself. Doesn't matter, I'll still be able to get some sleep. I need some rest with what I've got planned today. I hope Jessie appreciates how much effort I've gone to, to make her comfortable. I'm sure we'll have lots of fun when I get back there after a few hours shut-eye. Just the thought of the surprises I've got in store makes me hard. She'll have forgotten all about that big hero once we're together. She's my dancer, not his. Makes me hard just thinking about it, but I don't dare touch myself. That'll be Jessie's job, soon, very soon.

Here it is. The Worst Eastern Motel. Geez, I'm a funny bloke. Just as well the car space for my room is empty. Some slant-eyed idiot parked in it yesterday. Had his car loaded up with his stinking wife and two yellow brats. I gave him what for...Asian prick. They're taking over this country, I swear.

God, it'll be good to hit the bed. I hate driving. A hot shower won't go astray either. Then I'll be nice and fresh for Jessie. Only a few more steps to the door…Wait a minute, who's this big bloke coming out of the shadows? What's going on?

"Excuse me sir, is your name Peter Bookman?"

What's this cop doing here? "No. That's not me. Sorry, officer."

"Well, the room you're about to go into is registered to Mr Peter Bookman. So, either you're Peter Bookman or you're about to break and enter someone else's room?"

Shit. How did they find me?

"Please show me your driver's licence or some form of photo ID, sir."

This big gorilla has got to be joking. No way. "I've left my driver's licence in my car, officer." *I've got to get out of here. Make a run for it. Run, run…*

"Stop. Put your hands behind your head."

Shit. What's with the other coppers and the guns? Where did they come from? "Okay. Okay. I haven't done anything wrong, officers. I was just going to get my driver's licence from my car." *Better keep my hands up, otherwise these trigger-happy bastards will shoot me.*

"Skip Norton. I'm arresting you on suspicion of kidnapping Jessie Hilton. Put your hands down behind your back."

Bastards! How did they find me? The big interfering hero. I bet it's his fault. Doesn't matter. They can't pin anything on me.

"You are not obliged to say or do anything unless you wish to do so."

The cops never knew what happened to Muffin or Chrissy or the others. The same will happen this time. Without Jessie's body, they can't prove anything. And I'm certainly not telling them where she is.

"Whatever you say or do may be used in evidence. Do you understand?"

Still, it would have been nice to spend some time with my dancer. Now what will I do? I don't dare touch myself.

CHAPTER 35

"*How* much further?" BJ gunned the Jeep along the country road while the pale light of dawn lurked over the ranges. Against his prior decision to find and beat the crap out of Skip Norton, he chose to find Jessie as soon as possible. If Norton was in town, the police would take care of him. If he was with Jessie, he'd do the job, with pleasure.

Richard clung to the door grip of the speeding Jeep. "Take that road. There. On the left."

Throwing the Jeep onto the dirt track, BJ hit a hollow and he, Richard and Whiskey became airborne in the cabin. Weathering a back-wrenching jolt, he hollered, "Where now?"

"Up there on that ridge." Richard's finger pointed north to a copse of eucalypt trees.

Roaring up the track, the Jeep kicked up clouds of red dust and scattered mobs of choughs in fluttering black swirls of feathers.

"Here. Stop here." Richard craned his neck. "This is it."

BJ scanned the landscape for access. Aside from hundreds of limestone boulders lodged in the slopes, he couldn't see anything except undulating hills covered in hardy, native grass. "Are you sure?"

"Positive."

"Where're the entrances to this cave system?"

"They're scattered across the ridge, about fifty metres or so behind those rocks." Richard pointed in a westerly direction to a line of oversized boulders resembling the backbone of an ancient dinosaur.

"How many entrances do you reckon?"

Richard grimaced. "Hundreds, maybe more."

"Okay. Let's go. Come on, Whiskey." He opened the back door and she bounded out. "Sit. Good Girl." He glanced over to Richard. "You get the bag out of the back and be ready to run."

On opening the zip lock bag containing Jessie's soiled socks, BJ held it under the dog's nose. "Find Jessie. Find Jessie." He prayed this was the right spot and that Jessie's scent lingered enough to trigger Whiskey's nose.

Taking a deep inhale, the dog quivered and smelled the air. Up, down, right, left, she sniffed, but remained stationary.

Doubt gripped him. "Come on, girl." He thrust the scent bag under her nose again. "Find Jessie. Find Jessie."

Sweeping her head, Whiskey sniffed and then launched to her feet. She dashed up the hill, with BJ and Richard running close behind, until she gained speed.

"Come on. Here give me the bag." BJ snatched it and pumped his legs harder to catch up with Whiskey, leaving Richard behind. Suddenly, the slope peaked, and the dog propped. Heaving gulps of air, he kneeled beside her. "Find Jessie. Find Jessie."

Whiskey hesitated, nose quivering. The dawn breeze suddenly died. Wee Jasper Valley held its breath one last time before daybreak. *Come on, come on. Where's the wind?* The three of them waited, tense and impatient. Then Whiskey's nose caught a wayward gust of wind, and she took off. Over the ridge and down, she picked her way through a blanket of sharp-edged limestone rocks.

"Good girl. Find Jessie." BJ spurred her on and the Border

collie continued in the most important exercise of her life. After another ten minutes of investigating the rocky terrain, the dog snorted, plonked her butt to the ground and alerted with a bark.

"Good girl." He marked the cave opening. "This looks like where he took her. Through here," whispered BJ, pointing out the entrance to Richard.

"You don't have to whisper. The caves have no echo. Even if Jess called out, we couldn't hear her."

BJ groaned. "Terrific. You wait here. I'm going in with Whiskey to see if we can find her." He wrestled his torch from his vest and flicked it on.

"Take this." Richard handed him a ball of thick-threaded string. "You'll need it, so you don't get lost. I'll hang onto it from this end. Those passageways all tend to look the same after a while."

"Will do. Thanks." He slapped Richard on the shoulder. "Don't give up. We'll find her." Pulling out the scent bag once more, he cued Whiskey. "Find Jessie."

"Be careful..." Richard wound the end of string around his hand.

"Don't worry. I'm bringing Jessie home. I promise." BJ's gut squirmed at the thought of breaking another promise. Failure wasn't an option this time. Giving Richard a final nod, he shone his torch beam into the cave opening. With Whiskey heeled beside him, he stepped into the passageway. Not much wider than a standard doorway and about half a metre lower. On either side, shards of razor-edged limestone jutted inwards making the thoroughfare narrow and dangerous. He hunched over, endeavouring not to hit his head on the uneven ceiling or connect with the walls. "Stay close, girl. I don't want you getting cut up." Progress was grindingly slow. At each junction where other passageways intersected, he waited for Whiskey's nose to lead the way. Standing in the dark with only a sliver of torch light, he sensed evil lurking in the blackness. Like the desert at night, this place was at once, magnificent yet malicious. Unravelling the string, he checked around for markers Norton must have made. If there were any, BJ couldn't see them. *This guy has put some effort into this, so he won't take kindly to being disturbed.* Using a high degree of stealth and a minimal degree of light, he guided Whiskey on her mission. The dog clung to his leg, sniffing and pushing forward on the scent trail.

Every movement proved challenging. Every edge primed to inflict damage. The thought of Jessie holed up with some maniac in this blackness, fired up his rage. He'd witnessed this strategy before. The enemy terrorises their victims in the dark. Not being able to see increases a victim's vulnerability and weakens their ability to fight back. Slow, painful and torturous, the horrors that sicko could have already inflicted on her made his blood run cold. If BJ found Norton before the police and despite whether he'd touched her or not, he would administer injuries severe enough to lay him out in hospital for months. *Better to ask forgiveness, than permission to beat the perpetrator to a pulp.* Something he never got the chance to do with the drunk driver who killed Rachael and Tiffany.

While his passion for revenge stoked his urge to move faster, Whiskey also pulled forward with more eagerness. In front of them the passageway opened into a cavernous space. Fingers of light filtered down from above. Whiskey looked up and alerted with a bark. Shining his torch upward, BJ glimpsed a figure hanging from an upward curving ledge. Moving closer underneath, he shouted. "Jessie, is that you?"

"BJ? Help me." She sounded exhausted.

"Is Norton here?"

"No, but he could be back any minute." Her voice broke. "Help me...please."

"Hold on." He shone his torch around the cave and flinched. The walls looked unscalable. He didn't know how she'd got up there. Even if he could reach her, he had no idea how to get her down. She'd trapped herself on the underside of the ceiling.

"Can you hang on a little longer? I'll have to go topside and rope down to get you." The last thing he wanted was to leave her, but there was no other way to save her.

"I'll try. But hurry."

"Okay. If you can, call out so we can hear you from the top." Before he finished his instruction, he rushed from the cave with Whiskey beside him. Speed replaced stealth, as did contact rather than care. The limestone rock tore his shirt and scraped his arms as he retraced his steps. Thanks to the string line, he exited in record time and launched out of the entrance.

"Jessie's hanging off a wall just under a hole in one of the caves in there."

"That's a daylight hole. The place is covered in them."

"We need to find that hole. I'll rappel down to get her. Let's go."

They sprinted up the slope onto a plateau above the cave system. Once they cleared enough space, BJ set Whiskey to her task once more. "Find Jessie. Find Jessie." He prayed his dog would pick up the scent above the ground and lead them to where Jessie hung underneath the daylight hole. If she had the strength to call out, the dog might hear her as well. More sniffing sent Whiskey east about fifty metres where the plateau changed into a steep slope. Galloping downwards, the dog skidded to the bottom where she plonked on her haunches and alerted with an abrupt bark. Right behind her, BJ slewed in with the reward. In front of them yawned a jagged-edge hole leading down into the earth. Whiskey barked again. Rolling onto his belly, he pressed himself to the ground and peered in. "Jessie, are you there?"

"Yes. Yes. I don't think I can hang on much longer." The fatigue in her voice galvanised BJ into action. He snapped to a kneeling position, opened his bag and dragged out the equipment. With a coil of rope over his shoulder, he ran to the nearest, sturdiest tree and began preparations. His hands moved at a feverish speed. Time was running out. In minutes, he'd rigged a contingency rappelling system, tested it with an almighty tug and laid a small tarp over the rim of the hole to protect his ropes.

"Hang in there," he shouted, while he locked the harness buckles, ready to rappel.

"Hurry…" She was fading. He could hear it in her voice.

He backed to the edge of the hole and balanced on the balls of his feet, testing the tension. Once satisfied, he called, "I'm coming down." He dropped like a rock. He slipped down the line, coming face to face with her within moments and snatched her around the waist.

"I've got you. I've got you." His sharp grip forced a shuddering breath from her lungs. He held her gaze, watching the trapped look of panic lift from her expression. With a weak smile, she slumped in his arms.

Titling his head back, he shouted. "I've got her, Richard. We're coming up." Engaging the retrieval system, he hauled them both to the top, where Richard helped drag Jessie onto the grass.

"Oh God, Jess. Are you all right?" He bent over his bruised and bleeding sister.

Sliding in beside him, BJ lifted her head and rested it on his lap. Covered in serious scrapes and bruises, she heaved a couple of ragged breaths of relief. Like a weather-worn doll, she lay in a crumpled mass of sticky sweat, torn clothes and dirty hair. But to BJ, she'd never looked lovelier. "You are one tough lady, Jessie Hilton."

Forcing a thin smile, she peered up at him. "Tell me something I don't know."

"I think I'm falling in love with you, Jessie Hilton."

It wasn't until Saturday afternoon, after the police finished with their questioning and Dr Bruen tended to Jessie's wounds that BJ was allowed to see her.

"Don't stay too long. After everything she's been through and the police questioning, she needs rest." Joanna patted his arm and lowered her voice. "Thank you for bringing my daughter home to me. I don't know what I would've done..." In a flurry, her hands flew to hide the tide of tears welling in her eyes.

"She's safe now. She's made of tough stuff. Like her mother I suspect." He wrapped an arm around Joanna's shoulder and comforted her.

She dabbed a tissue to her eyes. "No. Jessica is much tougher and braver than me." Defying the emotional overload, she straightened her back and left the Garden Wing.

He knocked at Jessie's bedroom door and poked his head around the corner. "Can I come in?"

"Sure." Her bandaged hand motioned for him to enter. Propped up in bed with white ruffled pillows stacked behind her head, she looked the picture of convalescing sweetness. Only her strapped arms and hands told another story, as did the brown blotches of Betadine marring the creamy white of her fair complexion. In defiance of her hardship, her eyes glittered their hazel beauty, alert and purposeful. Tumbling over her shoulders, brunette tresses framed her composed expression. He marvelled at her resilience. When she tapped the bed and shuffled over for him to sit, he obeyed.

"How're you feeling?"

"Taking everything into consideration, not so bad. I look and feel like I've been in a cat fight, but no real injuries. Nothing to stop me from dancing..."

"I doubt there'd be much that could stop you from doing anything after this."

"Thanks. But I don't want to put your theory to the test anytime soon."

The thought of all she'd endured wrung his heart. He lifted her bound hand. "Jessie, I need to know. Did he do anything to you?" He hated even asking, but he had to know.

"Not that I know of. He drugged me, but I don't think he touched me. He said it would be today. That's why I had to get out of there. Even if I died trying." She shuddered. "But you saved me." Her grateful smile acted like a balm soothing his guilt and need for revenge.

"No. You saved yourself. Richard and I were there to help you over the line. I promised to look after you, and I didn't. I'm so sorry." He bent down and kissed her hand. "My fault. I shouldn't have left you alone."

"You can't control another person's actions. You may have been able to do that when you served in the military, but you can't do it in everyday life. It was my fault not yours. I placed myself in danger by wandering off in the dark down to the river. It was me being foolish, not you."

"I disagree. I made a promise to you, and I let you down."

"What's done is done. I'm going to make a full recovery, and I'm sure Skip will be put away for a long time."

"No doubt about it. Angel will prosecute and with you as a witness, there's no chance he'll get off this time."

"At least that's some sort of justice…Now, where's the real hero? Where's Whiskey? I want to thank her for finding me."

"I'll go get her." Relief rushed through his body while he strode to the veranda and returned with his clever Border collie.

"Whiskey. Up." On Jessie's command, the dog leaped onto the side of the bed with her customary exuberance. Sitting upright, she presented her chest for a rub. "Good girl. Good girl for finding me."

"She did a terrific job. Without her, there's no telling what would've happened." He rubbed his beloved dog's lopsided ears and kissed her forehead.

"I think she's proven herself worthy of joining the search and rescue unit next year…"

"Me too. I'm sure she'll sail through the training, and we'll be in. I'm really proud of her."

"Lie down, Whiskey." Jessie shuffled over a little more for Whiskey to ease down on her belly for more affection. "Sorry, BJ. You'll have to sit on the chair." Laughing, she fawned over the Border collie.

Knowing his dog deserved the kudos, he dragged the old chair beside the bed. Catching a breath, he lifted the embargo on his feelings. "I meant what I said."

Jessie slanted him a look, an inscrutable expression gracing her blotchy face.

Faltering only for a second, he forged on. "I think I'm falling in love with you. I never meant to. I don't know if a relationship is right for me because I still miss Rachael and Tiffany so much. Ricky and Angel have been on my back to get on with my life, but I've been bitter and angry for so long, I didn't know how. Then you came along. Suddenly, I'm feeling things I never thought I would ever feel again..."

"Like what?"

"Little things. When I was waiting for you at Yass Hospital, I actually felt relaxed for the first time in years. When I told you about my military history, about being a sniper and shooting targets—you accepted it as part of who I am. Then talking and laughing about our lives and families, swimming with you in the river and just enjoying being here at the homestead. I feel like I belong again. That there is a place for me in the world and that place could be with you." His heart raced in anticipation of her response.

"I don't know if a relationship is right for me either," she said. "I get one shot at my career and this is it. Being in a relationship consumes so much energy and time, both things I can't afford. Yet despite all that, I feel the same as you. It's all a bit overwhelming."

Rising from his chair, he strode to the other side of the bed, where her raised hands beckoned him. "You mean this love thing is happening to you as well?"

"Yes. Whether you want to believe it or not, you saved me

through this entire ordeal. It was your voice in my head telling me my worst enemy was my own self-doubt, to keep going, that I was tough enough, and to just front up—just like you told me at the hospital when we first arrived."

"Oh, Jessie." Wrapping her in his arms, he inhaled her loveliness into his soul.

"Ouch," she said.

"Sorry." He released his over enthusiastic grip and gently held bandaged hands. Planting a tender kiss to each one, he revelled in the opportunity of a brighter future, literally resting in his hands.

A slight growl from Whiskey followed by a brusque tap, tap, tap broke the mood. "Hello. May I come in?" Aunt Hilda popped her grey-haired, cheery face around the bedroom door. "I made you some scones, dear." On top of an enormous country platter were a dozen steaming scones straight from the oven, accompanied by a bowl of strawberry jam and whipped cream. Beside them, steamed two mugs of freshly made tea.

"Aunt Hilda, aren't you wonderful." Jessie wiggled upright in bed.

"Now BJ, since Jessie can't use her hands properly yet, you'll have to help her. Here's the cutlery and some side plates. Enjoy."

"But aren't you going to join us Aunt Hilda?"

"Oh no, my dear. I think you and your young man should have some time together." The twinkle in Hilda's eyes darted from Jessie to BJ.

"Thank you, Mrs Hilton. That's very kind of you."

"Oh no. You're the one who's kind. I knew it the moment I met you. I know you'll look after our Jessie. See you later, dears." Reminding him of the fairy godmother in one of the nursery rhymes his grandmother used to read him, Hilda turned and all but floated from the bedroom.

"These are the best scones you'll ever taste," Jessie said, eyes sparkling.

"You won't eat the breakfast I cook for you, but you'll eat your aunt's scones?" he teased.

"I normally ration myself to half, but after everything I've been through, I think I deserve a treat and might have a whole one." She flicked her hair behind her shoulders and eyed the platter. "You better start with the jam and cream because I'm starving."

He selected a plump, soft scone and tore it open. The delicious, freshly-baked smell wafted on the escaping steam, bringing a hungry grin to his face. Cocking a brow, Jessie tilted her head in an "I told you so" fashion.

"Okay. But everyone likes different amounts of jam and cream, so you'll have to tell me how you like it."

"You won't have to worry about that, Brad Jordan. I will most definitely tell you how I like it."

He caught her mischievous wink and chuckled. "That I have no doubt about." As he set about following her instructions, his mind delighted in the scene before him—Jessie and Whiskey, the two new girls in his life to love and protect.

a soft knock at the bedroom door roused Jessie from her afternoon nap. "Can I come in?" Richard peeped his head in.

"Sure. Help me up though…" She squinted as light splashed through the door.

Moving to the bed, he scooped her up and stacked some pillows behind her back. She patted the bed, motioning him to sit beside her.

"How are you feeling?"

"A bit sore, but not too bad…" She managed a smile as stiff as her body. "Thanks for coming to my rescue with Whiskey and BJ. Without you knowing the local cave systems, I would never have been found."

"Jess, there's something you need to know." His face slid in a landslide of remorse. "It was my fault all this happened."

"What do you mean your fault? Nonsense."

"That Norton fellow wouldn't have known where we lived or about the caves if it hadn't been for me."

"I don't understand?"

He lowered his eyes. "I went into Rosie's on Wednesday and this guy starts talking to me. I think he's trying to pick me up, so I blather on about our family, the funeral, anything to keep his attention. I had no idea he was pumping me for information about you. Really I didn't."

"Don't blame yourself. Even if you hadn't told him, Skip would've found out what he wanted to know from someone else."

Richard sighed heavily. "Maybe? But..."

"But it's a lesson learned, isn't it?" Tilting her head, she regarded him closely.

"What do you mean?"

"...to think with the head on top of your shoulders and not the one in your pants." She shot him a cheeky smirk, and he managed a strained smile in return.

"Yeah, you're right. This sex stuff is a mind-fuck. I'm not good at it."

"Well, you're just going to have to find a way through it all. You'll get the hang of it."

"I guess. But this whole episode has really made me think about my future and who I want to be. I've got a lot more growing up to do yet."

"Don't be too hard on yourself."

"Thanks for understanding. I love you." He leaned forward and embraced her in a gentle hug.

"Love you too. Remember you can always confide in me if you need."

"I know. Thanks. You get some more sleep. I'll see you later."

"Okay." Still fatigued, she shimmied down into bed, thankful for more rest.

~

"Thanks, Mum. That was delicious." Jessie dabbed a napkin to her mouth, clumsy though she was. "Your vegetarian lasagne is better than anyone's."

"I'm pleased you enjoyed it. After everything you've been through, I thought cooking your favourite dinner would at least build up your strength." Taking the napkin, Joanna stacked the tray and placed it on the bedside table. "How are you feeling? Really?"

"I'm okay. Nothing is broken, and I'll be dancing in no time."

"That's not what I mean." Joanna fidgeted with her hands, obviously uncomfortable with what to say.

"I'm okay. Nothing sexual happened, if that's what you mean." She heard her mother's relieved sigh.

"Thank goodness. Physical wounds are bad enough, but to have…" Again, Joanna baulked, unable to continue.

"Mum, can I ask you something?"

"Of course."

"I know that when you fell in love with Dad you accidentally got pregnant with me and that's why you never pursued your ballet career."

"But I don't regret having you, Jessica."

"Are you sure?" She gave her mother a serious look and waited a beat. "Sometimes I think you resent me for having the career you could have had?" There she'd finally said it out loud. The painful thought that had plagued her for years.

"I don't resent you. I'm proud of you and what you've achieved."

"Really? Sometimes I think I ruined your life and that's why you don't seem that interested in my career." Tears brimmed in her eyes.

"My darling, Jessica. Forgive me. I never meant for you to think that. I've been such a hard taskmaster on myself, I guess I'm the same with everyone else. I'm sorry. From now on, I'll try to be more understanding of your feelings. But believe me, I do not regret giving up my career to have you." Joanna fixed her with the most compelling look of love Jessie had ever seen on her mother's face.

"But because of what happened to you, I'm scared of falling in love with BJ and having to give up my career."

"But times have changed. There's contraception and…"

"No, not that, Mum. I'm already on the pill. I wasn't going to take that risk." Her lips tilted in a slight smile at the surprise blinking on her mother's face. Never had they had a serious mother-daughter conversation. Obviously, Joanna found some of Jessie's forthright discussion a little unnerving.

"I'm not sure what you mean then?"

"Love, Mum. Love. I don't want the growing love I have for BJ to take away from the love for my ballet. I'm scared that if I allow myself to fall madly in love with him, there'll be no love left for my career."

Joanna grasped Jessie's bandaged hands. "That will only happen if you allow it. You can fall madly in love with a man and still be in love with your career. One doesn't have to compete with the other. In fact, love compliments and compounds itself. It's like deposits in a bank. The more love you deposit, the more your love keeps multiplying."

"But you gave up your love of ballet to be with Dad and to have me?"

"But I wanted that more than my career. The choice I made was a conscious choice. I gave up my ballet career to raise a family with your father here at Coodravale."

From out of the fog of unworthiness, the revelation dawned. It wasn't Jessie's fault that her mother hadn't pursued her ballet career. Her mother had made a clear choice—family before career. A long, shuddering breath heaved from Jessie's chest as the guilt she'd carried for years slipped away. "But don't you ever think about what could have been?"

"Sure, I've wondered…But I stopped asking that question years ago. If I kept wondering how things might have been, I would never have been happy with my life here."

"So, you're saying that I could fall madly in love with BJ and not jeopardise my career?"

"Absolutely. Falling in love doesn't mean giving up your other loves unless you choose to. I'm sure Brad understands how important your career is and what ballet means to you. He doesn't strike me as someone who'll try to make you give up anything just for him. My advice is to take it slow. Keep your eyes on the goal of being a principal dancer and tell him how you feel. I'm sure he'll support you all the way. We all will."

"Thanks, Mum." She reached out and they shared an intimate embrace for many moments. At last, the relationship with her mother that Jessie longed for bloomed like one of Joanna's glorious roses.

"Now, sleep. You need as much rest as you can get. I love you…" She dropped a kiss on her forehead.

"Love you, too."

While Joanna cleared the tray and left the room, Jessie once more snuggled into her pillow as contentment nestled in her heart. A massive shift had taken place in her relationship with her brother and mother, despite the sadness of her father's death. For the first time since she could remember, she believed that they could finally be the loving, supportive family she'd craved.

Having slept for over twelve hours, Jessie woke Sunday far more bruised and battered than the day before. Although she'd endured horrendous after effects from punishing ballet rehearsals, today her muscles ached in unfamiliar ways. Unwilling to hobble around hunched over like an old crone, she straightened her spine to find significant resistance. Not only were her muscles objecting, her skin pulled taut as her wounds began to heal, making movement even more difficult. Bathing, breakfasting and general activities proved strenuous. By late afternoon, she still felt like she'd been hit by a bus.

"For goodness sake, let me carry you outside where you can sit and relax for a while." Clearly concerned about her painful, crooked shape lurching around the living room, BJ hurried to her side.

"No. I can do it. Really, I can." She pulled her shoulders back and winced.

"I didn't say you couldn't do it. I said let me help."

She lifted her head to meet his icy blue gaze and surrendered. "Okay. But go easy."

He bent down and scooped her in his arms. "You really need to eat more," he said, striding onto the veranda.

"You don't listen, do you? I get one chance at being a principal dancer and since I can't practice at the moment, I have to be doubly careful of what I eat."

She watched him shake his head in silent disapproval. His long, golden hair tucked back in its band, his sculptured, masculine jaw roughened with blonde bristles and the set of his powerful shoulders elicited a sexual stirring she'd not experienced for some time. While erotic arousal stirred in her body, wonder and delight set up residence in her heart.

Out on the lawn, he placed her on the garden seat under the heritage oak tree. "Comfortable?"

"Yes. Thank you." Staring past the target-practice poplar tree, she gazed to the far edge of the paddock and pointed. "Here they come?"

"What?"

"The flying goats."

"Flying goats? I thought you were only kidding about the goats on Wednesday, so I wouldn't do any shooting."

"Nope. Here they come. They belong to the Robinsons, our

next-door neighbour. We've got a sweetheart deal with them. We let their goats graze in our paddock, and they keep the grass down for us. In the afternoon, the herd wanders up here to the poplar trees."

BJ stretched out his legs, and clasping his hands behind his head, he watched the advancing herd of scruffy, angora goats. "Flying goats, you say?" He turned to her, a twinkle in his eye.

"Wait for it." Ignoring her body's resistance, she mirrored his posture. She knew the more she moved, the faster her healing. Flexing and pointing her feet, she willed her muscles to loosen and lengthen. She needed to move, to transcend the ugliness of everything that had happened. The afternoon sun wrapped her in its warm embrace melting some of her aches like hot candlewax. Nature's soundtrack of distant bleating sheep joined the chorus of kookaburras in a sporadic tempo which inspired her heightening mood. Rising from the seat, she waved her arms like willow branches waltzing in a spring wind. "Ah, that's better."

"Certainly looks good from where I'm sitting."

Pivoting to face him, she leaned forward. Resting her hands either side of his shoulders on the back of the garden seat, she lowered her face to his. "Are we going to give this a go?"

"If you want to, I'm ready."

"But let's take it really slow. Okay?"

"Whatever you want…"

Tentatively, she pressed a kiss to his mouth. Soft and tender, the touch was but a graze of skin. Parting his lips ever so slightly, he invited her further, his warm breath a subtle caress. Energy sparked. Instead of being responsible, of keeping herself in check, she abandoned her fears and kissed him—truly, madly, deeply. A tremulous breath transported her to his lap where he cradled her against the thudding plane of his chest. Enfolded in his arms, she melted into a mind-numbing swirl of joyous, blissful, empowering love. Not just for him, but for herself, for her life and for her future. Never had she imagined such effervescent passion.

Yielding into it, she wished for time to stand still. Just a little longer. Eventually, in perfect synchronicity, the kiss ended, and he returned ownership of her lips. Dreamily, she opened her eyes to see his blinking; swimming in pools of tears. She cocked her head in an unspoken question.

"Tears of redemption." He crushed her to his body.

Snuggling into his chest, Jessie wanted to stay like this forever. Safe in his arms, secure in his protection.

"Well, I'll be damned." A tone of surprised amusement tinged his voice.

Swivelling on his lap, she turned in the direction of the paddock. "See, I told you. Flying goats."

"But what are they doing?"

"They climb onto the branches of the poplar trees and because they can't climb back down, they just leap off. No matter how high up the tree they get, they just jump off, landing with a terrible thud. That's why we call them flying goats."

The herd of about twenty, cute-faced goats took turns climbing and jumping from the poplar tee. Like lemmings, they followed each other up and off, time and again. Unconcerned with breaking limbs, they grazed and played like carefree children, while Jessie snuggled into the lap of someone she never expected to find.

"Oh God, that feels good." With her legs outstretched, she leaned back in the arm chair, her eyes shut and toes wiggling in delight.

"I'm pleased you like it."

"Like it? I love it. You must be the best foot and ankle masseuse in the world." Opening one eye she glanced down at him and snickered.

"Now give me the other one before I wear out." He reached for her other foot.

Over the next ten minutes, Jessie relished the attention and restorative power of BJ's hands. Beside him, Coodravale's official hero, Whiskey, took up permanent residence in the Garden Wing. Sprawled on the carpet, she too enjoyed her newly-earned privileges.

"Okay. I'm done. When your skin heals, I'll give those sexy legs of yours a proper massage if you like." He rose to his feet, leaned over and pressed a gentle kiss to her lips.

"I'd like that," she said in a husky voice.

"Yeah, well. Don't tempt me. It's bad enough I can only massage your feet with all that's on offer."

"Soon. When my skin heals."

"I know. Would you like a glass of wine?" He headed to the kitchen.

Jessie searched for a hint of judgement in his voice, but found none. "I'll just have a sparkling water, thanks."

Lingering at the doorway, BJ gave her a tender smile before proceeding into the kitchen. "I've spoken to Angel, and he's coming down in the morning. We'll meet him at the police station at ten." His resonant voice carried in warm waves of authority.

"He doesn't waste any time, does he?" Feeling remarkably supple after the massage, she shuffled upright and crossed her legs underneath her, being careful not to dislodge her bandages.

"He wants to get this started as soon as possible." He handed her the glass and folded into the opposite armchair with a beer. "He was terrific with Rachael and Tiffany's case."

She noticed a subtle shift in his mood. "Are you okay?"

"Yes. I just haven't spoken about it with anyone for a long time."

"You don't have to if you don't want."

"I know. But if we're going to give us the best chance, I need to tell you." Narrowing his eyes, he began. "We lived in Perth. Rachael and I met seven years ago. In a lot of ways, you remind me of her. Both brunettes, tall, beautiful and smart. Rachael and I had been married for three years, and Tiffany was one year old when…" Jessie watched his eyes glaze over as he drifted back to the painful past. "I was in Afghanistan on a snatch and grab mission when I got the call that they'd been in a car accident. DOA. Dead on arrival." Grim-faced, he slugged back a gulp of beer. "Some drunk bastard swerved onto the wrong side of the road. Killed my wife and daughter." Her heart ached for him, but she said nothing while he battled his demons. "No matter what I'd been through before, nothing compared to that. My life as I knew it was over. I left the army and spiralled into depression. Suicide looked like a bloody good option for a while there. If it hadn't been for Ricky and Angel, I probably would've punched my own ticket." Another hefty mouthful of beer steadied his voice. "But as they say, warriors don't die or retire, we just keep walking into danger." Pushing up from the armchair, he strode to his bedside table. On his return, he stopped next to Jessie, in his hand, a picture frame. "This is the photo of Rachael and Tiffany I took with me on my missions. It goes everywhere with me."

She looked down at an attractive, young woman with a blinding smile and long brown hair. Around her neck clung the prettiest little girl with golden curls and dazzling blue eyes. The same striking colour as her father's. A lump rocketed into Jessie's throat. With hot tears burning her eyes, she titled her head up to look at him. "It's all so awful."

"Yes. It is." Still holding the frame, he kneeled beside her. "But then you turned up and things changed again. I've anguished over Rachael and Tiffany for so long. I won't ever forget them or replace them. But I know I've got to start a new life. I'm hoping it will be with you, if you can put up with a broken soldier?"

She cupped his handsome face in her hands. "You're not a broken soldier. You're my warrior hero." Pressing a kiss to his lips, she prayed he would find the healing he needed. Her physical abrasions were easy to mend, whereas his emotional wounds were deeper and longer lasting. She hoped, not irreparable. "We don't have to tell my family any of this, you know."

"At the moment, I'd rather keep it like that. Thanks." He rose and returned the frame to his bedside table drawer. "I'm getting another beer. Do you want another drink?"

"No, thanks. I'm fine."

With another chilled bottle of Crown lager in hand, he returned in a lighter mood. "You've haven't had much fun either. There's all this crap with Skip Norton and the eventual court case, whenever that'll be. Then there's your father's funeral on Tuesday. How are you holding up?"

"To be truthful, I haven't had much time to think about it. There's been one thing after the other and just when I think everything is settling down, wham! Something else turns up." She took a beat. "The most terrifying thing though was being trapped alone in the cave and wondering when Skip would turn up. That constant fear of someone lurking in the shadows, touching me, whispering horrible things to me and my not being able to escape. It reminded me too much of my nightmares. Out of everything that's happened, that sense of helplessness and hopelessness has been the worst. To be at the mercy of someone else is…" Her skin cringed at the recent memory. She rubbed her neck as best she could with bandaged hands.

"It sends sheer dread through your heart, you're boxed in and your destiny is in the hands of the enemy." The fierce intensity and haunting recall with which he spoke dampened her anxiety. It was good to speak with someone who understood. "But remember, you conquered your fear and got out. It's over now." He stroked a stray tendril off her face, hooking it behind her ear.

"Thank God. I'm just pleased Skip won't be frightening other women like that again."

"Angel will see to that."

She hesitated, twisting her lips.

"What is it?"

"I'm concerned about Mum."

"Why? What's wrong?"

"When Dad took out a loan to buy Coodravale, it included an extra one hundred thousand dollars, which he then loaned to Uncle Frank. Mum found their loan agreement when she was going through Dad's papers. It seems Uncle Frank hasn't paid back the loan after all these years. She's really worried he's not going to pay. Now with Dad gone, she needs as much money as possible to keep on top of things around here."

He scowled. "What's she going to do?"

"She's going to discuss it while they're here and get it sorted out. But she didn't seem very confident about it. I know you think Mum is made of tough stuff and I guess, in some ways, she is, but she'd come to depend on Dad for so many things. You know, she gave up her career as a ballerina when she accidentally fell pregnant with me."

"Is that why she barks at you at times?"

"Up until I talked to her today, I always thought she resented me for ruining her career."

"And?"

"She said she never resented me or regretted choosing family over career. I've been carrying around this guilt about ruining her life, but in the end, her giving up her ballet career wasn't my fault at all. She wanted me more than ballet."

"Well, there you go. I knew you two would sort it out."

Talking in a softer voice, she held his gaze. "But I'm not my mother. My career must come first until I achieve my goal. You understand that, don't you?"

He reached out and traced his thumb along her cheek. "Of course, I do. You're the career warrior she never wanted to be."

Jessie moaned, a half-smile tipping her lips. "Oh, God. That means you and I are both warriors…"

"There's nothing wrong with that. That's what attracted me to you in the first place. We just better make sure we're on the same side and not get in each other's way."

"I'll drink to that." She raised her sparkling water.

"Cheers." Chiming his bottle to her glass, he winked. "Now, since we're sitting on the property Banjo Patterson once owned, why don't I read you some of the old boy's poetry?

"Seriously?" She giggled.

"Why not?" He moved to the mantle. With leather-bound Volume One of the *Complete Works of Banjo Paterson* in his hands, he returned to the armchair. "Let's see." Flicking through the pages, a playful smirk tugged at his mouth.

Jessie regarded him, her chin resting in the cup of her bandaged hand. Despite everything that had happened, her ending up with BJ was a wonderful reward. On first impressions, some people might think they were mismatched, but they'd be wrong. She and BJ had endured much to reach their goals. Strong-willed and focused, they shared a certain compatible, yet flammable, energy that empowered them as individuals and, she hoped, as a long-term couple. With his support, Jessie was even more determined to reach the pinnacle in her profession and be the Company's principal dancer next year. And having healed years of unspoken feelings with her mother and brother, an emotional weight lifted from her shoulders.

"This has got to be it." BJ launched from his chair and took centre stage in front of the fireplace. With the book splayed open in the palms of his hands, he cleared his throat. Flashing a theatrical smile, he read aloud. "The Billy-Goat Overland." He added a wink.

"Come all ye lads of the droving days, ye gentlemen unafraid, I'll
tell you all of the greatest trip that ever a drover made,
For we rolled our swags, and we packed our bags, and taking our
lives in hand,

We started away with a thousand goats, on the billy-goat
overland.
There wasn't a fence that'd hold the mob, or keep 'em from their
desires;
They skipped along the top of the posts and cake-walked on
the wires..."

And while he continued reading, she cheered from the
sidelines.

CHAPTER 37

I'm not sure how much more of this I can take. Back and forth. Back and forth.

"What's a person supposed to do to get a drink in this place?" I'll die of bloody thirst in here before these cops bring me a glass of water. Smug bastards. Two nights I've been stuck in this cell with their shitty food, and I still haven't been appointed a lawyer. It's all the hero's fault. Him and his stupid dog. *I hate dogs.* If it wasn't for them, my dancer would still be there, waiting for me… forever. Even though the cops arrested me, they wouldn't have been able to pin anything on me. Not without a body. But no! The hero sticks his nose in— again and rescues her. That's what the cops told me. Now I'm fucked!

"What is it you want this time?"

He reminds me of that big, lumbering idiot, Salvatore Bacci. Another one who thinks he's hot shit. "If it's not too much to ask, Sergeant, can I have some water?"

"Sure."

Prick. "When's my lawyer coming?"

"I don't know. But when he or she gets here, you'll be the first to know. I'll get your water."

She? Now that would brighten my day. Not that she'd be as graceful or as beautiful as my dancer, but still...She might be able to get me off with just a slap on the wrist. Once I tell her about my childhood and how my mother used to beat me and lock me in the cupboard under the stairs, she might take pity on me. A woman lawyer... I get hard just thinking about it, but I don't dare touch myself.

CHAPTER 38

*B*J strode into the Yass police station with Jessie by his side. Like most country town police stations, the place lacked the hustle and bustle of its city equivalent. Bulletin boards advertised the local police benefit, CWA meetings and the Yass Primary School fete, all with dates long since passed. On the counter, three mugs of stale, half-drunk coffee and the crumbed remnants of a muffin on a chipped saucer indicated Monday mornings were typically slow. In BJ's opinion, being a copper in rural Australia seemed an uneventful job. He suspected the kidnapping case of Jessie Hilton added much needed excitement, and the opportunity for the police to exercise their arrest and capture skills. *They'll dine out on that story for years.*

Dressed in a grey Armani pin-striped business suit, lilac shirt and purple tie, Angel rose to greet them. "You certainly know how to attract trouble, don't you?" Gripping his mate's hand, Angel pumped a few times. BJ shrugged, grinning sheepishly. Angel switched his attention to Jessie. "And how are you after this ordeal?"

"I'm doing fine. Thank you so much for handling all this."

"My pleasure." He clasped her bandaged hand cautiously in

both of his. "Why don't we go to the café down the street and grab a coffee so we can talk." He turned to the officer at the desk. "I'll be back in about an hour or so, Sergeant Clark."

"Take your time. That creep in there won't be going anywhere, anytime soon." The Sergeant nodded to the closed door behind which BJ assumed were the lockup cells.

"I still can't believe it. Inoffensive, bungling Skip, a stalker and kidnapper…" Jessie shook her head.

"I've had a good read of his file and it seems Skip Norton has been a sick boy for a long time. Family and community services were called in on many occasions when he was at primary school. His mother was suspected of abusing him, but it couldn't be proven. No mention of a father. Even if he was abused, it's likely he'd stay silent. Kids normally don't tell on their parents particularly if it means they'll be taken away from the only family they've ever known—no matter what horrors are perpetrated on them at home."

"So sad," Jessie said in a quiet voice.

"In my experience, most murderers, rapists and violent offenders are made. It's tragic, but everyone has the choice not to play out what's happened to them. Despite Skip's upbringing, he had no right to threaten or kidnap you."

"I know, but I can't help feeling a little sorry for him." Jessie's gaze travelled to the door separating her from her perpetrator.

"In your case, the State will accuse him of coercion, stalking and intimidation, false imprisonment, assault and battery. There's a lot to get through before we go to trial but for now, it's time for coffee." Guiding her in front of him, Angel stepped in stride with BJ. "She's one hell of a young lady."

"Tell me something I don't know." His beaming grin said it all.

"What is this I see? You and Jessie?"

BJ nodded, and he was surprised at how much pleasure it gave him to admit it. "Yeah, me and Jessie."

"About time. I'm happy for you. And from the little I've seen, she's a good match. Determined, disciplined and passionate about what she does—a mirror image of you, my friend." He clapped BJ on the shoulder.

"Yeah. We'll see. As we used to say in the forces, the easy day was yesterday. Being with Jessie will not be an easy day…"

"But you don't like taking it easy. Need I say more?" He laughed, and they followed her onto the footpath.

With the mid-morning sun slanting through the trees, the rosiness of the day matched BJ's spirits. He tilted his face to the sun's warmth and breathed in his new life. Listening to Angel and Jessie chat about mundane things like the weather, his drive to Yass and the town's history, the promise of a brighter future gripped him. For the first time in years, life was good.

The cheery ringing of the café's doorbell signalled their arrival. He scanned the room, searching for the table he always chose in any venue—the one closest to the quickest escape route, where he could sit with his back to the wall, so he could see the movements of the other patrons. The disappointment at his table of choice already being taken, instantly turned to delight.

"Buddy, over here." In a matter of a few fast-moving steps, Ricky Alvarez clasped him in a tight bear hug, slapping his back. "I leave you alone for a few days and look at the trouble you get yourself into."

"What are you doing here?" He held his mate at arm's length, pleased to see him.

"What? You expect me to stay in Melbourne when all the action is happening out here in the sophisticated, trend-setting town of Yass? Give me a break."

BJ hugged his best mate, laughing heartily with him.

"Jessie…" A high-pitched voice squealed from behind Ricky. BJ turned and watched Jasmine throw her arms around Jessie's neck.

"Ouch, not too hard." Jessie winced, and Jasmine hugged her with less fervour.

The girls glided to the table chatting, and the three men ordered.

"It's on the house," the middle-aged man behind the counter said. "It's the least we can do what with everything Jessie and her family have been through."

"Thanks." BJ popped a twenty dollar note into the tip jar with a wink.

Once coffees and an assortment of muffins, chocolate brownies and custard tarts landed on the table, the conversation settled.

"What's the plan?" Ricky stirred a dollop of foam into his coffee and reached for a brownie.

"Dad's funeral is tomorrow morning..." Jessie declined Ricky's offer from the pastry platter.

"I don't have to be back until tomorrow night for the show, so it means we can stay if you like. Moral support and all that," Jasmine said.

"We?" Jessie cocked an eyebrow at her girlfriend, who pulled apart a steaming blueberry muffin.

Jasmine blushed. "Ricky drove me here. We could both stay. Isn't that right, Ricky?" She battered her eyelashes at him.

"I've got nothing urgent on, so we can stay for the funeral tomorrow then head off." He glanced at Jessie. "If that's okay?"

"That would be great. But we've got family at Coodravale, so we can't put you up there. Sorry."

"Not a problem. We'll get a room in town here." He cast a cunning smirk at BJ, who merely raised an eyebrow and grinned.

"Any news yet?" Jessie asked Jasmine.

"Not yet. Tabitha may be off for the entire season. She's really damaged some ligaments. David is ropeable..."

"I bet..." Jessie explained the current stalemate over the female principal role for next year to Angel and Ricky.

"The job could still be yours if Tabitha remains out. When do you think you're coming back?" Jasmine asked, between mouthfuls of muffin.

"I don't know. As soon as I can after the funeral, and we get things sorted out at Coodravale. But in my current shape, I couldn't dance anyway. It's better David doesn't know I'm injured, okay?" She regarded Jasmine with a shrewd look.

"Got it. He won't hear anything from me." She mimed locking her lips and throwing away the key.

"Right. If everyone is finished, let's get down to the business at hand, shall we?" Angel flipped open his yellow legal pad and steadied his pencil. "If you'll excuse us, Jessie and I need to go over a few things."

While Jasmine explored the main street to find a motel in which to stay the night, BJ and Ricky loitered outside the café.

"What a clusterfuck this has been for you, buddy." Ricky leaned against the red brick wall, watching the local traffic cruise along the main street.

Standing like a twin beside him, BJ folded his arms. "I've never seen so much shit go down so fast since we were on tour. It's like the whole world conspired against Jessie to see if she could be broken. But she's still standing." He shook his head thinking back on the past weeks.

"Anyway, it's worked out. Skip Norton got arrested. Lucky for him you didn't get to him first…" Half-smiling, Ricky shot his mate a sly glance. "Jessie seems to have come out of it pretty unscathed, and you seem to be more like the bloke I used to know."

"What do you mean?"

"You don't look like you're going to kill the next poor bastard who looks at you sideways. Correct me if I'm wrong, but could you and Jessie…?"

"Jessie and I have decided to give it go."

"Give what a go?"

"A relationship."

"God, you make it sound so bloody calculated. You don't give a relationship a go." He stepped in front of his mate, locking him in a demanding stare. "Do you love her?"

"Well, it's probably too early to…"

"Shit, man. It's a simple question."

"Yes. I think I do."

"Good. Glad to hear it. Now make it work."

"Just a minute." BJ pushed himself off the wall, usurping Ricky's position of power. "Isn't this the pot calling the kettle black? What did I see going on with you and Jasmine?"

"Just the usual. You know how it is…" He danced a two-step deflecting his buddy's intense stare.

"Not so quick, Tricky." BJ's big paw clamped down on his mate's shoulder. "Am I sensing another arrow in the air? Someone aside from me, falling under the spell of love?"

"Cut it out." He slapped BJ's hand away. "Well, maybe."

"I knew it. About time you thought of settling down."

"There's something about these dancers. Don't you think? They're just so damn sexy and …"

BJ raised his hand. "I hear you, Ricky. They're a breed unto themselves. A bit like us."

"Roger that." He took a beat before his gaze settled across the road. "Hey, look, the RSL Club is open. Why don't we go in and have a beer for the troops?"

"Sounds like a plan. Let's go."

By the time he and Jessie returned to the homestead, flaming colours burned the dusk sky as if forewarning the imminent bushfire season. Although the day faded, its heat refused to wane.

Even the wind making it daily pilgrimage from the Goodradigbee River sounded cranky and hot. Galloping to meet them, Whiskey whined a hello and was duly rewarded with praise for guarding the property in their absence.

Jessie puffed out a breath. "I'm beat. I'm going to have a quick shower. Then we'll go in for dinner. No way we can get out of it tonight."

"Fine by me. I'll play with Whiskey for a while, feed her, then I'll freshen up, and we'll go in."

Within thirty minutes, they wandered back to the main residence for a family dinner. Pausing at the front door, he traced his thumb along her chin. "Take it easy. Okay? We can leave whenever you want. You've got a big day tomorrow."

She reached up and kissed him on the lips. "Thanks. Let's see what dramas are in store for us tonight?" She dredged up a sarcastic smile and opened the door.

Inside the dining room, the atmosphere crackled with a killer heat and strained conversation. Small talk occupied the prickly silence. Frank, Hilda and Tom didn't mention Jessie's ordeal or Ken's funeral. Instead, they skirted the obvious topics, chatting about unimportant things—Tom's possible new promotion, Frank's interest in vintage cars and Hilda's plans to vacation on the north coast. Joanna, Richard and Jessie responded politely while attending to their guests' drinks needs. Even the creaking floorboards winced under the weight of unspoken words. By the time everyone took theirs seats for a light dinner of cold chicken and salad, the atmosphere dampened further as if smothered by a wet blanket.

"What time are we leaving tomorrow, Mum?" Jessie broached the most pressing subject.

"We'll leave here at eight and drive to the cemetery. Father Conlon will meet us there at about nine-thirty, ready for the funeral at ten."

The clatter of Frank's fork to the floor rattled already jangled nerves. He cast an apologetic glance to the others and reached to collect it. Righting himself, he looked down his nose and vigorously rubbed the fork with his napkin. "Father Conlon you say?"

"Yes. It was Ken's wish to have Father Conlon preside over his funeral."

"But Ken's not been a practicing Catholic for years, decades even."

"Yes. But it was one of the last things Ken said to me in hospital. Why? Is there a problem?"

BJ watched every head turn towards Frank.

"No. No. Of course not. I just thought it strange, after all these years that my brother wanted a Catholic funeral."

"I thought it was a rather strange request as well." Distracted, Joanna pushed her food around the plate. "But he kept saying something about when Jessie and Richard were young and how helpful Father had been to him."

Unbeknown to the others, BJ wasn't the least interested in giving his attention to Joanna. He was far more absorbed in monitoring Frank's reaction to the whole Father Conlon revelation. On first meeting Frank, BJ's sixth sense had alerted and now as Joanna finished, Frank's face paled like he'd been stuck and drained of blood.

"Have you met Father Conlon before, Mr Hilton?" BJ seized the moment.

"I may have done, years ago. I can't remember." Frank fidgeted, obviously shaken to be questioned by a relative stranger in such a direct manner. "Anyway, it doesn't matter. It's Ken's funeral, and we have to respect his wishes."

"And those of Joanna." All heads snapped in BJ's direction. He'd intentionally installed himself in a power position in the family, making an unmistakable declaration as Joanna's ally. While the Hiltons scrutinised him, he deferred to her and waited.

"Why thank you, Brad. That's most appreciated. It's rare to find respectful young men these days."

Everyone exhaled, except Frank who remained wooden, barely able to hide his contempt at being usurped.

"Are we doing a wake for Dad?" Jessie's voice cracked with sadness.

"Yes, darling. We'll just have a morning tea in town with friends, and then we'll come home..." Joanna lowered her cutlery to the table, murmured her apologies and left the room.

Jessie scurried after her mother, leaving BJ and Richard to manage the awkward meal with Frank, Hilda and Tom.

Sawing into his chicken, BJ glanced over at Tom. "Tell us more about this promotion you might get."

Delighted to talk about himself, Tom regaled them with a lengthy soliloquy. By the time he finished, the plates were bare. Aided by Richard and BJ, Hilda cleared the table, obviously pleased for the assistance. As expected, Frank and Tom retired to do something other than help in the kitchen.

When BJ returned to the Garden Wing and readied to watch some television, Jessie shuffled through the French doors, red-eyed and slump-shouldered. Into his arms, she sobbed in small hiccups. "Poor Mum. I feel so sorry for her. I don't know how she's going to cope here all alone."

"I'm sure she'll work it out. Everyone needs to get through tomorrow first. Funerals are the hardest. Then we can think about what happens after that. Okay?" Thumbing her face upward, he bent down and pecked a kiss to her nose. "You need some rest. I'm putting you to bed."

He escorted Jessie to her bedroom, where she changed into her pyjamas and climbed into bed. Rolling the covers back across her chest, he leaned closer. "What time do you want to get up in the morning?"

"If I'm not up by six thirty, you better wake me. I'm not sure I'll get much sleep though."

"You will. You're exhausted. Good night." He brushed a kiss on her cheek.

Sliding her bandaged hand behind his neck, she pulled him closer, sealing her lips on his in passionate kiss.

"Whoa. This is not the time to be making love…" he said, although the stirring in his groin disagreed.

"But…" She pouted.

"Jessie, when we make love, it will be when we're both happy. Definitely not the night before a funeral…especially not your father's funeral." He yearned to climb in with her. But not now, not like this.

"You're right. When we're both happy, deliriously happy. Good night."

He waited as she rolled over. In no time, her breathing slowed and after a final stroke of her hair, he left the room.

Even from the dark depths of sleep, her scream woke him. Leaping out of bed, he sprinted to Jessie's bedroom to find her sobbing, her head buried in her hands. Sliding in, he cradled her in his arms until her trembling subsided.

"It's only a dream. A nightmare…" He reached over to switch on the bedside lamp.

Inclining her head upward, Jessie's torment etched her face. "I'm so sick of these nightmares, and I'm so tired. I can't think straight. Round and round it goes in my head. Some man chasing me, touching me, telling me ugly secrets. When will I be free of all this?" Renewed sobbing shook her shoulders.

"You're just wound up and worn out. It'll pass. Is there anything I can do?"

"Will you sleep with me? Keep me company? Maybe with you beside me, I won't dream…"

"Shuffle over." He climbed into her bed. "How's that?" He

reached his arm around her shoulders, and she snuggled onto his chest.

"Wonderful. Just wonderful…"

"Now go to sleep. Everything will be fine." He breathed in the fresh scent of her— soap, shampoo and enticing sexuality. Within moments she fell asleep, leaving him to his throbbing groin and gathering thoughts. He'd forgotten how good it felt to have a woman cuddle up next to him in bed. The simple joy of being the yang to a woman's yin. That's how Rachael used to describe them. *Rachael. My darling, Rachael.* Tonight, the familiar ache at her memory didn't rent his heart in two. It didn't fill his mouth with bitterness. Instead, the memory tasted sweet, wholesome. Rachael had blessed him with her love, giving him Tiffany and an insight into how extraordinary life and love could be. Now with Jessie in his arms, he might just get another chance.

CHAPTER 39

On the morning of Ken Hilton's funeral, life in the Wee Jasper Valley overflowed like effervescent champagne as if in defiance of his death. The four of them sat in silence in BJ's Jeep on their way to Yass Cemetery. All that remained for Jessie was dealing with the unknown—the service, the burial, the wake —all essential elements to farewelling a good man. Despite his sometimes detached exterior, her father had been a good man, a good provider, a good brother and a good father who she'd loved. Now, when his life was over, she realised she never knew him very well at all.

Free of their bandages, her hands lay limp in her lap, much like she imagined her father lay in his coffin. She flicked the thought away. Instead, she gazed out the passenger window, admiring the scenery along the top ridge overlooking the Murrumbidgee River. "How are you holding up, Mum?" She stuck her hand between the front seats towards Joanna who sat in the back with Richard.

"I'm okay…" She tweaked Jessie's outstretched hand. "I'm pleased to see your scrapes and scratches healing up so well. A principal ballerina must have unblemished skin, my darling." Without warning, Joanna sobbed.

Swivelling in her seat, Jessie cooed sympathetic sounds. "Oh, Mum…" She stared at Richard who hurriedly embraced his mother, his own eyes filling with tears.

"Come on now. Come on," he said into Joanna's bowed head.

Straightening, she blinked and dabbed water from her cheeks. "Sorry. I'm fine now." After a few more sniffles, she continued. "Thank you, Brad, for driving us in today."

"Yes, thanks." Richard reached over and clapped a hand on his shoulder.

Jessie squeezed his thigh in appreciation of his presence during this awful time.

"Not a problem," he said. "Anything you need, just ask."

In a cheekier tone, Richard directed to his sister. "Am I right in assuming you and BJ have become a bit of an item since arriving at Coodravale?"

"Richard, don't be rude," his mother said. "It's none of our business."

"It's all right." A sunny smile replaced her melancholy expression. "Actually, we have."

"Oh, that's wonderful." Joanna hesitated. "But that doesn't change your plans with the Company does it?"

"Absolutely not. There's no way Jessie isn't going to get the top job. I'm behind her one hundred percent of the way."

Jessie pursed her lips. "I can answer my own mother's questions, thank you very much."

Joanna and Richard chuckled.

"Watch yourself, BJ. Jess may come off as meek and mild, but she can be a real firecracker when she wants to."

"I found that out the first night I met her." A duly chastised expression spread on BJ's face, and unable to resist, Jessie leaned over and rested her head on his shoulder for a moment.

"We're just going to take our time and see how it goes." She rubbed his strapping forearm, admiring the shape and strength of his muscles.

"A very sensible approach," Joanna said. Despite the solemnity of the day, a more hopeful silence descended on the Jeep's occupants.

On a steep hillside overlooking the town of Yass, the cemetery prostrated itself down the slope. Each level told the story of people dating back as far as the 1850s who chose this small town as their final resting place. Famous explorers, pious nuns, young drovers, old women and precious children joined the afterlife together from this vantage point.

"Drive on. The new cemetery is down the road a bit more on your left," Jessie said. As the poplar-tree-lined road wound on, the cattle in the paddocks to the right peered at them with expressions of indifference. He turned onto a gravel driveway into the modern section of the cemetery and parked beside a wall of sculptured acacia trees. Creeping in beside them, Frank pulled up in his sturdy Holden sedan.

Silent and pensive, they stepped out of the Jeep, Jessie and Richard flanking their mother, with BJ beside Jessie. Under clipped arches of massive acacia hedges, they walked into the sprawling lawn cemetery covering acres of land. Neat rows of concrete pathways crisscrossed the occupied burial blocks, ensuring visitors remained off the grass and the dearly departed. Decorated with meticulously manicured red and white rose bushes, each burial plot's brass plague shone in the sunlight like a beacon, showing the angels where to find the souls of the dead.

In the near distance, under a towering eucalypt tree, Father Conlon waved. "Joanna, my dear. Jessie, Richard, it's so wonderful to see you again." Drawing each one to his chest, he kissed them politely on the cheek. "It's a sad day indeed. Ken was a good man. He'll be missed."

"Father, this is my boyfriend, BJ." Jessie tingled. Calling BJ her boyfriend added seriousness to their blossoming relationship. One she liked more than she expected.

"Pleased to meet you, Father Conlon."

"And you too, BJ…"

"You know Ken's brother, Frank, his wife Hilda and their son Tom…" Joanna stepped aside to allow the priest to greet the rest of the family. His smile stiffened slightly, but he graciously gave his condolences.

"Let's sit here under this tree to wait for the other guests. We can talk and give thanks for the good life Ken lived. Come, Joanna…" With her mother seated between Father Conlon and Richard, Jessie led BJ to the garden seat on the east side of the contemplation garden.

"It really is a beautiful day," she said, as they sat down. "Dad would've loved it. He always enjoyed spring and summer best. The flowers, the bees, the land. He was happiest at this time of the year."

"Did your father and Frank get on?"

"It's hard to say, but I don't think so."

"What do you think of your Uncle Frank?"

"To be honest, I never really liked him much. He's full of himself. Dad wasn't like that. He didn't try to big note himself. I remember when Uncle Frank, Aunt Hilda and Tom used to visit us at Christmas when we were all kids. Aunt Hilda is what you'd call, a good Christian woman. She loved to celebrate Christmas. She used to spend lots of time in the kitchen, cooking with Mum. But Uncle Frank locked himself away in the old shearing shed. I remember Dad and Uncle Frank yelling at each other over something to do with the shed. I can't remember what it was, though. But it made Dad angry as hell. He burned down the shed years ago. It's that charred spot on the bank near the wombat holes. Anyway, it all seemed to blow over, and they patched things up. Now poor Mum's got to get the one hundred thousand dollars back from Uncle Frank that Dad lent him. I can't see that being an easy job."

"Who's that waving to you?" He pointed towards a cluster of red rose bushes around which two young women appeared.

"Goodness. It's Mia and Kate. I went to school with them."

Still bright-faced under mops of red hair, the identical twins rushed to Jessie with effusive, straight-toothed smiles. Throwing their arms around her, they alternated between exuberance at seeing their friend and sadness of the occasion.

"Girls, I'd like you to meet my boyfriend, BJ." She liked how that sounded. *Boyfriend.*

"Hi..." he said, obviously confused as to who was who.

"I'm Kate. I've got the curly hair. This in Mia, she has the straight hair."

"Got it. Kate, curly. Mia, straight." He gave them a good-natured smile.

"We all went to school together. We usually catch up once a year when I come back home for Christmas." Jessie stepped between her friends.

"We're so sorry about your dad." Kate clutched Jessie's hands, making her wince.

"Did that happen when that madman kidnapped you?" Mia asked.

"How do you know about that?" Alarm rose in Jessie's voice.

"The *Yass Tribune* broke the story in today's paper."

"Oh, God." Just as Jessie was about to say more, a noisy disturbance to their left interrupted.

"Jessie Hilton. Oh, Miss Hilton. Can we talk to you about your kidnapping? What did it feel like? How are you feeling now?" Rushing towards her like a freight train, a group of photographers and reporters hurried along the pathway. Pulling away from the pack, Ricky and Jasmine sped forward. BJ dashed to meet them. "Jasmine, you go to Jessie. Ricky, you're with me."

While the men marched back towards the melee of unwelcome

intruders, Jessie dropped onto the seat with Mia, Kate and Jasmine, hiding her as best they could.

Holding up his hand like a crossing guard, BJ advanced. "Stop right there. Miss Hilton has nothing to say. For God's sake, this is her father's funeral. Leave her alone." The force of his command brought the media ruck to a halt.

One smart-mouthed, young reporter stepped forward. "I'm from Channel Nine News in Melbourne, and we just want a statement from…"

"I don't care if you're a bloody angel from heaven. Get out of here." His voice growled deep and low. Knowing too well what the menace in his tone meant, Jessie grimaced.

"I suggest you all do an about-face and leave. Otherwise, there may be more than one burial today." Ricky stood shoulder to shoulder with his mate. An imposing pair.

"Are you threatening us?" some prissy woman with too much make-up asked.

"Not at all," Ricky said. "It's just a recommendation. Call it a best health practice."

When Jessie peeked through the barrier of her friends, she saw BJ push a television camera out of his face and snarl. Stalking like a wild leopard, he advanced, and the reporters scattered like frightened gazelle. Once satisfied they'd retreated to an acceptable distance, he nodded to Ricky, and they paced back to the contemplation garden.

"My goodness." Father Conlon blinked up at him.

"Sorry, Father, I'm not one to start a fight, but I'll finish one when it's needed. I couldn't let them intrude on Jessie or her family."

"Quite right," the priest conceded, although visibly shaken by the unexpected drama.

"Thank you." Joanna reached out a grateful hand. BJ leaned down, pecked a kiss to her cheek and returned to Jessie. "Are you all right?"

"Yes. Thanks," Jessie said, although the scene had unsettled her nerves.

"Vultures, all of them." Jasmine sneered. "It'll be across all news platforms now. What do you want to do with David? Do you want me to speak to him for you or what?"

Jessie's composed posture slumped. *How would he react to all this coverage?* That one of the senior artists had been kidnapped while on leave for her father's death would horrify him. David didn't believe that all press was good press. He staunchly adhered to the theory that bad press could kill a ballet season. Yesterday it all seemed so simple to keep the kidnapping and her injuries a secret from him. Now it'd be exposed for the world to see. But what could she do? *Nothing.* She pulled a face.

"What? What is it?" Jasmine asked.

"To hell with David. I'm through worrying about what he's going to think. It's not my fault I got kidnapped. Don't say anything to him when you go back. If he asks you, tell him the truth. I'm uninjured and ready to return to work once I sort out family matters. Tell him I'll see him on my return."

"Good for you," Jasmine said. "About bloody time you didn't take any more crap from him or Tabitha Simpson for that matter. I don't like to say it, but this kidnapping saga has shown you how strong you really are. I'm proud of you." She threw her arms around Jessie's neck and squeezed tight.

"Second you on that." BJ patted Jessie's knee.

"Who's David?" Kate asked.

"And Tabitha Simpson," Mia said.

Explaining the behind-the-scenes workings of a ballet company, Jessie found some humorous respite before the invited funeral guests arrived.

With BJ and Ricky standing guard against the media scavengers, the priest gathered the fifty or so mourners to Ken Hilton's graveside for the service and burial. While Father Conlon spruiked Ken's qualities, achievements and contribution to the local community, Jessie fixated on her father's coffin. Suspended above the hole in the ground on strong, durable bands and decorated with a massive spray of red and white roses, Ken Hilton's highly-polished, honey-coloured, timber coffin shone in the sunlight. *Inside is so dark and lonely, like being trapped in a limestone cave forever.* She clung tighter to her mother's hand. Glancing over to her brother, she noticed he looked dazed and insecure. They'd all been set adrift by Ken's death.

When he finished, Father Conlon nodded to Joanna. She stepped forward and sprinkled earth on the coffin as the cemetery workers lowered it into the grave. Down it went, deeper into the darkness. Still tearless, Jessie accompanied Richard to the grave side, and they sprinkled dirt onto the descending coffin. *I'm never getting buried. Never. Cremate me. Burn me up. But never leave me in a dark hole.* Locked arm in arm, she, Joanna and Richard steadied themselves before the mourners filed past. Ever poised, Joanna accepted condolences from friends, while Jessie and Richard managed thin smiles in appreciation. Slipping away after a suitable time, she and Jasmine headed to BJ and Ricky who patrolled the perimeters.

"You okay?" BJ tucked her under his arm.

"Yes. I think the worst is over now. The sooner we get out of here the better."

"Agreed." He leaned closer and whispered, "Love you."

"Love you too." She kissed his cheek.

"Come on you two. I think it's time to go." Hand in hand, Jasmine and Ricky moved to leave.

In a final farewell, Jessie returned briefly to her father's grave with BJ by her side. "Goodbye Dad. I love you. I wish I'd known you better. I'll miss you." Scooping up a handful of rose petals from the memorial basket, she raised her hand high, sprinkling them into the grave. The graceful, silky white and red petals danced on their way to the coffin—elegant in their beauty, unafraid of their destination. *For you Dad, next time is for you.*

CHAPTER 40

*T*he temperature inside the community hall was hot enough to roast a chicken. While the ladies dabbed handkerchiefs at their glistening faces trying to stem the flow of perspiration, the men fanned themselves with Ken's funeral programs. Stationed against the far wall, BJ and Ricky hung back from the cake-eating, tea-drinking group, watching them share happy memories of the deceased.

"What do you think?" BJ sipped a cup of tepid instant coffee poured from the urn.

"The coffee sucks." Ricky curled his lips and discarded the half-drunk cup on a nearby table.

"Not the coffee. The uncle." Expressionless, BJ did his best not to draw any attention to their tête à tête.

"After everything you told me. I agree. There's something off about him." Assuming the same disinterested expression, Ricky lounged beside him feigning casual conversation.

"Aside from obviously brow-beating his wife and turning his son into a budding narcissist like himself, Frank Hilton has stayed clear of Father Conlon the entire morning, at the cemetery and now here. I think it's odd he hasn't spoken to the priest at all." He set his unwanted cup down next to Ricky's.

"Yeah, I noticed."

"Did you also notice Father Conlon hasn't gone anywhere near Frank?" They both cast a furtive glance towards the ageing priest.

Ricky frowned. "Yeah. It looks like there's something between Frank and the priest that neither wants to dredge up."

"Something that Jessie's dad knew all about, or at least suspected, because it was Ken's dying wish for Father Conlon to preside over his funeral. Maybe Ken hoped that bringing Frank and the priest together would expose whatever that something is."

"Would you boys like one of my scones?" Aunt Hilda trundled up to them, holding a platter of freshly made fruit scones, slathered in butter.

"Thanks, Mrs Hilton." BJ grabbed two halves and nudged Ricky. "These you have to try. Best scones ever."

"Thanks, Mrs Hilton." Ricky politely selected one plump scone half.

"You'll be sorry you didn't take two." Having devoured the first half in record time, BJ wiped butter from his mouth and smiled with contentment.

Within moments, Ricky wore the same expression. "Bloody great scones." He licked his fingers while scanning the room for Hilda Hilton. On spying her, he noted the platter was already empty. He pouted and grumbled in disappointment.

"I told you to take two." BJ licked his fingers. "When are you leaving?"

"Straight after this, so Jasmine can make the show tonight."

"And last night? How did that work out?" He cocked an enquiring brow.

"No sex if that's what you want to know." Ricky pouted again.

"Are you seeing her again since she's not putting out?"

"Yeah. Sex or no sex, I'm interested. Jasmine's like no woman

I've met before. She tells it like it is. Calls a spade a spade. I like that. A lot."

"Well, I'll be damned. The old dog is learning new tricks." BJ sniggered.

"Yeah, yeah, yeah, very funny." Ricky nudged his mate in the ribs. "What's your plan once this has finished?"

"Drive back to Coodravale. See what happens then. Joanna's got to get the money back from Frank over the next day or so, and I want to be close by when she speaks to him. After that, we'll see how quickly things work out. I know Jessie wants to get back to Melbourne as soon as possible."

"Let me know if you need anything, okay?"

"I will. But I figure it should all be straight forward from here."

BJ unloaded the sympathy flowers from the Jeep and helped Richard carry them inside the homestead. At his feet, Whiskey bounded and whined, eager for attention. "Sorry to leave you alone again, girl. I'll get these flowers put away, and we'll play soon." Reaching down, he ruffled her ears, sympathetic to his dog's escalating boredom over the past couple of days.

The strong smell of lilies, roses and other sweet floral fragrances greeted them as they entered the house. He placed the last of the floral tributes where Joanna indicated on the sideboards. With the kettle on the boil in the kitchen, Jessie busied herself setting up the cups and saucers on the dining room table, ready for service.

"Thank you, Jessica." Joanna settled into the chair at the head of the table.

"You relax for a while, Mum. Jess and I will look after everything," Richard said, then followed his sister into the kitchen.

"Brad, come sit next to me for a minute." Joanna patted the

chair to her right. "You've been a wonderful help here at Coodravale, with Jessica and with Ken's death. In fact, with everything since you've arrived." She paused for a moment. "Has Jessica told you about the money?"

"Yes, she has." He noticed how the backdrop of pretty, pastel flower arrangements accentuated her blanched face and reddened eyes. But her strength of will remained undefeated.

"Good. I've decided not to let sleeping dogs lie. I'm going to broach this with Frank as soon as they arrive. Ken's funeral is probably the best time to appeal to Frank's better nature. I'd like you to stay while we have this family meeting."

"Are you sure? I doubt Frank will be impressed."

"I'll be telling Frank in no uncertain terms how unimpressed I am that he still owes us one hundred thousand dollars— particularly since it's such a long outstanding debt." The annoyance gripping Joanna's face foretold of a battle she ready to fight.

"Of course, I'll stay and support you."

"Thank you."

"It's none of my business, but can I ask something?" BJ shifted in his chair.

"Of course."

"Do you think your husband expected this money to be repaid? I mean, it seems unbelievable that Frank never paid his brother back."

"I've asked myself this question many times. I'm sure Ken reminded Frank over the years, but Frank is a bully. He probably thought Ken would eventually let it go. But I can't afford to. I need that money now, more than ever." A bright blush coloured her cheeks.

"Don't worry, whatever you need, I'm here."

The sound of Frank's car tyres crunching on the driveway filtered through the open front door. She stiffened. "Jessica, Richard, bring the tea. I'm going to talk to your Uncle Frank."

Frank, Hilda and Tom wandered into the dining room, as Jessie and Richard carried in the tea tray. Remaining in her chair, Joanna waved her hand. "Please, everyone, let's sit together. Frank, you sit next to me on this side."

Clever woman, BJ thought, *putting her adversary directly opposite me.*

"Jessica, you sit next to Brad, Hilda next to Frank, Richard next to Jessica, and Tom next to your mother." Joanna lined up both sides of the Hilton family across the table. An unmistakable cue that something serious was about to happen. "Jessica, will you and Richard pour the tea, please?"

No one dared to refuse. Joanna Hilton was the grieving widow and whether they wanted more tea or not, today wasn't the day to deny her wishes. Once everyone had a dainty cup and saucer in front of them, she began. From an attaché folder nestled on the floor beside her, she produced a document that she slid towards Frank, eyeing him suspiciously. "Do you recognise this, Frank?"

He glanced at the folded paper, then turned away. "Perhaps."

"What is it?" Hilda craned her neck trying to see.

"Be quiet, woman," he said.

Joanna looked directly at Hilda. "It's a loan agreement in which Ken loaned your husband one hundred thousand dollars when we first bought Coodravale. Back then, we took out a higher bank mortgage, so Ken could loan Frank this money. We've paid off the mortgage, but Frank hasn't paid back any of this outstanding loan."

"What?" Hilda's hand flew to her throat. "That's over twenty-five years ago, Frank?"

The pallor of Tom's face turned chalky white, while Frank's ruddy complexion deepened to the purplish hue of eggplant. Under the table, Jessie clutched BJ's hand, yet neither broke from their sombre expressions. Richard's wide-eyed stare contrasted with his mother's cool composure—all of them staging a striking tableau worthy of an artist's brush. Remaining stony-faced, BJ admired Joanna's approach. *Blunt, no nonsense. She sure knows how to kick the hornet's nest.*

"I'd prefer if you and I discussed this matter in private, Joanna." Frank puffed out his chest.

"And I prefer to discuss this in front of family."

"He's not family." Frank jabbed a finger at BJ who merely cocked an eyebrow.

"He soon will be. He and Jessica are getting married."

"What?" Richard listed from his chair.

"Richard, be quiet. You don't know everything that goes on." Joanna quashed her son's shock, while casting Jessie a haughty smile. BJ squeezed Jessie's hand tighter under the table, and with a little shake signalled all was well.

"Therefore, Brad will stay for this meeting. As I was saying, you currently owe us one hundred thousand dollars as per this loan agreement. I'd like to know when I may expect to receive it in our bank account. Considering this debt is well overdue, it's disappointing I need to bring up this matter on the day of your brother's funeral."

BJ leaned back in his chair, wondering why Joanna even needed him there. She was an assassin, in the nicest possible way. Everyone waited while the tea turned cold. Dumbfounded, Hilda and Tom leaned forward, blinking at the head of their family.

By this public inquiry, Joanna had cornered Frank as surely as a mouse in a maze. With no other alternative, he changed his approach, fawning over his sister-in-law. "Joanna, please. It slipped my mind. I'm sorry. I forgot all about it, and Ken never reminded me."

"Don't take me for a fool, Frank Hilton. I've no doubt Ken asked for this money over the for years. When will you deposit the money into our account?"

Frank launched from his chair, bellowing like a wounded bear. "How dare you question me? What right do you have to insist on anything? You are nothing more than…"

Pushing to his feet, BJ rose swift and sure. With muscles flinching and jaw set, he glowered.

Beside him, Jessie leaped to her feet. "How dare you speak to my mother like that?" She wagged a scolding finger at her uncle.

"Be quiet. You wretched girl."

Jessie staggered back into her chair.

Gritting his teeth, BJ snarled and turned to check she was okay. With a vein throbbing in his jaw, he swept his gaze back to Frank, whose pompous demeanour appeared almost comical. Leaning forward, he rested his clenched fists on the table. "You're not the one giving orders here. Answer Joanna's question. When can she expect to receive the one hundred thousand dollars in her bank account?" If only Frank would make a move. Just one. A cool touch on BJ's hand broke his focus, and he stood down.

"Thank you, Brad," Joanna said. BJ stowed his rage and folded back into his chair, leaving Frank brushing himself off in deliberate strokes. Again, she quizzed her brother-in-law. "Well, Frank?"

After more bluster, Frank resumed his seat. "I don't have that sort of money available in one lump sum. What if I deposit ten thousand dollars each month for the next ten months?"

"What about you go away and come back with a better plan." Her smile was as distasteful as Frank's offer. Turning to Hilda, she softened. "This should've been finalised years ago. There are so many things I need to reassess now Ken is gone, and I can't afford to have the strain of this on my shoulders as well. Please. You must come up with this money, somehow."

"Really, Frank, it's bad enough that poor Joanna has just lost her husband, without having to worry over this money business." Hilda directed a withering scowl at her husband and pushed to her feet. "We'll get this sorted out, Joanna. I promise." She turned and marched out of the room. Fidgeting in his chair, Tom delayed, obviously uneasy with his mother's fierce and uncharacteristic reprimand of his father.

"Very well. I'll see what I can do." Frank rose like royalty, while Tom scampered to his feet, like the court jester. Without another word, they departed.

When the door closed behind them, Richard expelled a long exhale. "When are you two getting married?"

"It was a ruse, Richard, so that Brad could stay for the family meeting." Smirking, Joanna stuffed the loan document back into her folder.

"You're cleverer than I thought, Mum."

"Mothers usually are."

"Are you okay?" BJ stroked Jessie's trembling arm.

Blotches of red flashed up her neck and warmed cheeks. "He makes me so mad. How dare he treat us like that?"

"Don't worry, Jessica. Hilda is a good woman, and I'm counting on her to apply the right pressure on Frank to repay the money as soon as possible. Now, I'm going to lie down." She rose, as did everyone else. "It's been a horrible day. I'll see you all later."

"I think I'll do the same." A frown creased Jessie's brow. "I still can't believe we just buried Dad."

"Neither can I." Richard put his arm around his sister's waist, and they hugged each other a few moments longer.

"Once the shock settles, that's when reality sets in. An afternoon sleep is a good idea. See you later." BJ guided Jessie out of the dining room, away from the miserable realism of the day.

Holding hands, they strolled back to the Garden Wing with Whiskey dancing happy circles around them. Stopping at the bottom of the stairs, he faced her. "Get some rest, and we'll watch the sunset together."

"Sounds lovely. See you then." She touched his cheek. "Thanks for being with me today and for standing up to Uncle Frank."

"Not a problem. Later…" Clasping her shoulders, he spun her around and sent her on her way.

As she padded up the stairs and along the veranda, he admired how even after another emotionally gruelling day, her inherent poise remained unruffled. Tilting his head, he smiled at her departing image. *I'm a lucky man. I can't wait to put all this behind us and get back to Melbourne to start our new life.*

His Border collie's expectant face nudged him. "Okay, Whiskey. Your turn, girl." Winging the ball she dropped at his feet, he focused his attention on the other female in his life.

CHAPTER 41

*C*heck it out. I made the front page of the Yass Tribune.
"Melbourne man, Skip Norton, has been arrested in connection with the kidnapping of local woman, Jessie Hilton. Miss Hilton is a soloist in the Australian Ballet Company and grew up at Coodravale in Yass. She began her career..." *What the fuck!* The story is all about her. What about me? I did all the planning, preparation and execution. Blah, blah, blah... "Miss Hilton was rescued by her brother, Richard and a family friend Brad Jordan and his dog, Whiskey." *I can't bloody believe.* There he is again. The interfering hero and his dog. Brad bloody Jordan is his name. That guy really pisses me off. *I hate dogs.*

"Hey, when is my lawyer going to get here? Is there any bastard out there who can hear me?" *That'll get the serg' in here quick smart. I can hear him lumbering along now.*

"Listen here, Norton. There'll be none of that language in my lock-up. What is it you want, now?"

"Did you see this? The bloody *Yass Tribune* only mentioned me once. Once!" "You do realize that this is not a competition to see who gets their name in the paper the most times. You've been arrested on some serious charges. Do you understand that?"

"All I know is that I'm stuck in this hell hole while I wait for a lawyer."

"Well, you won't have to wait too long. He's on his way."

"He? I was hoping it would be a woman."

"I bet you were. The court has appointed you a Mr Stephenson."

"Is he any good?"

"I've got no idea. He should be here soon so I suggest you think about what you're going to discuss with him so he can represent you in the best possible way."

"Yeah. Yeah. Thanks, Serg'."

Shit! None of this has worked out the way I wanted. I lost my precious dancer, the cops nabbed me and now I get a male lawyer. There's no way I'm going to jail. No way. All those men cooped up together, touching each other, sucking each other's cocks. Freaks, the lot of them. My mother made me do that to her boyfriends when she brought them home. She said that if I did it, they'd stay and look after us. But they didn't. They all ended up leaving no matter what I did. Mum's men were bastards. Them and their fucking dogs, laughing and barking at me. I'm not going to jail. I'm not going to suck cock in jail. I've got to find another way…

CHAPTER 42

*W*ithout the in-laws, Joanna, Jessie, BJ and Richard breakfasted alone, which suited Jessie just fine. Uncle Frank's presence upset her more the longer he stayed at Coodravale. She wondered how poor Aunt Hilda put up with him all these years. As far as Jessie was concerned, if she never saw Uncle Frank again, it would be too soon.

Clearing away the last of the dishes, she shot a serious look at her mother. "Have you heard anything more about the money?"

"No. I expect he's trying to explain to Hilda what the money was for in the first place and how he's going to repay it." She flicked a lace doily on the table under an arrangement of white lilies that Richard held aloft. The dining room looked so festive with all the scented sympathy flowers, yet their beauty only added to Jessie's melancholy. Cheerful flowers for a miserable occasion.

"When will you speak with him again about it?" Richard busied himself by twisting and turning vases.

"It'll have to be sometime today." Joanna pushed the chairs into the table, so their backs lined up evenly.

"Do you need anything from us?" BJ stayed out of everyone's way.

"Thank you. I think I might speak to Frank alone this time. See if I can't get a better response. In the end, he has the leverage in the matter. I need the money as soon as possible. All I can do is push a little and hope it works."

"Well, let us know if you need anything, Mum." Jessie reassured her mother with a hug.

Joanna motioned for Richard to join them. Clutching their hands in a one-for-all grip, she held them steadfast. Her cool, grey eyes drifted between her children. "I am so proud of you both. You have given me much joy, love and support. I know I don't say it enough, but I'm saying it now. Without you both, I don't know how I would've got through all of this. If your father was still here, he'd be proud of the considerate young adults you've become. And you, Jessica, after everything you've been through with that terrible Norton fellow, you're still unflustered and in control. I don't know how you do it…really, I don't. And my dear boy Richard, you've been a rock to me. I know you dislike still being here at Coodravale, but soon you will go off to start your own life and be successful in your career. I love you both dearly. Know that Coodravale will always be your home." Embracing in a group hug and pledging their love for each other, they formed the new Hilton family of three that Jessie had hoped for.

"Now off you go. I think I might make some tea and take it to them. Then have my chat with Frank." Joanna turned on her heel towards the kitchen.

"I'm off for a ciggie out the front. I'll see you later." Richard kissed Jessie on the cheek.

"Okay. We'll be down by the river, so join us once you've finished if you like."

"Thanks, but I have a couple of things I need to take care of first." With his cigarette pack already in his hands, he marched towards the front door.

"Just you and me, kid." BJ winked at her.

"And Whiskey," she said.

"And Whiskey." He took her hand, and they sauntered outside in the direction of the river.

Unlike the previous days, today bore the threat of the rainy season. Across the Brindabella Ranges, foreboding clouds gathered as if in consultation of where to unleash the first downpour. Even the birdsong sounded muted. Like the end of a holiday when happy campers pack up before the storm, the energy thrummed with the panic of a swift departure.

"What a great life Whiskey has." With a wistful smile, Jessie envied the dog's happy mood. "Every day is as wonderful as the day before or the day following. She lives in a perpetually happy state."

"I guess so. But that doesn't mean she has no feelings. Whiskey feels everything we do, love, happiness, sadness, anger, loneliness. It's just that when she has a choice, she always chooses to be happy. Dogs are smart. She was the best thing that happened to me after Rachael and Tiffany died. Whiskey helped bring me back from the brink. She loved and trusted me..."

"And she saved me..." Jessie flashed a grateful grin at the Border collie.

"That she did. She's a damn fine friend and protector." Pulling the ball from his pocket, he threw it along the riverbank. "Whiskey. Fetch." Bounding after her reward, the dog played the game repeatedly until she lay panting, worn out and contented.

"She's like a dog with two tails." BJ rubbed her belly.

"What do you mean?"

"It means she couldn't be any happier if she tried."

Gazing down at the dog's blissful face, Jessie longed for two tails herself. An unexpected temperature drop sent a shiver up her arms. "It's getting cold."

"I'll run up and get your coat if you like?"

"Thanks. I'll wait here with Whiskey." She watched BJ's brow crease. "Go on. No one's going to kidnap me. Skip's locked up, remember? Off you go."

CHAPTER 43

When BJ walked out the French doors after getting Jessie's coat, a noise to his left alerted him of someone's presence. He stopped and retreated from view as Frank rounded the corner, heading towards the main house. The pompous look on his face signalled Frank was up to something. BJ waited until he passed and then followed him. Striding through the side veranda doors, Frank disappeared into the main living room of the house. The curtains fluttered closed, but the doors remained opened. BJ considered his options. Eavesdropping wasn't something he usually condoned, but he convinced himself that if this was the meeting Joanna alluded to having with Frank, she probably wouldn't mind. He hoped not. Deciding to take advantage of the situation, he slipped up to the open doors and listened.

"Very well, Joanna. Let's see if we can't come to some arrangement."

"As I said Frank, you owe us one hundred thousand dollars, and I would appreciate it if you could pay it back as soon as possible."

Through a crack in the curtains, BJ glimpsed her sitting in a red velvet armchair, hands clutched in her lap.

"I understand, but I don't have that sort of cash lying around. I did offer to pay it back over ten months."

Men like Frank irked BJ. When they had the upper hand, they metaphorically waved it around as a weapon. Frank clearly enjoyed this game.

"Yes, but Ken loaned you this money years ago. He took out a higher mortgage on Coodravale to help you. Why don't you take a second mortgage on your house? That way you could repay me and be responsible for your own debt?" BJ glimpsed Joanna lift her chin to match the rising indignation in her voice.

Frank's tone turned ominous. "Did you know that if it wasn't for me, you and Ken would never have been able to afford to buy Coodravale in the first place?" He paused. "Because Ken had a low credit rating, I went guarantor on the property all those years ago. It was me who secured this property for you, your husband and your family. So, I suggest you show a little more respect and appreciation for our family ties."

BJ flinched.

"We appreciate your help, but that's all in the past. There is a current debt of one hundred thousand dollars which you owe. Can't you repay it faster than over ten months?"

Frank's leering face came into view as he leaned closer to Joanna. "Perhaps we could come to another arrangement? A more private and personal one?" His hand trailed over Joanna's shoulder.

Bastard. BJ's fingers flexed and balled into fists, as he prepared to use them on Frank if he went any further.

Joanna sprang to her feet and glowered. "How dare you. I'm offended by your lewd suggestion. Paying the debt off over the next ten months will be suitable. I'll write up a short letter regarding our agreement and should you renege, I'll instigate legal proceedings. Now if you, Hilda and Tom are ready, I think it best if you leave today." She snapped a turn and left the room.

BJ light-footed it off the veranda and headed toward the lower paddock. Bad enough that Skip Norton had threatened and kidnapped Jessie with plans to inflict all sorts of sexual horrors upon her, but overhearing Frank's sexual advances towards Joanna was too much. *What the fuck is wrong with these men?* By the time he crested the knoll, he knew one thing for sure. Like Norton, Frank's primary rule of engagement was to belittle and victimise women.

CHAPTER 44

$\mathcal{P}$erched on a log, Jessie tugged her coat tighter while she and BJ flapped their feet in the icy water of the Goodradigbee River. Nearby, Whiskey slept off her game of fetch. Though the day approached noon, the sky darkened with voluminous grey clouds like a portent of doom.

"I don't know what's wrong with me. I must be an ice maiden." Jessie snorted. "I'm as cold as these Snowy Mountain waters." Staring at her chilling feet, confusion swamped her mind as to why she'd not shed one tear since her father's funeral. Despite an average night's sleep, and the loving moment she'd shared with her mother and Richard after breakfast, exhaustion and anxiety riddled her body. Uncle Frank's attitude over the money further stoked her bad mood. Why wouldn't he just pay it back? Although she loved Aunt Hilda, she wanted her relatives gone. *I just want to go back to Melbourne. Get back to my ballet.*

"Stop beating yourself up. Funerals are strange events, and everyone responds differently." BJ grabbed her hand. "Why don't you tell me happy stories about growing up here in Coodravale?"

Dredging up a stiff smile, she thumbed back through snippets of memories. "One of the happiest times was when I got my cat,

Penny. She was the runt of a litter that the Robinson's barn cat produced. Everyone thought she'd die because she was so small. But I knew she'd make it. Penny was a ball of tortoise shell fur, the tiniest squeak of a meow, and I loved her. She was my shadow. No matter where I went, she was there. She'd sleep on my bed, sit on the bathmat while I had a shower and curl on my lap when I watched TV or did my homework. God, I loved my little moggie. Come on, I'll show you something."

Rising to her feet, she slipped into her sandals and shepherded BJ across the river paddock, with Whiskey scampering behind. The smell of impending rain teased at her nostrils. The dry, cracked earth would soon be soddened. She thought of how the rain would drench her father's grave, and she shuddered at the image. Pushing the thought away, she tramped on. Tucked in the paddock's corner under a scattering of eucalypts, leaned a weathered wooden cross. She stared down and read aloud. "Penny, my best friend forever. Gone too soon."

"How old were you when she died?" BJ asked.

"Fifteen. I'd just got into the Aussie Ballet Company, and Mum called to say Penny had died in her sleep. I just cried and cried…" Staring down at the spot, she swallowed hard, but the long-awaited storm of emotion broke. She erupted in howls while hot tears rained down her cheeks. "I miss her awfully…" Crumbling to her knees, she lurched forward and threw herself over Penny's tiny grave. With her cheek resting on the cool grass, she sobbed and sobbed. Big, gut-wrenching gulps of grief rushed from her core finally finding freedom.

While she surrendered to the emotion, her mind picked through long-forgotten memories. The smell of the sweet grass reminded her of when she and Penny rolled on the lawn after her father mowed it. Overhead, the curved shape of the eucalypt leaves reminded her of Penny's ears with their pretty, tawny points. The taste of summer honey flooded back, reminding her of how she and Penny used to share a secret spoonful together.

DIANE DEMETRE

Jessie cried and cried. Buried emotion exploded within her, renting itself free. The sound of a distant creaking barn door reminded her of the shearing shed and the times she'd go looking for Penny inside and…

Time spiralled—and she struggled to breath.

A piercing scream shattered the afternoon silence. She thought it came from somewhere else, from someone else, but it didn't. It was her. Screaming and screaming, hysterically screaming. BJ crouched on the ground beside her, but his voice drifted in from afar, trying to soothe her. But nothing could sooth her now. She tugged at her hair and screamed, unable to stop, unwilling to stop. From the homestead she saw her mother and brother running in panic towards her. Dad. Where was her father? *He was the one who saved me. Where's Dad?* She sprang to her feet like a wild cat and bolted.

"Jessie, stop." But she didn't. "Whiskey. Go with Jessie." At his command and gesture, Whiskey galloped beside her, keeping pace.

"What's wrong?" Joanna tried to intercept her daughter.

"Jess, Jess, come back." Richard out-stepped his mother, gaining speed.

Her lungs burning, Jessie rounded the upper corner of the paddock. *Get away. Get away.* Circling back, she leaped up the stairs of the rear courtyard. She could cut through the house and be out the front door before… Skidding on her heels, she reared like a wild brumby, Whiskey beside her.

"What on earth is the matter, you wretched girl?"

Shrieking like a beaten dog, she stumbled and fell at the feet of Frank Hilton.

With a ferocious growl, Whiskey leaped in front of her prostrate body, bailing up Frank with a series of fierce barks.

"Get this bloody dog off me," he said, as BJ slid in to kneel beside Jessie.

"I suggest you control yourself, Frank. Any quick move of your part will simply make things worse." A long beat ensued. "Whiskey. Release." The faithful Border collie snarled once more for good measure and then retreated to rest by her master. "Jessie, are you all right?"

In a weak voice, she said, "Get me out of here. I don't want to see anyone. Please." She closed her eyes, feigning unconsciousness.

"Jess, are you okay?" Panting, Richard looked over BJ's shoulder.

"Brad, whatever is the matter?" Joanna kneeled on the other side of her daughter, patting her hand.

"She's fainted. I'll get her inside." He bundled Jessie in his arms and stood.

"What happened?" Joanna turned on her brother-in-law in a savage attack.

"Nothing. I just walked down the stairs, and she ran up like a wild thing, screamed and fainted."

"People don't faint for no reason, Frank. What did you do?"

"Nothing. You know Jessie has always been highly strung. Even as a child…"

"Don't say another word, Frank Hilton." Joanna hissed like a viper. "Let's take her inside, Brad."

In his strong arms, Jessie rested. A miasma of mixed memories and emotions tumbled in her mind. She needed time to think this through. She needed to be sure.

CHAPTER 45

"Okay, they're gone." BJ sat on the bed beside her and waited.

Opening her eyes, she cast him a feeble smile. "Thanks."

"Your mum is sick with worry. She's calling Dr Bruen to come out."

"Oh, no. She mustn't." She scrambled to sit up in bed.

Grasping her shoulders, he pressed her back onto the pillows. "Well, since you didn't 'come to'," he gestured air italics with his fingers, "your mother thinks there's something seriously wrong with you. I'm under strict instructions to tell her as soon as you wake up."

She rolled her eyes and slumped.

"What happened down at Penny's grave?"

"I'm not sure. One minute I was crying over Penny's death all those years ago, and the next I'm screaming and running, trying to get away."

"Get away from what?"

"It's pretty foggy, but it had to do with the old shearing shed..."

He watched her eyes glazed over. Then her lips clamped shut. Having witnessed some of his military mates return home with post-traumatic stress disorder, there was little doubt in his mind that Jessie had suffered some trauma in her childhood. The recurring nightmares, the sudden illness and death of her father, the stalking and kidnapping—all these unexpected and stressful events contributed to her unlocking something. He was sure of it. In her mind, she'd compartmentalised some past traumatic event and buried it away. Now, the secret was digging itself out, whether she wanted to face it or not.

"Jessie, look at me."

With a nervous twitch, she returned her focus to him.

"Do you remember anything else?" Careful not to push too hard, he kept his questioning light.

"It's all blurry. I know Dad was there, but…" Again, she drifted. A frown drew lines across her forehead while she searched her memory for something more.

"Listen. Why don't you rest? I'll tell your mother you're okay and there's no need for the doctor."

"Thanks. I am awfully tired." Without any further encouragement, she rolled over and closed her eyes.

Despite his negotiating skills, BJ had barely been able to convince Joanna to call off Dr Bruen. Giving her a believable reason for Jessie's panic attack had taken repeated assurances. Eventually, he'd convinced her it was the recent stress of everything Jessie had been through which caused her extreme anxiety. She just needed lots of rest and sleep for a couple of days. If she was no better tomorrow, he promised he'd drive her in to see the doctor. A deal of sorts had been struck, which now left him to his thoughts as he and Whiskey strolled around the gardens.

A persistent riddle gnawed at his brain. There was something else, something painful, something secret. He knew pain, intimately—the physical, emotional and mental torment of trauma, of unspeakable, body-breaking, mind-numbing pain. He knew how it looked, how it felt and what damage it could inflict, short term and long term. Witnessing Jessie's emotional pain escalate over these past weeks, he sensed a war of subterfuge at play. He needed to identify the real enemy.

BJ's mind raced over all the details he knew for sure. At dinner on Monday night, Frank's behaviour about Ken's request to have Father Conlon preside at his funeral struck BJ as suspicious. This was further compounded by neither Frank nor the priest going anywhere near each other yesterday at the funeral, perhaps indicating some past antagonism. Jessie had said her father and Uncle Frank didn't get on. There was a big argument one Christmas between them when she was a kid. Not long after that, her father burned down the shearing shed. Then there's the matter of Frank borrowing money from his brother and still owing one hundred thousand dollars. Yet no one in his family even knew about this loan. *What was the money for?* Earlier today, BJ witnessed Frank's predatory behaviour when he made sexual advances towards Joanna. Interwoven in all this were Jessie's ongoing nightmares which had haunted her since she was young. When Jessie regressed into her past trauma and hurtled headlong into Frank, she collapsed at his feet in shock. But he showed no concern or compassion. In fact, he said she was always a highly-strung child. *A highly-strung child...* The hairs on BJ's arms and neck bristled. Could what he suspected be true? The pieces of the puzzle certainly seemed to fit. He checked in with his gut instinct. That powerful sixth sense he'd depended on to stay alive in combat confirmed that as vile as it was, he was right. BJ drew breath.

He no longer noticed the glorious yellow rose and purple agapanthus blossoms at his side. He no longer heard the chattering birdsong or smelled the dusty sweetness of summer. A small muscle flinched in his jaw and a fine film of sweat sheened his skin. He'd been wrong at Yass Hospital when he thought danger was no longer his companion. He thought it was over when they arrested Skip Norton. But his gut had squirmed even then, telling him otherwise. There was something else going on, someone else. And now he knew. In long deliberate strides and with the stealth of an assassin, BJ moved to the Jeep. Unlocking the rear door, he opened the floor tray and lifted out his rifle case. Gripping it with unshakeable resolve, he carried it to the river to prepare for his mission.

CHAPTER 46

*W*hen BJ left her bedroom, Jessie threw off the covers and sprang out of bed. She peeked into the living room to make sure he'd gone. After a quick check at the French doors, she returned to the living room. She had to sort this out. And the only way she was going to solve this was to keep moving. She did her best thinking when she moved. Frowning, she paced from one end of the living room to the other, mulling over everything. *What the hell is going on with me? What happened down at Penny's grave?* The terror she experienced had virtually lifted her off her feet. Fragmented recollections caught in her mind, but none of them pieced together for a clear, unified image. She wished Jasmine was here. Her best friend seemed to get a handle on things better than she did. *What would Jasmine say?*

"What happened all those years ago that you're so scared of, Jessie?"

I don't know. But now I think it has something to do with my recurring nightmares...

"What about your nightmares?"

There's always a man in the dark, reaching out to me, touching me, licking my cheek and telling me ugly secrets.

"Where does this happen? Can you see where the place is?"

No. But I have a feeling it's somewhere I know.

"Can you see who the man is?"

I'm not sure. I can't see him clearly.

"For God's sake, stop putting up with this crap. Don't run away. Turn around and look." It was as if Jasmine was in the room with her, demanding she make a stand.

Determined to face whatever lurked in her past, Jessie thrust her chest forward and gulped a lungful of air. If she could escape Skip Norton, she could be free of this haunting. Mustering up all her grit, she spun around. Unexpectedly, she caught sight of BJ and Whiskey through the kitchen window. From a faded past, a Technicolor memory sharpened into total recall. She remembered. And she knew where they were going.

CHAPTER 47

BJ spied Frank, his eyes downcast and his brow furrowed, stalking around the rear courtyard. From behind one of the flowering citrus trees which bordered the private quadrangle, BJ watched him for a few moments.

"I knew I shouldn't have come back here for Ken's funeral," Frank said out loud. "What with the priest and all this shit with the money. Everyone needs to leave the past where it belongs." He stopped his private tirade and scowled at his feet. "Bloody ants." He ground his boot viciously on the flagstones. "Too many people punching above their weight around here."

Stepping out silently from his hiding place, BJ approached him, wearing a casual smile. "Excuse me, Frank. Joanna would like to see you."

Frank's eyes narrowed. "What? Now?"

"Yes. She's waiting down by the river and would like you to join her for an afternoon drink." BJ ladled syrup onto his voice, while his stomach churned.

"A drink you say? Well that sounds promising." Frank puffed his chest and preened. Full of self-importance, he strode down the steps to join BJ on the grass.

"I'll walk you down to where's she waiting. She's set the table in a different spot to usual." BJ kept his expression neutral while they strolled away from the homestead. "Lovely afternoon isn't it?"

"Yes. It is. I wonder what Joanna wants to see me about?" Frank's lips pulled into a smarmy smirk while he adjusted his trousers' waist.

BJ's tactical training prevented him from slamming Frank's face into the ground right there and then. *Avoid exposure. Exploit the enemy's vulnerabilities.* "She didn't say."

After a few more minutes of walking and listening to Frank's narcissistic comments, he slowed, with Whiskey heeled beside him. On a nearby knoll where the wombats lived, they stopped under the shade of a dozen or so coolabah trees.

"Where's Joanna?" Frank looked around, confused.

"She's not coming."

"What do you mean? What game are you playing at?"

BJ locked him in an intimidating glare and growled. "Don't speak unless you can improve the silence."

"How dare..."

Frank hit the ground before he saw it coming. Thump! After catching his breath, he rolled over onto his back, grovelling and terrified. His hand rubbed his reddening cheek where BJ's fist had connected. He could've easily broken Frank's jaw, but he didn't want to pre-empt himself, so he'd kept his touch light. BJ grabbed him by his shirt collar and hauled him to his feet. "You know, Frank? Silence here at Coodravale has its own sound." With him cowering beside him, BJ rough-walked him to a nearby tree. "Listen." He cocked his ear in demonstration. "The silence is broken only by the baying of the sheep, the warble of the magpies and the rushing of the river. Can you hear it, Frank?"

Panic-stricken, Frank nodded. His left cheek inflamed into a rosy rouge stain, adding the only colour to his whitening face.

"Do you know where we are, Frank?"

Frank glanced down at his feet and shuddered.

"That's right. This is where the old shearing shed stood. Whiskey. Defend." On her master's command, the dog bailed him up with an impressive display of threatening snarls and teeth-baring. "Don't make a move or she may do you some serious damage." BJ pivoted and strolled to a fallen log, on top of which coiled a length of rope. His rifle case lay next to it. "I've been thinking, and I'm certain I've solved the mystery." Selecting the rope, he returned, twisting and untwisting it in his hands. "Whiskey. Release." When she stood down, Frank virtually collapsed into his arms.

Pushing him hard against the tree, BJ roped him upright. With the cord biting into Frank's wrists tied behind the tree, he tightened its remaining lengths around his hostage's waist. "Now, before we begin, let me tell you what I think." He paused for effect. "I think you're one sick motherfucker." BJ watched Frank's expression infuriate, but he was smart enough, or scared enough not to speak. "I also think your brother and Father Conlon knew, or at least suspected what went on here, right on this spot." Despite his valiant effort at indifference, Frank couldn't hide his fear. "This is the spot where the old shearing shed stood. The shearing shed which Ken burned down after you and he had an argument. The shearing shed in which Jessie searched for her cat, Penny." BJ's gaze raked his hostage up and down, his disgust palpable. Only when Frank averted his gaze did he stride back to his rifle. With deliberate intent, he lowered himself onto the log and prepared his weapon.

"What do you think you're doing?"

"What does it look like? I'm loading my weapon." Without missing a beat, BJ flicked a cool, calculated glance from under heavy lids. "I'm going to shoot you, Frank."

"Are you crazy?"

"No. I'm not crazy. I'm an ex-SAS sniper." He straightened—rifle in hand, revenge in his heart. For him, the Coodravale silence was broken only by the internal surge of blood pulsing through his veins. Within and without, the ordinary world melted away. This was his world now, his special world. "So, Frank, I'm giving you a chance. A chance to confess what went on in the shearing shed…with Jessie."

Frank struggled lamely against the ropes, only tightening their grip with every movement. "You're mad. I knew it from the moment I met you. You're stark, raving mad." He lurched against his restraints, yelling wildly for help.

Smack! The bullet smashed into the tree just above Frank's head. Poleaxed by terror, he blinked, his eyes round as saucers. BJ was no longer a perceived threat. He'd smashed into Frank Hilton's reality like a sledgehammer, and now he had his full and undivided attention.

In cool deliberation, he loaded and locked another bullet into his .308. Meeting Frank's pitiful gaze, he shook his head in disappointment. "Frank, that was chance number one. Let's not waste any more time. What did you do to Jessie in the shearing shed?" With his patience oozing from him like blood seeping from a wound, BJ was gripped in an escalating scenario of do or die.

"Nothing. Really it was nothing." Tears leaked from Frank's eyes as he struggled to stay in control. "I didn't mean to. It just came over me."

"You didn't mean to do what, Frank?"

"It was so long ago. I've forgotten all about it. Can't we all just forget about it?" He ducked his head and closed his eyes, as BJ aimed his rifle, sending another bullet whacking into the tree. This time it whisked the grey hairs standing on Frank's head. His beleaguered cry could have been mistaken for a cockatoo screech. Not in the least out of place on a country afternoon when menacing rain clouds churned in the sky.

The sound mildly amused BJ. "You see, Frank, you may have forgotten, but it wasn't nothing." He locked him in a scathing stare. "That was your second chance. What is it you didn't mean to do?" Calm and calculating, he once more set to his task of reloading his rifle.

"Surely you're not going to kill me and risk going to jail?"

"I've killed many men in my life, probably far better men than you. If I have to kill you to give Jessie peace, I will. We have a saying in the army...Better to ask forgiveness than to ask permission. If this ends up with you dead, and me arrested for your murder, then so be it. I'd rather be asking for forgiveness than permission for killing a child molester."

Frank's face fell.

"This is your third and final chance..." He raised the rifle, butting it into his shoulder.

In a final attempt of bluster, Frank babbled. "I didn't do anything. You have no proof. You're no better than that Skip Norton who abducted that wretched girl. I'll have you arrested for this..."

No turning back now for BJ. When you call in the SAS, it's not to negotiate. It's to resolve the situation with violence. By Frank's reactions, he knew he was correct. *Time to rain down hell...for Jessie, for Rachael, for Tiffany.*

Cocking his weapon, he locked on his target. "Your life, as you know it, is over."

"No, wait," another voice yelled.

BJ glanced over his shoulder to see Jessie running towards him. "No. You don't have to do this."

"Jessie, thank goodness, you've arrived. This crazy boyfriend of yours was about to kill me. Untie me this instant."

Ignoring her uncle's demands, she reached for the rifle, pushing the barrel towards the ground. "It's all right. It's all right." She cupped BJ's cheeks in her hands. "You don't need to save me this time. I've got this."

"Jessie, I'm sure he..."

She nodded. "I know." She marched to the tree where her uncle was bound.

"It's about time, girl. Untie me."

"Don't you speak to me, you wretched man." A harsh, wire-taut voice hissed from her. "I remember. I remember everything." She paced backwards and forward in front of him. "I was only little, maybe five years old, and I came into the shearing shed to look for Penny. You were in there, drinking. You offered to help, but I didn't want to stay. I knew something was wrong. When I tried to leave, you grabbed me. You told me you had Penny in a hessian bag, and you wouldn't give her back to me unless I stayed. You picked me up and sat me on some sort of crate. Then you whispered how much you loved me, that I was your favourite. In that filthy shed you did filthy things to me." Utter disgust dripped from her voice as she rubbed the vile past from her cheek. Standing in front of her uncle, she snarled. "You licked my face, and then you touched me. You slid your hand into my pants and touched me." With hands clenched and eyes seething with rage, she screamed. "What kind of sick pervert are you to touch a little girl? Your own niece."

"It's a lie, it's a lie," Frank blathered.

BJ's fist connected deep in Frank's belly. "Speak again, and I'll kill you."

"It is not a lie," Jessie said. "Because of you, my life has been filled with nightmares and a feeling of never being good enough. You threatened that if I told anyone you'd kill Penny. Nearly every day that holiday I had to meet you in the shearing shed, and you did despicable things to me or Penny would die."

Frank groaned, his body hanging like a broken scarecrow from the tree.

Jessie grabbed his chin, shoving his face upward, so he had to look at her. "But Dad suspected something was wrong because he asked why I kept going to the shearing shed. And when I couldn't tell him, he followed me. That was the day Dad called me, and you walked out of the shed after me. That must have been what the fight was about. Dad suspected. But I just shut it all out, except in my nightmares. How could you do this?" She spat the accusation in his face.

Nothing. Nothing, but silence. No birds, no sheep, no wind. Even the gurgling waters of the river seemed to have quietened in respect for Jessie's painful catharsis. Storming off, she moved into BJ's open arms and breathed a series of short, sharp breaths. After a few long moments, she pushed out of the embrace, speared her fingers across her scalp and stormed back to her uncle.

"Stand up and be a man." The force in her voice demanded obedience. He struggled upright, silent and timid. "So, here's how it's going to work, Uncle Frank." The sarcasm she inflected on the last two words brought a proud smile to BJ's face. "You're going to find the one hundred thousand dollars you owe us and deposit it into Mum's account within seven days. If you don't, I'll be speaking to the state's prosecutor, Aaban Naser, about bringing child molestation charges against you."

Frank's mouth opened only to be snapped shut by a swift flick from BJ. "I suggest you let the lady speak."

She continued. "I won't press charges if you not only deposit the money, but you break all ties with my family. You'll leave this afternoon and won't visit Coodravale again, ever. But if Aunt Hilda wishes to visit, she is welcome. Unfortunately, you've already tainted poor Tom, so he's in no man's land." She took a beat. "Furthermore, I suspect your perversions with young girls probably still exist..."

Frank's eyes darted sideways.

Images of Tiffany danced in BJ's mind. To bring this perpetrator to justice, right here and now, would give him such satisfaction. He also knew it would only lead to his own self-destruction. Despite everything, he no longer wanted the smell of death on his hands. Dragging in a deep breath, he channelled every self-discipline technique he'd ever employed to manage his rage. Leaning in to Frank's face, he whispered his menacing question. "Is this true?"

Still with lowered head, Frank blinked the sweat from his eyes and bit his lip.

"And where do you do this? Online or in person?" BJ scrutinised every reaction Frank couldn't hide. "Both is it? But not here? Overseas perhaps? Is that what the money was for that you borrowed from Ken?" A flicker of Frank's crinkled eyelids and the escalating fear seeping from his pores signalled BJ had found the mark. "And your family believes that you're off on some buying trip for your vintage cars. It's vintage cars you're interested in, isn't it, Frank?"

Frank nodded feebly.

"But the trip isn't for the cars. It's for your sick perversions…"

He whimpered, unable to withstand the interrogation any longer. BJ spat at his hostage's feet, pivoted and strode away. If he stayed within reach, he'd surely strangle the freak. Try as he might, BJ couldn't swallow the filth swirling in his mouth.

Back at the tree, Jessie continued to dispense her own form of justice. "You'll surrender your passport to me, or I'll call the police."

Frank nodded.

"Where is your passport now?"

"At home."

"You'll post it to me here as soon as you get home. Agreed?"

Frank nodded once more.

"You'll also submit yourself to counselling, which I'm sure the crown prosecutor, who is trying the case against Skip Norton, will arrange. If you fail to attend these sessions, I'll press charges, which Aaban will be even more delighted to prosecute. Do you understand?"

Frank gave another meek nod of his head.

"Good. Break one of these conditions, and I'll rain down hell upon you."

BJ managed a half-smile at her use of one of his tactical

training terms. It pleased him enormously to hear it from her sweet lips. He stalked over to join his ballerina warrior.

"Let's not have any foolishness, Uncle Frank. The last thing you want is to be arrested, tried and jailed as a child molester. Jail is an ugly place for perpetrators like you."

Frank groaned. BJ suspected the old leopard may not change its spots, but the conditions under which Jessie cut this deal certainly provided opportunity for everyone to move on.

"Cut him loose."

BJ released Frank who slumped pitifully. No longer the blustering predator, he listed like a shipwreck.

"I'll say my goodbye now. I'll see Aunt Hilda and Tom before you go."

Lifting his head, Frank gazed at Jessie. "I know it means nothing, but I'm sorry, Jessie. I didn't mean…"

"Out!" She screamed the directive with a fierce snap of her arm. "Sorry will never make up for the horrors I've endured because you."

Skulking away, Frank hobbled over the knoll. As he retreated from view, BJ figured Frank had got a damn good deal. At least, he wasn't dead.

CHAPTER 48

*J*essie's body crackled like a bushfire. She'd come face to face with fear and won. With BJ standing beside her, they watched Frank stumble away. Battered and bruised, he collapsed on the ground and rubbed his welted wrists. A small part of her felt sorry for him, while another part hated him for the childhood he'd stolen from her. She gritted her teeth and stared hard into the distance. Finally, she'd escaped from the dark depths of her nightmares, from Skip's evil clutches and from years of anxiety. The haunting was over. She exhaled a long, pent up breath. She knew it'd take time to heal but knowing what happened all those years ago liberated her to begin the process. She inclined her head upwards and met BJ's wild blue gaze.

"I told you, you were tough."

She was too exhausted to speak.

"Frank. Frank, what's wrong?" Hilda's shrill voice rang out as she rushed to where her husband slumped on the grass. She kneeled beside him, examining his wrists. A few moments later, she raised her head. Her shocked expression could be seen from where Jessie and BJ stood. Frank shook his head and lowered it into his hands. Wrapping an arm around his shoulders, Hilda rocked him like a baby.

"I think he's going to tell her," BJ said.

"Why?"

"Because there's only a certain amount of shame any man can live with."

An anguished sound pealed through the valley. It reminded Jessie of a wounded bullock her father had had to shoot many years ago. Her uncle. His bellowing sheared Coodravale's stillness and the birds screeched on their startled flight towards the ranges. Tense moments passed until peace returned.

"Look." Surprise laced BJ's voice.

Jessie's eyes opened wide as she watched Aunt Hilda help Frank onto his knees. In the position of prayer, husband and wife knelt side by side and lowered their heads.

"She's making him pray." Jessie's voice choked with emotion. "She'd be asking for God's forgiveness for his sins."

"Do you think that's why your dad asked Father Conlon to preside at his funeral? Since your father couldn't prove anything, maybe he'd discussed his suspicions with the priest. That would explain the friction between Frank and Father Conlon."

"Maybe. When Father Conlon spoke to me at the hospital, he kept saying Dad tried to protect me. But I didn't understand what he meant."

"Father Conlon couldn't have said anything because of his vows. But if I had to guess, he and your dad had a pact of some kind to protect you, since nothing could be proved against our uncle."

In the distance, Hilda pulled herself to her feet. Lifting her chin, she stared in their direction. Jessie was sure her aunt looked directly at her. Hilda nodded once and waited. Jessie responded similarly. Bending over, Hilda assisted her husband to his feet and with her arm hooked around his waist, helped him back to the homestead.

"Thank you so much for your hospitality through this difficult time, Joanna." Sweet and gracious, Aunt Hilda embraced Jessie's mother with a kiss to both cheeks. "Frank will be depositing the money he owes into your account before Christmas Day, so you have no need to worry yourself further over it."

A spontaneous smile tipped Joanna's mouth. "Thank you. It's much appreciated to have this sorted out." She squeezed Hilda's hands in hers, obviously thrilled to have the debt behind her.

Jessie noticed her uncle didn't speak during the farewells. He barely managed a timid smile and a nod. Aside from these small responses, his body appeared devoid of life. Aunt Hilda's excuse of his being allergic to bee stings proved genius as the reason for the red bump on his cheek. *Clever woman, my Aunt Hilda.*

"Also, Frank's health has deteriorated quite badly with the travel, so we won't be visiting you again at Coodravale. But I might pop out to see you now and then. Or we can catch up when you visit Sydney."

Before Joanna could question Aunt Hilda's reference to Frank's health, Jessie wrapped an arm around her mother's waist. "That sounds fine, Aunt Hilda." With a tight squeeze and captivating smile, Jessie finished the conversation. "We'll see you soon then. Merry Christmas…"

Hilda leaned in and kissed Jessie with the lightness of a feather. In a departing whisper, she said, "Merry Christmas, my dear. Frank will never trouble you again."

Jessie mouthed a silent thank you.

"Merry Christmas, everyone. Come Frank. I'll drive while you relax." Hilda ushered an acquiescent Frank into the front passenger seat, while Tom farewelled his relatives with brief hugs and kisses. In no time, the Hilton family edged their car along the driveway, away from Coodravale.

"How odd." Tilting her head, Joanna frowned as she watched them go. "Whatever has happened to Frank?"

"Don't worry about it, Mum," Jessie said. "All's well that ends well."

"Yeah, forget about it. It's good to not have to listen to him go on and on about himself." Moving to one side, Richard tapped a cigarette from his pack and lit up.

"Aside from making the best scones around, Hilda is a remarkable woman, isn't she?" BJ shot a sideways glance at Jessie.

"She most certainly is." She inclined her head on his shoulder.

"Richard, do you really have to smoke?" Joanna asked.

"I do, if you want me to stay here and help you run Coodravale."

The three of them blinked and stared at him.

"What? I thought you wanted to get to the city as soon as possible?" Joanna said.

"That's what I thought too. But with Dad's death and everything else that's gone on here, I figure I can stay for at least a year to help you out. God, I'm only twenty-three. If a son can't help his widowed mother, what good is he as a man?"

Jessie did a double-take. For a moment, her brother looked uncannily like her father. He seemed to possess a quiet, inner strength. The same strength her father had obviously called upon the moment he'd suspected his brother was sexually abusing her and burned down the shearing shed. But because he didn't know for sure, her father had become tormented over his inability to prove anything. He withdrew and became a dour, embittered man. At the hospital, he'd kept saying he was sorry, and this is what he probably meant. He was sorry for not knowing, for not being able to prove the abuse and for not stopping it sooner. So many things started to make sense about her father now that she'd remembered that dreadful past. *Good things can come from bad times.* Shooing away the sad memories and welcoming the good, she returned her attention to the conversation.

Richard stubbed out his cigarette, picked up the butt and shoved it back in the empty packet. "What do you think about my staying around a little longer to help you out, Mum?"

"Oh, that's wonderful news. Thank you." Joanna wrapped her arms around his neck, hugging tightly.

He withdrew and regarded his mother seriously. "But there's one thing I have to tell you."

"Okay, what is it?"

"I'm gay."

Jessie squeezed BJ's hand tight. Neither of them moved.

"I see. But what has this to do with me, or with you're staying on here at Coodravale?" A sly smile lifted the corners of Joanna's lips.

"I thought I should tell you. You're my mother, and you should know about my sexual preferences..."

"It's no surprise to me, darling. I've known you were gay since you were about twelve years old. I've been waiting for you to finally speak about it."

"But how did you know?" He looked a little disappointed his news hadn't come as a shock.

"As I said before, mothers are cleverer than you think." She tweaked his chin.

"But what about Dad? Did he know?"

"I'd been telling him for years, so he sort of knew. He just didn't want to mention it to you in case it made you feel uncomfortable."

"And he didn't mind? About me being gay?"

"At first, he denied it, but he came to accept it. He loved you. You were his son."

Tears filled Richard's eyes as he hugged his mother close. "Oh, Mum. I love you and Dad..."

"We both knew you loved us. It had to be your decision to talk about it, not ours. After all, it's your life." She clung to her son's hands, exchanging smiles. "Now that everything is out in the open, why don't we all sit under the oak tree? Have a glass of wine to toast your father and the future. Come on, Richard. You can help me, and we can finally talk about you, the real you."

CHAPTER 49

*L*ounging on the bed with Jessie snuggled on his chest, and Whiskey snoozing on the floor, BJ considered the whirlwind of events that brought them to the end of this momentous day.

"Do you want to talk about any of this?" Stroking her hair, he breathed in the familiar scent of her shampoo.

"I'm not so sure that's a good idea. I've been having nightmares about it and playing it out in my subconscious mind for so long, I don't really feel like digging deeper or talking about it. Even the whole Skip Norton episode feels like the universe somehow conspired to push my buttons, to make me remember. Well, today I did. And now, I'd just like to let it go." She upturned her face, trading a smile with him. "I guess it's a bit like if I asked you do you want to talk about all the things you've seen and done when you were in the SAS."

"I understand. There's a lot of stuff I'd rather just leave alone as well. It's a bit like picking the scab off an old sore, it just keeps bleeding. You've got to let it heal."

"That's exactly how I used to feel every time I came home to

Coodravale. And now I know why. The whole coming-home experience was bittersweet."

"Maybe now you'll be able to come home, and it'll only be sweet?" He breathed her in and sighed.

"Yes, I think it will." She sprang up in bed and swivelled on her bottom to face him. "Would you have killed Uncle Frank?"

"No. But I wanted to."

"What stopped you?"

"You. Even if you hadn't turned up right at that moment, you were the one who stopped me…you and the life we could have together. And the life I had with Rachael and Tiffany. No matter how much Frank deserved to die, if I'd killed him, I would've sentenced myself to a worse death."

She cocked her eyebrow. "What's that?"

"Never being able to move on. Never being able to forgive or let go of a past not worth remembering."

Lunging forward, she wrapped herself into him. "And that's why I don't want to think about Uncle Frank and what happened in the shearing shed ever again. It's done. It's past. I want to focus on the future, my career, you and me—oh, and Whiskey of course." At the mention of her name, the dog snorted a loud snore. "Are you ready to leave tomorrow?"

"Yes, we'll leave straight after breakfast. You need to get back to Melbourne to see your artistic director."

"And once you get back to Melbourne, what do you need to do?"

"Look after you." Sweeping her in his arms, he leaned Jessie backwards, kissing her long and tender. She tasted sweet and forbidden, like extravagant confectionery. He yearned to devour her, but instead he released her from the delicious embrace. Fusing her in an intense gaze, he held her steady. "Are you happy?"

"Yes. Despite everything, or maybe because of it, I am."

"Well, let me know when you're deliriously happy."

When a frown wrinkled her forehead, he waited, wondering if she'd remember. The gold flecks in her hazel eyes glinted as a mischievous expression brightened her face.

"I remember…" Her lips tipped in a cheeky smile. "I promise I'll let you know when I'm deliriously happy."

The long-awaited balminess of a summer's night finally settled on Coodravale. The lone owl awoke and resumed hooting his mating call. Either he'd still not found a mate, or he lacked satisfaction. BJ felt a little sorry for him, for unlike the owl, he'd found a mate. Nevertheless, the passionate affection growing in his jeans indicated he too, lacked satisfaction. In this regard, he sympathised even more with his feathered friend. Disinclined to stay cuddling too much longer, he kissed Jessie's forehead. "I'm going to bed. We've an early start and a long drive tomorrow."

"Won't you stay?" The moist pout of her lips, her longing gaze and the creaminess of her skin tested his resolve.

"I want to, but we have an agreement. When we're both deliriously happy, we'll make love then. Anyway, whether you want to or not, I want you to give yourself some time. When I touch you, I …" He had no idea how to finish this sentence without making her feel uncomfortable. The last thing he wanted was to make love to her and for her to recoil because of the sexual abuse in her childhood. That'd be too awful.

"I understand. Let's give it some time. There's no rush. Deliriously happy it is." She reached over, cupped his face and kissed him—an endearing kiss, a kiss of promise and hope. "I don't know what I would've done without you through all this."

"You would've done what you've always done, Jessie Hilton— fronted up and toughed it out." Slipping out of bed, he pulled the sheet over her. "Now, no more nightmares, okay?"

"Okay. No more nightmares. Good night."

"Good night, my love." Sliding his hand on the wall, he flicked off the lights and left her to sweet dreams.

Opening the French doors, he stared down at Whiskey. "Righto, girl. Out you go. It's too hot in here for you to sleep." His faithful Border collie circled three times in her bed on the veranda and plonked down with a grunt.

Once he locked up, undressed and climbed into bed, he pulled the picture of Rachael and Tiffany from his bedside table drawer. With the frame in his hand, he traced his thumb over the faces of his two favourite women of his past. "I love you so much. But Angel and Ricky were right. It's time for me to move on. Rachael, I know you won't be mad. I know you'd want me to be happy, and I think I can be with Jessie. At least, I'm willing to give it a try. And my baby girl, Tiffany. You were gone way too soon, but maybe you'll come back to me?" His eyes shone with tears as the intensity of asking permission from his dead wife and daughter caught in his chest. "You'll be with me always. My girls. My precious girls." Clutching the frame to his heart, he closed his eyes. Tighter and tighter he squeezed them, his chin tucked into his chest. Finally, he exhaled and opened his eyes. *Letting go is tough.* A wave of acceptance washed over him while he kissed their images. He rolled over and slipped the picture into the bedside drawer. Without a moment's thought or hesitation, he reached up and turned off his bedside lamp. The darkness threatened him no more.

CHAPTER 50

*L*ike a great gift from heaven, the sun spread its luminescence across the countryside, highlighting its lavish smorgasbord. Even at this early hour, shadows retreated leaving nothing but a vivid, light-enriched landscape of brilliant blue and green hues. Hauling bags onto their shoulders and with Whiskey in tow, Jessie and BJ farewelled the Garden Wing. She stood on the veranda, gazing out through the poplar and crab apple trees towards the Goodradigbee River. The familiar sound of distant rushing waters, bleating sheep and laughing kookaburras loosened her thoughtful expression. "It's been a helluva ten days."

"I'd say, more like hell. Full stop." He slanted a glance in her direction.

"Yes. But it's over now." She sighed, releasing the last fingers of the past on her breath.

"Mostly. Just the Skip Norton court case, but with Angel at the helm, it should be straight forward. All you'll need to do is front up. And you know how to do that already…" He leaned down, and turning her mouth up to meet his, she accepted his kiss.

"Off we go then." She trotted down the stairs, eager to get on the road. Little topped the hope which fluttered in her heart. Like the story of Odette in Swan Lake, Jessie had been under the curse of an evil sorcerer all her life and now the spell was lifted. She was free. Sensing her life had taken a one hundred and eighty degree turn over these past few weeks, she renewed her faith in a future of her choosing.

With BJ and Whiskey beside her, she sauntered to the Jeep where Joanna and Richard waited. Beaming as bright as the morning, she grasped her mother's hands. "So, we'll be back to spend Christmas Day with you and Richard, okay?"

Joanna turned to BJ. "But what about your family? Don't you need to spend Christmas with them?"

"Mum has spent many Christmases without me. Besides, since I've been back from duty, I've spent Christmas with her. It'll be fine. Anyway, I want to take Jessie to meet Mum in the New Year." He hugged Jessie closer, and her skin tingled. She longed to get back to Melbourne, so it could be just them.

"See you then, Jess. Thanks for everything." Stepping forward, Richard hugged her tight.

"I love you, Richard."

"Love you." Releasing her, he shook BJ's hand. "Good to have you here, mate. You look after my sister, okay?"

"That's my job. And you take care of your mother."

"That's my job." He winked.

"This is for you, Jessica. Your father wanted you to have it." Joanna dropped a fine gold chain on which hung a gold swan into Jessie's palm.

"It's my ballerina necklace. You and Dad gave it to me one Christmas when I was little. I wondered what happened to it."

"Your father found it in the shearing shed a long time ago. I don't know why he kept it all this time and didn't give it back to you then." She shook her head obviously confused by Ken's actions. "But when he was in the hospital, he told me where he'd kept it and asked that I give it to you."

Holding the chain up, Jessie nodded at BJ to fasten it around her neck.

With a delicate touch, Joanna stroked the gold ballerina medallion resting on Jessie's throat. "I know I've been tough on you. But I want you to have the career you deserve. I want you to fulfil your destiny, without distraction. And you're doing just that. You're the best daughter a mother could ever have. I'm so proud of you." Enclosing her in her arms, Joanna caressed her daughter's hair with long, loving strokes.

"And you're the best mother. I promise I won't let you down or myself for that matter. Watch this space, there's more to come yet."

"I've no doubt." Joanna swiped away her tears and turned to BJ. "Now, you get my daughter back to Melbourne safely. We'll see you for Christmas lunch. Richard and I are looking forward to having you back here." Reaching for her son, she wrapped an arm around his waist with a tug.

"See you then." BJ leaned over and kissed Joanna goodbye. Glancing over his shoulder to Jessie, he cast a brilliant smile. "Let's hit the road."

After a brief exchange of more hugs and kisses, Jessie slid into the Jeep with Whiskey propped in the back, and BJ behind the wheel. For Jessie, the growl of the engine as it came to life was like an overture, signalling the beginning of a new performance, a new opportunity. The curtain had come down on her past, and now she leaped onto a new stage, into a new future.

As the Jeep pulled away along the gravel driveway, the blossoming flowers nodded in approval. Clouds of bees thrummed as they darted to-and-fro, oblivious to Coodravale's history, charm and family secrets. Jessie hung out the window, waving and calling goodbye. "I love you. See you soon. I love you."

Joanna and Richard chased the Jeep up the driveway, echoing her farewells. Once they reached the gate, mother and son linked arms, turned and strode back to the homestead. *If only Dad was here,* Jessie thought. But deep inside her, she knew he was.

Reclining back in the seat, she blew out a breath. "I love Coodravale, but I can't wait to get home to Melbourne."

"Me, too." With raised eyebrows, he cast a sideways glance. "Since I wasn't woken up last night by screaming, I assume you didn't have any nightmares?"

"No. I had a great night's sleep." Finally, she could say this simple fact which other people took so much for granted. She'd had a good night's sleep. Not because she'd done a yoga class, but because she was done with the drama.

"Good to hear." His cobalt blue eyes sliced through her just as they'd done on the first night they'd met. *My God, he's gorgeous.*

Unable and unwilling to drag her gaze away, she realised she was returning to Melbourne with a man in her life. But what woman wouldn't want this handsome, muscled, protective warrior as her man? She'd not gone searching for him, but here he was, an unexpected gift of love. A bolt of appreciation and anticipation raced up her body, searing her groin with yearning. Home. He was taking her home, back to her unit, back to her ballet and soon, back to his bed. Stretching her legs deep into the foot well, she spent the six-hour drive wide awake in happy conversation and delirium.

"Here you go. Home at last." BJ dumped her bag onto the floor.

Scanning her unit, a grateful smile graced her lips. Gone were the police tape and all hint of the break-in. Her little home had returned to its normal persona thanks to Ricky and Jasmine who'd cleaned up in her absence.

"I must say they did a fine job, those two." Hands on hips, he scoped her unit.

"Yes. They did. Everything is just as it used to be." She strolled around, running her fingers over her furniture. Even a quick glance in the bedroom proved Jasmine had tidied everything to within an inch of its life. "Jasmine is the best friend a girl could have…"

"And Ricky, the male counterpart."

She wrapped her arms around BJ's waist in an affectionate squeeze. "Do you think they'll get together?"

"Hard to say. Ricky's a player. I'm not sure if he's the settling down kind. But I do know he's quite taken with Jasmine. I guess we'll have to wait and see. But enough about them…So what do you want to do? I need to get Whiskey home."

"You go home with Whiskey. I'm going to stay here and organise myself. We'll catch up tomorrow."

"You sure?"

"Yes. I need to have some time by myself."

"Call me tomorrow. But if you need anything, you know…"

"I know where you are. But I have a feeling I won't need saving again, if that's okay with you?" She shot him a cheeky smile.

"Perfectly. See you then." Cupping her face, he pressed a long, lingering kiss to her mouth. "Tomorrow…"

"Tomorrow…"

Once she closed the door, she lifted her bag and headed for the bedroom. Hazy mid-afternoon light filtered through her windows. Up until now, she'd peered out these panes, wondering what life was like on the other side. Back then, she'd lived with a fretful tightness in her chest. Now, a fluttery lightness danced inside her. Where fear and anxiety had previously dwelled, the strength of certainty now resided. *This is my time. It's now or never.* A glimmer of sunlight reflected off the opposite building's window, blinding her for a moment with its glare. *My time…*

She continued to her bedroom to unpack, and within the hour, she sat propped on her couch, a mug of tea in hand. Spread on the coffee table in front of her were the four photos of her and her father that she'd selected for the funeral. Beside them was an assortment of ballet programs and professional career shots she'd rummaged out from a box in her wardrobe. Her eyes rested on the collection of memorabilia. With pen and paper, she wrote down the size picture frames she'd need to buy. If her life had been worth living, it was worth recording and displaying. She'd never keep anything hidden away again.

Placing her mug on the table, she reached for her demi-pointe shoes. Having showered, and now dressed in her ballet gear, Jessie slipped them on, tying the ribbons tightly at her ankles and tucking in the loose ends. Rising to her feet, she pushed over her insteps, arching each foot multiple times. She padded to the kitchen bench, her impromptu barre, to begin. Three hours of hard work lay before her. Her spirit soared.

CHAPTER 51

"Well, here we are at last girl. Home." BJ threw open the front door of his house and with the force of a droving dog, Whiskey rushed past his legs straight to the kitchen. Securing the door behind him, he wandered after her, detouring only to place his bag on the bed. With everything that had happened, it felt like he'd been gone for months—like he'd been on a tour of duty. In some ways, he had. The difference this time was that he was coming home victorious, without having killed anyone or destroying part of his soul in the process. He was returning home with someone special and with love in his heart. Despite his past happy home-comings with Rachael and Tiffany, this one held even grander promise and hope. For now, he no longer had danger as his constant companion.

"Okay, Whiskey. An early dinner it is." He opened the freezer door and pulled out a bag of bones. "You'll have to wait while I defrost one though."

Squatting her bottom to the floor, the Border collie followed her master's every move as he placed her dinner in the microwave. On the ding from the appliance, she sprang to her feet, bouncing with excitement. "Here you go." He opened the back door and with bone in mouth, she bolted for the grass to resume her usual dinner routine.

Propped in a deck chair, feet on the railing and beer in hand, he watched Whiskey with quiet appreciation. *Life's good.* Had anyone tried to convince him of this simple truth a month or more ago, he'd have grunted in disbelief. Now, no longer concerned with barricading himself against the world, he looked forward to living in the world again—this time with Jessie by his side.

He cracked the driving stiffness from his neck, placed his bottle on the table and stood. With hands resting on the railing, he scanned the back yard. *That's the spot.* Across the bamboo line, lay a wide strip of gradual sloping grass. Striding down the stairs and past Whiskey, he paced out the patch of land doing rough calculations in his head. He checked his watch. There were still a few hours of daylight left. *Plenty of time.* Within fifteen minutes, he stripped down to his shorts and drove a garden fork into the ground.

By nine o'clock that evening, BJ sat proud and pleased with himself, his fourth beer in hand. Not only had he turned over the soil, he'd been out, bought and planted the bee-and bird-attracting plants he needed to turn his compound into his own little slice of Coodravale. Drenched from a good watering, the garden of seedlings glimmered in the backyard floodlights. *I need softer garden lighting. Something subtle.* "Whiskey, your master is turning into a certifiable romantic." He reached down to stroke his dog's happy face and grinned. "Come on, girl. Time for a shower and bed. Tomorrow, we'll clean the Jeep."

Trudging into the house with Whiskey heeling at his side, he closed the back door and turned off the lights. "It's been a long day, girl. In fact, it's been a long few weeks. It's damn good to be home..."

CHAPTER 52

his lawyer seems a nice enough sort of bloke. He just sat there for the last hour taking notes and nodding his head. I decided there was no point in not telling him. So, I told him everything. About my mother and her rose switch beatings and locking me under the cupboard, about her boyfriends and their cocks, and how they used their dogs to bail me up until I did the things they wanted, about killing Muffin and drowning Chrissie, and about kidnapping Jessie. I gave him every detail I could remember. It felt good to finally tell someone. To get it all off my chest.

"So, that's it, Mr Stephenson. Do you think I'll have to go to jail? I can't go there. They'll do terrible things to me. I just know it."

"Well Mr Norton, I'll need to corroborate the details you have given me, but if they are confirmed, I can almost guarantee you won't be going to jail."

"Really? You mean you'll get me off?"

"No, I don't think that's likely. However, we'll plead you out before your case even goes to trial."

"Plead me out? What does that mean?"

"Based on the terrible sexual, physical, emotional and mental abuse you suffered as a child, I think the best course of action is to plead mental impairment."

"But I'm not mad. I'm not crazy."

"That's not for me to say, but you have experienced extreme damage from a highly violent and sexualized childhood. A trauma which you acted out time and again as you grew older. You began by being cruel to animals and then you progressed to humans. Mr Norton, you have suffered things no person, particularly a child, should ever have to endure. Do you know what retribution means?"

"It means payback."

"Indeed, it does, Mr Norton. You took revenge on whoever you could for what had been done to you. Yours is a very sad story. But can I ask you this? Why Chrissie and Jessie? You just told me how much you liked them both. Did it have something to do with them being ballet dancers?"

"Mum made me watch ballet on TV after her boyfriends left. She loved ballet. She said it was my fault she never became a ballerina. That's why I had to do those things to her boyfriends. It was my penance for ruining her life. Over and over, we'd watch the ballet. When the ballerinas danced, she'd tug at my cock and tell me I could never play with myself. That if I was more of man, maybe I'd get lucky one day and a ballerina would suck my cock instead of me having to suck her boyfriends' cocks."

For the first time since Mr Stephenson sat in this God forsaken cell, he stopped writing, put his pen down and looked like he didn't know what to say. *Poor Mr Stephenson.*

"Tell me, Skip, whatever happened to your mother?"

"The last I saw her was at my flat in Melbourne."

"Did she come to visit?"

I laughed. "Oh, no. She hasn't visited anyone in years."

Mr Stephenson blinked and looked more uneasy than ever. "Go on..."

"The last I saw of her was her lifeless eyes staring out of her fucking ugly, frozen face in my freezer. Her days of messing with me are through, Mr Stephenson."

CHAPTER 53

*I*nside the Australian Ballet Company's rehearsal studio and with her hand resting on the barre, Jessie was truly home. Her body dripped with perspiration and her muscles screamed in agonised delight. Across the aisle, Jasmine stood at the other barre. With her blonde hair captured in a top knot bun and her strong body wrapped in sweaty gear, she wore an expression of concentrated focus. Their eyes met, and Jessie winked at her best friend. Jasmine winked back. A quick, naughty respite from the gruelling morning's class. Their working feet lifted in long, slow *passés* while their supporting legs locked high on pointe. All the dancers resembled a flock of flamingos, graceful and slightly peculiar in stature.

"And one, and two, and three, close four." Counting out the tempo, the ballet mistress weaved her way between the two barre, inspecting the dancers' technique. Hesitating beside Jessie, she tinkered with her arm and leaned close into her ear. "It's good to have you back."

"Thank you, Miss." Inspired to work even harder, she stretched taller, sucked in her stomach flatter and managed a self-satisfied smile.

The sound of the door opening signalled a change of energy and, although no one broke movement, all eyes turned to see David Fitzgibbons stride regally into the studio. Without a word, he took his position in a straight-backed chair in the front of the class, crossed his legs and folded his arms. Jessie noted he remained like this for at least ten minutes watching her, only her. The more he scrutinised, the stronger she became. His steely stare would not faze her. This was her time.

"Thank you everyone. Take ten minutes, please." In a velvety, yet authoritative voice, David dismissed the company and rose from his chair. "Jessie, may I see you?"

With a quick sideways glance at Jasmine, she pattered over to him. "Hello, David."

"Hello. It's good to have you back. Please have a seat." He motioned to the chair beside him and when Jessie lowered herself to sit, he mirrored. "I understand you've been through a tough time? What with your father's death and the kidnapping…"

She noted his eyes surreptitiously inspecting her bare limbs. *Checking for damage. Can't have a blemished ballerina in the company.* Gluing a sweet smile to her face, she lifted her chin. "It was challenging, but here I am. Back and ready to dance my role of the Sugar Plum Fairy in tonight and tomorrow night's performances —the last two of the season."

Cocking a brow, he scrutinised her carefully. "Are you sure you're up for this? We've been without you and Tabitha all this time. Kelly has done an admirable job in the role in your absence. She can still dance the last two nights if you're not able."

"I'm sure Kelly has done an admirable job, but I intend to do a remarkable job. It's my role, and I'd like to dance it tonight and tomorrow. I'm ready to return."

Outside, she was all confidence and boldness. Inside, her nerves sizzled like party sparklers. *This is my time. This is my time.*

"Very well, Jessie." He rose signalling the meeting was over. Likewise, she stood. "You return to the role tonight. I'll inform the ballet mistress for rehearsals today." Leaning towards her, David clasped her shoulders and whispered close to her ear. "Dance like I know you can." Her skin tingled. When he pulled away, his smile seemed filled with hidden meaning. She knew that her future lay in no one else's hands except her own.

~

"Oh, Miss Jessie, I am so sorry Skippy did that to you." Salvatore fawned over her as she and Jasmine settled in for after-rehearsal coffees at his café.

"It's not your fault, Salvatore. You weren't to know Skip was planning anything. Besides, it's over now. Let's not talk about it." Shooting him a forgiving smile, she hoped he wouldn't continue. She didn't want her focus broken from her preparations for tonight's performance.

"Of course. Of course. Today, the coffees are on me. Enjoy." Although concern still creased his face, Salvatore made a gracious exit, leaving them alone.

"So back to the Sugar Plum Fairy tonight? I'm proud of you." Jasmine reached over, grabbing her friend's hand.

"After everything that's happened, I figured if I can get through all that, I can dance tonight and tomorrow. With Tabitha still off with her ankle, this is my chance to show David who should be the principal dancer for next year."

"That a girl. Show him what you're really made of. Once he sees you perform, I'm certain he'll give you the job. What else could he do? Tabitha may not be strong enough to do it anyway."

"But I don't want it by default. I want it because I deserve it."

"What does it matter? Don't think about why, just get it. In the end, it's all the same. It's yours." Jasmine lifted her coffee cup in a toast to her best friend. "Jessie Hilton, the Australian Ballet's next principal dancer."

Unwilling to suppress the confident smile stretching across her face, Jessie accepted her friend's toast. These next two nights were deal breakers for her career, and she intended to dance her way into the annals of the Australian Ballet Company.

CHAPTER 54

Surprised at how quickly the first two months of the new year had slipped by, BJ stood reminiscing in front of his bathroom mirror. Christmas Day at Coodravale with Jessie, Joanna and Richard had been delightful. Despite the absence of Ken, the Hilton family had enjoyed their time together. The trip to introduce Jessie to his family had also been terrific. Love at first sight for his mother and uncle when they met her. Having someone in her son's life to love and look after him had his mother crowing with pleasure—although he wasn't too sure if Jessie agreed with the 'look after' bit. Regardless, she'd been accepted with open arms.

He gazed down at the faithful black and white furry face beside his legs. "Tonight's the big night, Whiskey. We'll be home later to celebrate. You'll just have to hold the fort by yourself. Okay?" Taking the nudge of his dog's head as confirmation, he resumed the last of his grooming.

The buzzing of his phone interrupted him. "Angel, what's up?"

"Good news about the Norton case. As I suspected, the accused's counsel has pleaded not guilty under the defence of mental impairment. The judge just handed down his determination, and he's sanctioned Norton under the mental health act. The case won't go to trial. Norton will be institutionalised. Case closed."

"Wow, that's terrific news."

"Certainly is. I just called Jessie, and she's relieved."

"I bet. She really didn't want to relive the whole thing in court, although she was willing to do it."

"You know. The abuse Norton went through as a child is beyond comprehension. It's no wonder he turned out the way he did."

For a fleeting moment, BJ thought of what Jessie had endured at the hands of her uncle. "I hear you, but it's no excuse. I'm sure there are a lot of people out there who go through all sorts of abuse as kids. Some find their way out as adults, while others don't. It doesn't minimise the abuse or lessen the pain. It's just that some people put a different spin on it in their own minds. Redemption, rather than retribution becomes their MO."

"Yes, you're right. Who knows? Maybe with the right psychiatric help, Norton will find the boy he lost all those years ago."

"Stranger things can happen. Anyway, thanks for letting me know."

"You're welcome. See you later."

"Absolutely. Bye." He ended the call on a high emotional note. Bending down he ruffled Whiskey's lopsided ears. "With everything falling into place, wait till we start our search and rescue training next week. We'll top the class in no time. You saved me, girl. You kept me sane until Jessie came along. Then you saved her. You're the best rescue dog ever. Good girl."

Returning to the mirror, BJ finished the ritual with a splash of aftershave. Inspecting his reflection, he stepped back. If his smile widened any more, he felt sure his face would split in two. Happy, he was deliriously happy, and he hoped tonight Jessie would be too.

Next stop. The bedroom. While he slipped into his shirt, his eyes wandered to the bedside tables, where most of the photos were of him, Jessie and Whiskey. His favourite photo of Rachael and Tiffany still rested in full view—a changing collection of joyful memories, past and present. Stepping into his black trousers, he reflected on how he and Jessie had decided to let their relationship grow in its own time. Neither of them wanted to rush into anything. They wanted to get to know each other without all the drama which initially brought them together. But the sexual tension between them had now reached a tipping point, which was evidenced by the difficulty to zip up his trousers at the mere thought of taking her into his bed.

Black socks, patent leather shoes, bow tie and jacket finished the ensemble. "Okay Whiskey. Outside for you." Leading the way, he walked to the back door. When he opened it, he scanned the perimeters, taking delight in his top garden. The plants and flowers had begun to work their magic attracting a few birds and bees into the property. By next summer, more wildlife would abound in his back yard. "Maybe we'll even have wombats, Whiskey?" He chuckled and coaxed her outside. "See you soon, girl."

Between Angel and Ricky, he sat agog. Dressed in their finery, the three of them had entered the auditorium earlier to escape the crush. Now with the bell chiming the final call, they settled back taking in the civilised urgency of the occasion. Over three tiers of cutting edge, contemporary design, at least two thousand people whispered excitedly while they located their plush red velvet seats. Tense anticipation electrified the air in Hamer Hall for this special night—the opening of the Australian Ballet Company's season for the New Year.

"I don't know how she does it." Angel craned his neck,

scanning the auditorium. "Having all these people watching you must be daunting."

"I agree. Going into combat's easier than this." Ricky watched the hordes of people enter the main performance space of the Arts Centre Melbourne.

"Hello, Brad." From behind him a familiar voice spoke, and a hand tapped his shoulder.

Swivelling around, his face drew in a warm welcome. "Joanna. Richard. You remember Ricky from Ken's funeral, and this is Angel, the crown prosecutor who spoke with you on the phone." They exchanged hurried greetings.

"Thanks for buying our seats." Joanna leaned forward with a kiss to his cheek.

"You're welcome. Can't have you missing out…" He squeezed her hand and shot Richard a brotherly glance before settling back into his seat. "Check it out, fellas. That's my girl." The program of Swan Lake lay open in his hands. On the page, an image of a radiant Jessie leaped out to the reader with the caption…

Jessica Hilton Principal Artist
Jessica Hilton possesses a rare artistry. Her dancing is marked by superb grace and elegance, as witnessed in her debut performance of Odette/Odile, Swan Lake.

Before either of his mates could respond, the house lights dimmed, and an instantaneous hush fell over the auditorium. Applause echoed as the conductor took his position and quelled the orchestra. Silence settled, and a rush of energy flowed through the venue like a tidal wave.

"This is it," he said in a whisper.

From the orchestra pit, the lilting sound of the strings and oboes drifted on the auditorium's perfect acoustics. Their melancholy refrain of the theme of Swan Lake touched BJ so unexpectedly, his eyes moistened with tears. Surprised at his response, he swallowed hard, rubbing his palm across his mouth. In his chest, his heart thudded. Or did it cleave open? So much love, so much life, so much beauty. He'd not heard anything like it before. And as he fought to control the rising emotion, the last tenuous threads of anger, grief and revenge floated away as the heavy, proscenium curtain lifted…

CHAPTER 55

*S*tanding in the wings, Jessie fidgeted. She'd finally done it. She'd fulfilled the destiny she'd dreamed about and for which she'd worked so hard. Swan Lake, Act One, Scene One was underway and here she waited, ready for her entrance as Odette—the Swan Queen. Around her, a hive of activity buzzed as crew and dressers readied themselves for the first scene change. Aside from being on stage, she loved the backstage energy as it ramped up through a performance. Everyone had their job to do and each was integral to the other. Regardless of the star status the dancers may be given, she appreciated how many people got her to this point. Not just from her past, but also in each performance, every night.

Costumed in a hand-made tutu of white satin and tulle, lustrous beads, elegant pearl tiara and drop earrings, she slowed her breathing. As she batted her extravagantly long false eyelashes and pressed her ruby red lips together, she drew her focus away from the backstage logistics. Centring within, there was nothing left for her to do now except perform the role to which she was born.

Supremely fit, strong and flexible, she'd ensured nothing had distracted her from this moment over these past couple of months. Not even the new man in her life. Seated somewhere in the blackness of the audience he, Angel, Ricky, her mother and Richard waited—all of them supporting her, willing her on. She cast her eyes towards the lighting gantry hanging over the stage with its hundreds of stage lights. *This one's for you, Dad.* Instinctively her hand touched the top of her bodice above her heart. Sewn into the lining hid her childhood gold swan necklace. *Thanks for getting me here safe and sound...*She glanced down at her perfectly manicured nails, delighted that she no longer chewed her cuticles. At last, she was unblemished.

Scene one ended. Like a hot air balloon escaping the earth, her spine stretched upwards, her muscles lengthened, and she channelled the energy. The *corps de ballet* fluttered onto the stage in the blackout, taking their places. She intuited a glance in her direction from Jasmine and smiled a silent thank you in return. In the moments of deathly silence which followed, she prepared with a deep breath and final over arch of her pointe shoes.

Moving forward in the wings, she concentrated on embodying the character of the Swan Queen—graceful, entrapped and forlorn. Around her all movement stopped. The lighting changed and on the beat of her choosing, she stepped delicately onto the stage bathed in an eerie, blue light. One, two, three, four, five, six, seven, eight steps and prepare. Arms poised like the wings of a swan, she tilted her head downward and surrendered to the music, the dance and her destiny.

Over the next two hours, raw passion surfaced in her performance. The pain and suffering experienced by the character of Odette surged through every cell of her body. The desperate love between Odette and the Prince and the cruelty of their inevitable doom struck a chord in her heart, bringing real tears to her eyes as she danced. Enraptured in the performance, she reached into the brimming well of her emotions, baring her soul for all to see.

By the time she'd taken four curtain calls, accepted the praise heaped upon her backstage, showered and changed, she was elated and exhausted. All she wanted was to see BJ and go home to his place with friends and family for a post-performance celebration.

Sitting in front of her private dressing room mirror, she unpinned the tight bun of her hair. Mingled with the scent of dozens of roses and other flowers celebrating her opening night of the season, the smell of success filled the room. Taking a deep breath, she wanted to remember this moment, forever. She paused, filling her senses. Tap, tap, tap.

"Come in." Casting her gaze behind her in the mirror, she blew out a breath.

"Congratulations." Tabitha Simpson stood just inside the door, her mouth pursed. The words obviously tasted bitter.

"Thank you." Jessie gave a smile sweet enough to attract bees. "How's your ankle doing?" She plucked the last pins from her hair.

"Much better. I'll be dancing your part of the Swan Queen in no time." Her mouth curved upward in an unattractive sneer.

"Only if I injure myself." Jessie's voice sounded bright and breezy.

"Well, you never know…"

Jessie spun around in her chair. "You know what Tabitha? I wouldn't bet on that happening anytime soon. Now, if you'll excuse me, I have to finish dressing." With another spin, she faced the mirror. Keeping her gaze glued on her own reflection, she brushed her hair in long, even strokes. Tabitha slinked from the room without a sound. *About time, too.* Having put Tabitha in her place and out of her mind, Jessie seized her career as a principal artist. No more looking over her shoulder or worrying about what other people thought. This was her time.

With her usual enthusiasm, Jasmine popped her head into

Jessie's dressing room. "I'll meet you in the foyer when you're ready. Take your time. You were incredible, of course. But I always knew you would be." She blew a kiss and left.

Jessie zipped up her clinging black cocktail dress and stepped into a pair of strappy black stilettos. Slashing a lick of hot pink gloss on her lips, she grabbed the dozen red roses BJ had sent for opening night. Closing her new dance bag, another gift from him, she stifled a laugh. Inside the bag, hung her keys secured on a leather strap. "Now you can find your keys easily," is what he'd said, when he presented her with the bag. Shaking her head, she clucked at his caring ways and at how lucky she was.

With the bag hauled onto her shoulder and the bunch of roses crushed to her chest, she rushed to the foyer. Shouts from the media greeted her, as did David Fitzgibbons' guiding hand which ushered her to a couch for a promised exclusive interview. Knowing the periphery obligations which came with the job, she responded to the media's insistence with grace and humility. Once they'd got their all-important news, they vanished like vampires into the night.

"Jessie you were truly wonderful. Congratulations." David kissed her on both cheeks.

"Thank you, David. Thank you for giving me the chance."

"You deserved it. I'd wanted to give the role to you for some time. I was just waiting for you to step up and claim it as your own." A caring smile tipped his lips giving her the rare opportunity of seeing inside the artistic director. A dancer like her, he lived for the stage regardless how business-like his approach. "Go enjoy time with your friends and family. I'll see you back here tomorrow night for another superb performance."

She dashed towards the stairs leading down to the lower foyer. By now, most people had left and only a few die-hard fans remained. She signed autographs, all the while glancing out of the corner of her eye. *Where's BJ?* The last straggling fans departed, leaving only a small group of people at the bottom of the stairs.

All eyes turned to her as did the big guy in the centre of the group. She gasped. There he stood, immaculate in his black dinner suit, looking like a famous movie star on the red carpet. But it wasn't just the dinner suit. Tonight, he was less GI Joe and more James Bond. His trademark scruffy beard and pony tail were gone. *Oh my God, he's breath-taking.*

"Jessie." His rich, velvety voice ascended the stairs.

Spellbound, she could do nothing, but admire the most handsome man in the world climb the staircase towards her. Without his beard, the planes of his face cut an exquisite symmetry highlighting his splendid genetics. A dimple, which she'd not noticed until now, etched his chin adding a boyish impudence to his ruggedness. Shaped into a modern, executive cut, his hair sliced into the nape of his neck while a wicked bang of blonde and golden tints contrasted against the bronzed skin of his forehead. No longer competing against straw-coloured bristles and strands of hair, the striking blue of his eyes shimmered like artic ice as he fused his gaze with hers.

"My love. You were spectacular. I had no idea..." Enveloping her, roses and all, he pressed a passionate kiss to her mouth. She trembled at his delicious touch.

"Look at you..." Tracing her fingers across his clean-shaven face, she couldn't tear her eyes away from his magnificence.

"For you. The principal artist of the Australian Ballet Company can't be seen with some shabby bloke by her side." His soft chortle lightened the mood.

"But..."

"It was time. Time to stop hiding myself away. Time to let you and the rest of the world see me, the real me. Do you approve?"

"Oh, yes. Very much." She stroked his smooth cheeks and flicked the wisps of hair from his brow.

"Besides when I make love with you tonight, I don't want to scratch your delicate skin."

Faltering slightly, she grabbed his arm. "Tonight?"

"I figured you'd be deliriously happy after tonight's performance. I am. So, tonight's the night. What do you think?

"Deliriously happy is most definitely how I feel."

"Then let's go home and celebrate."

Whiskey was sound asleep in her bed when midnight chimed and the last of the happy revellers departed. Leaning against the front door, BJ locked her in a heart-stopping gaze. Having discarded his jacket and tie when they got home, he looked even sexier with his shirt's top buttons undone. Jessie's breath hitched as he stalked down the hallway towards her. Pinning her to the wall, he leaned down and plundered her mouth in a ravenous kiss.

"Still deliriously happy, my love?" His fingers toyed with the straps of her dress.

"Oh, yes." She squirmed hard against his body, feeling his excitement grow. Without another word, he scooped her up and carried her into the bathroom, where he lowered her to the floor. "What's all this?" Filled with dozens of flickering, perfumed candles, the bathroom resembled a luxurious private guest spa, shimmering in a romantic glow.

"I thought you'd like a relaxing spa after the show, so I set this up for us." He leaned over the steaming water and switched on the bubbles.

"But how? Jasmine and Ricky have only just left?"

"Everyone was in on it. If you noticed, no one used the bathroom over the last thirty minutes which gave me time to sneak in and set up." A devious smile curled his lips. "Now enough about logistics…Time to undress. Allow me."

At the touch of his magic fingers, she bowed to his will and he unzipped her dress. With every deliberate stroke, his lips enhanced the movement—first nibbling the nape of her neck, next pressing a kiss to her shoulders and then butterfly kissing each vertebra as the zipper bared the length of her spine. Her dress finally puddled on the floor, leaving her naked except for a black G-string and towering stilettos. Feeling a little self-conscious, because as a ballet dancer she had no body fat and therefore no full breasts, she bit her lip praying he wouldn't be disappointed.

Tracing the delicate musculature of her shoulders and torso to her pantie line, he groaned. "I've waited so long for you. You're more beautiful than I imagined." He spun her to face him and raked every inch of her body. "Look at you. You're perfect. I love you, Jessie Hilton."

Springing into the air, she wrapped her legs around his waist and peppered his face with kisses. She combed her fingers through his freshly-cut hair and said, "I love you, too, Brad Jordan. I think I loved you the moment you looked at me with that wild, blue gaze."

Unravelling her legs, he set her on the side of the spa. "Time to get naked, my love…" Reaching out, she touched the planes of his muscled chest as he shrugged off his shirt. He slid his belt from his trousers and unzipped, letting them fall to the floor. Clothed only in underwear, his buff, bronzed body twitched.

Her eyes widened. "For me?"

"For you." He kneeled at her feet and unfastened her shoes. "At last, I have your long, luscious legs to myself." After discarding each shoe, he trailed his tongue up one leg and then the other. She wished for more legs.

Her hands fluttered across his inked back and shoulders. "By the way, I never did ask you. What's with the fire-breathing dragon tattoo across your back?"

"It's a promise of things to come, when I breathe fire between your legs, my love." He glanced up at her, a wicked gleam in his eyes. "Now, G-string…"

She peeled it off, while he stepped out of his underwear.

Within moments, they were locked in a passionate embrace in the welcoming warmth of the spa.

"I need to touch you." Slipping his hand between her legs, he caressed her, tender yet deliberate. She gasped. The candle flames blurred and danced like dozens of fireflies. Lost to everything except his touch, she closed her eyes and surrendered. All too soon, her back arched, her body exploding. Never had she experienced such a mind-emptying, body-breaking orgasm. Never had she had such a talented lover. Never had she imagined she could feel this way. Spent and smiling, she drifted into the comforting warmth of the bubbles.

"That was wonderful…" she said.

He whispered in her ear. "But we've only just started." He eased her onto his lap, and her sex-loosened muscles melted around him like rich, hot chocolate.

She groaned. "Oh God, that's so good."

"You can have as much of me as you like, when you like." With his powerful hands encircling her waist, he set a slow, steady tempo. Moments drifted into minutes while she rode him into a shared sexual nirvana. Eventually, she opened her eyes and cast him an impish smile.

"What?" His brow knitted, while his hands fondled her breasts.

"If this is opening night as a principal dancer with the Australian Ballet Company, then bring it on."

"Your wish is my command. Let's fire this baby up?" Wrestling her into his arms, he rose from the spa like an ocean god. "It's the bed for you." In long strides he headed to the bedroom, leaving a trail of sudsy water through the house.

Slung over his shoulder, she giggled. "And what do you plan on doing to me?"

"Look closer…"

Face to face with his tattoo, she laughed and prepared for the delectable onslaught of the fire-breathing dragon—her modern-day warrior.

THE END

I hoped you've enjoyed reading *Retribution* as much as I did writing it.

If you have, please consider leaving an honest review on the retailer site where you purchased the book.

BEHIND THE SCENES

SPOILER ALERT

Retribution is romantic suspense, a genre where the suspense element and the romantic relationship are equally important to the plot. I wanted to give an emotional depth to the story by constructing complex character arcs in a story that merges the deeper elements of life, love and hope.

This story is my way of paying tribute to the people who've endured more than most. Those who've lived hellish childhoods, those who've fought for our freedom, those who've experienced unimaginable trauma and those who may never recover from their suffering. With the overarching theme of forgiveness and redemption, *Retribution* pays homage to the human condition in all its glory and misery.

Having trained in ballet and worked as a professional dancer, choreographer and director, I knew my protagonist had to be a ballerina, as they possess the qualities I needed for my story. Tough, disciplined and ambitious, she had to be driven to achieve her dreams, even against the worst odds. As a lover of the Australian Ballet and having access to past students and dancers, I created a protagonist who fit the role of an Aussie Ballet soloist. Soloist is the final step before becoming a principal dancer, which is the highest position in any ballet company. For those who have the talent, dedication and grit to make it, the transition from soloist to principal is a career highlight. The incomparable Amber Scott from the Aussie Ballet was my inspiration. https://australianballet.com.au/artist/amber-scott

My hero had to be her match; a man with equal power, passion and fortitude. Since I've always had great respect and gratitude for the men, women and animals of our armed forces, I knew my hero would be one of them. They're a rare breed who place themselves in harm's way to fight for our freedoms and way of life. A uniquely Australian character, my hero needed to be a professional soldier with a damaged past and worthy of finding love again. Inspired by Chris Hemsworth in the lead role of Thor and then clean-shaven in a dinner suit from his modelling days, he represented the two incarnations of my hero.

Thus, Jessie Hilton and Brad Jordan were born.

I set about researching my main characters by watching documentaries on the SAS, reading autobiographies of snipers and talking with professional ballet dancers and students. Having worked for over three decades in the live entertainment industry, I had first-hand experience of what happens onstage, backstage and in a dancer's mind, giving me a unique insight into Jessie's character and that of the secondary 'ballet' characters. I've met many talented ballerinas like Jessie who suffered from misplaced feelings of unworthiness. As for Brad, I've inherently found writing from the male point of view (POV) liberating. Getting inside the head of an alpha male who is at once, powerful and vulnerable is a writing space I thoroughly enjoy.

Then there is BJ's dog, Whiskey, who's integral to the story and a true hero. Being a besotted animal lover with a furry family of three dogs, I fashioned Whiskey on my own Border collie, Gypsy Rose, who I named in honour of a famous American burlesque dancer. Whiskey possesses the same enthusiasm and gentle nature as Gypsy, though my collie isn't as well-trained as Whiskey. You

can see pictures of my puppies on my blog.
https://dianedemetre.com/blogposts/

Because *Retribution* delves deeper into the human psyche and explores how people deal with their emotional past, I wanted to set Jessie's past in the context of a real location. I needed a small rural town within a six to seven hour driving distance from Melbourne, where the Australian Ballet Company is based. I also needed this town to be quintessentially Australian, with an historical bed & breakfast on its outskirts and a believable lair nearby for the antagonist. My husband, who has travelled by road throughout most of Australia suggested a little town called Yass. A place I'd never heard of. Bingo! Not only did Yass look like the town I imagined when I began plotting *Retribution*, it had a nearby homestead, perfect for Jessie's childhood—Coodravale Homestead. Yes, it is real, as is its history which I weave into the story. My thanks go to its owners John and Rosemary Robinson for their help during my research.
https://www.coodravalehomestead.com/

To truly capture the essence of Coodravale and the town of Yass and its surrounds, my husband and I set off on a fourteen-hour drive from our home on the Gold Coast to the gateway of the Yass Valley. When we finally arrived, I hung out the window taking photos like an excited kid, while he drove up and down the streets. We visited the hospital, police station, RSL Club, coffees shops, the cemetery and a variety of other places that feature in the book.

The scenery heading out of Yass to Coodravale was truly inspiring. It exemplified what Icehouse sang in their 1989 hit, Great Southern Land, which I have playing as I write this. Icehouse not only captured the landscape of Australia, but its history and spirit in this song. I tried to do the same with my setting descriptions in *Retribution*. The location details I describe in the story are true, at least they were when we did this trip in 2016. My research notebook is full of moments when we stopped

the car, and I jotted down my feelings, observations and thoughts.
For example, these are some of the rough notes I jotted down on
that trip...

*A flock of low-flying yellow-crested cockatoos lifted in a cloud of
wings as the Jeep sped toward them.*

*Tracing odd geometric shapes, sheep tracks criss-crossed the grassy
hillsides.*

*...lined with wisps of spinifex that whispered the details of the
passing vehicles.*

The scene when Jessie and Brad arrive at Coodravale is
authentic right down to the lopsided sign, the driveway, and the
first impressions of the property. It's a glorious place filled with
history, charm and a bountiful supply of possibilities for a writer.
We stayed for three days in the Garden Wing during which time
the plot developed further. John and Rosemary were generous
with their time, answering my questions, taking us on walks
around the property and ensuring we saw the flying goats. True
story, as is the rifle practice scene. In fact, I asked a friend of mine
who owns a .308 to teach me how to shoot it, so I could
experience what Jessie does in the story. I posted the clip from
this fun bit of research on 23 September 2016 on Facebook
https://www.facebook.com/dianedemetreauthor In fact, I kept
the spent casings and shooting target from that day as souvenirs.
Again, here are some of the notes, I jotted down after that
experience as I tried to steady my trembling hands...

*Holding a lethal weapon in my hands sent distress signals to
my brain*

*Even with earmuffs, the sound of a single gunshot was unexpectedly
loud*

*After firing the rifle, I wanted to be rid of it, to return to my peaceful
self*

Then there is the antagonist, Skip Norton. On purpose, I
switched POV for his scenes as I wanted you, the reader, to be in
his head. What a delight he was to write. I know that sounds odd,

but he appeared so clearly in my mind, I felt I knew him. As his past grew into the sordid history it ended up being, I was repulsed by Skip's behaviours, while feeling great sympathy for him because of his horrendous childhood. Once he became fully formed, I went on the research trail as to his personality type. It seems Skip is a violent malignant narcissist. The statement Angel makes about most murderers, rapists and violent offenders being made is based on current psychology. What a child experiences in their formative years fashions their adulthood. And if you're a dog owner like me, you know that your dog is probably the best judge of character you could have. Beware of who your dog dislikes.

The Wee Jasper Caves proved to be the perfect place for Skip's lair. These amazing limestone caverns tunnel under the earth for miles and are spectacular. The owner of Carey's Cave, a cracking bloke named Geoff Kell, took us on a private tour. He regaled us with all the details I needed. He even turned off all the lights, sending the caves into pitch blackness. Too spooky for words. It proved a dramatic and major turning point in Jessie's journey. If you're ever in this part of Australia, put these caves on your must-see list. And say hello to Geoff for me
http://www.weejaspercaves.com/

In summary, *Retribution* is about the abuse Jessie, Brad and Skip experienced in their childhoods, whether physically, sexually, emotionally, mentally or a combination of all. Brad's father blamed him for Tony's death, Jessie's Uncle Frank molested her (this is based on a true story of a friend of mine) and we all know what Skip went through with his crazy mother. I wanted to explore how these harrowing events colour people's lives, affect their futures and the decisions they make. Then there is the guilt...of Ken who could never prove his suspicions, of Father Conlon who could never break his vows, of Frank who eventually showed signs of remorse, of Joanna for being too tough on Jessie, of Brad over Tony's, Rachael's and Tiffany's death, and the list goes on. Guilt from the past is interwoven in just about every character in the story. If you reread *Retribution* you'll probably notice it, quietly gnawing away at the story.

Then I needed a provocative headline for the book cover. It's a question few of us consider. *Who would you kill to escape your past? What decision would you make if you were pushed to the edge? Would you choose good or evil?* This is the ultimate choice my characters had to face when confronting their pasts—to either choose for redemption or retribution. In the end, their choices fashioned their futures, as do the decisions we make every day in our lives.

If you enjoyed reading *Retribution*, please consider leaving an honest review on the site where you purchased it.

Keep up-to-date by signing up for my no spam newsletter here
https://bit.ly/ddNews
For more information please connect with me at…
www.dianedemetre.com
https://www.facebook.com/DianeDemetreBooks/
https://www.instagram.com/dianedemetrebooks/
https://twitter.com/DianeDemetre

www.ingramcontent.com/pod-product-compliance
Lightning Source LLC
Chambersburg PA
CBHW021405110726
47901CB00008B/2063

* 9 7 8 0 6 4 8 3 3 2 4 4 2 *